The Silen.

International bestselling author Anna McPartlin had her first novel published in 2006. In recent years she has turned her attention to scriptwriting for TV serial dramas featured on BBC UK, RTE Ireland and A&E America. She lives in Ireland with her husband and dogs.

the
silent
ones

ANNA McPARTLIN

First published in the United Kingdom in 2025 by

Canelo Crime, an imprint of
Canelo Digital Publishing Limited,
20 Vauxhall Bridge Road,
London SW1V 2SA
United Kingdom

A Penguin Random House Company
The authorised representative in the EEA is Dorling Kindersley Verlag GmbH. Arnulfstr. 124, 80636
Munich, Germany

A CIP catalogue record for this book is available from the British Library.

Print ISBN 978 1 83598 245 7
Ebook ISBN 978 1 83598 246 4

Cover design by Jet Purdie

Cover images © Shutterstock

Printed and bound in Great Britain by Clays Ltd, Elcograf S.p.A.

Look for more great books at
www.canelo.co | www.dk.com

To the real Mary O'Shea—

My aunt. My inspiration. My mother.

The past is a foreign country; they do things differently there.

L. P. Hartley

Until our very recent past, the beautiful, culturally rich and storied country of Ireland was a cold house for women. Teenage girls growing up in the 1980s were shaped by a pious patriarchal society terrified of female sexuality and determined to control it. During this time, real and terrible events highlighted how far the Irish had fallen, how difficult life for women and girls had become and the cruelty at the heart of the Irish Church and state.

The case of Baby Crónán is a fictional story inspired by a real event. In 1984 the body of a murdered baby boy, Baby John, washed up on a beach in Kerry. What happened afterwards was tantamount to a witch-hunt: a young single mother was erroneously charged with the child's murder, and although the charges were later dropped, the events that followed caused great harm to her and her family. It took the Irish state thirty-six years to formally apologise for the 'appalling hurt and distress caused'.

In March 2023, DNA tests confirmed the identities of Baby John's parents, but their names have been withheld to protect their privacy, as they have not been charged with any crime. The investigation remains ongoing. Mary Shea is a fictional character, born to explore what it is to be a woman attempting not just to survive, but to thrive in a man's world; she questions how differently the cases involving the death and murder of Irish women and children would have turned out if the women of that time had power to effect change.

Prologue

There's a strand shaped like a crescent and made of white sand, powder to touch and so fine that when disturbed, it flurries unseen into the air before gently settling once more. That's where he was found, in a dune not far from the lifeguard tower and straight as the crow flies. It was the smallest drift, sunken, surrounded and fanned on all sides by tall marram grass. Till then an anonymous patch of ground, but afterwards and forevermore that small dune would be known as *the cradle*.

In the midst of surreal horror and terrible beauty, I'll focus on the latter for now. He was tiny but sturdy too, his hands balled into fists, ready to fight for his life. He had dimples above both knees and was a chubby thing, pale as the dawn and with perfect little feet. Ten toes with translucent nails that were already turning black at the base and tips. His eyes were grey, a mirror of the heavy sky above him, and he stared far beyond it and the people gathered around. It was undeniable he had come to a violent end and so they were weeping and whispering, shocked utterances of how and why and who could do such an evil thing, while staring down at his beautiful, angelic face. He was gifted with rosebud lips that no doubt would have delivered a devastating smile had he been given the chance to muster one. He was clean; I could smell the bleach wafting my way as I approached, and his black tuft of hair was rancid with it. He had been wrapped in a blue towel rough from overuse. It had slipped from around him so he lay on it, naked.

It was catching, this baby Medusa. One look at him and we were all turned to stone – at least outwardly. Our humanity shrank to accommodate the practicalities of the job at hand, but inside, every one of us, from the best to the worst, screamed. How could we not? For my part, I wanted him to know that someone cared for him; I wanted to shout to his soul high above the clouds, to where God's choir sings, but what could I say? So I remained silent as the grave while my emotions ran riot and my mind ticked over. Who was he? Where did he come from? Why did he die? By whose hand? That was for us to investigate, but first we called upon Father Cunningham to perform the rituals to pave this tiny creature's way to heaven while he lay there in the cradle – and to do that, he needed a name. He was christened Baby Crónán, an ancient Irish name, meaning little dark one.

CHAPTER ONE

Monday, 21 January 1980

Day One

I ran around my tiny rented one-bed cottage, which was in reality a converted cowshed on a farmer's land. The walls were plastered, the floor tiled, and indoor plumbing had been installed but despite many attempts to rid the place of the musky odour of cows, it remained in the air, stubbornly refusing to shift. Once I'd conceded defeat, I got used to it, even found comfort in it, but the galvanised steel roof was harder to tolerate, as I was a light sleeper and it made a terrible racket when it rained.

It had been raining for four days and nights, so I'd slept barely a wink. Bone-tired, I smoothed down my freshly ironed uniform, knotted and tied my wet hair in a bun at the nape of my neck, and covered my head with a hat; I checked my tights for ladders and my shoes for dirt, while eating a slightly burnt slice of toast I was holding in one hand and grabbing my coat from the rack just inside the door with the other. I was a skinny thing, often described as a tall glass of water: blonde hair, watery blue eyes. I suppose I had a pretty enough face, the kind with small features, but my height became an issue early on. Despite my mother's prayers to Saint Anthony, I stood at five feet seven-and-a-half inches in stockinged feet by the age of fifteen. Boys didn't like looking up at girls, and men weren't too fond of it either. The end result? I was no prize at the fair.

I was running late. The rain had finally stopped at 4:15 a.m. and as soon as the noise relented, I'd finally slept in the silence. Too soundly, because the alarm clock rang just over an hour later and one or both of my arms decided to react independently of my brain by knocking it to the floor. I don't remember it happening, I simply woke to find the evidence of my action and saw from the wall clock that I'd overslept. I couldn't be late for work. Everyone else at the station seemed to breeze about the place as and when they liked, but I was held to a higher standard than those fellas. If I was a minute late it was noted, shouted aloud for all to hear. Grumbling and the shaking of heads would follow. 'Probably too busy doing her make-up,' one or another would say. I didn't wear make-up, a fact that went unnoticed by those detective geniuses. I would pretend to make no mind. I'd just offer to make a pot of tea, thinking what a bunch of ignoramuses they were as I poured it.

I left the house that morning and got into my second-hand Ford Escort, which smelled of peat briquettes, and had a tear in the driver seat's leather upholstery and an artfully mangled steel hanger that replaced the long-gone radio aerial. I was on the early shift, six a.m. to two p.m. It was already five fifty-five as I drove speedily to the station in the dark, half-concentrating on the road ahead, half-daydreaming of the outfit I'd be wearing to the disco that the farmer's son, Seamus, was taking me to the following weekend. Seamus was as handsome as the devil – at least that's what my mother said the first time she saw him. He was tall and lean but fit too, from all the work he did on the farm. He kept his chestnut hair long enough to sweep back and had the most extraordinary aqua-blue eyes – they made him stand out in any room. Some girls would look at us with obvious envy when we were together, not realising that I was far from his type. That suited me just fine. I was more interested in having the opportunity to wear the brand new, beautiful, embroidered blouse Mammy sent me as a birthday gift than Seamus, but he was kind company and he fixed things around the cottage that needed attention. I daydreamed of the blouse, the music, the lights and spinning around to Blondie or The Police, arms in the air, dancing. I loved to dance. Seamus would hole up at the bar and mind my handbag, and I'd boogie the night away until the sweat rolled off me and my head felt lighter. I was looking forward to the weekend and losing myself in pop music as I pegged down those quiet roads, nestled where the mountains met the sea in the town of Nead Mara, a quiet haven in God's own county of Kerry. Speeding along the winding roads, past quaint stone cottages, unflinching against the ravages of time and high tides, and the beach that swept out into the North Atlantic Ocean, I ratcheted the window down and inhaled the soul of the place.

Despite my hurry and the trepidation that came with every working day, I felt at ease with the world.

Donal 'Dicey' McCarthy made it through the gate of the carpark just before me when I arrived at two minutes to six a.m. I'd broken every speed limit and maybe even set a few records in getting there. He was a big wide bear of a man – his broad frame and heavyset shoulders were at odds with his lean, wiry face that seemed to belong to another body, and his thick head of fair hair definitely looked like it belonged to another head: nothing about Dicey added up. He snarled more than he smiled but when he did, it was disarming. He had a hearty laugh too; I'd hear it echoing about the place when he talked with the lads. He'd always talk *at* me, not *to* me, but I pretended not to notice. Now, he checked his watch as though he was my superior. He wasn't, he was just on the regular like me, but he didn't act like it. I parked close to the building entrance to be sure I made it through the blue door before him. Aside from the cleaner, who was pushing sixty and came in twice a week, I was the only woman in the station. Women were as welcome in the Irish police force as a fart in a space suit but I had managed to slip through the net by sheer force of will, sneakiness and the fact that my father was a high-ranking assistant commissioner. I adored my job, even the mundane stuff – and so falling in love was not an option, because love leads to marriage and if I got married, I'd be fired. That would be the end of doing the thing I felt I was born to do, and at the age of twenty-eight I felt I had so much more to give.

–

Liam Kenny was already inside, standing at the desk, coughing and spluttering. He was in his uniform but his grey pallor and shiny forehead suggested he was a sick man needing his bed and comfort. He was only thirty but his balding head and having lost a few teeth he'd failed to replace, when he played hurling in the minors, made him look twenty years older. He wasn't the brightest man in our unit but he was the sweetest, and although he wasn't my friend, he was friendly to me and it meant a lot. Dicey arrived in a step or two behind me, just enough time for poor old Kenny to cough and splutter right into his face.

'For the love of God, what did you do that for?' he shouted at Kenny. Dicey was close to fifty and although he was still on the regular, he acted with authority so that even the Station House Officer, Brian Keating – a small, quietly spoken but firm man – was almost submissive to him. He had that kind of presence, one which took up more space than everyone else; his size, his voice and his aura were vast and he wasn't one bit apologetic about it.

'Sorry… God… Sorry, Dicey. I'm dying over here,' Kenny said, wiping his nose ferociously.

Dicey took one look at him. 'Well, you're not going home. Keating has a hospital appointment with that knee of his.'

'Oh, I'm ready to work,' Kenny said, lifting his arms into the air as if that made a difference. He was pumping sweat and wavering right in front of us. *Ah, Kenny, you're as sick as a small hospital*, I thought to myself, hoping to God I wouldn't catch whatever he had. Influenza was not a part of my plan for the weekend, so I stepped back, hoping he'd do the same. He didn't. He pushed forward. 'I'm here to work,' he assured us, hawking all over Dicey, whose gaze raked over him, from his head to his toes, before he leaned over the counter to take a sniff. Kenny pulled back so quickly, he almost lost his footing but steadied himself just as quickly. He looked towards me anxiously. I was still shielding behind Dicey so in the absence of doing anything helpful, I gave him the thumbs up.

'You've got the waft of a coffin ship about you,' Dicey said.

'I can work,' Kenny said.

'So stay here and answer the phones. I'm not having you in the car with me,' Dicey said, before looking my way. 'I suppose it will have to be you.' He sighed as though sharing a vehicle with me was the worst thing in the world. I'd been working in that station for five years and it was only the third time I'd be in the car.

Ten minutes later, we were driving by a house inhabited by a man known to beat his wife. Apparently, Dicey liked to drive by and flash the blue lights to remind the brute that he was watching. The wife had never made a complaint, but that wasn't unusual. In a small town like Nead Mara, she didn't have to. Town gossip reached our door daily, and the reports of Ann Buckley's beatings were regular. I'd heard from Kenny that Dicey's solution was to threaten the fella with his size and deliver a few punches when he stepped out of line. He was a factory worker, locally referred to as Dave 'The Wave' Buckley. He was a surfer at one time but gave it up when he lost a few toes in a lawnmower accident. We passed by and Dicey hit the blue lights just as he was getting into his car to go to work. A neighbour was leaving at the same time and he stared at us, then looked over at Dave The Wave, waiting for some sort of verbal or even non-verbal explanation.

'Everything all right, Dave?' the neighbour said, feigning ignorance, as Dicey slowed almost to a standstill outside the house.

'Shag off… You nosy feckin' article,' snarled Dave The Wave to his neighbour, who was now fumbling for the keys of his car, desperate to make his getaway. Dicey laughed but I didn't find his action funny or constructive.

'You're just rising him,' I said.

'Excuse me?' he said, anger immediately injected into his tone.

'Look in on her, be kind to her but leave him alone,' I said, but Dicey wasn't used to people telling him what to do. He stewed on what I'd said and as soon as we were away from the street and out of sight, he pulled in at the side of the road with a dramatic swerve, then turned in his seat to address me.

'You haven't a clue.' He scoffed. 'He's scared of me. That's what he needs.'

Dicey was what my mammy would call a galoot. Thinking he was saving this woman from the hell and torment she lived in, congratulating himself for being the big man. But he was a fool if he thought that. And I, being a different kind of galoot, felt an obligation to let him know as much.

'I see Ann Buckley in the supermarket with bruises on her arms, moving slowly and guarding her ribs. They've got four kids, and she's never going to call for help. All you succeeded in doing just now is making good and sure she gets a hiding tonight.'

Dicey's mouth fell open, and he was momentarily lost for words. 'You're one cheeky bitch,' he snapped, and although I had a lot more to say on the subject, I stayed quiet long enough for him to voice his grievance.

'I'm sorry I didn't put up with Kenny's diphtheria, it would have been less painful than listening to a foolish woman.' Then he leaned in to me, grabbing my leg with his hand and holding my thigh tight in his grip. 'She's alive because of me. He might give her a few slaps but he knows the line.'

I didn't move, not an inch. I just held his eye as I let him sink his fingers in the flesh of my thigh, hoping to God my tights didn't rip, because I didn't have a spare set with me. *Don't say a word, Mary. Not one word, just breathe.*

I waited, steeling myself for what may come. Then, slowly and deliberately, he let go, put the car in gear, and we were off – him in a temper, me in fear. That's when the radio crackled to life. I grabbed it like a drowning woman clutching a buoy and answered. It was Kenny. His voice, as alarmed as it was, offered some reassurance.

'Is Dicey there?' he said.

'No, I'm in a French woman's knickers,' Dicey retorted, his temper dampening and ego soothed as Kenny pretended to laugh.

'Eh, listen, just got in an interesting call… Some woman, she was bawling, hysterical really…'

'And the sky is blue, Kenny, so what about it?' Dicey said.

'She said she's on the beach… There's a baby there… Thing is, Dicey, she said it's dead.'

Dicey grabbed the radio from my hands. 'Did you say dead?'

'Yeah. Gave her name as Nora Fitzgerald. She rang from the phone box on the top road. I told her to go back to the site, where she said the baby lies, near the lifeguard tower. The one closest to the main entrance, you know, with the carpark.'

Dicey didn't speak after that but threw the radio back into the holder and bolted along the narrow winding road, despite the wet and at a speed that made it feel like we were on rails.

We arrived at the beachside carpark just after six thirty a.m. and the woman who was waiting for us looked to be in her late twenties, small in stature with a chubby frame and a round face. She was wearing a coat too light for the weather, and her body trembled and her teeth rattled from either the cold or the shock of her discovery. Black mascara tracks lined her cheeks and her dog was at her feet, silently awaiting instruction as she wiped her tears.

As we approached, she pointed to the dune behind her and Dicey ran towards it as I slowed to speak to her.

'Are you Nora Fitzgerald?' I asked and she told me she was. 'Is that where the baby is?' I said, pointing to the dune that Dicey was scrambling to.

'He's in there, it was Prince who found him,' she confirmed, presumably referring to her dog. I looked up in time to see Dicey turn to me with his mouth gaping and his eyes wide. Suddenly, I was walking to him as though he were a magnet. He tried to stop me.

'No. Don't,' he said, his hands raised as if to ward me off. 'You won't stomach it.' His tone wasn't mean, and there was a quiver in his voice from barely contained tears, as though he was already regretting what he'd seen and wished to spare me. But I wouldn't be spared. This was my job. I was determined to do it.

'I'm a member of the force, just like you.' He let me pass and that's when I first saw him. A tiny baby boy, hurt beyond words, stabbed repeatedly until the life flowed out of him, leaving nothing but dark wounds. It was in that moment my heart ripped asunder, and he found his way past the tear, searing himself into me. The anger rose within me, fury burning in my throat as I tasted the tears that I swallowed. I would not be seen crumbling. Dicey had paled and I noticed his hands were trembling, but I was determined to keep mine steady. I retreated down the dune, past Nora and her dog, and back to the car, where I used the radio to call in. 'We need a coroner and the lads from McGuire's funeral home.'

'So it's real,' Kenny said, his voice laden with disbelief. I watched as Nora bent double, clearly in a bad way.

'It's a baby boy, Liam,' I said quietly. Kenny didn't reply, presumably taking in the information. I continued, more firmly now, 'We have a witness in shock here, is the ambulance on its way?'

'Oh God… I'll call it now. Was he…?' He tapered off, as though he couldn't bring himself to say the word – that, or his sickness was getting the better of him.

'Murdered?' I said, before confirming that he was.

'Oh Lord God… A little boy.' Although I couldn't see him, I was aware he was blessing himself.

'We'll need to call the Super so he can put a call in to the lads from Dublin, and don't forget the State Pathologist.'

'Leave it with me and… well… God rest the poor creature,' Kenny said, and I hung up the radio and grabbed the tape from the boot of the car, passing poor Nora again, now crouched, hugging her dog. I paused briefly to assure her that help was on the way.

'For the baby?' she queried in surprise.

'For you,' I replied.

'The baby's gone,' she muttered, hopelessly.

'He is.' I confirmed what she already knew, my heart as heavy as a rock. As I turned to leave, she grasped my skirt. 'They'll need a statement,' she said.

I nodded as I politely corrected her. '*We* will.'

'I'll give it to you, then?' she asked. I hesitated, knowing it wouldn't be popular. 'Just you,' she insisted.

I was grateful to be there for her and ever more so that she wanted me to.

As I reached Dicey, he was just staring at the baby. 'Oh, dear God,' he muttered. I handed him the tape. *Don't look at the child, Mary. Focus on the job. He deserves your help. Don't let him down.* I kept my eyes averted.

'Come on,' I said, 'we've got a crime scene to preserve and a witness I need to take a statement from.'

He looked at me as if I were an alien. 'Have you no heart, woman?' he asked, and I almost laughed at the response in my head: *No heart? What am I supposed to do, Dicey McCarthy, cry my heart out so you can call me names? What are any of us to do?* Aloud I asked, 'What would you have me do? What is the right reaction to a murdered baby?' I was genuinely interested in his response.

'Are you a woman at all?' he retorted.

This time a bitter yelp of laughter fell from my mouth.

'I am, and that's why if my hands shook as yours do now, it would be derided as weakness.' He was shocked; I could see it. I was shocked myself. Truth be told, seeing his hands tremble transformed the beast in the car into a vulnerable human standing before me. But that question, in that place at that time – it was as though he'd wielded a knife of his own. My insides were blackened with grief, but I pushed through *because* I was a woman. The sight of the dead infant had done something to me and the anger I felt growing within me was set to explode. I tempered myself before I burst into flames and went on before he could interrupt me. 'Nora wants to talk to me alone,' I said. Then I walked away and left him with the roll of tape. For once Dicey McCarthy seemed to take up a little less space in the world.

CHAPTER TWO

The shock had got the best of Nora but I needed to do my job, so I sat her in the back of the car and I climbed in beside her. The dog wouldn't rest until he was between us, making it a tight squeeze. She stroked Prince's back and the motion appeared to calm them both. Recalling the incident by returning to that scene in her mind – as she had stood on the edge of the dune, looking down upon that tiny boy – was clearly difficult. She sobbed at the thought of his wounds and of what had been done to him, and she cried as she pointed through the window at the dune where he still lay. She rambled too, and even when she could gather her thoughts enough to string a sentence together, her words seemed to run into one another. With just a pen and paper, and my knee for a desk, it was hard enough to get it down right but I needed to, so I was patient with her and myself.

Extracts from the statement of Nora Fitzgerald – 7:02 a.m., Monday 21 January 1980

I walk the dog every morning on the beach at six a.m. He plays in the dunes and he's always come to my call but this morning at 6:10 a.m. he refused to budge, and instead he stared into the dune. I worried if he didn't come soon I'd be late for work so I made my way to him. It was then I saw the baby. I didn't know what to think it he was at first… except maybe one of those life-like dolls, but then I remembered if it was a doll the sight of it wouldn't turn my dog to stone. I ran and stumbled and fell and hurt my knee, but I made it to the phone box at the top of the road. I phoned the station and I kept having to repeat myself because every time I spoke, the garda coughed and spluttered and he couldn't seem to hear or understand me.

So I shouted to him, 'The baby is dead!' Three times I said it. Why couldn't he have just shut up and listened, not to have me repeat that terrible thing? That's it. That's all I know.

By the time I had finished taking Nora's statement, the ambulance was approaching. It was clear she needed medical attention. She was white as a ghost, and her head had dropped to her knees as though her blood pressure was about to hit the floor. She was still holding her dog and crying softly, but otherwise silent, except for the chattering of her teeth.

We heard sirens piercing the cold, still air and saw red lights flashing, casting a crimson hue on the white sand as the ambulance skirted across the empty beach. I looked at my watch so that I could note the time of arrival as 7:34 a.m. One hour and twenty-four minutes after Nora had made her grim discovery. They had come from across the border, and with only a distressed woman in shock to treat, we weren't as high on the list of calls as one might have thought.

'You're all right now,' I said and I led her to the ambulance as the back doors opened to reveal a man I was used to seeing.

Jimmy Nugent gazed up at the dune and then to me. 'So it's true, it's a baby up there?' he asked.

'I can't say,' I replied, knowing well he'd question Nora in the van. He sighed and shook his head, taking my vagueness as confirmation. 'God almighty,' he said before looking at Nora. 'Come on, girl, we'll get you checked and get you home.' He looked at the dog. 'You too, big fella… come on, get in, this is my last call, I'll be cleaning the wagon anyway.' The dog jumped into the van after Nora, and I waved them off – I was glad the ambulance was taking her away from this now terrible place, but sorry the distraction was gone. I turned back to the dune where he lay. Dicey was joined by poor Kenny, who'd arrived at the scene while I was helping Nora. He had his back to me, hunching over, and it sounded like he was coughing up half a lung into his hands. The entrances to the beach were taped off, and some lads called in from the station in Killarney were already manning them. I walked up to the men.

'The statement's done.'

'Go back and type it so,' Dicey said.

'I'm going nowhere,' I said, looking to Liam Kenny, and then to Dicey. 'Liam is on the desk today, not me.'

Dicey looked at me with a hint of mild hatred. Then Kenny coughed and a ball of rich bottle-green snot leaped from him. He apologised profusely as he held it in his hands. I took some tissues from my pocket, four fresh squares, folded them and handed them over. Dicey shook his head. 'You're a disgrace, Kenny. A living feckin' disgrace.' Kenny, too sick and disheartened to defend himself, was dispatched off. So then it was Dicey McCarthy and myself, standing over the tiny corpse and waiting for the local priest and the boys and the pathologist from Dublin. Until they arrived, we were alone, and neither of us spoke. Dicey turned his face away, but I couldn't. I was desperate to take him in my arms, to wrap my coat around him and hold him close to my beating heart, thinking… *If only the sound of it could raise him.* But I couldn't, and it wouldn't. Instead, I held him with my eyes and spoke to him in my mind. And as the sky cleared, I imagined holding him, soothing him and singing him a lullaby. But I didn't stir, not once, because Dicey kept glancing my way and I knew he was waiting for me to crack, to do something stupid, to cry or break down and to reveal all the reasons why I didn't belong in the job. So I said nothing out loud. *We're here with you now, you are safe, beyond hurt, beyond pain.* And as I repeated my silent mantra, I noticed Dicey's hands creep together, his fingers intertwining, and from the corner of my eye I saw his lips move ever so slightly as he prayed to himself.

Father Cunningham, the local priest, arrived on his bike. He was in his early seventies by then and had been serving the parish for twenty years. He was a fat, bald man with chubby, flushed cheeks – and yet, not being a driver, he'd remained fit enough to travel everywhere on his bike. He'd be seen cycling for miles in all weathers, up and down hills, without it seeming to take a puff out of him. He cycled along the sand towards us, his pale face grave, and it could have been the wind, but even from this distance, I could see the tears in his eyes. Dicey waved down at him. He nodded and dropped the bike, stepping over it and heading for us, his expression stern, rosary beads in his hands. I saw his mouth twitch ever so slightly when he saw me standing there. He only addressed Dicey.

'Sad day,' he said.

'And deeply troubling, Father,' Dicey said. Dicey was a great man for pointing out the obvious. Father Cunningham looked beyond him and towards the baby. 'Oh, Mary Mother of God,' he said, blessing himself. 'Pray for us.' He mumbled to himself, his rosary beads knocking each other, making a loud clacking sound that cut through the low rush of the curling and coming tide. His face paled, his knees buckled and he dropped, and there he was, on his behind. Dicey scrambled to try to pick him up, but Father Cunningham waved him away. 'I just need a minute.' He seemed unashamed of his weakness that manifested in the folding of his knees.

'Of course, it's understandable,' Dicey said before offering up a deep sigh. 'A terrible thing like this marks a man.' They exchanged empathetic glances, nodding together while steadfastly ignoring me, as I continued to hold the child with my eyes.

Finally, when he was ready, Father Cunningham was helped to his feet by Dicey and then he mentioned the flask of whiskey he kept in the lockbox on the back of his bike. 'For times like this...' he said, and that's when they both looked to me. They didn't have to ask. It was implied I'd be the one to go fetch it. I walked towards the bike and thought about having a nip of it myself. I was freezing in my sheer tights, whereas they were dressed up in nice warm trousers. I was practically bare-legged. *Don't do it, Mary, they're probably watching.* I brought the flask back to Father Cunningham. He offered a nip of it to Dicey. He took it gladly and then the priest drank greedily. When the men were done drinking, Father Cunningham declared he'd be christening the child to save him from purgatory. 'It's only fair he gets the chance to land straight into God's loving arms,' he said, and I hoped for the child that he was right. 'We will need a name to christen him.'

'Who are we to name him?' Dicey said.

'We're the only ones to do it,' I said to their backs.

'It doesn't seem right,' Dicey said to the priest as though the air, not I, had spoken.

'Baby Crónán,' I said without really meaning to – the name just tumbled out of me. That caught their attention.

'Crónán?' Dicey said, followed by a snort. 'Where did you get—'

'Little dark one,' Father Cunningham said, explaining the name's meaning. He pondered, raising a finger to his lips as a warning not to interrupt him. All eyes were now on the baby, observing his tiny rosebud lips and shock of black hair. The priest finally blinked. 'Baby Crónán it is.' He bowed his head. 'Let us pray.'

–

Superintendent Lynch eventually arrived from Tralee, having driven to the beach with Brian Keating, who'd abandoned his hospital visit and could be seen limping behind the Super towards us. It was nearly eleven by the time they got there. Brian had brought flasks of tea, which I was grateful for, because I was blue with the cold by then. The men stood around, shaking their heads. 'Lamb of Jesus,' Superintendent Lynch said more than once. Then he told us the boys were on their way from Dublin.

'Who's coming, do you know?' Dicey asked.

'Detective Matt Foley is one of them,' Superintendent Lynch said. I had no knowledge or impression of the detective but Dicey reacted badly.

'Balls anyways,' he said.

Superintendent Lynch nodded. 'He's known to be a tricky fecker, all right,' Lynch said and I wondered what they meant. I must have been wearing my curiosity on my face, because the men offered a quick offhand glance before walking away together, leaving footsteps in the damp sand. They stood facing one another, talking shop and smoking cigarettes, leaving Baby Crónán and me to ourselves. I tried to raise a smile for him, hoping its warmth might reach him as I sang once more, this time in a whisper the breeze carried away: 'Hush now, don't you cry…'

It was just after noon when Detective Foley and his team arrived on the scene. He was as tall as Dicey but not half as fat. He was well built, with a sharp jaw and a full thick head of brown hair to match his brown eyes; his suit was navy and worn away on the left sleeve, where two buttons had been replaced that didn't exactly match the originals. He wore a light blue shirt under the suit, the top buttons open and the navy tie with light blue diamonds on it loose. As dishevelled as he appeared, he had a commanding presence. The pathologist, Frank Waters, had arrived alongside him, having taken a lift with the Dublin boys. Foley moved us all back. 'I'll take over from here,' he said and I noticed he didn't seem to react at all to Baby Crónán. I wondered if he was so inured to death in all its forms that it was just another day to him, or was he holding everything in, afraid to break? I followed the men across the sand to the carpark at the entrance. They spoke to one another as though I wasn't there. Dicey was doing much of the talking, filling Detective Foley in on the events that led to the discovery of the dead infant.

'So you took the witness statement, right?' Detective Foley said in a Dublin accent that sounded rough to my ears.

'No, it was hers,' Dicey said, nodding his head back towards me. 'The woman was half-mad, so…' Dicey trailed off when Detective Foley gave him a look.

'Mad how?' he asked.

'Crying and screaming,' Dicey said.

'Well, the woman had just come across a baby covered in knife wounds. Crying sounds about right to me, or am I mad?' he said and there was an edge to his voice. Dicey McCarthy almost shrivelled up and died. It was a glorious moment and, despite myself and the desperate situation, I could tell I was grinning like an eejit, so I bit my lip in case anyone bothered to look my way. It was a good thing, too, because it was then that Detective Matt Foley turned his attention to me.

'Talk me through it,' he said, so I did. I told him exactly what Nora had told me.

'Do we have any idea of a timeline?'

'The baby wasn't there at six a.m. yesterday morning,' I answered.

'How do you know that?'

'She walks the dog here every morning at six before she goes to her job as a teller in the bank. That dune… Her dog likes to roll in it. Every morning, like clockwork, until today.'

He nodded. 'Right. Is the beach busy this time of year?'

'Not till a good bit later,' I supplied, 'and the weather's been bad. We've had rain for four days and nights solid. This morning's the first break in it. Very few come out when it's so wet, especially when it comes with a cold wind, which it did.'

He looked at me, surveying me. 'Go on.'

'There are three entrance points to this beach: two have houses opposite, one is quiet enough, down the end of a long, empty road. But there's a shop at the top of that road, run by a woman called Celine

Ford, who likes to sit by the door and smoke. There's not much she misses.'

'Doesn't look like there's much you miss either,' Detective Foley said. Dicey made an involuntary grunting sound.

'What do you think happened here?' Detective Foley asked me.

'Well, a baby was born into this world and someone violently took his life. He did nothing to no one except come into being, which makes me suspect he wasn't wished for.'

'You think a woman did this?' Detective Foley asked.

'I think if she didn't, she certainly knows who did,' I said. 'So what now?'

'We go door to door,' Dicey said, trying to reinsert himself into the conversation.

'Well, now, that's bloody standard, isn't it?' Detective Foley commented, shooting Dicey down once more. I could see why the lads thought he was tricky, but so far, I liked him.

He asked us our names. Dicey swallowed hard before he answered. Detective Foley then turned back to me.

'Mary Shea,' I said.

'And what do you think, Garda Shea?'

His wanting to know what I thought was a shock to Dicey and me. I ploughed on as if it wasn't, while Dicey made a face as if he were sucking a raw egg. 'We talk to the local GPs, the local hospitals, we get a list of the pregnant women. Judging by the baby's weight and size, he was almost full term or over it.'

Detective Foley nodded in approval, then sighed deeply, his eyes dimming, 'God rest him and God help us.' He gave his nose a good rub, then moved the thick gold band that he wore on the fourth finger of his left hand with his thumb, which seemed to restore him. 'All right, then.' He turned to Dicey and looked at his lads. 'McCarthy, you willing to do a little overtime?' he asked, and Dicey perked up, agreeing enthusiastically.

'Good man yourself, go door to door with the lads,' Foley directed. Dicey's face turned to stone. Detective Matt Foley cast his gaze in my direction. 'Well, lady, how about you?' he asked.

'I'll work day and night till we find who did this,' I said earnestly. He seemed to appreciate that; a hint of a smile tugged at his lips as his thumb absentmindedly nudged again at his wedding ring – a small repetitive movement he'd been making since we'd been gathered on the sand. We all waited for his direction. He gestured to me.

'Grand, then, you're with me.' My heart skipped an actual beat. Detective Matt Foley had looked right at me and suggested I was fit to do my job when it mattered most.

'Good,' I heard myself mumble, trying hard not to sound as intimated as I felt. The Superintendent interjected. 'Dicey McCarthy is one of our best,' he said in a voice that suggested he wasn't at all happy with the detective's choice.

'I'm sure he is,' Detective Foley said and then he pointed me towards his unmarked car. 'Let's go.'

'Where are you off to?' Superintendent Lynch demanded.

'We're going to talk to a few GPs and then we're going to pay a visit to some women,' Detective Foley answered. Then he added, 'Your station big enough for an incident room?'

'Not really,' Brian Keating said from behind me. I'd forgotten he was even there.

'You have a hotel with a boardroom in it around here?'

'There's one at the top of the town, just across from the station, the Bonham,' Keating replied.

'Grand, book us in there and start setting up the room.' He looked at me. 'Keep up.' We walked away, leaving the lads with their mouths hanging open wide enough to catch flies. I was only short of swaggering, but I didn't, because a baby was dead and as nice as it was to be considered capable, the image and loss of him were uppermost in my mind.

–

There were three GPs in the town, and the most popular for women of childbearing age was a man named Dr Gerry Pierce. He was the first man to practise in the town and now, in his early seventies, he had brought half its population into the world. He was also known to be less handsy than the other fella, Dr Fredrick Boyne, who was in his forties, had a wife, kids, a gammy eye and was known for making women strip naked whatever their complaint. The last GP was a woman named Dr Ciara Crosby, and she was only new to the town. Her client list was small; Dicey remarked that he'd rather be treated by a monkey than a woman. He wasn't alone; many of the patients had transferred to Dr Pierce upon learning that a female doctor had acquired the practice. I imparted the necessary information, leaving out the bit about the monkey, to Detective Foley as he drove, and he listened and nodded along.

'So we'll head to Dr Pierce first. And, Mary, call me Matt,' he said as we drove along the coastal road, following the signage that would lead us to town.

'I'd rather not,' I said. *We're not on a date*, I thought.

He laughed to himself. 'Call me Foley, then.' *Foley… Foley… Fine. Foley.* I nodded my agreement.

'So you're Assistant Commissioner Shea's daughter?' he said, focusing on the road ahead, and didn't wait for my reply. 'Is that how you got the job?' he asked without fear or hesitation. Most people simply treated me with the contempt that comes with perceived nepotism, but they dared not say it to my face. It took me off guard.

'I got this job in spite of him,' I said, which was the truth.

'Right,' he said. 'How's that, then?'

'He doesn't want me in the force, he thinks it's no place for women,' I admitted.

'Yet here you are.'

'Only because I went behind his back to get the interview.' My father had been so unsupportive, so unhelpful. I'd gone to him with the application, hoping against hope that in the absence of him having a son to follow in his footsteps, he'd be thrilled he'd inspired his first-born daughter to do so, but he dismissed me. It was ten years earlier and he was sitting in his favourite battered wooden armchair with soft faded green cushions that faced the bay window overlooking my mother's well-manicured rose garden. I was eighteen: strong, athletic, my grades were good, I was well capable. As his daughter, policing was in my blood. I challenged him, sat on the hard red-and-navy diamond carpeted floor beside his battered chair, legs crossed and appealing to him. 'Why not?'

'There is horror out there, and horror is men's work,' my father responded.

'Why?' I asked.

'Because women are weak.' He wasn't trying to be offensive. His eyes were soft when he said it. I wanted to tell him to feck off. I didn't. It would probably have killed him, hearing those words out of a woman's mouth, my mouth. Instead, I told him that he was wrong. 'Women are strong, stronger than men,' I insisted. He laughed at me.

'You don't know what you're talking about.'

'Really? How many babies have you witnessed being born?' I asked, knowing the answer was none.

'That's women's work.'

'That's right,' I said. When I was ten, I had helped my poor mother give birth to my sister, with no one else around. I saw her white sheets turn red as she tore apart, her pain and agony undeniable, with the chilling notion that my sister, who was coming way too early, would die in my arms. I was the one who opened the door to the doctor, covered in her blood, and heard him swearing and running past me; I heard my mother cry as he sewed her up while I held my newborn baby sister, wrapped in a blanket, rubbing her back and pacing while we waited for the ambulance. I had a much better understanding of that work than my father did. 'Women's work is horror,' I said. 'Being a woman is a horror.'

He looked at me then and something crossed his eyes; maybe it was anger or maybe it was doubt, but he shouted at me to leave him in peace and as he shooed me from the room and closed the door, he mumbled again, 'You don't know what you're talking about.'

Matt Foley wasn't the first person, and wouldn't be the last, to assume I got that job because of my father, but the truth is I became who I was because of my mother. It was Mammy who helped me fill out the endless forms; it was she who drove me to the interview and spoke to me all the way, telling me how great I was and not to worry at all, because she would deal with Daddy. It was she who pulled in at the side of the road when I threatened to be carsick and who played my well-worn Simon & Garfunkel tape so loud that the car shook all the way to Templemore. We sang 'Bridge Over Troubled Water', 'Cecilia' and 'The Boxer' until our voices were hoarse. When she told a silly joke, we'd laughed ourselves empty and by the time I'd got to that interview, I felt like nothing or no one could bring me down. The three men behind the desk made a good go of it, with faces like wet blankets. Not one of them had a smile for me. They didn't introduce themselves, but instead looked me up and down; one of them, the middle one, spoke to my boobs. They talked at me, telling me all the reasons I had no business wasting their time. They joked about me being only good enough to make tea and when the fella on the left with a face like a bear's behind said I had nice *tit—eeth*, the others laughed. It was then I interrupted their fun to ask if someone had a question for me. They didn't like that.

'I'll conduct this interview as I see fit,' the middle one said.

I didn't come here for this, I thought. 'Interview implies that one of us asks questions and the other answers them. So far all you three have done is tell me how great you are and how awful I am, all the while looking at my boobs and dribbling tea,' I said before looking at my watch. 'We've been here fifteen minutes. I am applying for a job, not looking to be turned off matrimony, although you've succeeded in doing that, so fair play to you.'

The middle fella slammed down his mug of tea on the desk, his moustached lip twisting to reveal a black sharp tooth. He was an awful-looking eejit. 'Listen here you...' Boiling with temper, he spat the words out.

Oh no, this is going all wrong. Flip it anyway. I had run my mouth when I'd sworn to myself I wouldn't. My back was to the wall. *Feck it*, I thought. It was then I mentioned my father's name. 'I'm listening. My father, Assistant Commissioner for the Southern Region, Eric Shea, always taught me to listen well.' That put a stop to his spluttering. His eyes finally reached mine for the first time.

'Assistant Commissioner Shea?' he said.

'That's right, it's been his long-held wish that I join the force,' I said, lying through my back teeth.

'Right,' he said. 'I should have copped the name but I would have thought we'd get some prior...' he stammered.

'Warning,' I supplied, finishing his sentence. He didn't confirm or deny his intended word. The others said nothing at all and just stared down at the table. I'd had enough and stood to leave. 'It's been lovely to meet you all. I look forward to talking to my dad and filling him in on how professional you've all been.'

I'd sworn I wouldn't trade on my father's name but my dream was unreachable without mention of him, and they'd treated me so unfairly. So I did it, and I'd do it again.

'Well, thank you,' the man in the middle said, his voice a mere whisper now. His colleagues remained silent and looked like they'd rather be anywhere else. I held the middle fella's eye, thinking, *Nothing to lose now… except maybe control of my bowel…* 'Of course, the formal offers won't go out until next week but, subject to a medical, we look forward to you joining the ranks,' he continued.

'Thank you,' I said, offering those lads my most winning smile before turning and running.

Mammy was waiting for me, sitting in the car, smoking. She jumped out as soon as she saw me.

'Well?'

'I got in,' I said and we ran to one another and she picked me up, which was difficult enough because I was taller than her. She dropped me fairly quickly and we screamed together, dancing around like wild women. She brought me out for lunch in a roadside restaurant, and the food was terrible and the service worse but we didn't care, we were giddy as goats. 'I couldn't be prouder of you,' she said more than once that day. In the ten years since I joined the force, my mother's words – 'I couldn't be prouder of you' – have carried me through the intense training, the first five challenging years in Cork city and now here in Nead Mara, when I considered giving up multiple times a day. I didn't. I wouldn't, or couldn't, because of what she said. Foley was wrong; it wasn't my father who secured my position, though his name opened the door. It was my mother who ensured I pursued my calling. I survived, despite all that was thrown at me, because I was smart enough to play the game, strong enough to withstand the ensuing storm and calculated enough to navigate around those intent on destroying me. In all the ten years I was a guard, I'd been a tea-maker, a typist and a cleaner mostly. I answered the phone, I typed the reports, I endured the jibes, the name-calling, the put-downs, the slapped arse, and waited for my moment to shine, to show them who I was and of what I was capable of.

My father never gave me a word of encouragement or advice. Upon learning I'd secured the job, he had a huge row with my mother, resulting in them ignoring each other for three weeks. He finally caved, unable to go another day without a roast dinner. While he didn't stand in my way, he didn't help me either.

'Well, however you got the job, he must be proud,' Foley said.

'He's not, and if you are half as smart as you purport to be, you already know that,' I said.

He laughed. 'They say you're hard work, all right.'

'And what do they say about you?' *Tricky fecker.* His laughter faded to a grin. He drove on and the rain began to fall, and I fervently hoped the pathologist had finished his cursory work and McGuire's lads had Baby Crónán in the back of their hearse. I knew he'd never get warm but I was desperate he didn't get wet.

We arrived at Dr Pierce's office just after two p.m., when I should have been home already and warming myself by the fire. His secretary was very apologetic, but Dr Pierce was away on a long weekend, a golf trip. He wasn't due home till the next day.

Foley didn't seem to mind; in fact, he seemed almost relieved. 'No need for him, just information from his files,' he told her. She was twenty if she was a day, not really sure what to do with a detective from Dublin flashing his badge at her while she glanced curiously at me. As many times as the women of the town saw me in uniform, they still reacted with a combination of surprise and uncertainty. 'I can't, because of patient confidentiality,' she said. Foley said nothing. He just stared at her. 'It's the law,' she stammered.

'I'm the law,' Foley said. 'And patient confidentiality doesn't mean anything when there is a murdered baby and a woman who is possibly in need of urgent medical attention,' he said gravely, maybe aiming to shock her into compliance. In a small town, word of the grisly horror would spread like wildfire, but it was evident this was the first she'd heard of it. Her eyes widened and her hand fluttered towards her face. 'Oh, my God.'

'I'd like the names of the women on the books who would be…' He looked at me.

'Over seven months pregnant, to be safe,' I said. She looked from him to me and then back to him, before nodding her agreement. 'And make a note of anyone who was struggling.'

'Struggling?' she said, attempting to grasp my meaning.

'If any of the women mentioned they were unhappy or scared or finding things difficult.' Again, she looked from me to Foley. He nodded his approval of my suggestion. She turned to walk away. 'And note their marital status,' I added as she scurried off. I joined Foley, who had headed to the chairs by the window.

'That was good thinking,' he said.

'Thank you.'

'You're not as useless as they say you are,' he commented, his tone amused.

'I'm far from it,' I said, while internally basking in the backhanded compliment.

'You've got a lot of feckin' confidence, I'll give you that.'

'You're no stranger to it yourself,' I retorted. He wasn't so enamoured with that, so I shut up.

He picked up a magazine, rolled it up and tapped out a beat with it, clearly playing in his head. I just sat in silence, hoping my stomach wouldn't rumble; the burnt piece of toast had proved an inadequate breakfast and now I'd missed lunch. The girl approached us, holding a list in her trembling hands. 'I hope I'm doing the right thing.'

'You are,' Foley told her, and with that, we left.

I read through name after name, their due dates, their ailments. As I'd expected, all had husbands, and most were on their third or fourth child. No one jumped out. Then I came across Bridie Fitzmaurice, thirty-seven years old, due date 8 March. Pregnant with her fifth child, she suffered from swelling around her ankles and was described as depressed. It was the reason for her depression that stood out: she'd been recently widowed and her eldest son had died too. The notes stopped there, failing to provide a cause for their deaths, but I knew their story – the whole town did. Theirs was a recent tragedy, still murmured about as poor Bridie passed on the street, with her head down and mind God knows where.

'That's where we'll start,' he said and then he had me read out the names of the other women to Kenny over the radio, so he could send the lads out to make sure they were all still pregnant or at home with their babies.

I guided him to the street where Bridie lived and we parked outside the old brick council house. It had a small garden that had been cemented over and there was a pot by the door with more weeds than flowers in it. A child opened the front door, one of the girls, aged fourteen. She was a whippet of a thing, her second-hand clothes swallowing her slender figure.

'Can I help you?' she asked, scanning me in my uniform and the strange man from Dublin, who was holding up a badge. Behind her I could see the steep staircase that led upstairs; the hallway was dark, with a frayed carpet completely worn away in places.

The place was clean, though – even from the door, the smell reminded me of something… A hospital, back when hospitals smelled sterile.

'We're looking for your mammy,' I said to the girl, whose fear and mistrust were evident in her wide eyes and trembling hands.

'She's not well,' she said, unable to meet our gaze, her voice faltering. We looked at each other. *Could it be that easy?*

I was vaguely aware of the girl; I'd seen her around and I knew her sister, Lisa, well. Her name had slipped my mind but she told me it was Debbie.

'Debbie, we need to see her,' I said and I pushed my way inside without invitation.

'Take us to her,' Foley added, following close behind.

'Why? What do you want from her?' she said, her voice climbing in alarm.

'It's adult business,' Foley told her. We were standing in the hallway, and Debbie quickly closed the front door and turned to face us.

'She won't like it,' she said as she gazed up the stairs. 'She's in bed. You shouldn't be here,' she pleaded. It was obvious she was hiding something, but what?

'Who else is here?' Foley asked, examining the confined hallway.

'My sister Lisa. My brother's in school.'

'Why aren't you?' I asked as Foley pushed on the sitting room door, then the kitchen, confirming the house was as empty as reported.

'Mam's not well. I have to mind her,' she said, her voice hardening. She glared at me; it was evident she was on the verge of tears.

'And what about Lisa?' I asked. She looked at me as though I had two heads.

'She's slow. She can't mind my mam, she can't mind herself.' I knew what Lisa was like. God knows, everyone from Kerry to the Cork boundary knew Lisa Fitzmaurice. She was a wanderer, and there wasn't a month that went by without a call-out looking for her.

She was always found safe and untroubled, leading me to think she was more capable than her family gave her credit for. She was a happy, bubbly thing, who seemed to love the feel of the earth under her feet and the taste of freedom. Seventeen years old but she had the mind of a ten-year-old.

'You should be in school,' I heard myself say to Debbie.

'It's my job to mind Lisa and my brothers—' She corrected herself, 'I mean my brother...' Tears formed in her eyes. She was a pathetic sight, this stick of a girl dressed in someone else's clothes, wiping tears from her eyes with a wool sleeve that was so worn away she had stuck her thumb through it.

The last time I'd seen her was when I went to the funeral home and shook hands with the family, the whole town did, but then we all went off about our business, forgetting about them and the enormity of their loss. In that moment, it was impossible to escape. Her pain trumped my self-loathing.

'I'm sorry for your loss, Debbie, can I ask what happened?' Foley said. I hadn't mentioned they'd both drowned, afraid it would appear unprofessional and like gossip. Men often spoke of events around them unchallenged, but as a woman, I knew I had to be more careful; the same words falling from my lips were often deemed frivolous. It was a tightrope walk. In this instance I figured it would be best if the family circumstances came out in the interview and hoped that Foley didn't feel blindsided.

'My dad went out fishing. He took Tommy with him. They drowned,' she said.

'When was that?'

'Four months ago,' she said. Foley scowled at me; clearly, he thought drowning might have been worth mentioning. *Damn it, Mary, why didn't you speak up?* Foley started for the stairs, but Debbie intercepted his path.

'Debbie, you have to move out of the way now,' I said as gently as possible.

Debbie bit her lip and shook her head from side to side. 'She's bad,' she said and everything in me screamed we were in the right house. Foley must have felt the same; he gave her a serious look, placed his hand on her shoulder and, without one word spoken, she turned and led us up the stairs, her feet heavy like lead and the climb as arduous as if she were scaling Mount Everest. We followed her up to the tiny diamond-shaped landing that led to three doors. There were footsteps from behind the nearest door, then banging, and a voice shouting, 'Let me out. Let me out.' There was a key in the lock.

Debbie turned to us, horrified and embarrassed. 'That's Lisa. I locked her in there. I can't look after her and Mam when Mam's this bad,' she said by way of explanation and apology. 'Still running away?' I asked, already knowing the answer. Debbie nodded. 'She'll be the death of me.' She leaned on her mother's door while we stood on the landing, calling to her. 'Mam, there's people here to see you.'

'Send them away,' came the hoarse voice from the room.

'I can't,' she said. 'It's the guards.' The word caught in her throat.

She opened the door and we peered inside. Bridie was in the bed, lying on her side. The curtains were closed, and there were no lamps in the room. The only light came from a red bulb forming part of a framed Sacred Heart electric picture mounted on the wall behind her. All we could see was her shape in the bed and, above her, the face of a Jesus Christ photo drenched in the red glow. She stared at us blankly as we moved towards her in the dark, as if we were figments of her imagination. Debbie opened the door wider to allow light from the small hall to seep into the room. She covered her eyes as though this low light hurt her.

'Sorry to disturb you,' Foley said, walking to the end of the bed.

'Is this about my husband, about my boy?' she asked without moving to look at us.

'No,' he said regretfully.

A fat tear formed and fell from her eye. 'The weather was fine, you know. No storms, no reason for them to find trouble. They were strong swimmers. It doesn't make sense. It's a crime.'

'If it is, the guards will find out, Mrs Fitzmaurice,' Foley said. I wasn't sure if he was trying to comfort or threaten her.

'Not if it was the devil,' she said. Her eyes flicked to the ceiling as she screamed out, 'You *evil bastard*!' The venom in her voice took me aback. Debbie's knees seemed to buckle and she held on to the door, tears drowning her big blue eyes. 'Please, Mam, stop.' She looked petrified by her mother's words.

'Has the devil called recently?' Foley said, as though it was a normal thing to say. This caught her attention.

'Oh, he's here all right,' she said. 'We've been cursed.'

'How's that?' he asked.

She lay there, eerily still, her eyes wide and staring through us.

'First there was Lisa, the devil took her sense and any kind of future we'd hoped for her. And then he stole my husband and Tommy, my beautiful, brave boy.' Her face softened and I could see her disappearing into a warm memory.

'Who cursed you?' Foley said, pulling her right out of it.

'What do you want?' she said, snapping awake. Blinking her blood-shot eyes, she leaned heavily on one arm, trying to push herself up into a sitting position. She was pale, her face so gaunt that her skin clung to her bones.

'Have you had your baby, Mrs Fitzmaurice?' Foley said.

'Do I look like it?' she said.

'You'll need to sit up for us to know.'

'Why would I do that? What's that got to do with my boys?' she asked and she seemed distant, as though she was mentally sliding away to somewhere else entirely. I noticed the small brown bottle of tablets on her locker.

'Is this a test?' she asked, her unfocused eyes trying hard to find Foley's face. 'Maybe you're the devil.'

'I'm not,' Foley said. 'If I was, I'd have a nicer car.'

'Well, he's here in this house,' she said and Debbie sobbed.

'Ah no, Mam,' Debbie said. 'Ah no.' She backed out of the room and into the landing. I could hear Lisa start to bang at the door again. 'Let me out. Let me out.' Bridie heard her too and she was mentally back in the room. 'It's all right, my girl. Debbie will take you for a walk.'

Debbie called in from the landing, 'I can't, Mam. She'll run.'

'Put her on the reins. She needs to get out, she needs to run and to breathe. Let her out,' Bridie said and then she was sitting up. The blankets still covered her.

'We'll need to see you,' Foley insisted. She had her back to me as I moved towards the locker. I picked up the small brown bottle. It was half-full, labelled 'Valium', and prescribed to Fidelma Regan. I noted the name in my notebook.

I could hear Lisa's door unlocking as Bridie slowly pulled off the blankets, revealing her legs and swollen ankles. Slowly, she stood up, the blankets falling away as she fixed her nightdress. She struggled to her feet, her stomach so full of life, it was fit to burst.

'What now?' she asked impatiently. 'Would you like me to sing a song or dance a jig?' she snarled before slumping back down onto the bed. 'What is this?' she asked, and it was clear she hadn't heard about the baby on the beach. She had probably been in her bed all day while Debbie ran the house and Lisa banged the door down. I had been so sure we'd solved the case at the first house we knocked on. I felt silly but also relieved for poor Bridie; her husband and son were gone, but she still had her other children and the baby. It was something. My mind wandered back to him – Baby Crónán, naked and alone, his grey eyes staring up at the dark sky. I promised him justice and I was determined not to fail him.

'No, thank you, Mrs Fitzmaurice. We are sorry to disturb,' Foley said as he made to leave.

'You look like you could give birth at any moment,' I said. 'Mind yourself now.'

She lay down. 'Where's Lisa?'

I'd heard Lisa follow Debbie down the stairs. 'Debbie's taking her for a walk.'

'Oh,' she said as though she'd forgotten. 'Tell her to bring Lisa to the church to light a candle for her daddy and Tommy.'

'I will,' I promised.

'Will you leave us now?'

'We will,' I said. 'Except to say once more that I'm sorry for your loss.'

Bridie looked at me and a tear rolled down her cheek. We left her alone after that. In the kitchen, Lisa was wrestling with Debbie, who was trying to put a pair of welly boots on her feet.

'I don't like them,' she said. She was older than Debbie, stronger too, and she squirmed like a worm on a hook. Debbie, who looked tired and haggard, was struggling to keep a hold on her.

'Well, you'll be soaked through in anything else,' Debbie said, still close to tears. She had the look of a girl who just wanted to run. I knew that look well; lots of women and girls wore it. They rarely ran, though; for them there was nowhere to go. Lisa saw me and smiled. She had piercing blue eyes and presented with classic Down syndrome features. Her hair was cut into a bob and that day she wore two pretty pink clips, pinning her growing fringe to the side.

She was short but wide, built like a tank. In contrast to her sister, she had lightness to her. Her big, rosy cheeks glowed, and she looked like her mind and heart belonged somewhere else, somewhere less troubled.

'I know you,' she said and grinned at me.

'I know you too,' I replied and she giggled.

'We should go,' Foley said, taking no interest in the child before him.

'I want ice cream,' Lisa whined.

'I'll buy you ice cream,' Debbie said dully. 'Even though it's freezing,' she mumbled.

At the front door I took it upon myself to ask Debbie not to leave her mother for long. 'That baby will be here any minute and she doesn't seem in a fit state to handle that business herself,' I said.

'We won't be long. Lisa gets scared when it gets dark,' Debbie said. 'And my brother, Richard, will be home from school soon.' I nodded, and Foley and I took our leave.

We didn't speak in the car. Instead, we listened to a terse report on the local radio: a baby was found dead on the beach. Our silence was heavy with unspoken thoughts. We knew that was only the start of it; soon, the press would descend upon us, baying for answers, answers we didn't have. We arrived at Dr Fredrick Boyne's practice and knocked on the door. He was there, unfortunately. He was a tall, broad-shouldered man with a full head of dark, curly hair; he should have been attractive but the expression on his face rendered him ugly. He wore his spectacles halfway down his nose, likely to look over them in a patronising way, as he did now. He would prove difficult early on, and later, despicable. He sat down behind his desk. 'I have no intention of sharing personal information about my patients,' he said, unimpressed by my uniform or Foley's badge.

'Give us the names,' Foley demanded.

'Or what?' Dr Boyne said.

'Or I'll arrest you.'

'On what grounds?'

'On the grounds that you are refusing to co-operate with our investigation,' Foley said.

'Nonsense,' Dr Boyne said and his arrogance nearly tipped Foley over the edge. His hands curled into tight fists and his nostrils flared. I thought he was going to grab him by the scruff of the neck and punch him right then and there. He didn't. Instead, he placed his hands on the desk, leaning over Dr Boyne. 'A woman could be in dire trouble and if she is, and something happens to her, I'll have your licence.'

'And if there isn't some woman in terrible distress and this scenario is a figment of your imagination?' Dr Boyne countered coolly, seemingly not the slightest bit intimidated.

'Then I'll make sure that there isn't a day that goes by where you won't be forced to engage with an officer of the law,' Foley said.

'That's a threat, you heard him,' Dr Boyne said to me.

It is and I did. 'I've no idea what you are referring to, Dr Boyne,' I said.

Dr Boyne hissed at us, 'There is no list.' He revealed that he only had one pregnant woman on his books, Linda Thomas, and she'd given birth to a healthy baby girl that afternoon. I noted the woman's name. Foley pushed him for a list of all his female patients and, after much back-and-forth, he finally conceded. The list was short; his reputation ensured that.

Our final call was to Dr Ciara Crosby. She was around my age – maybe a year or two younger – and wore her hair in a brown bob, accentuating her angular face and thick eyebrows. She was a few inches shorter than me, with an athletic build. She had a nice smile, warm and welcoming, and she wore three delicate gold necklaces around her neck, one longer than the other, with charms on them. She was happy to help, without need for a threat, but revealed that she didn't have any pregnant women on her list; in fact, she had very few women at all. 'It appears that women are as uncomfortable with a female doctor as men. Ironic, really,' she said as she printed off her patients' list. Foley asked her about the hospitals. 'Most women go through their GPs. The closest maternity unit is in Cork. I trained there, I can make a few enquiries, see if I can find out anything helpful,' she offered, and Foley told her he'd be obliged and took out a card with his name on it. 'What's the station phone number?' he asked me. I told him and he jotted it down. 'If you could phone the station and let us know.' He handed her the card.

'I will,' she said and we headed for the car.

'What now?' Foley asked.

'We go to the hotel, liaise with the boys, see if anything came of knocking on doors,' I said, quietly amazed to be asked for my suggestions.

'And the woman who found the baby...?' he said.

'What of her?' I said, not quite catching on quick enough.

'Is there any chance she could be the mother?' he asked, and the question caught me by surprise.

I was completely unprepared for the idea. Surely not? 'No... although...' I needed to think. She was a big girl; she could have been pregnant, and she was pale as a ghost and near fainting. She was rambling… screaming, shouting, incoherent sometimes but crystal clear at others. But her behaviour made sense after what she'd seen. I'd put it down to shock, but what if…? He was staring at me. 'No,' I said. 'I doubt it, but then… maybe?' Lots of women hid their pregnancies, I knew that. She was stiff when she walked; I thought it was the fear running through her, but what if she was sore? She'd kept dropping her head like she was dizzy too. 'Thinking about it…' *When she doubled over, was it pain, grief, guilt? Is there any way she could be that child's mother?* 'It's possible,' I admitted.

'We'll have to talk to her and she'll need to be examined. No doubt she won't go willingly. Are you all right with being a part of that?' he asked.

'Yes,' I agreed, without even thinking about it. I had to show him I had the stomach for the job, and God forgive me, I did have the stomach for that and so much worse.

CHAPTER THREE

The press landed in town: we spotted three vans sporting the RTÉ television logo parked in the square, and familiar faces were vox-popping locals on the street. Foley wanted to steer clear of the media circus for as long as possible. We were both hungry, so I brought him to a small place on a little side street that would be missed by anyone but locals. The place was filled and buzzing with talk but as we entered, it descended into silence. Every step that led us to the counter was scrutinised. We ordered two ham-and-cheese sandwiches and two cups of tea. We sat at the back of the room at a cramped table covered by a plastic tablecloth embossed with pink roses. The chair seemed a little small for Foley, whose knees hit the underside of the table. Our audience were still gawking at us. It made for an uncomfortable scene. Finally, a fella in his sixties with a peaky cap shouted over to Foley, 'Are you from Dublin?'

'Yeah,' Foley said without looking his way.

'Do you know who did it?' the fella asked.

'Not yet,' Foley said. 'But we will.' It was then he raised his eyes to meet the man's gaze, before he looked around the room at every one of them, studying them just as they had studied us. They seemed to shrink back, all eyes averted. The waitress approached shyly, bringing our tea and sandwiches to the table. He grinned at her, thanked her and she sloped off. No one looked our way after that; instead, they disappeared into their own murmurings. Still, we didn't talk about the case; the place was too busy and the people next to us too close, even a whisper would be heard by the attentive listener. I was happy to eat in silence, the sandwich was going down well. Hunger is a good sauce, goes the saying. Foley didn't seem such a fan of the quiet.

'How long have you been working here?' he asked.

'Long time,' I said.

'Any man in your life?'

'No,' I said. I couldn't stand small talk. If he realised that, he didn't care.

He cocked a brow. 'Why wouldn't a girl like you have a man in her life?'

Here we go. 'What's a girl like me?' I challenged.

'A pretty one,' he said and my temper rose. *Would you say that to one of the lads? No, you wouldn't…* My face flushed hot. He noticed my expression immediately.

'It was a compliment, nothing more.' He raised his hand to make the peace sign. *Shove your compliment,* I thought, but of course I wouldn't say that. I wanted him to understand me. I believed that he actually might be capable of such a thing. 'I like my job,' I said, my eyes drawn to his ring, which he was once more fiddling with. He caught me looking and stopped twisting it.

'I suppose you think it's unfair that I can marry and stay doing this job, and you can't,' he said and he was absolutely right.

I hummed. 'I do.'

'But what about children?'

What about them? I thought. I'd watched my mother go through six miscarriages before the birth of my baby sister nearly killed her. 'It takes two to make them, it takes two to rear them,' I said. His lips tightened and he folded his arms across his chest.

'In what world?' he asked before finishing off his tea. I didn't answer, as I doubted he cared to hear what I had to say. We left soon after and as we made our way to the car, I was worried about the press descending upon us. I hadn't been involved in anything like this before. It was disconcerting.

'The press will want answers,' I said.

'The press can wait.'

'Will you be doing a conference?' I asked.

He grunted. 'Tomorrow, when we have something to talk about. They can stew tonight.'

'What do you think we'll have to say by tomorrow?' I asked as we got into the car.

'Probably not much, just that it's an ongoing investigation. I'll ask people to come forward if they know anything,' he said.

'Every fantasist in the county will show up with a story then.'

He rubbed his eyes at this and then started the engine. 'That's why we hold off and try to establish key witnesses early on. Then we cast the net wide. Anyway, with or without a statement, it will lead the *Six O'clock News*, and we'll be hearing from those fantasists of yours by the first ad break.'

'Oh,' I said. *This is huge. What am I doing in the middle of a story shown around the country this evening?* Foley seemed to sense that I was daunted, because he took a moment to school me, to make me understand.

'This is the big leagues, lady, are you sure you're up for it? Because it won't just be the locals watching, it will be the whole of Ireland, maybe even the world,' he said.

'The world? Couldn't be,' I said naively.

'It's a baby, murdered, laid out on a public beach in a quiet costal town. It doesn't get more terrible than that.' He was right. It didn't, and the more terrible a thing was, the more interest it garnered.

The food didn't stay down well. It was hard to digest, when the prospect of the whole world watching and waiting for us to find out who hurt Baby Crónán was looming so large. I couldn't fail him. My mind slipped to thinking about Nora Fitzgerald. *Was* she *his mother?* My stomach was tied up in knots, which was doing unmentionable things to my guts. I was still contemplating what I'd do if my bowels gave way, as Foley banged on the pale pink hardwood door of Nora's two-bedroomed pretty cottage. It was just after five by the time we got there. The garden was bereft of flowers, stunted by winter, but it was well-manicured and dotted with evergreens. I could imagine it in bloom as we waited and heard shuffling behind the door.

'Hello,' called out an older female voice I didn't recognise.

'Hello, it's the gardaí,' I shouted. 'Is Nora in?'

'Oh… Right so…' came the voice. 'Just a second,' she said, and Foley and I stood while she rummaged for a key. Then we heard it hit the lock and the door slid open. Nora's mother, Lena Fitzgerald, was opposite us, probably only in her late fifties but she might as well have been ninety; her face was wizened and her hair pure white. Behind her was the staircase that formed part of her sitting room. From the door I could see the small kitchenette through an archway, the walls painted in delicate colours, and a sweet scent of lavender came rushing forward.

'Is it about that poor baby?' she asked, her tone riddled with anxiety.

Foley nodded. 'It is.'

'Nora's asleep. She's had a few stiff drinks.' She opened the door for us to step inside.

'We'll need to wake her.'

'Okay so,' Lena said. She wasn't going to argue with a big man from Dublin. She wasn't going to stand in the way of an investigation, either. 'Sit down over there.' She pointed to the sofa. She moved to turn away, but Foley stopped her.

'I'd like to ask you a few questions first,' he said.

'But sure, I wasn't there at all.'

'I know, but these questions are about your daughter.'

She looked from him to me quizzically. 'What about her?'

'Sit down, Mrs Fitzgerald,' Foley said, and the woman sat on the cosy floral armchair that seemed to mould to her shape. We sat, as directed, on the sofa, facing her.

'How has your daughter been?' Foley said.

'Well, she's in a terrible way after what she's seen.'

'Not since this morning... before that?' he said.

She frowned, uncertain. 'I don't know what you mean.'

'Health-wise.'

'She's fine, nothing at all wrong with her,' Mrs Fitzgerald said as her complexion paled. I could see the penny was dropping...

'You don't think that baby was my Nora's?' she said in a voice that suggested the very thought was outlandish.

'We wouldn't be doing our jobs if we didn't consider it,' Foley said.

Nora's mother blessed herself before continuing with a firm voice. 'That child is not my daughter's. Nora lives here with me and works by day in the bank. She walks her dog on the beach at six in the morning and in the park across the road at six every evening. Aside from that, she reads in her room. She doesn't have a man in her life. She has one friend who moved to Cork. She talks to her on the phone every now and again, but that's it. That's my daughter's life, Mr...'

'Detective Foley,' Foley supplied.

'Detective Foley, my Nora's life is a very simple one.'

'I'm sure it is. Can we see her now, please?' he said and she stood up slowly, her head shaking from side to side, disbelieving but yet unable to do anything to protect her already traumatised child from what was to come.

36

'I'll get her so.' We watched her make her way up the stairs as we sat quietly together on the sofa, and I thought about how empty Nora's life sounded. At least she had a dog... And a friend in Cork. I had no dog. My mother was my only friend now.

For five years, the girls I boarded with in Dingle – the ones I lived, laughed and discovered myself with – were my whole world. Sharing a dorm made our bond feel unbreakable.

Then we graduated and scattered to our hometowns. I joined the guards; they got married and started families. Slowly, that unbreakable bond bent into a loop – held together by geography for some, but more often by shared domestic lives, husbands and children. I found myself out of that loop.

My parents were Kerry people, born and bred, but they lived in Bantry, in a house my mother's aunt left her when she died. Aunt Nuala was a childless widow. My mother was one of three – she had two brothers – but Nuala didn't have much patience for them. Mammy was the light of her life. In a world where inheritance usually passed down the male line, Aunty Nuala bucked the trend, and two years after my parents married, they found themselves the owners of a fancy home in County Cork.

They thought about selling up and using the money to buy in Kerry, but Daddy was a guard, and Bantry was just over the road from the county bounds. It was better he didn't live and work in the same place. So he agreed to settle there on the condition that their children would be educated in Kerry, ensuring he wouldn't raise Corkonians – there would be no greater sin for a Kerry man than that. As a result, I had little connection to my hometown of Bantry, certainly no enduring friendships. When I started training for An Garda Síochána, there were three women in my class at Templemore. Two of us made it through training and we remained friendly enough, until she too got married and was forced to quit. That was the end of that.

Being a guard didn't exactly help me fit into life in Nead Mara either. The women in the town didn't like that I was a police officer. I could feel the temperature change when I walked into a room; they weren't unkind, they just weren't sure what to do with me. So I let it go and made peace with my loner status. When it came down to it – and aside from attending a disco once a week with Seamus, as his beard – I was adrift; untethered by human connection, as insubstantial as gossamer

37

in the wind. As I noted what Nora's mother had said, it occurred to me that if Nora's life seemed empty on the page, mine would read far emptier.

Nora walked down the stairs dressed in a white cotton nightgown and a belted white towelling housecoat, pulled tight. Fluffy purple slippers covered her feet. She was pale, wide-eyed and bleary. Her mother followed close behind.

'You think the baby was mine?' Nora said in a voice that sounded like a screech.

'We have to make sure it wasn't,' Foley said. Nora didn't look at Foley but instead looked at me.

'I'm telling you it's not mine. I would never. How could I? It's not mine,' she said, voice pitchy and growing desperate.

Foley spoke. 'Who's your GP?'

'Dr Pierce,' she said, still staring at me.

'He's away,' I reminded Foley without breaking eye contact with Nora. 'I'm sure Dr Ciara Crosby could see Nora.'

'For what? I told you. It wasn't mine.' There was a note of panic in her voice.

'You'll need to be examined,' Foley said, and it was then she registered it. She didn't have a choice. This was happening with or without her consent. She sank into the chair beside her, silent. I was on my feet and by her side in moments, but the trust she had placed in me was broken. I was the enemy now – she didn't want my help. She batted me away and reached for her mother, who had moved to her side. 'It's all right, Nora. Just do what they ask, and they'll leave us alone,' her mother said softly, squeezing her hand. I waited while she dressed herself and then escorted her to the car and into the back seat. Foley radioed the station about the need for a GP and as I sat into the front seat of the car, he picked up the radio to receive word that an appointment had been made with Dr Fredrick Boyne.

'What about Dr Crosby?' I said as evenly as my temper would allow.

'What about her?' Foley said and that was the end of that conversation. I wanted to point out that Boyne had a reputation for being *off* with women and Dr Pierce's practice was twice that of Boyne's for a reason, but I didn't. Foley was allowing me in, and I couldn't rock the boat, so I kept my reservations to myself. I watched her in the mirror, wondering if it was possible this decent, scared-looking woman could be capable of hurting an innocent. It didn't seem possible. *How could she? How could anyone?* My mind drifted back to him – Baby Crónán. I was thankful to know he'd be indoors now, in a place with heating and light. Of course it wouldn't matter to him, but it mattered to me.

–

When we arrived at Dr Boyne's office with Nora, he was waiting, leaning against his open door. He nodded to Foley and cast his eyes over the top of Nora's crown to the tips of her toes. 'Come in,' he said. She looked from him to me, wide-eyed and terrified.

'No need to be scared, I'm a doctor,' he said and all of a sudden, the hairs stood to attention on the back of my neck. He was a creep, no doubt about it.

'Do you want me with you?' I said urgently, as she stepped through the door.

'That won't be necessary,' Dr Boyne said without even looking my way. *The bad bollocks.*

'I can go in there with you,' I repeated, ignoring him. She nodded vigorously to indicate she wanted me there. I wasn't going to let her down. *No way.*

'Good. I'll go in so,' I said.

Boyne made an exasperated sound. 'That's highly unusual.'

'Well,' I countered, 'I think we can all agree the circumstances are highly unusual.'

'It's not a problem, is it?' Foley said to Dr Boyne. If he was aware of the tension, he ignored it. Boyne simply shrugged his concession. I slipped my hand into Nora's and together we followed him into the office.

He made her sit on the bed. He asked her to strip off her jumper. She was shaking as she did it and then she was sitting there in her vest.

'Vest off too, please,' he said.

'Why?' I asked.

'Why?' He looked at me as though I was stupid. 'I'm examining her,' he said, his tone dripping with condescension, as if I were a ridiculous woman. He turned to her. 'Vest off.' I wanted to argue that if he couldn't feel what he needed to through a thin piece of cloth, he certainly wasn't going to manage it through a thick stomach wall. But I didn't. I stayed quiet. There was Nora, sitting in her bra, weeping quietly as he poked and prodded at her stomach.

'Doesn't appear to be any evidence of a pregnancy, but to be sure I'll need to do an internal.'

Nora's low whine turned into sobs. I didn't know what to say or do. It felt wrong. All of it, but I was helpless, not having any real insight into what was and wasn't appropriate.

'Take your skirt off and pull your knickers down, Nora,' Dr Boyne said, and it was the way he said it. *He's pure sleaze*. I should have spoken up, but my voice had all but disappeared, my vocal cords as paralysed as the rest of me.

He patted the bed. 'Come on now, knickers off. The sooner you do it, the sooner it will all be over.' *Is that what you say to your wife?* I damn near wanted to cry.

'Oh God,' Nora said. 'Oh God.'

I said nothing. He waited and watched as she pulled down her pants and lay on the bed. He placed his hand on her thigh and she sobbed loudly at his touch. 'Now spread your legs for me, Nora. Good girl,' he said and it took everything in me not to slam his head into the wall. It was when her legs were parted and her hands were covering her streaming eyes that he turned his back on her, went to his sink and washed his hands. Only then did he look for his gloves – all the while leaving Nora lying there, exposed. I stood, mute, in shock I suppose. I knew what an internal was, but I didn't expect Nora's dignity to be disregarded in such a cold and callous manner. Before I knew it, my hands were working and I was unbuckling my jacket. I pulled it off and swung it over Nora's legs, and she looked at me with gratitude as the tears slid down her face. Dr Boyne turned to see that I had covered her and he wasn't best pleased.

'What's this?' he demanded.

'It's respect,' I said, my voice steady, despite how appalled I was.

His lip curled and his jaw stiffened. 'This is an exam, and I am doctor,' he said.

'If you are then you've taken the Hippocratic oath. How does it go... First do no harm?'

'No harm has been done,' he sneered.

'Nora's tears suggest different,' I said.

'Women cry, that's what they do.'

40

'Not in Doctor Pierce's practice. It must be why his list is four times the size of yours,' I said. Nora's tears were tapering off by then; the tension in the room had shifted and it now lay between me and Dr Boyne. As he approached her, I told him that he could leave the coat where it was.

'You want me to examine her blind?' he scoffed at me. I looked him straight in his beady eyes.

'Oh, now… a professional like yourself, I'm sure you're well capable of finding your way,' I said and I really didn't know where that kind of sass came from. Inside I was trembling. He decided it wasn't worth the argument. He placed his hand under my coat, and Nora called out in pain, squeezing my hand tightly. When he pulled his hand away, he barely glanced at her as he said, 'Knickers on now, Nora. Good girl,' and discarded the gloves he'd torn off into the bin. I shielded Nora as she pulled on her smalls and her skirt; then after she put on her jumper, I placed my jacket over her shoulders and put my arm around her, awaiting the verdict and feeling her shuddering beneath my touch.

'Well?' I said, but he ignored me and walked out of the room, closing the door on us both. Nora was white as a ghost. I reached for her trembling hands and took them in mine.

'It's over. You can start forgetting it now,' I said.

'Do you think that child is mine?' she asked me.

'No.' Just one look at her, and I knew she hadn't given birth. And I knew that… bollocks, Boyne knew it too.

'Thanks.' She seemed relieved and grateful, which twisted my insides, because hadn't I brought her here? Knowing what Dr Boyne was like, I should have insisted on going to Dr Crosby. I needed to do better – what if it had been Dicey here with Nora instead of me? What trauma would she have endured then?

When she was ready to face the men, we walked out of the room and into the waiting area where Dr Boyne was standing with Foley.

'Well?' I said to Foley, but it was Dr Boyne who spoke, in a jokey, overfamiliar tone.

'There was only one virgin to have a baby,' Dr Boyne said. 'And her name wasn't Nora Fitzgerald.'

Nora's humiliation was written on her face and when Foley laughed, it hurt me more than it should've. He'd treated me as a professional, so I'd hoped for more from him.

'Let's get you home, Nora,' I said. Foley thanked Dr Boyne. They shook hands. We drove back to Nora's house in silence. When we arrived, I walked her back inside to her waiting mother's arms.

'It's going to be all right,' I said as I took my leave of them. Nora squeezed my arm in gratitude.

'I hope you're right,' she whispered. I wished I'd done more to protect her. I was sorry for that. Nora and her mother closed the door on me. It was just after six p.m. I'd been on shift twelve hours. When I got back into the car, Foley took a look at me. 'You're exhausted, I'll take you home,' he said, putting the engine into gear.

'What are you doing?' I asked.

'The lads have set up an incident room at the hotel. I'll head over to see where we are,' he answered, before taking a sharp turn and following the long country road away from Nora's home.

'I'd like to come,' I said.

'You're done for the day.'

'Okay, but I'd like to come to see where we are, then I'll go,' I said. 'My car's at the station, I can take myself home.'

He thought about it as he drove onwards, heading towards town. 'I've never seen an incident room for something like this before,' I said.

He nodded. 'Fair enough, I suppose you've earned it.'

–

The Bonham Hotel was an old Victorian-style small establishment that had been renovated in the late fifties. I used to think the only thing they'd changed since then were the lightbulbs. It had a worn red carpet covering the entire place and a blue-and-white flowery wallpaper on the walls. In the reception area, there was a large, plush, bottle-green velvet chaise longue, balding along the seams and positioned next to a writing desk with a small drawer missing. Beside it stood an oak hall stand, complete with a bevelled mirror and a compartment for gloves. The antique reception desk, crafted from rich, dark mahogany, featured ornately carved edges and delicate scrollwork running along the front panel. A small brass bell sat neatly on the countertop, its surface smooth after years of use. There was always a smell of cigarette smoke in the place – that and yeast and strong perfume, but it was the turf fire in the bar area that provided the strongest aroma. I could hear it crackling and felt its warmth a whole room away. No one was manning reception when we arrived, but we didn't need help to see that the incident room was situated in the old dance hall at the end of the corridor. The doors were open, and the sound of men and movement echoed around the place.

When we reached the room, Foley closed the door behind him. He looked to those assembled there. The only face I recognised was Dicey's.

'Keep this closed. I don't want garda business becoming town business,' he said and some of the lads mumbled apologies. There were chairs and desks all placed in the middle of the room; a few of the lads were sitting at those, two of them typing. Another man was sitting on a table nearby, his legs crossed, talking quietly on the phone. There was a large chalkboard at the top of the room. Foley surveyed it. There was a long list of witness names scrawled across it.

'Where are the statements?' he said.

'The lads are typing them up now,' Dicey said and he stood up to reveal himself. Foley told him to make sure they were typed up as soon as possible. 'Sure Nora can do that, she's a great little typer, she'll get through it in no time,' he said.

'The word is typist, and she's going home. You should have done it already,' Foley said. 'Time for you to clock off too.'

Dicey suddenly looked like he'd chewed a wasp. 'I'm fine here,' he said.

'Go home, McCarthy,' Foley repeated before turning to me. 'You'll be on for six a.m. again tomorrow?'

'I will,' I said.

'Okay to do a double again?'

'I told you I'm happy to work till we catch whoever did this,' I said.

'Good work today.' He opened the door and that was my cue to leave. I nodded and walked into the hotel corridor. There was a girl at the reception desk now, probably no more than eighteen, with dark eyes and her long black hair in a ponytail – a petite little thing in a skirt, blouse and matching jacket that were too old for her. She nodded and smiled at me.

'Good evening, Garda,' she said.

'Good evening…'

'Jenny,' she supplied.

'Good evening, Jenny,' I said and we smiled at one another. I walked out into the evening air. The chill had returned and I hugged myself as I crossed the road towards the station. I heard Dicey's heavy footsteps before I felt his hand on me. He grabbed at me roughly, groping at me, trying to get a grip on my shoulder. I'm not sure what came over me in that moment – the loss of Baby Crónán or the assault on Nora Fitzgerald – but I grabbed his hand and squeezed it as hard as I could. He shouted out in pain.

'Christ almighty, what was that for?' he whined.

'Don't touch me,' I sneered.

'I was only trying to catch you,' he said, as though he was as innocent as the driven snow.

'I don't want to be caught by you or anyone. If you want me, use your voice, not your hands.'

'We all know you don't want to be caught, not by a man anyway,' he said. I ignored the barb, not wanting to follow him where he wished to lead me. I walked on.

'I saw the smile you had for Jenny,' he said, walking in step with me.

Pig. 'What do you want, Dicey?' I said.

'The question you should be asking yourself, Mary, is what does Foley want, because it sure as God isn't your insight or experience now, is it?' he said before turning and walking away, leaving me to stand and watch him head into Healy's pub. I found my feet and reached my car. I knew what he was implying and I told myself I didn't care. I didn't drop into the station but rather just drove home, past the beach and the entrance where a car with two guards sat in it were guarding the site from the press photographers, who were camped only a few feet away. I didn't stop to say hello, I don't think I even waved at them – instead I just drove, keeping my eyes focused on the road ahead. I parked up outside the house and opened the door. I walked into the bathroom and ran a bath. I sat on the loo and waited for it to fill and then without taking off a stitch of clothes, I sat in it and cried for Ireland.

–

Time meant nothing; I'd fallen into the fog. I don't remember the water going cold. But then there I was, in my full uniform and sitting in freezing bathwater, with Seamus looking down at me. I hadn't heard him come in, or pound at the bathroom door. My eyes were open, I was sitting straight up but I wasn't there, not in spirit, not in mind.

'Oh, Mary!' he said and that woke me. I grabbed for my hand and I could see that my fingernails were blue. I saw him, Baby Crónán, his tiny wafer-thin fingernails. I wanted to vomit but there was nothing in me to purge. Seamus hauled me out of the bath, pulling off my coat and covering me with the big bath towel he pulled out of the airing cupboard. He looked me in the eye and I was a zombie of a thing. He held my shaking shoulders and talked to me like I was a child.

'Mary, I need you to take off your wet things. Nod if that's okay?' he asked. I looked into his beautiful, gentle eyes and nodded.

'Grand, I'll get you some clothes. Okay?' he said and I nodded again. Then he was gone. I stood, shuddering, shaking and waiting, until he returned with fresh dry clothes and ordered me to put them on. It was then I finally found my voice.

'Thank you,' I said as he closed the door behind me.

When I finally made it into the kitchen, he handed me a cup of tea with brandy in it. He sat me down and then he picked up a glass of whiskey and raised it.

'The whole country needs a drink tonight,' he said, sitting opposite me. I drank deeply from the cup and we sat in silence as I processed the day's events, beginning with that first sight of Baby Crónán and ending with Nora, crying her eyes out with her legs spreadeagled and that man… talking down to her, shaming her. Seamus offered to top me up with brandy and I took it gladly.

'You won't say anything to anybody about finding me in the bath?' I said after a time.

'I won't.'

'You won't think badly of me?'

'Why would I?'

'You know why. It's weak,' I said, imagining Foley, Dicey and the others somewhere warm and dry, probably enjoying a pint, and Dicey telling some of his favourite mother-in-law jokes. He was mad for them.

'You're far from weak,' Seamus said, and I could see by his kind eyes and soft expression that he meant it. 'I suppose you won't want to go to the disco on Saturday night.'

'I will,' I said immediately. It was a full six days away and I'd been saving my new blouse and looking forward to it. 'Dancing is the only thing that takes all my cares away.'

He grinned. 'Okay,' he said and maybe it was the two brandies I had in me, but I found the courage to ask him, 'Why do you take me?'

'You like to dance.'

'So?'

'I like to have a few pints and watch you,' he said and I looked at him sideways. He blushed. 'Not like that, for God's sake, you're just a good dancer is all.'

I smiled at the compliment, conceding that I did a mean electric slide. And then, warm with whiskey and with me at my weakest, he propositioned me.

'Look, it's my first cousin's wedding next month, I've no way out of it. I was hoping you'd come with me,' he said. My mouth fell open. If he registered my shock, he didn't show it.

'It's not a date, is it?' I finally said.

'You know it's not,' he said quietly and then he drained his glass. He ran his hand through his hair, his eyes glued to the floor, and whispered, 'You know what I am, Mary.'

'I do,' I said softly. It was the first time we'd spoken so directly, but I knew.

'You won't arrest me?' he asked and he looked up at me, attempting to grin, but the sadness that dwelled in his beautiful eyes gave him away.

'No, I won't, but there's some that would,' I said. I knew how the fellas in the station talked about the likes of Seamus. Some of them would tar and feather him and drag him through the streets. The things they said, I used to wonder about them. They sounded more like twisted criminals than trusted police officers.

'Oh, I know that.'

'Do you want to tell people that I'm your girlfriend?' I asked. *Where did that come from? Have you hit your head, Mary Shea?*

He thought about that question for a moment or two. 'If you wouldn't mind. That would help me a lot,' he said and I nodded my agreement.

'That's fine,' I said, remembering Dicey inferring that I was a lesbian. A rumour like that would end my career, so I thought it would help me too. He stood up to go.

46

'You're going to be all right,' he said.

'I know,' I said. *But I don't feel all right. How could I?* I finished my tea.

I'd known Seamus for two years and it was the most words we'd ever spoken so plainly to one another. He left me alone with his bottle of whiskey and I poured out a glass that I drank neat before I dared go to bed.

CHAPTER FOUR

I lay in bed, staring up at the ceiling, my eyes refusing to close as I listened to the rain that had started up again. I wondered what the locals who had been canvassed had said to the officers, and if any of them had provided a lead in the case. Maybe Celine Ford had been sitting outside her shop, watching all who passed, and spotted someone who didn't look right. Maybe Dr Crosby had spoken to the hospital and got the names of more local pregnant women. Maybe they'd already found the child's mother and were banging down her door as I lay in bed, pickled.

I was shattered, body and soul. But my mind wouldn't rest. I recalled how exhausted I'd been the previous morning when the drumming rain had kept me awake all night, until it eventually stopped at four fifteen.

And then I remembered something.

The baby wasn't wet, which meant he had been left in that dune between 4:15 a.m., when the rain stopped, and 6:10 a.m. when he was found by Nora Fitzgerald's dog, Prince. That reduced the timeline to just over two hours. I made a mental note of it, and despite the rain – and because of the tea, brandy and Seamus's whiskey – I finally disappeared into sleep.

Day Two

I woke at five a.m. The drumming above my head had long ceased and was replaced by gentle birdsong. I thought of him as soon as I became aware I was awake. His little face, his grey eyes and his balled fists filled my aching head. I swallowed two paracetamols, washing them down with a glass of water while the kettle boiled so that I could make a nice hot cup of tea. When I was dressed, I ate some toast and sipped on the tea, and I was out the door by five thirty. I dropped into the station, where the Station House Officer, Brian Keating, was in his office. He saw me and called out.

'Close the door,' he said. I closed it and sat down where he gestured. He leaned forward, putting his elbows on his desk. I could see the lines ingrained in his forehead, the shine from his bald head and the single black hair dangling from his left nostril. I could smell his breath; it wasn't unpleasant, just strong, he smelled of mints. He had an addiction; he was never without a mint in his mouth. I could hear it rattle against his teeth as he spoke.

'Now what's this, Mary?' he asked and I wondered what he was getting at.

'What do you mean?' I said.

'The man from Dublin has his eye on you,' he said frankly. I said nothing. 'Romantically,' he clarified as if it needed clarification. *Of course that's what you'd think.*

'Does he?' I said.

'Does a bear shit in the woods?' he said in a mild and pleasant enough tone. I didn't respond. 'He's a married man.'

'Why are you telling me that, Brian?' I said, holding his gaze. 'Why do you feel it necessary to say what that man's marital status is? What has his personal life anything to do with me?' I asked him and suddenly he looked around for an answer, his head bobbing like a bird looking for seed.

'Brian?' I said, not wishing to let his ignorance pass.

'Well, because he has his eye on you,' he said finally.

'I doubt that very much,' I said. 'And if he did, wouldn't it better to talk to him?'

He didn't like that, his lips curling into a sneer. 'Well now, Mary, the fact is he doesn't work under me. You do.'

'I'm only interested in doing my job and maybe, just maybe, Detective Matt Foley values my insight,' I said.

He chuckled to himself. 'Ah, stop,' he said as if I'd cracked a joke. 'Go on, go. Just don't let yourself get caught out...' he continued, his tone softening. 'Not by him or anyone.'

He was warning me because, even though he was as bad as the rest in some ways, he did have a fondness for me.

'I will,' I said and I took my leave of him.

I left the station, marching, internalised rage spurring me across the road and into The Bonham Hotel, passing the unattended reception desk, towards the door, where I paused for a moment to steel myself before opening it to a room full of men. It was a different place to the one I had visited the night before: the old dance hall had well and truly been claimed, and it was now a proper incident room, organised around blackboards filled with information. Foley wasn't there yet but Dicey was, staring at me from under his hat. I walked up to the first blackboard and started reading it, then the next and the next. I moved over to the table where the statements were fresh off the typewriters, and I grabbed hold of them and started to read. Out of the corner of my eye I could see Dicey stirring, standing up, flexing, taking up space, and I knew what was coming.

'Any of you boys like a cup of tea?' Dicey asked out of nowhere.

'I'll have one,' one of them said.

Here it comes…

'Yeah, go on, then,' another said.

He looked over towards me. 'I'll have one sugar in mine,' he said.

That's when Foley came in. 'Mary's making tea. You want some?' Dicey said.

'Milk, two sugars,' Foley said.

Of course.

I dropped the statement I'd been reading, made the tea and handed it around. By then Foley was standing at the top of the room, talking to us about what we knew and didn't know from canvassing all the people who lived in the area, and specifically in the roads that led to and from the beach. As far as those that answered could tell, none of them were pregnant or saw anyone in a heavily pregnant state passing by on the night in question. I resumed reading through the statements as Foley asked questions to the men who had spent the previous day canvassing. There was a lot of talk but nothing that helped. I was listening with one ear while reading one statement after another, most of them short. The interviewee hadn't a clue – wasn't home, saw nothing and didn't know anything relevant at all. But then, three or four statements down in the stack, I found one from a woman named Mrs Irene Lacey. I read through it and spotted something interesting. I shot up. The lads turned around to see if I was having a fit or something. I held up the statement.

'This could be something,' I said.

'Oh, for the love of… We've been through them.'

'Go on,' Foley said, looking towards me and ignoring Dicey. I addressed Liam Kenny, who had just taken out a fresh hanky to wipe his nose. 'Liam, you canvassed her, a Mrs Irene Lacey.'

'I thought you were on the desk yesterday,' Foley said.

'I was and then our Station House Officer, Brian, sent me out with the lads,' Liam said.

'Right, well if there's a plague, we'll know who to thank for it,' Foley said before he addressed me. 'What's caught your eye, Shea?'

'She saw a woman in front of her house, barefoot, in a nightdress on Potters Road between midnight and morning.'

'Potters Road… Is that somewhere near the beach?'

'Close enough,' I said.

'Just a nightdress and barefoot?' Foley said.

'She was soaked through, according to the statement,' I said.

A few of the Dublin fellas made comments under their breath. I couldn't hear them, but judging by the look on Dicey's face, their remarks were far from complimentary.

Suffice it to say, the Dublin boys thought of the local lads the same way the local lads thought of me: useless.

'Why didn't you highlight it?' Foley demanded, and Liam looked from Foley to Dicey and back to Foley. Dicey wore a face like thunder and I knew he would have dismissed the statement, but Liam would take the fall.

'So sorry, eh… I…' Liam sneezed and a couple of the Dublin fellas laughed. 'Sorry,' he said again. Dicey sat back and folded his arms. Foley reached out for the statement. I crossed the room, all eyes on me, handed it to him and sat further away from the trestle table that held the kettle. Foley read the statement. He was fast, went through it like a buzz saw through wood. We waited. He looked to Liam.

'And you couldn't confirm a clearer timeline than between midnight and the morning?' Foley said, his voice hinting at a sneer. He pushed the statement into Liam's hands.

'Well, no, she's very old…' Liam said before reviewing the statement.

'Mrs Lacey is eighty-eight. Her eyes are half-shot and her mind is too,' Dicey said. He was out of his seat and behind me now. I knew he was fuming by the tone of his voice.

'How so?' Foley said, looking to Dicey.

'The batty old girl thought it might be her daughter, Tara, coming home to her,' Dicey said.

'And I take it she was wrong.'

'Well, seeing as Tara died of pneumonia in 1968, I'd say she wasn't right,' Dicey said with a flourish.

Some of the lads laughed. Foley wasn't amused. He turned to me.

'What strikes you that didn't strike them?' he said, pointing at me before shifting to indicate the men in the room.

'Maybe her mind is shot – she's old and lonely, and it was sometime in the middle of the night – but she said she opened the window and called out, and the woman ran.'

'She could have been dreaming,' Foley said.

'Maybe, but the window was open when Garda Kenny took the statement. She asked him to close it,' I said.

He glanced at the page, his thumb rolling over his wedding ring. 'You're saying you have a gut feeling, Shea?' He was testing me. Everyone knew it. I didn't need to think about it.

'I think she saw someone.'

He massaged his forehead before addressing a young Dublin fella, standing with chalk in hand having taken control of the board.

'Irene Lacey goes on the board,' Foley said and then looked around the room.

'Anything else?' he asked.

'The baby wasn't wet,' I said.

'Finally! Someone mentions the obvious,' he said, noting the time on his watch. 'No, he wasn't.' The lads' heads all went down. 'So, what does that mean?' he said and now it felt like we were in a lecture hall, not an incident room. Poor Liam was right in Foley's eyeline so he just buried his head in tissues. I would have paid money to see the look on Dicey's face.

When no one spoke, I continued. 'Well, it's rained for nearly four days solid, but there was a break that night. I was driving home around eight fifteen... one minute it was so heavy I was having trouble seeing the road ahead, and the next thing I know the sky clears and it just stopped.'

'And of course Mary Shea knows the exact time...' Dicey mumbled to himself.

'The local weather reports indicate it was around that time,' Foley said. I could hear Dicey shuffle uncomfortably in his seat. Foley was still looking at me. 'So what are you thinking?'

'The rain took off again around nine forty-five that night. I was getting ready to go to bed and remember hoping it wouldn't keep me up all night. I have a galvanised roof, you see, the rain clatters on it like tap shoes on an empty stage. The noise keeps me awake.'

I was conscious of the eyes on me but I focused on Foley. 'It didn't stop until four fifteen the next morning and I know that because as soon as it did, I looked at the time and saw I would have little more than an hour's sleep before getting up for work.'

Foley nodded. 'Shea's right. Local weather reports note that it rained from nine forty-five Sunday night until just after four on Monday morning. Baby Crónán was dry and so was the towel, and although we can't be absolutely certain, it does suggest he wasn't exposed to the rain.'

'So what are we saying?' a Dublin detective who'd been introduced as 'Quinn' asked. He was a quiet man, average in size, average in looks; the kind of man you'd meet a few times and forget entirely.

'We're saying that the baby was placed in that dune between four and six in the morning. So we concentrate on those 120 minutes. Quinn, I want you and our lads to scour all the statements, especially the ones the locals discarded, for anything else that might have been missed.' Quinn nodded. The Dublin boys mumbled between them – I wasn't sure what they were saying but I had no doubt it was at Dicey's and Kenny's expense. Foley looked back in my direction. 'You're with me.'

'Right,' I said, and as I stood up, I heard Dicey hissing under his breath. I tried to pay no notice but it was clear Foley's attention to me had got his back up.

–

Our first stop was at the local hospital, where the pathologist Frank Waters had commandeered a small sterile back room – that's where he and Baby Crónán had been since I last stood with them on that beach. I felt hesitant walking inside and my chest tightened; my heart ached at the thought of seeing him again. There was a smell of bleach with a hint of lemon in the air, making my eyes sting as I followed Foley into the place where Baby Crónán lay. Inside, we were greeted by the sight of Frank huddled over a small wooden table, doing paperwork. He glanced up at us over the rim of his spectacles, resting on the tip of his nose. With a deliberate motion, he pushed them up to his bridge before standing.

'Good, I'm glad you're here, I've a train to catch,' he said, grabbing a white coat that was hanging on a nail on the wall behind him. He put it on and pointed to the sheet that covered the cold steel table and the tiny lump concealed by it. *Oh...* I closed my eyes, for a moment, to steel myself in the temporary darkness and if the men noticed I was a little shaken, neither commented. I felt my legs fill with lead and suddenly heavy, so I focused on lifting my knees a little higher when following them towards his steel resting place. Frank Waters pulled away the white sheet that covered him and I saw the wounds had been cleaned. He had been further violated, in a bid to find answers, cut from stem to stern, then resown. Seeing his vulnerable, maimed body, I wanted to dress him in warm cotton, soft to the touch, a sleepsuit in blue, with a little train stitched into the chest and with feet to keep his little toes snuggled. I wanted to put a hat on his head, maybe a striped one, made of soft wool. But there were no clothes to put on him, only that stiff white sheet that offered no comfort; it was simply to hide him from the world.

Frank pointed to Baby Crónán, describing the weapon: a knife – his guess was a typical kitchen knife. He measured its width, using his fingers. 'About one-and-a-half inches,' he said.

'So you could find it in any home in Ireland?' Foley said.

'That's right,' Waters said.

'How long was he dead when Nora Fitzgerald's dog found him?' Foley said.

'I'd say just shy of twelve hours.'

'Anything on the blood group?' Foley said.

'That will be done in Dublin, it'll take a few days.'

'And the baby?'

'I'm done with the poor creature, he's all yours,' he said. He covered Baby Crónán, slowly, carefully. 'I've spoken to the local priest, the fella who blessed him, Father...' He struggled to remember the name.

'Cunningham,' I supplied.

'I've spoken to the local undertakers also, they'll do right by him. He'll have a wake, a funeral and a proper burial,' he said.

I heard myself exhale. 'Good. That's very good.' The pathologist, who'd seemed cold and callous, turned out to be a kinder, better man than he initially appeared.

'Hopefully the mother will turn up. Best to put this one to bed... fast,' he said to Foley, who nodded thoughtfully, spinning his gold ring around his finger. But I was stuck on something he'd said.

'The funeral, will it be open to the public?' I asked Foley.

'It will, and to the press. We want as much pressure piled on the killer as possible,' he confirmed.

I didn't like that, the idea of Baby Crónán being a spectacle, but I understood the opportunity it presented.

–

Foley drove down a narrow road with tufted grass breaking through the old tarmac and forming a line in the centre of it. We passed through rolling hills, flanked by dense forest, and hit potholes every few yards.

'Maybe if you drive around them...' I said, worrying that the tyre would burst or the suspension would go.

'Drive around them? There is no road around them.' He hunched over the wheel. He did slow down, though, and we drove in silence. I became lost in the spell that nature casts, watching the leaves dance in the dappled light, inhaling the resinous scent of the spruce trees looming above us.

'What next?' I said as we arrived in town.

'We go to the local girls' school, see if we can sniff out any potential young mother there,' he said. I didn't like the way he'd said it. *Sniff?* But I nodded anyway. 'Good idea.'

Dr Crosby confirmed there was no hospital record of anyone else from the area having been under medical care for pregnancy.

'Maybe the person wasn't from the area,' I said.

'Maybe, but in all likelihood they were.' He didn't explain further.

–

We arrived at St Joseph's, the girls' secondary school, just after eleven. Principal Kelly was a stocky woman with wide shoulders and a thick back, a square face and short grey hair. She wore pale blue, head to toe, which made her look like a nun, except for the trousers that were clearly too tight and a wedding band on her ring finger.

We were directed to her office. She was surprised to see us and midway through drinking a cup of tomato soup. Foley made the introductions.

'Sit,' she said in a commanding tone. We did as we were told, pulling the two heavy wooden chairs that were carefully tucked under the desk, and scraping them along the tiles.

She folded her hands, knitting her fingers together.

'What can I do for you, Detective Foley?' She paid no heed to me at all.

'I need a list of girls who were potentially pregnant up until two days ago,' he said and her face drained of colour.

'You surely don't think one of my girls gave birth to and killed that baby?' Principal Kelly said.

'I'm not sure, but part of our investigation is asking hard questions to try to find out,' he said.

'None of my girls were pregnant.' She spoke so firmly that she unfurled her fingers, forming a small fist, and tapped her knuckles against the desk. It was more of a tally-ho gesture than an act of aggression, but either way, her confidence didn't carry much weight.

'You're so sure?' He ignored the knock. 'Any girls missing form school since yesterday?'

'No,' she said triumphantly.

'Any missing school before that and maybe for a considerable amount of time?' he said and her eyes darkened.

'There's two I can think of,' she said, suddenly moving back in her chair, tugging open a drawer and pulling a large ledger out. She opened it out on the table in front of her with such gravitas that it was as though she was handling the *Book of Kells*. As she fixed a pair of tiny round spectacles on the bridge of her nose, Foley glanced my way, raising his eyes to heaven. I bit the inside of my lip to stop myself smiling. We waited as Principal Kelly scanned page after page of names, before shutting the ledger up tight and placing it back in the drawer. She nudged it shut with her knee and interlocked her fingers. 'Yes. That's right. Two girls.'

'Who are they, Principal Kelly?' he said in a tone that suggested he'd had enough of her stalling.

'Debbie Fitzmaurice… Her father died a few months ago.'

'Yes, we know of her. Who else?' Foley probed. Debbie was so slight that she couldn't have carried a bag of sugar, never mind a baby.

'Joyce O'Reilly stopped coming to school three months ago. I spoke to her parents and they said she was needed to work in the family business,' she said.

'Did you believe them?' Foley asked.

'I had no reason not to.'

'Did you try to talk them out of it?'

'Of course, education is important, but she was sixteen and not obliged to go to school by law.'

'So you never saw her after that?'

'No. I'd have no reason to.'

Foley hummed. 'And before she left, how did she look to you?'

'Not pregnant, if that's what you're asking.'

'Is she a big girl?'

'What do you mean by that?' she said immediately, insulted possibly due to her own shape and size. Foley didn't seem to notice or care, and instead he decided to spell it out for her.

'I mean, does she look anything like you?' he said.

Oh no! You didn't just say that. Principal Kelly's head nearly rolled off her shoulders. I didn't know where to look.

'She's a sixteen-year-old girl, so no, she does not look like me and how bloody dare you,' she said, her face flushed with outrage.

Rather than being contrite, her words were like water off a duck's back to Foley. 'Grand, then, we'll take her address,' he said.

Without another word, she gave us the address and we took our leave. As we crossed the yard, heading for the carpark, I asked him, 'Was that necessary?'

He immediately knew what I was referring to. 'It was,' he said.

'You insulted her.'

'Well, then, she's easy to insult,' he said.

'Or maybe you don't mind insulting people.'

He looked at me and scoffed. 'You're being childish.'

'Oh, am I?' I said, my tone veering into petulant territory, so I quickly changed tack. 'It doesn't cost anything to be kind,' I added, unsure why his comments had bothered me. Or why I wasn't worried about repercussions from telling him so.

We didn't speak during the next part of our journey, except when I gave him directions to O'Reilly's Scrap Metal Yard – ten miles from town inland and far from the coast.

–

We turned onto a road and ahead of us was a painted sign that read 'O'Reilly's Scrap Metal Yard, two miles' nailed to a wooden post by the roadside.

'This is us,' I said, pointing the way. The road to the premises was flanked by towering trees on one side, their branches arching overhead, and a sprawling field on the other. It looked more like the entrance to a grand old English estate, and not what you'd expect from a scrap metal place at all. Then the road parted into two smaller roads: one signposted the house, the other, the business. Foley followed the sign that led us to the yard – presumably guessing the O'Reillys would be at work – and we found ourselves driving onto flat, muddy land and immediately surrounded by tractors, ploughs, combine harvesters, cars and bikes. Some were ancient-looking, rusty and tired, and others clearly damaged. Sitting amongst the discarded machines were three grapples. As Foley parked, one was opening its jaws, reaching for a small red tractor. I watched as it clamped down and lifted the vehicle, preparing to haul it beyond the large, once-silver galvanised shed, now browned with rust. Inside, two men dressed in overalls were stripping a large combine harvester for working parts. It was one of two sheds – the second, smaller and made of stone, had a chipped black wooden door closed over, concealing its contents. Beyond that, there was access to a field in which a third shed was just about visible in the distance. We stepped out of the car to a cacophony of sound. As we made our way through this machine park, I could hear a radio playing from inside the shed, blasting Pink Floyd's 'Another Brick in the Wall'. Foley rapped his knuckles on the wooden door, though the sharp hiss and faint crackle of solder meeting metal drowned out the sound. Uninvited, we entered and approached the man wielding the tool. He was hunched over a long metal table and wore large safety glasses, gloves and an apron. Foley waved to get his attention.

'I'm looking for the boss?' Foley said. The fella nodded towards a makeshift timber-framed box in the far corner of the long shed. It was a shed within a shed, with a simple timber door fitted with metal hinges. Scrawled across in black spray paint was the word 'Office'. I followed him, weaving around table after table piled with metal parts, carefully avoiding eye contact with the four workers now staring our way. Foley rapped on the door, and this time we heard the word, 'What?'

Foley pushed the door open, and there, behind a small desk on a well-worn soft-cushioned armchair, smoking a cigarette and holding the phone to her ear, was a rotund, rosy-cheeked woman with a head of blonde curls and perfectly applied red lipstick.

'Is this about stolen parts?' she said, taking in my uniform. 'Because I have documentation for everything.'

'Are you Mrs O'Reilly?' Foley said.

'Yes,' Breda O'Reilly confirmed.

'We were told your daughter works here.'

'Well, yes,' she said before standing up. 'What is this about?'

'Can we speak with her?'

'She's at home today.'

'On a work day?'

'She's not well,' she said and I could see her demeanour change as she spoke, her initial confidence dissolving. Beads of sweat formed along her hairline as her complexion slowly drained of all natural colour, until her thick make-up sat in stark contrast to her ashen pallor.

'What do you want with her?' she asked, stumbling over the words.

'We want to talk to her,' Foley explained.

'Is this about the baby?' Her voice was so low that it was almost a whisper.

'It is,' he said, holding her gaze.

Shock distorted her face. 'Why my Joyce?'

'I have a suspicion,' Foley said. He was watching her intently. She couldn't escape his eyes, or mine. Breda O'Reilly swayed to one side before steadying herself, but she didn't speak, waiting for Foley to continue.

'Where is she?' he asked and she just stared at us for what seemed like the longest time.

'Mrs O'Reilly, is Joyce up at the house?'

She nodded.

'And your husband?'

'Ray's at the yard, and my son Thomas is with him,' she said. By now she was trembling, and I gently urged her back into the chair.

'Mrs O'Reilly, did your Joyce give birth to a baby?' Foley said and her eyes met his, full of tears.

'I think she might have,' she whispered as those tears tumbled down her cheeks.

–

Foley marched out of the office and instructed one of the boys in the shed to grab Raymond O'Reilly, Joyce's father, and her brother, Thomas, as a matter of urgency. While we waited, Breda took a long drag on her cigarette, sucking as much nicotine as possible into her lungs. Foley went to the car to radio the station while I leaned against the wall, thinking about Joyce and what she could have done.

Raymond was in his early sixties and had a head of grey curls; his son shared the same curls, though his were sandy brown. Both were blocks of men, wide as they were tall, with hands like shovels. I'd seen Thomas before, with Seamus, at the discos. I knew they had played hurling together, and something about the way they looked at one another often made me wonder about them – about what they meant to one another.

'What's this?' Raymond O'Reilly said. He appeared aggravated but perhaps he was scared. He glanced at his trembling wife.

'It's about Joyce having a baby,' Foley said.

Raymond's eyes darted from his wife and back to Foley.

'A baby?' he said, almost laughing.

'Where is the baby, Mr O'Reilly?' Foley said, serious.

'Have you lost your mind?' Raymond exploded.

Thomas had been silent until then but now piped up. 'Get out of here!'

'Answer my question,' Foley pressed on, ignoring Thomas.

'Say nothing, Dad. We have rights,' Thomas said. Raymond seemed shocked into silence but he nodded to his son.

Foley decided he wasn't getting what he needed from Joyce's family. 'I'm going to the house,' he said and strode out past the two men, leaving them and the crying woman behind. I followed, mumbling,

'Excuse me,' and Thomas touched my arm as I passed him by. 'Why Joyce?' he asked me.

'I can't answer that yet,' I said.

Breda O'Reilly must have rung ahead because, as Foley and I arrived at the house, Joyce was standing in the doorway, tears streaming down her face. She had the build of her older brother and father, wide, but she was a shorter version of them: boxier, with the same sandy curls, except hers were well below her shoulders. She had brown eyes, a plain face, freckled – and even standing there, by the open door, I could see how visibly shaken she was, but the thing that gave her away was the way she guarded her empty, yet swollen, stomach.

Raymond and Thomas pulled up in a filthy white Toyota HiAce van behind us. Raymond jumped out of it, waving his hands in the air and shouting to her, 'Don't say a word.' Breda O'Reilly drove a red Ford Escort in, behind the van. She stepped out in time for Foley to look at all four of them in the face and tell them that they were being brought into town for questioning, the whole lot of them. Breda and Joyce were huddled together and bawling. The men stood quietly. Foley went out to the car and radioed for backup. We waited inside the kitchen of the old farmhouse – a warm, inviting, open space. A pleasant place now sullied by our presence. Aside from the odd squabble with their neighbour over noise, the O'Reillys lived a good life, wanting for nothing. They were charitable too, often sponsoring the local Gaelic Athletic Association teams, and they always gave generously to the church. They weren't the sort of people who got arrested, and yet here we were.

The O'Reilly men sat on the bench at a long table made of solid wood. Joyce sat on the window seat with her back to us. Breda stood by the counter, staring into space. I made tea. The women didn't drink it but the men did, including Foley. I had a cup myself; I was parched. It felt strange, us all sitting around drinking tea under the circumstances, but that's what we did. Foley ordered silence; the family complied and so no one spoke. I watched Joyce and I could see the maelstrom of emotions taking hold of her, so palpable I could almost reach out and touch the pain, confusion, fear and sadness in her and in those around her. The boys arrived one by one. Joyce sat at the back of our car, Dicey took Raymond in his, Thomas ended up with Quinn, and Breda with Liam Kenny. Foley wanted them kept separately. We drove out first;

the others followed in procession and it felt like a funeral. Joyce sat in silence; fear had taken hold of her, and she was exhausted, sickly looking, slightly green around the gills. Every pothole Foley hit seemed to cause her extreme discomfort; something would shoot up through her, and she jumped so high she was only short of hitting the roof, not that she said a word or called out. She just endured. I watched her through the mirror, and I wondered, *What did you do?* No one spoke in the car.

Mercifully, Foley kept the radio off. We drove and let the quietness of the countryside be our guide. As soon as we hit town, it erupted: the press were waiting to pounce and, looking back, the spectacle of four cars driving in procession wasn't the greatest or most forward-thinking of plans. As we drove into the station carpark, they crowded around, cameras flashing from all sides, suddenly blinding us, and so we covered our eyes and tried to cover the O'Reillys' faces as they ducked away, and the lads ushered them all inside, away from those clamouring and calling to them.

'Who are you?'

'What's your name?'

'What have you done?'

'Did you kill that baby?'

Then as I held Joyce, her face pressed against my chest, pushing her forward and trying to conceal her identity with just my hand, I heard it. Across the road, a group of locals had gathered, and they were screaming at her: 'Killer. Killer. Killer.'

–

Once inside the station, we locked the door. Brian showed the family to the back rooms and took Raymond into his office. Then Breda was brought into the tea room. Thomas was left in the main office. Joyce was brought into the holding room for questioning. That's when it began, the degradation and humiliation of the O'Reillys, and I knew in my gut from the moment that child sat in front of Foley that she didn't have a chance. None of the family did. I could feel it, the terrible tension inside the station, the expectation outside. The townspeople's anger and vitriol growing by the minute – this dead infant had drawn the eyes of the country and the world upon them, and shown us all up in the poorest light, and they didn't like it. Then there was the press, baiting and waiting for the gardaí to find the baby's murderer, for the story to unravel to a satisfactory end. Justice, that's what they thought they wanted, but revenge was in the air, and walking into that station, I felt it – the hatred, the viciousness – and I didn't expect to feel such pity and compassion for the girl shuddering in my arms, but I did. And I thought of him on cold metal, his round face, rosebud lips, his black tuft of hair and his little grey, empty eyes; and I looked at this young girl, with a square face, boxy shape, sandy hair, brown eyes filled with terror. They looked nothing alike but then the saying goes that babies come out looking like their fathers so they can't be denied. *Who is he?* I thought. *Where is he?* No one else seemed so concerned with the answer to that question. As it turned out, my colleague had decided from the moment he saw the broken girl in the doorway that she – and maybe the entire O'Reilly family – was both capable of and culpable for the murder of Baby Crónán. As a result of this sincere belief and the family's unwillingness to co-operate, they endured great indignity that day and suffered terrible violence later that night.

CHAPTER FIVE

'Well, we can't conduct interviews in this kip,' Foley said with great disdain, referring to the station where I worked, offering no apology as we made our way outside. As soon as he pushed on the heavy blue door, letting in the light, I was momentarily blinded by a thousand flashes. The photojournalists sprang into action like ninjas, appearing from everywhere, determined to document our every move as we waded through them. Just outside the station grounds, on the footpath, stood a bank of TV cameras and hungry reporters, thrusting microphones in our faces. I tucked myself in behind Foley, who stood tall and wide. He looked down the lens of the camera that would later deliver his face onto the *Six O'Clock News*. This wasn't new territory for him. He knew the press and they knew him well enough. The questions were fired at him like bullets, and he placed his finger to his lips, nice and slowly, and the adults complied and soon there was silence.

'Okay, then, this is what we know. A baby has been found murdered moments after coming into this world. A girl has been identified as being the potential mother. We have nothing else to share at this time.' He moved to walk away but the press descended like a horde of zombies. We were surrounded. Random journalists shouted over each other, their voices blending into a chaotic barrage.

'Can you confirm it's the O'Reilly family?'

'And the girl is Joyce O'Reilly?'

'Did she kill the child?'

'Was the family involved?'

These same questions were repeated in different ways and out of the mouths of many as Foley beat a path across the road, pulling me along with him, as though he was saving me from a raging tide. It was only when we got inside the hotel and the door closed behind us that they stepped away and accepted that no more would be said to them that day.

'You all right?' he said as I fixed my coat that had been nearly pulled off me.

'I'm fine,' I said. 'You?' His answer came in the form of laughter. *Of course he's all right, he's Matt Foley.* That annoyed me. *If you were ice cream, you'd lick yourself*, I thought as I followed him into the incident room. That's when I met Joe O'Neill for the first time. He was sitting on the edge of a desk, looking up at the blackboard. Foley greeted him fondly.

'O'Neill,' he said, injecting warmth into his voice, looking relieved to see him. O'Neill turned to face us and winked at his boss. He was striking: good teeth, dark hair, tall, athletic, he wore a smart suit and clean shoes, had deep green eyes and an easy smile. I learned later that we were the same age; he'd just turned twenty-eight the week before. My stomach fluttered, the colour rising in my cheeks. I turned away, hoping my face hadn't betrayed the fact I found him handsome.

'Well,' Foley said. 'Did she have it?'

Have what?

'She did,' he said.

She did what?

'Boy or a child?' He said, grinning at his own joke.

Oh, I thought. *Of course.* I hadn't looked at his ring finger to see if he was married, so lost was I to the rest of him.

'A child,' O'Neill said with a wide smile. Foley clapped him on the back.

Good. That's good. I had no time for distraction. Still, a part of me, the tiniest part, was just a bit gutted. I knew a relationship would mean the end of the career I loved, but I was still a human woman with human woman feelings, emotions and needs, and it had been a while since I looked upon a man who sparked something within me the way Detective Joe O'Neill had on first appearance.

'Good man. What are you calling her?'

'Lorraine,' he said.

'Fine name.'

'The missus likes it.'

As they talked, I could see Joe O'Neill taking me in, waiting for his moment to ask why I was standing by his boss, but Foley wasn't giving him the space to do so. He carried on talking as though they were alone. 'You should have taken the time off. Are you sure about working this case?'

'What do you mean?' O'Neill seemed perplexed.

'Well, with it being a baby,' Foley said in a hushed tone, afraid the other men might hear him.

'Are you messing?' Joe said, his lips curling into a smirk, as if the idea of recent fatherhood affecting his work – or him being remotely moved by the baby in the morgue – was preposterous.

Foley smiled. 'Good man,' he said, slapping O'Neill on the back. 'We've got her anyway.' I wanted to intervene, because I thought it was a bit premature, but I said nothing, knowing my opinion wasn't wanted nor would it be heeded.

'She admit it?' O'Neill asked.

'No, they've all clammed up but it's only a matter of time.'

'Who's they?' he asked.

'The girl, her mother, father, brother.'

Dicey appeared out of nowhere and sidled up to join the conversation he wasn't a part of. 'There was another one of them, Ricky, he left for America over a year ago,' he said. O'Neill just nodded to him.

'Did they ask for a solicitor?' O'Neill said to Foley.

'No, thank God, they don't know their rights,' Foley replied.

'Good. We need to get working, it won't stay that way for long.'

Dicey didn't know where to put himself, so he just slunk back a bit and found a seat somewhere, and he made a fuss of shuffling some paperwork.

'You and Quinn interview the father and the brother,' Foley told O'Neill before looking my way. 'We'll take the girl and then the mother.'

'We?' O'Neill said, staring past his boss at the lanky blonde in uniform. *Me.* I think I might have waved at him.

'This is Garda Mary Shea.' Foley pointed my way and O'Neill looked at him as though he'd lost his mind. 'You're bringing the girl in?' *Girl?* I thought. *I'm no more a girl than you're a boy.*

'She's got her head screwed on and I need someone who speaks the language,' Foley said.

'Are they foreign?' O'Neill said, slightly confused.

'No, Joe… They're women,' Foley said, amused, and O'Neill smiled at the joke but that smile quickly turned to a frown. He looked at me. 'Are ya sure about this?' he said to Foley.

'If she's not able for it, she'll tell me,' Foley said. 'Not behind the door about talking up for herself, this one.' I stood there, listening to them speaking about me as if I were a child. Did I want to bang their heads together? I did, and I fantasised about it. I could even hear the cracking sound they made as their skulls connected.

O'Neill examined me, taking me in. I kept cool, remained silent. There's a time and a place for talk. This wasn't it.

'You're the boss,' he said to Foley but it was clear he thought his boss was barking mad for including a woman in their big case. O'Neill didn't seem so handsome any more.

–

As the local police station was too small to try to keep the family apart, Brian Keating made enquiries and we were relocated to a station in the town of Tralee, which was less than thirty miles away. The family were all moved in separate cars; it was a bit of a palaver, with the press on our doorstep, but we managed it. Everyone knew who the O'Reillys were by then; the locals were shouting their names and the press were taking notes. We tried to conceal their faces but it was too late; the boys with the flashing cameras had captured them and now they'd be on the hunt for that one photo of the girl, before all this, that one image that would define her in the minds of the whole country. They'd be knocking on doors and someone, somewhere, would give them what they wanted. The wall of sound dissipated with the slamming of the car door and the burning of rubber, courtesy of Joe O'Neill, who was suddenly the designated driver. Foley sat in the front seat. I was demoted to the back with Joyce, who was locked inside her own darkness. Nothing could touch her now that she'd given into it.

–

The station was huge and there was a corridor of cells beneath it. As soon as we were inside, Superintendent Lynch was there to meet us. He and Foley moved off together down the hall, leaving me standing there with O'Neill while a young garda escorted Joyce, terrified, to an interview room. O'Neill stared after him before turning to me.

'He wants you in there with him. You sure you're up for this?' They were the first words he spoke to me directly.

'I am. Are you?' I countered.

'You're a strange one,' he said and I wondered how he could know that by my uttering four words.

Foley opened the interview room door to reveal Joyce hunched into a ball in the corner. He sat on a chair and directed me to the seat next to his, before pressing record on the tape machine. He spoke clearly into the speaker, recording the date, time and who was in attendance. When he was done, he directed his words to Joyce.

'Joyce, you can sit on the chair if you'd like.'

She didn't say anything.

'Did you have a baby, Joyce?' he asked and she rocked a little but stayed silent.

'I can have the doctor here in less than fifteen minutes. Would you prefer him to examine you to confirm it for us?'

This got her attention and she looked up, wild-eyed, and shook her head. 'No.'

'Did you have a baby, Joyce?' Foley repeated, and Joyce nodded.

'What happened to it?'

Silence again.

'Did you kill the baby?'

Silence.

'Did you kill your baby?'

Nothing. Foley slammed his hand on the table and I all but leaped out of the chair. She curled into a tighter ball, but Foley wasn't having that. He was up on his feet, crossing the room in less than three strides. In an instant, he had her hauled up by the back of her collar, leaving her dangling like a freshly caught salmon, thrashing around. Before I could even process what was happening, he had her slapped down into the chair in front of us. She was wild with fright, her mind overcome and her body unable to contain the tempest within her. She was vibrating, only short of levitating, and I thought if anyone was ever going to burst, explode or disintegrate in front of me, it would be this girl. The fear was catching, and I battled hard not to become infected by it. *Do your job, Mary. Don't let yourself down now.* I sat on my hands to prevent them from trembling.

'Enough,' Foley said when he'd plonked himself down in front of her. 'It's time to talk.'

Her eyes were round and swollen, her cheeks puffy, and tears tumbled from her as though a dam behind her eyes had been breached. She tried to talk but no words came, her very breath catching in her throat. I thought she might choke. It was then, as soon as I was sure my hands were steady, that I reached across the table and I laid them on hers. She jolted backwards initially but then responded to my gentle touch by meeting my eyes. I was sure to keep my expression soft. When I spoke, it was in a calm and measured tone, not too loud but loud enough for her to hear me over the tumult in her own head.

'Joyce, I'm sorry for what's happened,' I said and she blinked. 'I know it's hard and I can't imagine what you've been through, but you need to tell me what happened to you and your baby.'

'The baby's dead,' she choked out after another long moment of silence.

'Did you kill the baby, Joyce?' I asked.

She looked at me – no, she looked *into* me. 'I don't know,' she admitted. Foley nodded for me to go on.

'Your mammy, was she there?' I asked.

Joyce shook her head. 'I was alone in the sorting shed.'

'Did you stab the baby?' I asked, and her eyes widened, her expression changed and I could read the confusion in her eyes.

'No. Of course not. No. Why would you say that? What are you talking about?' She was almost screaming the words. I could tell she wasn't far off hysterical; I needed to steer her away from madness, because I was afraid once she'd given into it, I'd have an awful job getting her back.

'Okay, okay...' I soothed. 'Can I ask you who you told about the baby?' I enquired to lead her thoughts in a new direction.

'Nobody,' she said.

'Did you hide it from your daddy and your brother?'

'From everyone.'

'What about the father of the child?' I asked.

She slowly shook her head from side to side. 'I told no one.' I took her in. She'd given birth and, yes, she was a big enough girl, but the curve of her stomach, her shape, suggested a pregnancy. Maybe it might not have been obvious to most but to a boyfriend, if there was one… 'Joyce, who is…' I began, feeling that identifying the child's father was important at this juncture, but Foley interrupted me with a question of his own.

'Did your mother know about the baby?' he asked. She was staring at my hands covering her own when he asked. Her eyes flicked up and locked with mine, and in that moment it dawned on me: her pregnancy may not have been obvious to men, but to women – especially those who had experienced pregnancy – it would have been unmistakable. Foley knew it. Her mother would have seen it. She would have known.

'Do you think she knew, Joyce?' I asked.

Joyce nodded. 'I think so.'

'You didn't talk about it?'

She shook her head.

'Why do you think she knew?'

'She saw me.'

'She saw your swollen stomach?' I said and she blinked away tears. 'When?'

'I was going to bed last week, and she walked in and she saw me.'

The word 'she' hitched in her throat. She was trembling, every inch of her. Even her hair was standing on end.

'What did she say when she saw it?'

'Nothing. She wouldn't look at me or talk to me at all.'

There was a knock at the door. It was Rory, another officer. 'The doctor's here,' he said and Joyce looked from Rory to me, letting go of my hands. She pulled away, sinking into herself. 'No. No. No,' she cried out. 'No. Please. No.' She was sobbing now, her face, neck and chest soaked in tears.

'It has to be done. We need to confirm the pregnancy and make sure you're all right,' Foley said.

'No,' she cried. 'I don't want to.' She was screaming now.

'Shush,' I said lightly. 'No one is going to hurt you.'

'It's so sore,' she cried, and I knew instantly she was torn, maybe like my mother was when she gave birth to my younger sister, or maybe worse.

'I'm sorry, Joyce, but it's dangerous. We have to know you're all right,' I said, trying to assure her.

Rory led her out of the room, her shoulders heaving, her teeth rattling. The door closed behind them, leaving us alone, her cries, now muffled by the solid concrete wall, fading to nothing.

'That was good,' Foley said after a moment or two.

'Was it? We don't have much more information than we started with.'

'We know she had a baby, she's not sure if she killed it and her mother knew she was pregnant. It's a lot more than we knew before we got in here.'

'If she stabbed a baby, surely she'd be aware of that,' I said.

'Maybe she was in a frenzy, not sure of anything.'

'She was confused. Stabbing is a deliberate act. She'd remember it.'

'You don't know that,' Foley said and he was right, I didn't know for sure.

'Maybe not, but my gut—'

He raised his hand to stop me from finishing my sentence. 'You earn your gut… comes with experience, of which you have none.'

'But earlier you asked me what my gut feeling…' I began to say but he shook his head.

'Earlier you were right. Now you're just getting ahead of yourself,' he said, then pulled out a hankie from the inside of his pocket and blew his nose. He examined the contents before folding it over and placing it back in his pocket. 'Maybe it was the mother,' he mused, before standing up and stretching. We took a break for some tea and sandwiches. The boys were still busy with Thomas. Raymond and Breda were being held somewhere else. Once we'd eaten, Foley turned to me. 'Right, time to bring Breda in.' I returned to the room while he went to collect Breda, but he took an age, clearly doing more than he'd said. Doing something he didn't want me to know about, going over my head.

Foley returned with Breda O'Reilly by the arm. She was sullen, shaken, of course, but she contained her fright. She was cautious now, her eyes searching the room, searching me, searching Foley. She sat of her own accord. Breda, with her blonde curly hair, her plain dress and manicured hands, had managed to wipe her face clean of make-up. Foley slurped from a fresh cup of tea before turning on the tape recorder.

'How long had you known that your daughter was pregnant?' he began without any pleasantries.

'I didn't.'

'That's a lie. One more chance or I'll lock you up,' he threatened.

The blood drained from her. 'I didn't know for sure.'

'But you saw it for yourself.'

'I thought I saw.'

'And you didn't talk to her?'

She shook her head. 'What would I say? What would I do?'

'But you did something?' Foley said.

'What do you mean?'

'You killed the child,' he said as though it were fact. She balked, pulling her chair back, its metal legs making a high-pitched screech as she shifted position.

'I did not,' she said, appalled.

'So Joyce did it,' he said and she started to cry, because she didn't know the answer to that.

'You're saying you weren't there, Breda?' Foley said and she shook her head.

'I didn't even know she'd had it.'

'She's walking slow, guarded and with a slight limp,' I said. 'Have you not noticed she's in distress?'

'No. She said she was tired, stayed in her room,' she said. 'I'm very sorry but I didn't.'

'And her brother, Thomas, what does he know?' Foley asked.

'Nothing, he wouldn't have known.'

'How are you so sure? You didn't talk to her.' She squealed a little at this; a kind of high-pitched whine came out of her.

'What about your husband?'

'No. No. He didn't know.'

'Maybe he saw and ignored it too,' Foley said.

'He wouldn't have ignored it. He would have lost his mind and then he'd have sent her away.'

'So what were you planning to do when the baby came?' Foley said.

'I don't know, she wasn't that big, I thought there was plenty of time. I just needed to think.'

'Or maybe you thought the problem would go away.' She fell into a deep silence after he said that. He tried to get her to talk but no amount of aggression or fearmongering seemed to touch her, so I intervened.

'Mrs O'Reilly, I'm sorry, this must be a terrible thing, but you see…
the baby we found, something terrible happened to it,' I said and she
looked at me with curiosity.

'The papers are saying the baby was stabbed with a knife?' she asked
and I looked to Foley, not sure whether I should confirm it or not. He
took over.

'The baby was stabbed in the back with a kitchen knife,' he said
incorrectly. 'Who stabs a baby in the back?' he asked. *Why did he say
that? That's wrong. What was he doing? Was the truth not terrible enough? It
was a chest wound.*

She covered her gaping mouth. 'Oh no,' she said. 'Oh God, no. She
wouldn't… My Joyce… She couldn't.'

'Are you sure your boy or your husband didn't know previous to her
giving birth, or maybe found her in the immediate aftermath?' I said,
and that's the moment I cast doubt in the woman's mind about her own
husband and children. I could see it happen in real time. I could see her
process the terrible information and the doubt creep into her eyes, and
it was a terrible thing to see but I told myself I was doing my job. She
needed water. She said she felt faint. Her blood pressure had dropped.
Foley could see it too. He called an end to the interview. She needed
a break. We all did. I felt hot, my skin burnt. My head felt heavy. I
needed air. He met me outside as I lay against the wall, the cold stone
cooling me down, the air filling my lungs so that I could breathe again.
He stood beside me, taking in oxygen. 'Those rooms are hard,' he said
after a moment.

'Not as hard for us as for those opposite us,' I said.

'True,' he said. He took out a packet of cigarettes and offered me
one, which I declined. He lit up and as he took a drag, the acrid bitter
odour of his tobacco filled the air. I inhaled his second-hand smoke
before asking after the girl and was told she was in the hospital. The
doctor had discovered a tear that needed fixing. It was no surprise,
judging by the way she held herself. I wondered how it was missed
by those who loved her, but women and girls had a way of hiding in
plain sight, and looking back, it was only when her secret was exposed
that she'd truly given into her pain. Foley told me that Liam Kenny was
watching over her, making sure she didn't make a break for it. I thought
about him inside a hospital room, sniffling and coughing his guts up.
It wasn't the smartest move, but I suppose the only one he'd infect was

poor Joyce, and a nasty cold would be the least of her worries. Foley glanced at his watch. 'You've completed your second shift, go home,' he said.

'What about you?' I asked.

'I think it's going to be a long night.' He flicked the burning tip of the cigarette with his finger. The lit tobacco hit the ground, he stood on it, then pocketed the remaining part of the unsmoked cigarette into the box.

'Why did you say Baby Crónán was stabbed in the back when it was a chest wound?'

'I wanted to see her reaction.'

'And what did it tell you?'

'She was surprised.'

'So?' I asked.

'So, let's see how it plays out,' he said. I had no idea what he was getting at. He looked up at the sky. 'Yeah, a long night,' he mumbled and made his way back inside.

I drove down the darkening road, thinking about Joyce and wondering if – and how – that shivering wreck of a girl was capable of doing such a terrible thing. I couldn't imagine her committing such a heinous crime. My own prejudice kicked in, and I rushed to judgement, deciding that the murderer had to be one of the O'Reilly men. By the time I parked the car up at the station and transferred into my own, I was sure of it.

CHAPTER SIX

Day Three

I washed and dressed, having not slept a wink, but despite that, I was energised. I had work to do and I couldn't wait to set about doing it. I ate a breakfast of buttered bread and two eggs. I wouldn't make the mistake of risking hunger again; the job was too great to do it well on an empty stomach. Seamus was in the field, fixing up a part of the fence that had blown down during a gale the week before. He cast a glance my way, his expression suggesting he was far from happy, as he slowly raised his hand to wave. I waved back, and I realised that he must know his friend Thomas was being held for questioning, and I wondered if the outcome would change things between us. It was only a passing thought before it was crowded out, and I was once again ruminating on the O'Reillys and what had been done.

–

I bypassed our own station and drove straight to Tralee Garda Station, eager to discover what the Dublin boys had learned in my absence. Liam Kenny met me at the door; he seemed healthier, his nose was returning to a normal colour, and he had more energy but he was nervous and a bit off in himself.

'You okay, Liam?' I asked.

'Grand,' he said, but he couldn't look my way. I detected a tremble in his voice, making it clear he was far from it. It set me on edge, sensing a man was about to crumble like that.

'What's wrong?' I pressed again just as Quinn passed behind me in the corridor. Liam's eyes grew wide and he shook his head from side to side vigorously, and between that and the terrified look on his face, I knew to keep quiet until Quinn was out of sight.

75

'Let's take a breath of fresh air,' I said and Liam looked almost relieved. He followed me outside and we sat down on the wall.

'What did they do?' I asked him quietly. I'd heard enough to know that the Dublin boys could be heavy-handed. The rumours were rife, and having witnessed Foley picking up Joyce and shaking her like a rag doll, I couldn't help but worry about the fate of the O'Reilly men.

Liam shook his head. 'They hurt them, Mary.'

'Who did?'

'Those boys from Dublin. O'Neill, he was the worst. Quinn gave Raymond a few good clatters but O'Neill gave Thomas an awful leathering.'

'What about Foley?'

'He just kept asking questions as the boys were beating on them – kept shouting, shooting question after question. I've known those lads my entire life. Raymond's a good man, Thomas the same, and I just stood there.'

'What else could you have done?' I said.

'Oh, I don't know, something… anything. They really hurt Thomas.'

'I thought you were in the hospital with Joyce?' I said, trying to piece the events of the previous evening together.

'I was but then Dicey took over, and they asked me to come back here.'

'Why?' I asked, it didn't make much sense.

'I don't know, maybe they've heard that Dicey has a mouth. God knows if he was there the whole town would know what had happened,' he said. He was right. Dicey would have bragged, because the actions of the Dublin boys were in line with what he thought of as real police work. No doubt he would have joined in – any chance to be the big man. My thoughts briefly flitted to Ann Buckley, and I wondered how many bruises our Monday morning visit had earned her.

'I'd love a cigarette,' he said. I fished a box of ten from my pocket. He looked at me, curiously.

'I thought you gave up.'

'I did. These are for comfort, just to know I have them in case of emergency.' I had fought the instinct to smoke since the moment I laid eyes on Baby Crónán. I opened the seal and handed him a cigarette, then plopped one in my own mouth. 'Feels like an emergency,' I said, grabbing my lighter and sparking them both. We inhaled deeply, experiencing the rush of nicotine to our brains. The birds were suddenly singing a little sweeter, the grass appeared a deeper green, the sky seemed to be turning from grey to blue.

'God, I needed that,' he said.

I exhaled, releasing all that stored-up pain and tension from my body. 'Me too.'

'Your dad's going to pay a visit, isn't he?' Liam said. I nodded, and we both took another long drag of our cigarettes.

'What do you think he'd make of this?' he said.

'I don't know, Liam,' I said honestly. 'Is the baby really hers?'

He nodded. 'The doctor confirmed it.' That took a moment to sink in. *What happened, Joyce?*

We continued smoking, enjoying the last of our cigarettes before he'd go home and I'd go inside.

'What kind of questions did they ask?'

'Who knew and who was there, who wielded the knife,' he said.

'What did they say?' I asked.

'The men wouldn't talk but then Breda called for Foley, from the cell they were keeping her in. She said it was Joyce who did it. Her husband and Thomas knew nothing about it. She said Joyce had the baby in the processing shed and she murdered it there, stabbed it in its back and she used her bike to cycle to the beach...'

My eyes widened. 'She said Joyce stabbed the baby in the back?'

'That's right,' he said. *But that wasn't true, that's just what Foley told her.*

'She said Joyce put the baby in the front basket and covered it with a blanket.'

'Did she say what colour?'

'No, I don't think so.'

'Did Foley mention the baby being covered with a blanket before Breda mentioned it?'

'I don't know.' He sighed. 'I missed a lot of it. By the time I arrived at the station, the O'Reilly boys were good and bloody, and Breda had already started to talk.'

It was then Foley emerged; he'd been sleeping in a side room. He looked like the wreck of the Hesperus. He called out to us, and told Liam to go home as he lit a cigarette of his own.

'Good work last night,' he said to Liam as he walked away. He looked at me and at the cigarette in my hand. I flicked it out, grounding the butt with my foot.

'You didn't say you smoked,' he commented.

'I didn't say I didn't either,' I replied, defensively. He studied me for a moment before shaking his head.

'Liam told you, then?'

'He mentioned Breda's confession, all right,' I said.

'Right, and what did he say about it?'

'Joyce stabbed the baby, cycled to the beach and dropped him off.'

'That's right.'

'How did Breda know? Was she there?' I said.

'She said she saw her put the baby in the basket and she found the knife in the processing shed.'

'Except that Joyce said she gave birth in the sorting shed.'

'Well, Joyce is a woman of loose morals, so lying is not beyond her,' Foley said. That infuriated me.

'She's still only a girl, and her morals are no looser than all the men I've ever had to listen to as they brag about their nights out and the women they've conquered,' I shot back.

He fixed me with a sharp disapproving look, as though my words left a bad taste in his mouth. 'Those men you speak of – no doubt your colleagues – they've never stabbed a baby to death.'

'You're so sure that Joyce did this?' I said.

'I am,' he said.

'She stabbed him in the back?' I said. His eyes narrowed.

'You mislead Breda, hoping to catch her out, but now she's lying, using your words to make up a story...'

'Why would she do that?' he shouted, his face red with temper.

'She was scared. You were hurting her men,' I shouted. He took a step back. Recalibrated. I knew I was pushing it, the adrenaline pumping around my body told me so. I lit another cigarette.

'I admire your guts and your passion, but you're wrong. If you care to read the report, you'll find there was a knife wound on the baby's back,' he said calmly. This took the wind from my sails. I almost crumpled – the only thing holding me up was the cigarette in my hand. *Shut up, Mary. You know nothing...*

I had read the report. There was a cut on the baby's back – just a cut – but I knew I wasn't going to win the argument. He'd say it was semantics and that I was being a difficult woman. And it didn't mean that Joyce was innocent, or that Breda's confession was entirely built upon the information he gave her… But the complete lack of deviation from his account – that was troubling. I didn't argue further. I took a deep breath, counted to three and let it go.

'Fair enough. You should go to the hotel, rest, wash up,' I said, attempting to change the subject.

He seemed grateful I'd moved on. 'Oh, you care now?' he said, his tone playful, all signs of aggression gone.

'My nose does. You smell like a bag of dirty washing.'

His grin faded as I walked away from him. I half-expected him to call out, to tell me to leave and not come back, but he didn't. Instead, he took a whiff of himself. He must have conceded I was right because he left soon after. While he was gone about his personal business, I took the time to visit the cells where they were keeping Thomas and his father, Raymond. I found them sitting on the thin mattress on a metal frame bolted to the concrete floor. Raymond caught my eye first; aside from a swollen lip, he didn't seem too bad. He was nursing Thomas, who was in a terrible way: his arm was twisted and I knew instantly it was broken. His face was a mess, his eyes so swollen he couldn't open them. Raymond stood up as soon as he saw me.

'Help,' he pleaded. 'Help him, please.' He was desperate, the poor man. He looked nothing like the one who had stood in front of me the day before. It was then my eyes truly met Thomas's. He looked gaunt, a shadow of himself – even his curls seemed lank. We had known each other well enough to exchange hellos; once, he'd helped me lift a heavy bag of washing out of my car, when he was passing on his way to knock on Seamus's door. But now, we felt like total strangers. The gap between us was greater than any door or set of bars could create.

'Okay, it's all right. I'll call the doctor,' I said. 'If one hasn't been called?'

'There's no one coming,' Raymond said. 'He's been like this since eleven o'clock last night. He needs a hospital.'

'Okay,' I said, and I spun around and took the stairs two by two from the basement to the ground floor of the building. O'Neill was at a desk, fresh-faced and in a clean suit.

I immediately spotted his knuckles were slightly swollen from punching the boys. I walked up to the desk.

'Have you called a doctor?'

'For who?' he said as if he didn't know.

'For Thomas – that arm of his is broken,' I said, trying not to let the words sound accusatory. It was hard to look at him, especially with the smug expression he wore.

'Since when have you a medical degree?' he asked.

'I don't. What I have are eyes and sense, and they tell me that Thomas O'Reilly needs that arm set,' I said again, maintaining a lightness to my tone.

He regarded me with a kind of contempt. 'Is that right?' he said, unmoved. I couldn't have that – I couldn't have Thomas O'Reilly agonised and crying out for help while we did nothing. So I did it. I mentioned my father's name. I hated myself for it, but Thomas needed tending to.

'O'Neill, my father will be visiting, and I can tell you one thing about him: if he sees that man with a broken arm left unattended, he'll come looking for a head.'

'You forget I know him too,' he said and that threw me. He didn't know him – not personally, not even professionally, to the best of my knowledge. I played it calm and cool.

'Well, then, you'll know that if a conviction is thrown out of court because of something as stupid as not tending to a witness, he'll cut your balls off,' I said evenly and with a smile.

That hit a nerve. My father was renowned for his zero tolerance for incompetence. Under his watch, the Kerry guards boasted the best results in the county. That seemed to work. O'Neill winced a bit. We faced off. He thought through his options. I waited. 'Go ahead,' he said finally.

'No problem,' I said. I leafed through the phonebook and found a doctor close by. I rang and asked his receptionist to have him come to the station as a matter of urgency.

I explained that a young man in the cells had a broken arm and would need it set, so he should bring everything he required.

'Sure, he needs to go to a hospital,' she said.

'Hospital is not an option.'

'Is it one of the O'Reillys?' she asked.

'That's garda business,' I said.

'Oh, it is so. I'll get him down there straight away,' she said. She was calling his name before she hung up the phone. By then, Quinn had materialised from somewhere and he was leaning over me.

'You don't have the right to make that call,' he said.

'I have every right and you'll be glad, because now that Joyce is officially a suspect, a solicitor will be appointed. Best Thomas isn't screaming in agony or dead from acute shock when that solicitor arrives to question him,' I said. Quinn didn't know where to look. I was on a roll – Daddy used to say that was when I was at my most unlikable.

'She's right,' O'Neill said, and Quinn backed off. 'We've got her pinned down, no need to upset the apple cart.' He smiled and it was a genuine enough smile. 'Good work,' he said, his perfect white teeth on show and his eyes lit up as though he was genuinely happy with me. I couldn't make him out at all. What I did know was that he believed Joyce had killed her baby. I knew he believed that subjecting the boys to brutality was the most efficient way of bringing this terrible matter to a close. He saw himself as a hero. I wasn't so sure. I wondered if Thomas's arm would have been broken if O'Neill's wife hadn't just had a baby. That kind of violence stemmed from a place of rage. I knew he'd seen the photos of Baby Crónán. He'd pretended it was just another image of just another victim, but he couldn't truly conceal the horror as it washed through him. Maybe he was a good man, doing the best he could to fight evil. Maybe I was the devil's fool. I acted with assurance, but I felt none.

I reflected on a telephone conversation I'd had with my mother the night before. I'd stopped at the phone box near the beach and fished out a pocketful of twenty-pence pieces I always kept handy. I placed the call and when she answered, my heart felt instantly larger as tears stung my eyes. She warned me: Daddy was Assistant Commissioner, it was a big case, he'd turn up, but I'd have nothing to worry about.

'The Dublin man in charge, he's letting me work on it closely with him,' I told her.

'I'm so proud of you,' she said without missing a beat and, from the warmth in her voice, I knew she meant it. She loved that I loved what I was doing, even if she didn't understand why I did it, especially at times like this.

'I hope Daddy doesn't make life difficult,' I admitted, scared he'd say something to belittle me in front of Foley and the Dublin boys.

'He won't be let back in the house if he does,' she said and that made me smile, because I knew she'd be true to her word. I looked through the large glass panels; the wet path glistened with the sheen of water, reflecting the dim light of the street lamp that was only a few feet away.

'Tell me something nice,' I said.

'You're nice,' she said, and it made me chuckle.

Judging by the way O'Neill and the rest of the Dublin boys looked at me, they would strongly disagree.

–

The doctor arrived within twenty minutes of my calling him. I led him down to the cells. Raymond stood back from the bars to allow us in. I entered too and the door locked behind us. I wasn't scared to be in a cage with the O'Reillys after what had been done to them; they knew those same Dublin men were only a floor away. Doctor Kinsella – a small, slight man with a big moustache and thick round spectacles – gave Thomas an injection of morphine and we waited a few minutes for it to take effect. We sat there in silence.

Not a word or utterance between us. Once it had kicked in, it was obvious, because Thomas's brow relaxed and his teeth unclenched.

'How do you feel?' Dr Kinsella said.

'Better,' he said, but his eyes were still watering.

'I'm going to have to straighten it,' Dr Kinsella said and I worried for Thomas, because it was fiercely crooked.

'Okay,' he said and even though he was dull with morphine, I could hear the fear in his voice.

'I need you to hold him, Mr O'Reilly.' Raymond swallowed his concern and held his son in position. I turned away, but I heard the sickening crunch and Thomas's scream.

'That's it. That's it,' Dr Kinsella said, wrapping the arm in stockinette and roll padding. He took out some casting material, drenched it in a bucket of lukewarm water and, after wringing it out, he wrapped it carefully around Thomas's arm.

'Bend it for me slowly,' he instructed and Thomas did as he was told. He was to hold it in place for fifteen minutes while it set. Thomas nodded and thanked the man. Then Dr Kinsella checked Raymond's lip and his head for concussion, feeling his skull for signs of trouble. 'No lumps, no bumps, no cuts around the eyes. He'll be fine,' he said to me. As we left, Thomas was still holding his freshly cast arm; he rested his head against the concrete wall and he was somewhere else, lost in a morphine haze, while his father Raymond sat, crying softly.

–

When the doctor had been paid and was gone, and the lads from Dublin were busy with their paperwork, I made my way to Breda's cell in the basement. I unlocked it and walked inside to sit with her. Neither of us spoke at first. I just followed her gaze to the opposite wall. We were quiet for a while. She was the first to speak.

'How is Thomas?' she asked.

'Better,' I said. 'His left arm is in a cast, his eyes are swollen, his ribs are battered but unbroken – he'll be fine.'

'And Raymond?'

'He has a split lip, he'll be fine too.'

'He has a bad a heart, you know,' she said. I didn't know, not till that moment.

'He's fine. Honestly.'

'And Joyce?' Her voice was quivering now. Her curly hair, a mess; her plain dress, wrinkled; and she'd aged ten years overnight.

'She's still in the hospital but she'll be making an appearance in court later today. She'll be kept in the cells below it.'

'They're charging her with murder,' she said in a dull tone, heavy with despair.

'They are.'

She was heartbroken; one look at her told me she might never recover.

'Can I ask you something?' I said and she nodded. 'What was the baby wrapped in?'

She didn't look at me. 'It was a white blanket.'

'You're sure?'

She thought about it for a minute. She hunched her shoulders. 'I think the blanket was white.'

But it wasn't a blanket, it was a towel. The towel wasn't white, it was blue, and the child wasn't stabbed in the back, he was stabbed in his chest. It didn't add up and I was worried about that.

Foley returned after an hour or two away. He was clean and wearing a different suit; it was as old and battered as the previous one, but fresh nonetheless. I wondered how bad a housekeeper his wife must be to let him out like he was a homeless stray. He called me over to him, seated at a desk, reading through Breda's statement. I stood there, waiting for him to finish. He handed it to O'Neill – who was dressed to perfection, in sharp contrast to his boss – before turning to me. 'I hear you called the doctor,' he said.

'I did,' I replied.

'Did he ask what happened?'

'I explained it was garda business.'

'Good,' he said. 'Good. Is Thomas okay?'

'He has a broken arm,' I said, once again careful not to let on that I judged them, or that I was angry, even though I was steaming over it. Seeing the O'Reilly men in that cell, as vulnerable as they were, made me furious. We were supposed to protect people. We were supposed to be a moral authority.

'I want you to visit Joyce. She'll be charged later today but it would be good to get her confession too,' Foley said, pulling me from my thoughts.

'Has anyone spoken to her since her mother's confession?'

'No.'

'And you want me to do it?' I asked, a little amazed that he was entrusting me with such an important task.

He nodded. 'You're good with her.'

'You really think she did it?' I asked, after a moment.

'I've no reason not to,' he said.

'What about the towel around the baby?' I asked.

'What about it?'

'When I asked Breda, she said it was a white blanket, but it was a blue towel.'

This seemed to irritate him. 'So she was mistaken. It was traumatic – her daughter had just given birth and murdered her own child with a kitchen knife. She can't be expected to remember every detail. There is no such thing as a reliable witness, Shea. Not really. Traumatised people can't think properly, can't see what's really going on. They shut down, their focus narrows, it's human nature to make mistakes,' he said, his voice raised, his colour rising too.

He was right – there were no reliable witnesses. People made mistakes all the time, especially when traumatised. But still… I didn't argue. I nodded and agreed to go to the hospital before he changed his mind about extending the invitation. He and O'Neill were going back to the house to search for the murder weapon. The house and the business were already locked down as crime scenes. It was time for them to find evidence to put Joyce O'Reilly away for murder.

I arrived at the hospital mid-morning. Dicey was sitting outside a private room. When I said I was there to interview Joyce, he looked at me like I was a fish on a bicycle.

'You?' he scoffed. 'You're here to interrogate her?' He looked around to see if the boys were pranking him.

'Yes,' I said. 'Would you like to go to the nurses' station and make a call just to confirm?' I asked in a tone that suggested he'd be a fool to do it.

He thought about that. 'No. If it's okay by Foley, it's okay by me.'

'That's good to know,' I said and I entered the room. Joyce was lying on her side, staring out the window at the carpark below. I sat in front of her, blocking her view. She didn't blink.

'Are you all right?' I asked her.

'They tore me again, then they stitched me,' she said dully.

'You must have been in terrible pain,' I said and lifted her chart from the end of the bed and read it. The tear was described as a fourth-degree laceration. I didn't know what that meant but it sounded bad.

'Joyce, can you tell me what happened?' I said.

'I had a baby and it died,' she said.

'How?'

'I don't know.'

'Where did you have the baby?'

'The sorting shed.'

'Is that the same as the processing shed?' I asked, just to be sure.

'No. The processing shed is the first one as you come in, with my dad's office in it. The storage is the stone building behind it.'

'Was your mother there at any stage?'

'No, I told you. I was alone.'

'What happened to the baby?'

'I don't know,' she said. 'It just went wrong.'

'Tell me what happened, you felt pain and then what?'

'I was in my room and the pains started. The house was quiet, Dad and Thomas were in the pub and Mammy was sleeping. I stayed there for a long time but then it started getting really bad and I was scared to cry out. I got my raincoat, my boots and my umbrella, and I walked to the storage shed. I had a key for it and it was far enough away from the house. I was there for a long time, hours maybe, but then she was coming.'

'She?' I said and my heart leaped in my chest. *SHE?!*

'Yeah,' she said.

'Joyce, you had a little boy,' I said.

'No, I didn't. I had a girl. She was a girl.' She was crying again. Joyce had been home, in bed, when the news broke about Baby Crónán. Had she missed it? It made sense her mother would say nothing to her, knowing she was with child and afraid to talk about it. Men rarely spoke out loud about anything that didn't involve a ball. Did she even really understand what she was being accused of? I didn't know what to say. My head was spinning. *Was she right? Or just confused?* 'What happened then?' I asked.

'She was stuck, I couldn't push her out. I put my hands inside and I tried to pull and pull, I was screaming, wild with the pain… and the blood kept coming. I thought I was going to die and then she just came away in my hands. I had her by the neck, you see.'

'Was she breathing?' I asked, nearly forgetting to breathe myself.

Joyce was trembling now, her hands fidgeting, her eyes filling. She shook her head and as she did, tears spilled.

'No… She wasn't moving… She was still.'

'Where is she?' I asked.

'In the yard.'

'Where in the yard?'

'I don't know. It was so dark and I was so tired and the pain—'

'Joyce, you need to remember – what did you do with her?'

'She wasn't alive. I put her in a plastic bag and under the hood of one of the tractors,' she said. *Oh, sweet God, another creature*, I thought.

'Under the hood?' I asked.

She nodded, a never-ending stream of tears falling from her. 'I planned to bury her in the woods – somewhere nice, quiet and sheltered. I was going to carve something into a tree so I could visit. But I was so sore, and I felt so sick. Then you came and found me.'

'Joyce, your mammy told us you gave birth to a boy and you stabbed him to death,' I said and her eyes widened.

'What? No. I didn't.' She was horrified. She couldn't believe the words coming out of my mouth.

'Joyce, you are to be charged with the murder of a baby boy.' I spoke slowly, and she stared at me, watching my mouth, trying to wrap her head around the words coming from it. 'Joyce, it's important that you request a solicitor. After that, don't say another word to anyone but him. Tell him what you've just told me. Do you hear me?'

She nodded. 'Yes.'

'Not a word to anyone else until you speak to your solicitor. Understood?' I repeated and she nodded again.

'Good,' I said and stood up. 'We'll keep this conversation between us. I'm so proud of you.' My mother had said this less than twenty-four hours earlier and now I was putting my job on the line. *I'm sorry, Mammy.* I made my way to the nurses' station, where I asked to speak with one of Joyce's doctors.

'It's Mr Mahon and he's very busy,' the nurse said.

'Well, I'm Garda Shea and I'm very busy too. A girl's life depends on it so I'll sit and wait, but I don't expect to have to wait long,' I said and she got moving after that. Dr Mahon presented himself ten minutes later.

'I hear you want to speak to me about Joyce O'Reilly?' he said in a posh accent, so posh it was hard to understand him – it sounded like he was gargling rocks.

'Describe for me a fourth-degree laceration,' I said.

'It's a very deep tear. In Joyce's case it extended into her rectum.'

It was like he was talking French. 'I don't understand.'

'She was torn from her vagina to her rectum,' he said slowly.

'Oh God.' It sounded horrifying.

'We needed to close up and separate the vagina from the rectum,' he said. He seemed fond of repeating those two words. I wasn't fond of listening to them.

'It will take time to heal but she'll be fine.'

'Can I ask you… Could Joyce have cycled a bike…' I thought about the distance between the yard and the beach. 'About ten miles or so after sustaining that kind of laceration?'

He laughed. 'Not for all the tea in China,' he said and he walked away.

—

When I returned to the station, I called Foley into a side room. 'She didn't do it,' I said, conscious he had a press conference organised to announce that the case was solved, once Joyce had been charged.

He grunted. 'Don't annoy me.'

'Not trying to. Joyce O'Reilly gave birth to a baby girl.'

That put a stop to his gallop. 'Excuse me?'

'In the storage shed. The child was dead when she finally pulled her out of her. She put her in a plastic bag and under the bonnet of a tractor in the O'Reillys' yard.'

'No,' he said. 'She's lying.' He was visibly rocked by this information.

'Maybe she's lying but it's our job to make sure of it,' I said and he didn't like that.

He pointed in my face. 'Don't get cheeky with me,' he said, and then he rubbed his temple and stewed on things for a minute. He pointed at me again. 'Fine. Feck it. You're with me, we're going back to the yard.'

—

We drove in silence, and he put the radio on to drown out the sound of our collective breathing. Michael Jackson's 'Don't Stop 'til You Get Enough' was playing. It felt surreal: driving to the O'Reillys' scrapyard to search for another baby, seated beside Foley, who despite his frustration – or perhaps because of it – was humming along to the lyrics. But there we were.

First, we stopped at the house, where Foley asked Quinn if they'd found anything.

'We found the knife – well, five of them, but two look like they could be the murder weapon,' he said.

'What did Breda say about the murder weapon?' I asked Foley.

'Nothing,' he said. Then he asked Quinn, 'Where are they?'

'The knives? Bagged and labelled in the boot of the car.' Quinn pointed outside. 'With everything else.'

'What about blue towels?' I asked.

'Am I the lead or you?' Foley said in a tone that suggested I may shut up.

'I just want to know,' I said, not taking the hint. Quinn looked to Foley for permission to answer my question. Foley signalled for him to go ahead.

'No blue towels. They might have only owned one.' He addressed the answer to Foley.

'Right, then, you finish up here,' Foley said to Quinn, before looking to me. 'Let's go see this shed.'

The place was silent as the grave. We headed into the stone sorting shed. There were two tractors, mostly stripped for parts – one yellow, one red, both rusted, both ready for the crusher. Foley looked from the tactors to me. 'She mention a colour?' he asked and I shook my head. If I knew him better I'd think he was stalling. 'Okay, then,' he said and walked up to the yellow one and tried to open the bonnet. He inspected the latch mechanism.

'It's sealed shut,' he said. I looked around and spied a wrench sitting on a timber bench. I reached for it, handed it to him. He looked from me to the wrench. 'What am I supposed to do with that?'

'I don't know, hit it,' I said.

'It's not a broken TV,' he said, glancing around. Spotting what he needed – an oil can – he grabbed a handkerchief from his pocket, soaked it in the oil and used it to manipulate the rusted latch, rubbing it until the bonnet finally popped open. He pulled back for a moment before leaning in to look inside.

'Nothing.' He moved swiftly on to the red tractor. That was easier to open and, again, there was no baby to be found. 'She's lying to you, Mary,' he said but I was already on the hunt for more tractors – outside, the way we came in, there were at least four. He followed me and we checked all of them. Nothing. *Maybe it was a van or a car... She was just confused.* I walked around again, checking under the bonnets of every car and van I could find. No baby girl.

'Satisfied?' he said and he seemed relieved. I didn't know what to feel, except that everything felt wrong.

–

Joyce was taken from her hospital bed by O'Neill and Dicey, and escorted to the court, where she briefly met her state-appointed solicitor, a well-dressed, round-faced, balding, heavyset man in his early sixties by the name of Joe O'Callaghan. She was charged with the murder of her child and brought down to the cells beneath the court. Later – at an agreed time, outside on the steps – Foley stood, surrounded by cameras and microphones, flanked by O'Neill and Quinn, and I watched as he gave his account of how Joyce O'Reilly gave birth in O'Reilly Scrap Metal Yard sorting shed and then stabbed her baby to death, before cycling to the beach with the corpse in a bag in the front basket. He went on to describe how she laid her child to rest in the small dune to be found early the next morning by Nora Fitzgerald, who'd been walking her dog. When the statement was finished, he asked those gathered if they had any questions. Every one of them shouted at once, and amidst the clamour and chaos, the dominating question was: 'Anyone else in the family involved?'

'The mother is a witness.' He shouted the answer above the other questions being fired at him.

'Will Breda O'Reilly be prosecuted for perverting the course of justice?' came one question from a fella near the front.

'She is a co-operating witness,' Foley said.

'What about the baby's father?' someone yelled and Foley looked down at the man. 'No one has been identified but whoever he is, he's also a victim of this crime.'

My stomach churned as I watched him, every one of my senses on edge as he smiled down the camera and assured the people of Ireland that he and his team had solved this horrific atrocity. Later, when I stopped at Miley's Newsagent, I picked up an evening newspaper from the fresh pile, and my stomach churned again. There she was on the front cover – in a blurred, low-quality photo – Joyce leaning against a corner wall in flared cords and a tight white T-shirt, no bra. Her hair was messy and she had a kind of gawping look on her face. She was much prettier than the photo suggested, much more intelligent than it depicted. This wasn't the girl I spoke to in the hospital; it was someone else entirely. This photo was chosen for a specific reason: this version of Joyce was someone people could easily judge, willingly hate – someone capable of a heinous act and deserving of the nightmare to come.

CHAPTER SEVEN

As we entered the incident room back at the hotel, it was populated by many. Dicey was sitting on the edge of a trestle table drinking tea, but sure, when wasn't he. Liam Kenny was there, without a snot or a wheeze; he appeared almost entirely back to full health. He was placing down a telephone receiver, clicking it back onto its hook as he looked up at Foley.

'That was Brian, back at the station. He says he's after receiving a tip...' We all stopped, every head in the place now directed at Liam; he wasn't used to the spotlight, his face went from white to strawberry red to a deep purple in a matter of seconds. If he was aware of it, he didn't let it show. 'Dermot Mullen says that there was a girl in a white nightdress on Hillcrest that night.'

'Dermot Mullen the vet?' I said.

Liam nodded. 'Was she on a bike?' Foley asked, excitedly. 'Bloody hell, do we have an eyewitness?'

Liam hunched. 'He didn't mention a bike.'

I thought about the geography of the place: if Joyce had been cycling from the yard to the beach, she'd have gone well out of her way to end up in Hillcrest. I didn't say anything; Foley was on it now, clicking his fingers. 'What was in that statement, the one from the crazy woman who thought her dead daughter was knocking in for a visit?'

Liam answered him. 'Mrs Lacey, eighty-eight, saw a girl barefoot in a white nightdress, on Potters Road between midnight and the morning.'

'Anything about a bike?' O'Neill said.

'No,' Dicey said, scrambling for the statement. 'No mention of a bike, I'm sure of it.'

'So how far is Potters Road from Hillcrest? And can someone get me a map of this place,' Foley said, clicking his fingers again. Most of the lads looked my way, expecting me to go fetch it. So I did. In the hotel lobby I picked up a local map from the stand by the door.

'How much?' I said.

'Two pounds,' Jenny said. She was standing in reception in a pretty dress. She looked nice.

I fished into my pocket and handed her a five-pound note.

'I heard about poor Joyce,' she said, opening the till before handing back my change.

'It's nice of you to put it that way,' I said to her. 'Most people will want her hung, drawn and quartered.'

She nodded. 'I was in her brother Ricky's class... We were...' She smiled. 'Only for a while... before he went to America. Nothing serious... but I always liked Joyce. I can't really understand what she did or how, but I understand the fear,' she said. Then she whispered, 'This is no place to be for a pregnant girl on her own.'

I nodded. She was right. 'Still, girls can give their babies away,' I said.

'They'd still be shamed. So would their families,' Jenny said. 'Not that I can imagine doing what she did.'

'Well, she's charged but she's not found guilty yet,' I said and moved to walk away but she called out to me.

'Garda Shea?' she said.

'Yes?'

'Do you like your job?'

'I love it,' I said – and I did, even though up to that point in time I hadn't been given much of a chance to do it.

'I'd like to be something more than... well... what I am.'

'There's nothing wrong with what you are, Jenny, but if you do want more, don't let anyone stop you.' I left her with those words of encouragement, hoping she had a steel rod for a backbone because, if she ever followed my advice, she'd need one. I placed the map in front of Foley. He was arguing with Liam and Dicey over what could have transpired that night... all assuming that the girl gadding about in a nightdress was Joyce O'Reilly.

'So if she was seen by the nutty old one on Potters Road between midnight and the morning, and she was seen by the vet on Hillcrest that same night, what does that tell us?' O'Neill said.

'Potters Road is opposite the beach, but a direct route from the O'Reillys' would be through town and then onto the coast road. Hillcrest is out of the way,' I said.

'She'd want to avoid town,' Foley said.

'So she'd go via Henry's Road, past the convent and up around the pass. It's still more direct than going via Hillcrest,' I said but he ignored me.

'Let's just go and speak to this vet,' he concluded.

He grabbed the photo of Joyce I'd seen in the newspaper. The one that didn't look like her at all.

'You have the original photo?' I asked, and of course it was a stupid question, as I was looking at it in his hand. I was surprised is all.

'We took it during the search,' he said.

'You picked it? You gave it to the press?' I asked.

'It's part of the job,' he said, schooling me.

'There were no nicer photos of her?' I asked.

'It's not a beauty contest, sweetheart.' He knew what he was doing and it was unkind at best but at worst it was a deliberate attempt to demean her in the eyes of the public.

The gawping girl who lingered around corners in a tight T-shirt and no bra seemed to have loose morals, just by her stance. A girl like that was the perfect foil, capable of murder. That girl was capable of anything.

–

Dermot Mullen was waiting for us in the doorway of his surgery, smoking. Foley introduced himself, O'Neill and me. Dermot invited us to smoke with him. Foley took one and lit up; O'Neill accepted one and placed it behind his ear. I declined, despite the fact that I'd been craving one since I'd lit up with Liam.

'You said you saw a girl?' Foley asked him after exhaling a cloud of smoke straight into my face.

'Before dawn. I'd been up all night... Paddy Hickey called me to his farm around ten p.m. He had a labouring cow that wasn't doing so well. It came right in the end,' he said.

'And the girl?'

'I drove out the gates of Hickey's farm and there she was.'

'You say it was before dawn, but do you have an idea of the time?' Foley said.

'I didn't check my watch,' he replied.

'Was it raining?' I asked and he thought about that. 'It had been thundering all night but no, now that you mention it, the ground was sodden but the air was dry.'

'Can you remember what time you got home?' Foley said and Dermot thought about it before nodding to himself. 'I can't be sure, but maybe around five a.m. My wife's alarm goes off at five thirty and I was in bed and drifting off to sleep when it went off.'

'Okay, good. We're getting somewhere. How far is your place from Hickey's farm?' Foley asked.

'About a fifteen-minute drive with no traffic, but I was tired so I took it handy, maybe it took an extra five or ten minutes.'

'So, if you're right, you saw the girl at approximately four thirty, give or take a few minutes?' Foley said.

'If I'm right, then yes,' Dermot Mullen said.

Foley nodded thoughtfully. O'Neill was writing everything down so I listened, observed, looked at the man's face, instead of having my head stuck in a notebook.

'So start again: you were driving out of the farm at approximately four thirty, give or take a few minutes...' Foley said.

'I'd been driving for a minute or so when I saw her, a girl in a white nightdress walking in bare feet. I passed her and when I slowed down and looked in the mirror, she'd turned away...'

'And then what?' Foley said.

'There was fog on the road, and between that and the fumes from my broken exhaust... Well, I know it sounds stupid but... she vanished.'

'Vanished?' Foley said.

'That's why I didn't come forward before now. I thought she might've been a ghost.'

'A ghost,' Foley said.

'Do you believe in ghosts, Mr Mullen?' O'Neill asked.

'I've seen one or two in my day,' Dermot Mullen replied.

'Is that right?' Foley said.

'It is,' Dermot Mullen stated and, to be fair, he seemed very sure of himself.

'Can you describe the ghost?' O'Neill said and it wasn't clear if he was trying to be funny or not, but Dermot Mullen didn't seem to care.

'I couldn't tell you what her face looked like, because she kept her back to me, but she was tall enough, lean, you could almost see through the nightdress, almost see through her.'

O'Neill and Foley shared a look. Foley bit his lip; I could tell he'd expected the local vet to be a little less crazy than the eighty-eight-year-old they'd mentioned earlier. All I could think was that Joyce was neither tall nor lean.

'What colour was her hair?' Foley asked. Joyce had a head of sandy curls.

'Fair, I think. Not sure, if I'm honest, it wasn't her hair that drew my attention.'

'Any sign of a bike?' O'Neill asked.

'No,' Dermot Mullen said.

'Was she carrying anything?'

'Nothing at all.'

'Which way was she headed?'

'Not sure… Hillcrest is a long road that leads to a crossroads.'

'Was your girl soaking wet?' Foley asked Mullen.

'Bone dry,' he said.

'You're sure?' Foley said.

'If she wasn't, the nightie would have been stuck to her and it wasn't.'

Foley thanked Dermot Mullen, and he went inside. I followed the men to the car. Foley mumbled, 'Maybe he did see a bleedin' ghost, because the girl he described was not Joyce O'Reilly.'

—

After that, we went to interview Mrs Lacey. She lived in a large cottage on Potters Road, one of the first houses ever built there. A little red wooden gate with a black steel latch gave us access to her small wild garden, enclosed by a crumbling rock wall and divided by a neat stone path leading to a matching red wooden door. The whitewashed clay walls were covered in the vines of a dormant creeper. In the absence of a bell or a knocker, Foley rapped his knuckles, one, two, three times. Mrs Lacey was slow about answering but when she did, she smiled at us as though we were all old friends. Upon introducing ourselves, she invited us in and insisted we drink tea in her quaint front living room. It was filled with antique furniture that was too big for the space and probably would have cost a fortune if woodworm hadn't invaded every stick of it. She sat us on various chairs: Foley and O'Neill awkwardly shared a flowery soft two-seater, and I was directed to an oversized plush green velvet armchair. Mrs Lacey sat as upright as was possible for her, on the edge of a red chenille chaise lounge, passing around a photo of her daughter, Tara. It was instantly apparent that she had soft curly brown hair to her shoulders. This cheered Foley up no end. 'She could be Joyce O'Reilly,' he said, showing the photo to O'Neill. He nodded. I asked to see it. O'Neill begrudgingly handed it to me. Aside from her hair, she looked nothing like Joyce. She was exceptionally beautiful, with an ovel face and ever so delicate features. Joyce O'Reilly, standing at five-foot-two inches in her socks, was at least five inches shorter than the willowy girl in the photo.

'What height was your daughter, Mrs Lacey?' I asked.

'Oh, she was tall, like you. Believe it or not, I was tall once too.'

'You still are,' I said.

'Oh, no, I shrunk a few years back. That really happens, you know,' she said, looking around at us and nodding. 'Mark my words. It's all ahead of you.'

'Where exactly did you see the girl, Mrs Lacey?' Foley asked.

'Just outside my gate.'

'Was she walking by?' he asked.

'No. She was just standing there.'

'For how long?' he asked.

'Long enough for me to think my Tara had come home.'

'How long would you say that was?' I said, trying to help her along. She thought about it. 'About ten minutes.'

'Did she move at all?' Foley said.

'She was bent over for a little bit.'

'In pain would you say?' Foley said.

'Oh, I hope not,' Mrs Lacey replied earnestly.

'Right,' Foley said.

'And no sign of a bike?' O'Neill said. *Him and the stupid bike.*

'I didn't see one. I just saw the girl.'

'But not her face?'

'No.'

'And what happened?' Foley asked.

'Well, I called out to her. I said, "Tara, is that you? It's your mammy."
I know it sounds ridiculous, she's been dead for twelve years, but... If
I'm honest... Well, God is my saviour, but I do like to drink.'

'Right,' Foley said and O'Neill stifled a laugh.

'And you had a drink that night?' Foley asked.

'I drink every night, dear,' she said.

'Good to know. Well, thank you, Mrs Lacey,' Foley said in a bid to
wrap things up.

'Did the girl respond to you at all, Mrs Lacey?' O'Neill asked her as
we were leaving.

'No. She ran away as soon as I called out to her,' she said.

There was no way of establishing a proper timeline; it was clear Mrs
Lacey was four sheets to the wind, so between midnight and morning
was the best she could do.

In the car, the men were giddy with the notion that the girl outside
Mrs Lacey's gate was Joyce. Brown curly hair, doubled over in a nightdress... All that was missing was the bike. At least that's what O'Neill
said.

'Maybe she dumped the bike,' Foley suggested.

'It's a long walk if she did,' I said. *And when did she grow five inches*? I
thought.

'Not if she cycled most of the way,' O'Neill said. 'We need to find
that bike.'

I snapped. 'She wasn't on any bike. She wasn't able to be on a bike.
She was slit from one end to the other – had she sat on a bike, it would
have disappeared up into her,' I said and I shouldn't have been so graphic
but I was fuming. It wasn't their ignorance that was so infuriating, it
was how wilful it was. O'Neill nearly drove us off the road.

'God alive... There's no need for that,' Foley said and sighed deeply.

'Sorry,' I said. It was an unpleasant image, to be fair.

'Do you still think Joyce is as innocent as the driven snow?' he asked.

'No. I don't,' I answered honestly. I knew she was capable of lies, as
any of us are.

'But you are determined to cause trouble.'

'I just want to be sure.'

'Well, that's all any of us want. The bloodwork will be back in a
few days and that should help clear things up,' Foley said. Then O'Neill
looked in the rear-view mirror at me.

'Until then do us all a favour and only speak when spoken to,' he said. Foley didn't react. I just resumed looking out the window.

-

All hell broke loose when we arrived back at the station. Brian Keating was stood by the door, waiting for us. 'Joe O'Callaghan, Joyce O'Reilly's solicitor's inside,' he said, nodding in the direction of the one and only interview room we had. 'He's not happy.'

'So what?' Foley said, and he walked into the room and slammed the door behind him. He was in there for about fifteen minutes. It was getting late and I'd nearly completed a third day of double shifts. I was tired but not so tired that I could walk away not knowing whether Joe O'Callaghan was as good as I'd heard he was, or whether Joyce had given me away. Joe O'Callaghan had a reputation for knowing his stuff; he didn't suffer fools and while he'd fight for the innocent, he'd never truly put himself out for the guilty – at least that's what my father had said. Foley would need to bring his A game now. *Good*, I thought. *I'd like to learn something that doesn't amount to what not to do.* As soon as Joe O'Callaghan left the building, O'Neill and Quinn were all over Foley, wanting to know what was happening.

'He's spoken to Joyce, and she's still peddling the story about the baby being a girl and in the engine of a tractor.'

'So we'll show them it's not,' O'Neill said.

'He's secured the release of the rest of the family and now they've turned too,' Foley said.

'What do you mean?' O'Neill asked.

'Breda's recanted her statement, said she was afraid for her husband's life – her son's too. Said she lied to save them from injury.'

'Christ,' O'Neill said.

'We have a statement,' Quinn said.

'She said it was made under duress.'

'So we'll say it wasn't,' Quinn said and Foley looked at him like he was a donkey.

'Except that O'Neill broke Thomas's fu—' He stopped himself from swearing and lowered his voice. 'Except that O'Neill broke the boy's arm.'

'How was I to know he has bones made of butter,' O'Neill said. They were in a right tizzy.

'What about Joyce?' I asked.

'What about her?'

'She's still charged, right?'

'Yeah.'

'What if there is another baby and we looked in the wrong place?' I said. 'She's talking to her solicitor, she's telling him what she told me. Her family are home. If there is a baby to find, what if they go looking? We need to be there,' I said and Foley nodded.

'She's right. We need to go to the farm. It's still a crime scene.'

It was after six and I was into my third shift, but neither I nor anyone else cared. When we got there, the O'Reilly men were searching the yard. O'Callaghan was in the kitchen with Breda. Foley, O'Neill and I entered the house while some of the other Dublin lads went to find Raymond and Thomas, to aid in their search. Breda didn't have much to say to us. I didn't hold it against her, under the circumstances. O'Callaghan acknowledged me when I introduced myself. 'You're the assistant commissioner's girl,' he said. I nodded.

'I've heard good things.'

'I've no idea who'd have a mind to say good things, and that includes my father,' I said. That's when he gave me a knowing look – something that told me we shared a secret, that his young client had confided in him about what I'd said to her. It compromised me, I knew that much, but what was done was done, and there was no changing it. 'Joyce told me she placed the child under the bonnet of a tractor, but we looked under the bonnet of every tractor, car and van we could find, and she wasn't there,' I said. I was aware that by now the yard staff were back on site, working – despite the drama that was unfolding, there was a business to run.

'Where did you look?' Breda said.

'In both sheds, in the front yard.'

'What about behind the storage shed?'

'I didn't know there was anything behind the storage shed.'

'Oh yes, it's a field where we...'

'Where we what, Mrs O'Reilly?' Foley said, instantly noticing her face had turned to stone.

'Where we have the crusher.' She was running to her house phone as she said it, dialling the office. We could hear the dial tone. She looked at us with fear in her eyes. 'They're not answering.' We ran, Foley and O'Neill and I, into the car, and O'Neill drove like the clappers over the dirt road, hitting every bump, stone and pothole along the way. It only took a minute or two, but they felt eternal. We could hear the machinery buzzing and whirring and clanking. The yard was alive again. *Oh God. Oh God. Oh God*, I thought to myself as we scrambled from the car and ran through the yard, through the processing shed, the second yard, the sorting shed and bust out the small door that led to a field, only a short walk away to where the crusher was located. We could hear its hydraulics warming up, the loud rumbling engine noise, the banging, the clanging, the creaking, popping and twisting of metal. *Oh God. Oh God. Oh God.* We arrived in time to see what was once a large machine now flattened. My stomach felt instantly sick. My eyes stung. *How did we miss this?* Foley was running towards the operator, waving his arms as though it would matter if they stopped now. The man in the seat – a large, balding, burly fella named Jackie – looked to him, registering shock. Foley was shouting, trying to project his voice over the terrible noise. '*Stop. Stop!*' Jackie switched off the control panel as Raymond and Thomas ran over from the front field, where they'd been searching the vehicles we'd already searched earlier. Jackie turned the machine off as the O'Reilly lads reached us.

'What now?' Raymond said and he was almost afraid to hear the answer.

Foley looked from him to the flattened metal before us. 'Was that a tractor?' he asked, because it was so mangled, it was impossible to tell.

'It was a digger,' Jackie said as he jumped from the rig. Thomas sighed with relief. Poor Jackie didn't know what was going on.

'Oh, thank Christ for that,' Foley said.

'What's going on now?' Jackie said as Foley looked around. I'd already spotted the red tractor that sat in line to be crushed. Now we were both walking towards it, Raymond and Thomas following us. As we approached it, Raymond froze. Thomas was suddenly striding past us. Foley grabbed him by his good arm. 'No,' he said.

'This is my home, my land, my family,' Thomas said, shaking himself free. Before either Foley or I could react, he had the bonnet open. He stumbled back, his hand on his mouth, tears filling his eyes. 'Oh, Joyce,' he mumbled.

Foley was now by the tractor, looking inside, and blessed himself before turning to me. 'Go. Call Brian and get him down. And while you're at it, call Waters and tell him to get back on the train. We've got another body,' he said. I was off and running as Raymond and Thomas O'Reilly both sank to the ground.

–

O'Neill, Quinn, Brian, Dicey, Liam Kenny, Foley and I all stood around the tractor. It took me a while to look at her. When I did, I saw that her skin was blackened, her eyes closed; she had a head of fair curls, a square face – she was Joyce's girl, all right. She was in a far worse state of decomposition than Baby Crónán and yet she had not been violated, as far as I could see. *I'm sorry, little girl. Rest in peace, little one.* The lads would take turns to watch over her until the pathologist Frank Waters arrived on the first train the following morning. O'Neill and Quinn erected a tent over the tractor to keep her safe from the elements. Father Cunningham arrived to pray over the engine. He wasn't the better for it. He took a good long sip from his flask.

'As long as I've lived, I've known nothing like this,' he said, before we all bowed our heads to pray – the Dublin and the Kerry boys, the priest and I. The O'Reilly men were sent up to their house as soon as she'd been found. Both in need of a very stiff drink. I was sent home an hour later. 'You've done your bit for today, Mary,' Foley said.

'But what does it mean?' I asked.

'It's too early to say.' He looked back to the tractor and to the poor soul lying within it. 'It's just too early to say.'

We were all in shock. That Monday morning we'd found Baby Crónán and by Wednesday a second baby was found dead. It was surreal for everyone, even the seasoned Dublin lads. We were all deeply troubled by it. How could we not be?

It was eight p.m. and dark, when I got into my car. I drove home and I hadn't the heart to bathe or change or eat or do much of anything, except sit at my kitchen table with a glass of whiskey in hand. I heard a knock at the door. 'Come in, Seamus,' I said, knowing that news of the second baby would be all over town. He entered, still in his blue battered overalls and his big old welly boots. He held up a fresh bottle and plonked it on the table. Grabbing himself a glass, he pulled out a chair, sat down and poured himself a drink.

'Hard week,' he said, worry and fear etched into his handsome face.

I nodded. He drank. 'You're not going to drown yourself in the bath, are you?' he asked.

'I thought you said you wouldn't hold that against me,' I reminded him.

'I don't.'

'I'm not planning on it tonight,' I said. We both took a drink. 'How did you hear?' I asked.

'Thomas rang the house,' he said and I heard the hitch at the back of his throat when he uttered the name. I saw the softness in his eyes.

'Is he all right?' I asked.

'He'd be a lot worse if you hadn't helped him,' he said and he raised his glass.

'I just did my job,' I said honestly.

'And those boys from Dublin, what were they doing?' he asked, and I had no real answer for him, because what happened shouldn't have happened. Yet there were two dead creatures and one girl's family held the key to the answer as to what happened to at least one of them. 'Joyce didn't hurt anyone, unlike those animals you work with,' he said before he drank deeply.

'We won't know until Frank Waters tells us,' I said. There was no point in pretending that foul play was impossible.

That quietened him. 'I'm sorry,' he said after a long time and then, without knowing why, I asked him, 'Is Thomas O'Reilly the reason for your good humour these days?'

He didn't have to answer, his lips turned crimson, his eyes darted around in his head... He looked away, trying to hide from me.

'Be careful,' I warned him and then it dawned on me: if Frank Waters determined that child was murdered, they'd be bringing the O'Reillys back in to be questioned.

'You weren't with him that Sunday night, were you?' I said and he nodded. He was.

'Were you alone together?' I asked. He nodded. They were.

'Where were ye?' I asked.

'In my dad's old caravan. It's parked in the lower yard. With that bad leg of his, he never strays down there, so I did it up.'

'He was with you all night?'

'He was.'

'Joyce's solicitor, O'Callaghan, he'll get that out of him. He'll make him repeat it,' I said.

He froze. 'Why?'

'If the child was killed, he might need an alibi.'

'We played cards, we drank, we fell asleep,' he said. He couldn't look me in the eye.

'You know what they did to him. They'll do a lot worse if there's even a hint that you were—'

'What?' he interrupted, fire blazing in his eyes.

'At each other,' I said, searching for the right words and clearly not finding them.

'Jesus, Mary.'

'I'm only telling you what's in store.'

'Joyce didn't kill her child. Her family didn't kill it either. Thomas won't need an alibi. We'll be fine.'

'Nothing is fine,' I said, before I finished off the glass. 'And nothing will ever be the same again.' I rose from my seat and walked into the bedroom, closed the door, climbed onto my bed and left Seamus to drink his troubles away in my kitchen while I slept like the dead.

CHAPTER EIGHT

Day Four

'Crónán's bloods are back,' Foley said as soon as I walked into the incident room. He was talking to me, not at me, which was unusual. Foley wanted me to know something about the case I was working on. It was thrilling. 'And?' I asked, immediately engaged.

'He's an O. Joyce O'Reilly is an A,' he said.

'So we can move on,' I said and I didn't know whether I was upset or elated. I didn't want that broken girl to be capable of that kind of evil, but I didn't want anyone else capable of it either.

'Not so fast,' he said.

'Not so fast? Baby Crónán is an O and we've found Joyce's baby.'

'Maybe she was just one of Joyce's babies.'

'*What?!*' I said and I almost roared it.

'Have you never heard of twins?'

'You can't be serious,' I said, but of course he was. He told me the bloodwork doesn't have to be a match for the mother, or the father – it's the combination that makes sense of things.

I must have been looking at him like he was a madman.

'I'm not making this up, Shea,' he said by means of explanation.

'But even if that's true, twins?!'

'I know, I know.' He sighed. 'It's not likely, is it?'

'No. It's not,' I agreed.

'We'll have to hunt down and talk to the father of the baby girl, poor fella. Get his blood sample, clear up this line of investigation and move on,' Foley said. *Poor fella?* I thought.

'Poor fella?' I said, the words dripping in disgust. I couldn't help it.

'Yeah, poor fella, being dragged into all of this,' he said and I wasn't sure if I wanted to laugh or cry. *Poor fella, oh how my heart weeps for the poor, poor fella. Was he alone giving birth in a shed? Did he nearly rip in two pieces? Where was he, the poor fella?* Sometimes I wanted to pick up a hammer and smash something.

'You'll need to talk to her, she won't speak to anyone else. We need a name,' he said.

We should have had a name the first day but none of the men thought it necessary to drag the poor fella into it. I kept that thought to myself. I wanted to see Joyce again, to speak to her, to do my job and solve the case.

—

Foley, O'Neill, Quinn and I arrived at the O'Reilly household early enough; Raymond and Thomas were still sitting at the kitchen table, as though they hadn't moved an inch since last I saw them. Breakfast was served, although it looked like no one was hungry. The food was left to go cold. Thomas stood up as we walked inside. There was murder in his eyes, but then, any man who'd had his arm broken would feel rage at the sight of those responsible for such barbarism. I asked him how he was. His temper quelled a little as he answered that he was all right. Uninvited, Foley sat down on the armchair, making himself comfortable.

'We need to know who the father of the child could be,' he said, and the family looked at one another across the table. Thomas sat down.

'This is still my house,' Raymond said, looking Foley straight in his eyes.

'I'm aware,' Foley said.

'I didn't invite you to sit down,' Raymond said. Foley thought about this for a second or two before brushing invisible lint from his trousers and standing up.

'No problem, you don't want me sitting, that's grand. I still need to know who the father of the dead baby is… Or we can move this back to my house.' He emphasised the words *dead* and *my house* for effect. It clearly worked: Raymond visibly shuddered. Breda started to cry.

'If you know, please tell us? We'll be talking with Joyce later this morning but the sooner we can talk to the fella, the better,' I said, looking to Breda, 'We just want to clear all this up,' I explained. She placed her face in her hands. Her husband and son looked her way.

She directed her gaze at me. 'If she was seeing anyone, I swear on Jesus on the cross, she never told me.'

I looked to Thomas. 'Did she talk to you, Thomas?'

'We talked all the time but not about that,' he said and he looked hurt by all of it, and not just the business with the guards. Raymond was shaking his head. 'If we knew, we'd tell you. We want this to be over,' Raymond said. 'We want her home.' His voice cracked a little when he said those words.

I looked to Foley, who sniffed and nodded. 'Fine, then. We'll see ourselves out.' As we were leaving, Breda stood up. 'When will we find out what happened to the… child?' She struggled to bring herself to say it. I felt sorry for her, that baby was her grandchild.

'We're hoping to have news later today,' I said. Brian Keating collected Frank Waters off the first train. He'd have been working to establish cause of death since then. I moved to follow Foley. 'And how is Joyce?' she asked.

'She needed a medical procedure but she's the better for it. She has her colour back,' I said as brightly as I could under the circumstances.

'Oh. That's good,' she said and she bowed her head, the shame of the lies she'd told catching up to her.

'I'll tell her you were asking for her,' I said and tears slipped down on her face. She nodded.

'And tell her that I'm sorry,' she said. 'Will you tell her that I'm so sorry.'

'I'll make it my business,' I assured her. I looked to Raymond and Thomas, nodding to them. 'Thank you,' I said. I followed Foley out into the yard. He lit up a cigarette.

'What are you thanking them for?' he asked as we walked to the car. O'Neill had taken a second car so he and Quinn could go back to the yard to take another look around the place.

'For not killing us when we walked through the door,' I said. He stopped and looked at me. 'And why would they do that?' he said, genuinely miffed. O'Neill blew the horn as he sped away. Foley raised his hand to wave him off.

'Anger and injustice are a potent mix,' I said, visualising my hammer fantasy.

'Oh, is it now?' he said. 'And what injustice would you be referring to?' He took a drag.

'Their treatment,' I said. He coughed a bit at that. I was desperate for a smoke. *Blast it…* I pulled out the packet I had in my pocket and lit one up, inhaling deeply… *Oh, that's bass.*

'Listen here—' he said and I stopped him as soon as he started.

'Wait before you give out!' I said, waving my cigarette around. He waited. 'I'm not a judge or a jury, and you've been doing this a lot longer than I have. I'll give you that, but to say that emotions are high is no lie. You asked me a question, Foley, and I answered it. That's all.'

He thought about that while we finished smoking our cigarettes. I dropped the butt, quenching it under the sole of my shoe. He opened the car door and I sat in the passenger side. He flicked the butt of the cigarette over the bonnet of the car and into the thick, wet mud the car had laid fresh tracks on.

'Fair enough,' he said before settling into the driver's seat. We drove in silence from the O'Reilly home to Joyce's jail cell, thirty miles down the road.

–

Foley insisted I go in alone. He was relying on the fact that we had an established trust, Joyce and I. He gave me pointers, talked me through things, told me I could do it while warning me not to mess up. He was like a coach. *Go team,* I thought. I was of the opinion that Joyce belonged in a hospital bed, to be cared for by professional medics, but round-the-clock garda protection cost money and the more time that passed, the more riled the people of the parish became. Foley worried someone would try to do something foolish. 'She's safer in prison,' he'd said.

The news about the second dead baby was everywhere; those of the press who had left our small town had returned and brought more with them – the pressure was on. You could feel the weight of tension in the air. Foley was trying to keep his cool but I could see he was finding that hard enough; he wasn't crumbling by any means, but he wasn't as confident as he'd presented either. He told me to get straight to the point, not to deviate. We needed the name and address of the boy, and nothing else was to be discussed in this interview. I found that an odd instruction but, then, I hadn't been involved in this level of investigation before, and time was of the essence. A prison guard brought me inside to a small meeting room away from the cells. I watched Joyce struggle to walk towards me. She was washed and wearing a starched uniform belonging to the jail. It was a pitiful sight. It took a minute for her to sit on the hard chair. Pain and hurt creased her face; confusion and terror clouded her eyes. She was a broken thing. I wanted to reach out to her, despite everything. I wanted to comfort her and I wondered if that made me weak. We were facing one another but she was looking through me.

'How are you?' I asked. She didn't answer. *Fair enough*, I thought. After all, what could she say? 'Who is the father of your baby?' I said. There was no point in beating around the bush, as they say. Her eyes focused. She blinked and looked up to the ceiling.

'I don't know him,' she said.

'What do you mean?' I asked, genuinely baffled. She was focused, but not on me – her gaze fixed on the wall just beyond and to the side of my head. As she spoke, she began telling me a story about the carnival coming to town. She went with friends and rode the bumpers; other than that, she wasn't interested in the rides, everything was either too high or too fast. The others, her friends, they liked the danger, so they left her alone and while they queued for the swing boats and the Rock-O-Plane, Joyce played games by herself.

'I won a fish,' she said, brightening a bit. 'But it was dead by the time I got home.' Her brightness faded to gloom again. 'I suppose I must have left it in the bag too long.' Tears slipped down her face. 'I met him when I was queuing for ice cream. He walked up to me. We got talking. He seemed nice. So we walked together, just talking about things.' I let her talk. I let her remember. I stayed quiet. 'He was handsome. He asked me if I wanted to walk with him. I said yes. We ended up alone. He kissed me and then it happened,' she said, and more tears formed and fell.

'Where?'

'Behind a caravan,' she said.

Mother of God, I thought to myself. *Behind a caravan*. I almost died at the idea of it. I was a prude then – even at twenty-eight, the furthest I had gone with a boy or man was letting Alan White drop the hand, and even that was in a house with the doors and the curtains tightly closed.

'Was he local, was he a carnival worker?' I asked, shifting my mind back on track.

'I don't know,' she said and it was hard to make her out with all the crying.

'Did you want that to happen?' I asked.

'I don't know,' she said.

'Well, how did you feel afterwards?' I asked.

'I don't know,' she repeated once again. Then she thought about it. 'Scared.'

'Did he tell you where he was from?'

She shook her head.

'Did he have an accent?'

She thought about that. 'He did but I didn't recognise it.'

'Was he Irish?' I asked.

'Oh yes,' she said.

'Can you tell me what he looked like?' She thought about that for a while. Then she nodded.

'Describe him,' I said before telling her I'd be sure to have a sketch artist come to speak to her.

She described him as tall, dark and handsome. 'I'll need more than that,' I said.

'He had a nice smile.'

'What age was he?'

'He looked around seventeen, but he could have been slightly older or younger. It was hard to tell,' she said.

'Did you see him after that?'

'No. I went to see my auntie Paula in Wexford with Mammy the next day. When I came back, he was gone. I didn't see him again.'

'Did he tell you his name?'

She shook her head. 'No.' She seemed ashamed.

'Was he your only… encounter… of that nature?' I asked as politely as I could.

'Yes,' she said.

'You're sure?'

'What are you trying to say?' she asked, and it was the first bit of spirit I'd seen in her since we'd descended upon her family. It was good to see.

'I'm only asking because we need to find him,' I said.

'Why?' she asked.

'We need to rule out his blood group.'

'I don't understand. For what?'

'For Baby Crónán.'

She immediately reddened and teared up. 'The boy? You're not serious?' she said. 'How do you think…?' The words stuck in her throat.

'It's procedure,' I said in a tone that attempted to soothe her. She dried her tears with the back of her hand. 'Do you know how my baby died yet?'

'Hopefully, later today.' My mind was on Baby Crónán and the silent promise I made him. I wanted to move on and hoped this boy's blood results would allow me to do just that.

She nodded. 'Do you think I strangled her when I pulled her out of me?'

'I don't know,' I said truthfully.

'I should have called for help,' she said. 'I don't know what I was going to do. I didn't have a plan, it all just happened.'

'Did you think about hurting or killing her, Joyce?' I asked as gently as a person asking that question could ask.

'Oh God, no… No. No. I couldn't think past getting her out,' she said. 'But… I think I would have tried to hide her in life just like I did in death.'

'How long do you think that would have worked?' I said.

'Not long,' she replied. 'Maybe I would have run away with her, gone to England. I've heard of girls who ran away to England. I'll bet some of them weren't running alone. I'm a good worker,' she said, and she was running away with herself now. 'I'm a fast learner, maybe we could have been okay… If I'd asked for help, maybe she'd be alive… It's my fault. Did you see her?' she asked.

'I did,' I told her.

'She had fair curly hair, like my mother.'

I nodded. 'She was beautiful.'

'She was, wasn't she? I should have called for help.' She clammed up after that, so I moved to leave. She was exhausted, pale. She needed rest and respite. It was time for me to go.

'I spoke with your mother, she wants you to know she's so very sorry,' I said, and with that, a new spring opened as Joyce burst into fresh tears.

'Thank you,' she said. She called out to me as I put my hand on the door. 'Her name is Lily,' she said. 'Will you tell them her name is Lily O'Reilly.'

'I will,' I said. *God rest you, Lily O'Reilly.*

–

In the car on the way back to town, I read out her statement regarding the description of the child's father to Foley. He wasn't impressed. 'Tall, dark and handsome? That could be anyone,' he said. With the state of most of the men in the vicinity, I disagreed.

'Well, short, fair-haired, ugly people are out of the picture, as are Kerry men and probably Cork men – she'd recognise those accents,' I said and he gave me a sideways glance that suggested he wasn't happy with me at all. I needed to up my game.

'There is only one carnival that comes to town. The McNight's run it, they come from up north. Might be why she didn't recognise the accent. It sounded like the fella knew where he was going. If he was a worker...'

'Or one of the McNight's,' he said.

'We can get the lads in Donegal to pay a visit to the family. See if any teenage boy in the family or in their employment matches her description.'

'Well, if there are any fairytale princes living up there, we're in luck,' he said sarcastically. I ignored him. ''Course it could have been a tourist. The carnival comes to town in summer, half of the country visits the place then. It might not mean much to you, but every girl in the town would have spotted the fella she described. If we don't have any luck with the McNight's, we can canvass the schoolgirls. If he had an encounter with Joyce, he might have had another with someone else. Although...' I began, and I wasn't sure if I should say it or how it would be received.

'Spit it out,' he ordered.

'I'm not sure the encounter was consensual.'

'Did she scream and cry?'

'No. I'm not entirely sure she really knew what was happening until it was too late.'

'And what from her statement implies that?' he asked.

'Her repeating the words, "I don't know",' I said.

'Rape is a very serious charge.'

'It's why I didn't use the word,' I said.

'So what are you saying, Garda Shea?'

'I'm saying that girl wasn't out looking for a man to have relations with that night. Sometimes, as a woman, things happen that are not entirely within our control, yet for some reason, when it comes to these matters, the men of this world pretend that it's not only within our control, but it's entirely our responsibility,' I said.

He did a double take. 'Right,' he said, and we descended into now-familiar silence. It didn't bother me at all. I liked to look out the window at the passing rock walls, the ferns browning at their tips, the stony road and the grass verges that needed tending. From the ground and to the sky, where grey broke into blue, I could think my own thoughts, uninterrupted. As we drove that day, I thought about the baby girl with bouncy curls, who, if things were different, might be alive and on her way to England.

–

Frank Waters was in the same room we'd last found him in, only this time the covered bump on the steel table was a girl and not a boy. It felt surreal to be back there, standing over the small cloth.

'Can you tell me what happened, Frank?' Foley said.

'The baby was stillborn. Those lungs never breathed air.'

'Are you sure?' Foley said and I couldn't help but feel that he sounded slightly disappointed.

'As sure as anyone can be,' Frank said, fixing his heavy spectacles on his face. 'She didn't survive the birth and from the hospital report I've just read, it's a miracle the O'Reilly girl survived it,' he said.

'Right.' Foley massaged his chin. 'So what we know is that Baby Crónán is blood group O. Joyce O'Reilly is blood group A.'

'It will take another day or two before we receive the blood results of this little one. Any sign of a father will clear things up a bit,' Waters said.

'Her name is Lily,' I said. They both turned to face me. 'Lily O'Reilly.'

Waters nodded. 'I'll tell the undertaker.'

We left after that.

–

The coffee shop was empty, despite the town being full to the brim with journalists. They were outside the station, waiting for an update; a podium had been placed at the front door since early morning. 'Keeps them busy, waiting for one of us to step outside – they'd hate to miss us,' Foley said before he ordered two coffees and two slices of apple tart. He didn't ask me if I liked apple tart, he just presumed. It was a calculated guess. He paid for it. I took note of that. I'd be sure to pay next time. If there was a next time. We sat close to the door but not in front of the window. We spoke with our voices hushed so that the staff and the two locals couldn't hear us. The locals were staring at us and mumbling comments as if they were in front of their TV sets and we couldn't see or hear them.

'Do you really think it's possible that Joyce O'Reilly had anything to do with the birth or the death of Baby Crónán?' I whispered.

'It's hard to imagine,' he admitted. 'But, then, stranger things have happened.'

'Name one.'

'The resurrection of Christ.'

'That wasn't today or yesterday,' I said. He laughed at me and sipped on his coffee, before continuing.

'Two babies dead and discarded in one small town by two different women on the same night? It's almost as implausible as Joyce giving birth to both… But it happened,' he said.

'So what? She had Lily, she was dead. Then Crónán started to come, and she stabbed him?'

'Maybe it was the other way around. He was born first, she murdered him. The girl came second, she was dead, so…'

'But why? Why hide Lily in the yard and then cycle miles to display murdered Baby Crónán in a public place to be found? It makes no sense.'

'I agree it doesn't but, Mary, if I had a pound for every man or woman who did things that made no sense, I'd be a very rich man,' he said and he had a point.

'Okay, then, how? You've seen the medical report. How could she cycle or walk or even crawl that night? She was in a terrible way,' I said.

'Adrenaline, maybe?' he surmised.

'There would have been traces of her blood on the bike, never mind the ground leading from the farm to the beach. With the amount she was bleeding it would have been like breadcrumbs...' I said.

'You're forgetting the rain,' he said.

'The sheets on her bed were soaked and dried and then soaked again. The poor girl was bleeding long after the rain stopped.' I reminded him of her bedroom – a grisly scene.

'We're not just focused on the O'Reilly girl,' he said. 'We have other lines of inquiry.'

I hadn't seen them, but then I was only dealing with Joyce and her family. 'What are they?'

'We've had someone come forward with more information,' he said.

'Who? When?'

'Not now.' I looked up from our close huddle to see the waitress approaching and smiling at us.

'Can I get you anything else?' she asked.

'No, thanks,' Foley said. He stood up. 'Let's go.'

–

In the car I asked him what would happen to Joyce O'Reilly.

'Her solicitor will start to cause a fuss, if he hasn't already. He'll have her out as soon as procedure will allow. In the meantime, we track down that boy of hers.'

We parked at the station and crossed the road to the hotel. Jenny was at her desk.

'Detective Foley, Garda Shea,' she said with a smile. Foley ignored her, but I smiled and nodded her way. We entered the ballroom and there he was – my father, standing with Superintendent Lynch in the middle of the room. Daddy was speaking to a group of men gathered around him, trying to sound encouraging. He stopped mid-sentence as soon as I entered, but then addressed me directly, 'There you are. I was beginning to think we'd lost you.'

'Hi, Daddy,' I said, blushing in front of the boys.

My father was six-foot-four and lean – Mammy called him a bean-pole. He had a slight limp from a car crash during a high-speed chase. He'd saved a girl that night and won a medal for it. My father was impressive; he looked younger than his years, was bright and articulate, sharp and funny and revered. He was everything I wanted to be.

As disappointed as I felt in him, I didn't just love my father – I adored him. He winked at me, and I grinned like a stupid kid. He annoyed me too, more for the things he believed than the things he said. I knew I couldn't change him, so I had to choose to love him anyway.

The knot in my stomach unfurled the moment he leaned into my ear and whispered, 'Don't worry, Mai*me*, your mother has been very clear with the rules of our engagement,' he said. I couldn't say my R's till I was eight, so I referred to myself as Mai*me* Shea till then. He never stopped. My grin widened. 'Thanks, Daddy,' I said.

Foley walked up to him and extended his hand. My father clasped it in his and gave it a firm shake. 'Detective Foley, I hear you've been making good use of my girl,' he said.

'She's been of great assistance, Assistant Commissioner Shea,' Foley said.

'Really?' my father said.

'Really,' Foley confirmed.

'You're not buttering me up?'

Foley pretended to chuckle. 'Didn't think I needed to.'

'You don't,' my father said, and he started to walk in stride with Superintendent Lynch out of the room and down the corridor. Foley and I followed.

'This is a very difficult case, Detective,' my father said. 'One that this state has not seen the likes of before.'

'Infanticide happens more than we pretend,' Foley said.

My father turned to face him. 'Is that right?'

'We both know it is.'

'We both know that what matters is what's in the public forum and how we're seen to manage it. The whole country is watching, Foley...' he said and then he looked to me. 'Now don't hate me, Mai*me*...' My heart sank even before he turned to face Foley. 'Do you really think it's appropriate to have a woman leading this?'

I could feel myself shrink, my heart tearing a little. But I stayed standing tall – I raised my shoulders, lifted my chin and grew myself so that when the other men looked at me to gauge my reaction, I wouldn't seem small, no matter what my father had said.

'Garda Shea has been nothing but an asset to this investigation. The day she isn't is the day I'll make changes,' Foley said. My father smiled at him. It wasn't warm or friendly.

'You talk like you are a man with many days in front of him.'

'This investigation is a complex one. We are using all our manpower and it will be solved in good time,' Foley said. My father turned to Superintendent Lynch. 'Well, I like his confidence if nothing else.' He turned back to Foley. 'This is the kind of case that makes or breaks a career. I'd ask you to keep that in mind,' my father said. Then as he and Superintendent Lynch walked away, he called into the wind, 'Come to dinner on Sunday, Mai*me*. Your mother wants to see you.' Foley and I watched them go.

'I see where you get it from,' he said.

'Get what from?'

'All of it.'

I wasn't quite sure what he meant, but his standing up for me eased some of the pain my father had caused.

—

Inside the incident room, Dicey was waiting for Foley. He walked straight up to him. 'A woman bundled up in a heavy coat, scarf and hat was seen carrying a bag of some kind on Appletree Lane at nine fifteen that night.'

'I've been aware of that since first thing this morning, that's just one of seventy other sightings,' Foley said.

'Well, we just got a call, some fishermen found a bag with a coat, hat and scarf in it caught on some rocks, a mile away from shore.'

Foley nodded. 'Where is the bag now?'

'O'Neill and Quinn have gone to meet the lads to retrieve it.'

'And why did these fishermen think to call it in?'

'They saw you on the news... you said anything suspicious. They felt it might have something to do with the case.'

'God bless the public,' Foley said. Then he asked Dicey for details of the witness who had seen the woman with the bag on Appletree Lane that night.

'Seanie Keogh is his name. I spoke to him myself. I have his statement here,' Dicey said, pulling his glasses from his inside pocket to begin reading it.

'Give it to Mary.' He looked to me. 'You can read it to me on the way.'

Dicey froze. He wasn't used to being so rudely dismissed. 'I have it all here. I can assure you,' he said.

'I'd like to speak to Seanie Keogh myself, if that's all right with you,' Foley said and Dicey looked like he'd swallowed a fly.

'Of course,' he said and he stepped back.

'Shea, let's go,' Foley said to me. Dicey was a real hard pill of a fella but I couldn't help feeling sorry for him in that moment.

–

We met with Quinn and O'Neill in the station first; they had the clothes and bag laid out on an interview table. They were soaking – water was dripping from them onto the floor. O'Neill was taking photos with a Polaroid camera as we arrived.

'Dry them off, hang the coat up, get better photos for the press. See if we can find the owner,' Foley said.

'What about the witness, Seanie Keogh?' O'Neill asked.

'We're heading there now.'

'We?' O'Neill said, glancing towards me. The men shared a weighty look. It was clear O'Neill was as unhappy with my presence on the case as my father was, but Foley wasn't about to back down.

'Looks like the O'Reillys have lodged a complaint,' Foley said.

'Oh yeah, what are they saying?' O'Neill asked. It was the first I'd heard of it and I'd been with Foley since early morning.

'That you used unreasonable force and broke Thomas O'Reilly's arm.'

'Is that all?' O'Neill said.

'For now, but if you want it to blow over, best to keep your head down.' He grabbed the photos from O'Neill, pocketed them and I followed him out the door.

–

Seanie Keogh owned stables a few miles from town. He trained a few local kids and provided full livery for twenty horses. He'd been a celebrated jockey when he was younger, won a few races, before he fell and hurt his back. He could ride; he just couldn't compete. People thought it was a real shame – he could have been one of the greats. He was mucking out the horses when the car pulled in. He stopped and waved. A young fella took over and he made his way to us, his wellies crunching on the gravel beneath him.

'Detective Foley?' he said.

'You heard I was coming?' Foley said.

'Dicey McCarthy rang the house, said you were stopping by. He wanted to make sure I didn't go anywhere. Come in,' he said.

His house wasn't far from the stables, a beautiful old manor, well kept. Seanie Keogh came from money. He asked us if we wanted tea and called out to his wife, Siobhan, asking her to make it and to bring some ginger cake. He led us into the drawing room; two large bay windows looked out onto the sprawling land that included an arena. Two large comfy sofas sat opposite each other, an ornate coffee table between them, and a fire raged in the most expensive and beautiful marble fireplace I'd ever seen. We sat on one sofa, he sat on the other. I'd read the statement he'd made to Dicey McCarthy on the way over. His description of the clothes was spot on. Foley handed him the photos.

'Was that the coat, hat and scarf you saw on the woman who you passed at approximately nine fifteen on Sunday night?'

'Yes,' Seanie said. Foley took note of this.

'And the bag?' he said. 'It wasn't a sports bag? It was a big shopping bag.'

'That's it,' he said. Siobhan appeared, looking every inch the lady of the manor, carrying a tray and wearing a silk twinset, a plaid skirt and a string of pearls around her neck. Her porcelain skin and manicured hands gave away her easy life. She was pretty but not beautiful. She had a kind smile and eyes. She placed the tray down on the table, insisting on pouring us tea and handing around slices of ginger cake. Then she sat beside her husband. He looked to her. 'That woman I saw, her clothes were found, caught on rocks, by the coast,' he said and she looked to Foley. 'What does this all mean, Detective?'

'I don't know yet,' Foley answered honestly. He looked to Seanie. 'It said in your statement you were riding at the time?'

'Yes, Winnie. The younger ones aren't able for her. She likes to buck.'

'I keep warning him that she's no good for that back of his,' Siobhan said.

'But if I don't take her out, no one will,' he said.

'Do you normally go out so late?' Foley asked.

'No, but we had the in-laws for dinner and they wouldn't go home,' he said and grinned. Siobhan pretended to slap his arm. 'Stop it.'

'And you're sure you don't have any idea who this woman might be?' Foley said.

'I'm sorry, the scarf was up around her mouth, and her head was hung low. I was passing at a gallop. The only reason I said something was because it's unusual to see anyone on that road, especially after dark – that's why I ride there.'

'Why is that?' Foley asked.

'It's a dead end. It's communal land but the only place it leads to is around the side of Hickey's farm. That's private land.'

'Paddy Hickey's farm?' I said before Foley could.

'That's right.'

'It sounds like a big farm,' Foley said.

'It's one of the biggest in the area. One of his fields takes him close enough to the beach,' Seanie said.

'Is that right?'

'Developers have been trying to buy off Paddy for years but he's not interested. Still, as soon as he dies, his two boys will sell it to the first man who comes along.'

'Right down to the beach?' Foley repeated.

'That stretch is only the width of one field, it's rubbish land for farming but worth a fortune to a developer,' Seanie said. Foley looked to me before writing it down. *I should have known that.* I wanted to kick myself.

'We'll leave you to it,' Foley said. But Siobhan put her hand up and looked to Seanie.

'And you did say, you forgot to mention in your statement, that the bag looked heavy,' Siobhan said.

'That's right,' he confirmed. 'There was something heavy in it all right.'

'How do you know?' I asked.

'Just by the way she was holding it.'

Could Baby Crónán have been in that bag? I wondered. *And if so, who was that woman?*

'You've seen the news coverage about Joyce O'Reilly,' Foley said.

'I have, it's a terrible thing,' Seanie said.

'Is it possible that the woman you saw holding the heavy bag on Appletree Lane was Joyce O'Reilly?' Foley said.

'It's possible but only because it could have been anyone. I didn't see her properly,' Seanie explained.

'Thank you,' Foley said, and he stood up and shook Seanie's and Siobhan's hands. 'We'll be in touch.'

We sat in the car and I was waiting for a lecture, but instead Foley just took off.

'I didn't know Hickey's farm bordered the beach,' I admitted.

'Well, you're not a local, so why would you. Those other fellas should have known,' he said, and I appreciated it but I'd been there long enough. I should have known. 'So the vet sees a woman, or *a ghost*, in a nightdress dry as bone at approximately four thirty a.m. while he was leaving Paddy Hickey's farm on Hillcrest. But the jockey sees a woman on Appletree Lane —on the other side of Paddy Hickey's farm — in a coat, hat and scarf, carrying a heavy shopping bag, seven hours earlier. Is that about right?' Foley said.

'Yeah,' I confirmed.

'And then there's the girl in the nightdress, soaked to the skin, that the mad auld one on Potters Road saw between midnight and morning. What are we dealing with here, Shea? One, two or three ladies of the night, and where does this leave us with Joyce O'Reilly?' he asked.

'The times don't make sense. The woman with the bag in Appletree Lane can't be Joyce — she was in labour on the farm then,' I said.

'Unless she wasn't,' he mused.

'I believe her,' I said. Just then, as if on cue, the car radio buzzed to life. I picked it up — it was Liam Kenny.

'There's a local lad here with his parents. He says he might be the father of Joyce O'Reilly's baby.'

'You believe her, do you? She didn't know him, she said. He was from the carnival, she said.' He looked to me. 'She's a bloody liar and you're a bloody fool.'

Oh, Joyce. I thought. *Why would you lie?* I knew she was in terrible trouble.

CHAPTER NINE

Seventeen-year-old Eamon Kelly was the opposite of tall, dark and handsome. He had box brown hair and a face full of freckles; he was thin as a whip and of distinctively average height. He certainly wasn't from the carnival, and his family on both sides had lived in the town for generations. It was a surprise to see the principal of the girls' school, Emer Kelly, standing with her arm on the teenage boy's shoulder. Beside her stood her husband, Bobby, a bald man with a long, serious face. We were in the small interview room – Foley and I on one side of the table, Eamon flanked by his parents on the other. Principal Kelly was forthright to say the least. 'Stop crying,' was the first thing I heard her say to the boy. Instantly, his tears melted into his hot face. 'Thank you for coming,' she said, which was odd because this was our station and not her home or office. Foley read the statement the boy had made to Liam Kenny before looking up at Eamon.

'You had sex with the O'Reilly girl?' he said straight out of the gate. The boy was utterly gripped by fear, his every last nerve shot. He was petrified into an awkward gawping position.

'Speak up,' Principal Kelly said in a booming voice that almost broke the spell. He still couldn't speak but he nodded his head vigorously to indicate that he had.

'I'll need that in words for the tape,' Foley said to the boy, pointing to the tape recorder sitting on the table to his left. Eamon's eyes moved to where Foley was pointing and widened like saucers, as though he'd just been made aware of it.

'Open your mouth and talk to the man,' his mother said as the boy shook. His father just gently nudged him. He gulped and then found his voice. 'Yes,' he said hoarsely.

'How many times?' Foley asked. Eamon Kelly's face drained of all its colour. He looked from his mother to his father.

123

'Well?' Emer Kelly said. 'How many times did you and that scrapyard girl—'

'Principal Kelly, I'll do the asking of the questions,' Foley said, interrupting her. The boy remained silent.

'Answer the man,' she said.

'A few,' he stuttered.

'How many?' Foley said.

'I dunno, ten or eleven times, maybe more,' Eamon said with his head hung so low that he was in danger of tipping over.

'Ten or eleven! God almighty!' Principal Kelly roared. Then she gave him a clip around the ear. 'And raise up your head,' she said. The boy held his hand against the ear she'd just slapped. 'A few is three, Eamon,' Principal Kelly said to her son. 'Three and no more than three or have you forgotten your maths with all your sex.'

'Ease up, Emer,' her husband said at the mention of the word sex. 'There's no need for that.'

I caught Foley smiling to himself.

'When did you start having sex?' Foley asked. Principal Kelly glared at her son.

'Good question,' she said.

'About a year ago,' he said.

'About a year ago,' she repeated to herself, just so she could hear it again. She made a fist and banged the table – this was not the tally-ho gesture we'd witnessed in her office; this was a woman who wanted to break the table, if not her son. She nodded. 'Well, that's that, then,' she said.

'As you can probably tell, we were unaware of the situation,' Bobby Kelly said apologetically. 'He's been acting strange for days. Off his food… And when they found the child at the O'Reillys' scrapyard, that's when he came clean,' he explained.

'When did he come to you?' Foley asked.

'First thing this morning,' Bobby said.

'Did you know Joyce was pregnant?' Foley asked Eamon.

He nodded. 'She told me but I didn't believe her. I was always careful,' he said.

'Were you now?' I said in a tone drowning in sarcasm. All eyes turned to me.

'I thought I was,' he mumbled.

'So what did you do when she told you?' Foley asked.

'Is this really necessary?' Bobby Kelly asked, sitting up straighter, his shoulders back, his neck arched. *How dare you*, I thought.

'Well, a young girl nearly died in childbirth alone in a shed, so yes, I'd like an answer,' I said. Principal Emer Kelly turned her head my way; she had a look, a seriousness, a power about her that was impressive. I could see how she rose through the ranks to become principal, could see why her school was highly recommended. She didn't take any shit.

'I know Joyce O'Reilly. I know what she's like. She's flighty. Not to be trusted. I wouldn't be surprised if—' she started to say.

'If what?' I interrupted.

'If there were more than Eamon sniffing around her,' she said, staring me down and folding her arms.

'You seem to know a lot about Joyce. What do you know about your own son?' I asked, because just like Principal Kelly, I didn't take any shit either. She didn't like that. She turned to Foley. 'We came in good faith. We don't deserve to be treated with disrespect.'

'We'll need the doctor to take Eamon's blood,' Foley said.

'Fine,' she said. Eamon's red face instantly paled.

'Do you know what blood group he is?' Foley asked.

'No. He's never been sick a day in his life so it's not something we've investigated.'

'Thank you for coming in. We'll arrange the doctor to go to the house for your privacy,' Foley said. *For their privacy?* This boy would be offered privacy, but the witness, Nora Fitzgerald, had her legs parted and her most intimate parts displayed – where was her privacy? And Joyce… Her face was in print on every breakfast and dinner table in the country. She would have no privacy, but this boy, who had intimate relations with her, made a baby and then denied it – he would be afforded his dignity and privacy? No need to drag the innocent boy into it. No point in two lives ruined, not if unnecessary. No one saw the irony, the hypocrisy.

'You'll let us know if the baby is…'

'Eamon's?' I said. 'She does have the look of him,' I added, and she did. Her hair was lighter and curly, but her nose and chin were just the same.

'That's enough,' Foley mumbled before I could get another word out. They stood to leave. I remained seated as Foley took them outside.

I waited for him to return and berate me for my behaviour. He walked back in and closed the door. He sat down and put his hands on the table. 'You can't form attachments to suspects,' he said evenly.

'That's not what's happening,' I said.

'I hope not, because so far you have been an asset but as I said to your father, as soon as you're not...'

'I understand,' I said. He looked tired; he had bags and dark shadows under his eyes. I wanted to tell him to go home. He needed rest but he still had work to do, he still had a show to put on for the press. It was after six. I had worked my fourth double shift in a row.

'Go home,' he said, and so I went.

–

I wasn't home ten minutes, when Seamus knocked on the door. He held up a bag of veg, some meat. 'Are you hungry?' he asked. I hadn't eaten a proper meal in days.

'I am,' I said, and he pushed past me and into the kitchen area.

'Right, then, you go and change, and I'll make dinner,' he said, and he was already turning the stove on as I went into my room and got changed. By the time I returned, the veg was peeled, chopped and in water. He had a fist full of chicken giblets and searching for the bin. I pointed to it. 'Have you spoken to Thomas O'Reilly?' I asked.

'Last night. I told him it would be better if we stayed away from one another for a while.'

'Good idea,' I said.

'Well, it was yours.'

'That's why it's a good one,' I said. He chuckled.

'Did he mention he was making a complaint against the Dublin lads?' I said.

'Yeah, but if they let Joyce go, they won't take it any further,' he said.

'I hope not for their sake.'

'Is that a threat, Mary?' he said, injecting a little steel into his tone.

'It's a warning. He won't get very far and it's best to leave sleeping dogs lie,' I said.

'They broke his arm.' I could detect bitterness in his tone.

'A baby was murdered. Tensions were high,' I explained.

'Breda gave a false confession to save her husband and you're excusing it?'

'No. I'm not. I'm just telling you, the O'Reillys have been through enough. They might have more to go through.'

'What do you mean?'

'I mean this is far from over, Seamus,' I said.

'But it was on the news this evening. Joyce's girl was stillborn.'

'It's not over, Seamus, not until we identify the mother of Baby Crónán.'

'But what has that to do with Joyce?'

I'd said enough, maybe even too much; the notion that those two babies were twins was far-fetched, so there was no need to put that idea in his head.

'The funeral for Baby Crónán is tomorrow. Let's just see what happens after, okay?' I said.

'Okay,' he said. He made a nice dinner – I even enjoyed the parsnips. We didn't talk much, preferring to slip into our familiar silence. At the door I thanked him for dinner and closed it behind him.

Day Five

It was the day of the funeral and I was asked not to wear a uniform. Foley explained he wanted me to blend into the crowd; he and the Dublin lads didn't wear uniforms either, although it would be hard for him to pass, as he had been all over the TV screens for the past three or four days. Dicey was also told to attend in plain clothes, whereas the rest would attend in uniform. 'If the murderer turns up, they'll be focused on those in uniform. It's our job to focus on the crowd, to find that person who acts strangely – any slight hint of anything...' Foley said, pointing to us. 'You take note, make sure they don't leave without first identifying them. Arrest them if you have to. But remember, this is a funeral, a solemn and holy occasion, do not turn it into a farce,' Foley warned.

I steeled myself for what was to come – a funeral mass that would be open to the public, for the townspeople to grieve this terrible tragedy on their very own doorstep, a ritual that would bond them forever in horror and sadness. For the journalists, a chance to report so the nation could join the locals in solidarity – and, as it turned out, for the people of the country to express their anger at fallen women. *That old chestnut.* But for us, it was a means to find another suspect or maybe just to strengthen the case against the one we had, even though it made no sense. No sense at all. There would be no public burial; it was decided that would be handled privately. It was better that people didn't know where Baby Crónán's final resting place was – not amidst an ongoing investigation.

–

The church was filled to capacity. The crowd spilled out on the grounds and beyond the gate, onto the street and down into the town. We weren't prepared for that. Half of Ireland had travelled. Foley was in a sweat when I landed at the hotel.

'God almighty, we'll be overrun,' he said. It's easy to judge us now, the decisions made, but it's hard to foresee the effect one person – one case, one set of circumstances – has on the psyche of a nation of people. There had been much, and well-reported, pain and suffering on the island of Ireland, and never before had we seen or experienced this kind of outpouring. The journalists themselves were shocked; they too were being overrun. They'd set up as far away from the church as was dignified, but close enough to report on and photograph the event. However, as members of the public streamed in from coaches, trains and cars – parked and abandoned all over the town – their hard-won positions, that they'd vied for all week, were swarmed upon. The town was overwhelmed. 'We need all hands on deck,' Foley said. 'It's a feckin' stampede.' Brian was phoned; he was in the station and already on it, ringing around – he told us there'd be fellas coming from as far as Limerick. It was Foley who had decided a public funeral was a good idea, and this was the first sign of doubt I'd ever seen in him. He was troubled. 'We can't mess this up,' he said and I wondered if it was already too late for that.

I was in the church, on the balcony amongst the choir at the very back, and so I had a bird's-eye view of all those assembled within its walls. Of course it was mostly the back of their heads, but people turned around and to the side, every head arching, looking, searching to see who turned up and who was wearing what. I watched them watch each other. I recognised a lot of the locals. The three doctors were all in attendance; our witness, poor Nora Fitzgerald, and her mother sat quietly, holding hands. I was surprised to see Bridie Fitzmaurice accompanied by her daughter, Debbie. The last time I saw Bridie she was in bed and fit to burst. She was still fit to burst. Principal Kelly arrived and squeezed herself into a pew at the back of the room, with her husband Bobby and son Eamon in tow. Then there was the rest of the town peppered around the pews amongst strangers from God knows where. In the centre of the aisle, in front of the altar, he lay resting on a brass catafalque meant to hold a full-sized coffin, not this tiny white box with a red velvet sash draped over it. That stark visual instilled silence in those present. All that could be heard was the shuffling of feet, and the feeling of dread and loss was crushing. Father Cunningham stood before us, behind the lectern, dressed in purple vestments and hugging his Bible, casting his eyes on the baby in the box just a few short steps away. Foley had consulted with him on what he wanted him to say. Of course Father Cunningham had his own ideas, but this was about striking at a person's guilt, and both priest and detective could agree – they both knew a lot about that. So Father Cunningham raised his Bible high as he turned his gaze from the tiny coffin to the crowd. 'The Lord is our saviour. He is our creator, and He watches over us. He waits for us to return home. He did not have to wait long to receive Baby Crónán back into His arms, for that is where this innocent child now rests. He sees all. He saw what was done – the horror of it, He felt as though it was done to Him. He knows…' He glanced around the congregation, and as he did, so did I. 'He knows who you are.' Small noises rippled through the crowd, the atmosphere charged. An elderly woman placed her face in her hands and sobbed. I watched Principal Kelly swallow her tears; her husband remained stoic, unreadable, but her son, pale as a ghost and shaking like a leaf, was probably reflecting on his own sins. 'He will forgive the very worst deed but only if forgiveness is sought. Baby Crónán is safe in God's arms. Unconfessed, the person who murdered him will find themselves in Satan's lair. It's a short life here on earth, but death is eternal.'

I was scanning the room, when I saw Debbie leading her mother out of the church. Bridie's knees were buckling, and Debbie was only short of carrying her. *She's having the baby*, I thought. My eyes followed them to the exit, where Bridie stopped, short of breath now, too many people in her path. Debbie attempted to push them all aside and Bridie struggled to remain standing. She was sliding to the floor. I couldn't just leave them. I stood up and moved through the choir and down the wrought-iron staircase. I heard Father Cunningham say the words, 'Rest in peace for eternity, Baby Crónán,' as I pushed my way through the crowd to find Debbie, her legs about to give way as she put all her strength into holding up her crying mammy. I cleared a path as best I could, while the slip of a girl supported her elephant of a mother. Once the crowd's attention was drawn away from the man on the pulpit and his spell was broken, they moved aside to let us through. Together, Debbie and I carried Bridie outside to the carpark, where she collapsed on the ground. I don't know how Dr Ciara Crosby found us, but within seconds of my arrival, she was there. 'Hello, Mrs—'

'Her name is Bridie,' I said.

'She's having a baby,' Debbie screamed. She was in a terrible state.

'I can see that,' Dr Crosby said. Debbie looked at her mother and she was beyond distraught. 'I told you we shouldn't have come here.' God love her, she was pale and trembling, her tiny frame drowning in a raincoat that looked like it belonged on somebody else. I wondered when last she had eaten, when last she had slept. She was a pitiful sight.

'It's all right, Debbie,' I said, 'we're here, it's going to be fine.' I tried to assure her, but there was no way Bridie was going to make it through the dense crowd. 'That's a convent, isn't it?' Dr Crosby said, nodding her head towards the building behind the church.

'It is,' I said.

'Ah no,' Bridie said between short breaths. 'I can't give birth in a convent, we're unlucky enough as it is.'

'What are you talking about? Unlucky to be born in a convent – sure, wasn't our Lord born in a stable,' Dr Crosby said before looking to me and giving me a wink. 'I'd say you're about to give birth to the luckiest baby alive.'

'Do you think?' Bridie said. Her knees were buckling and, with the weight of her, so was my back.

'I do, what do you think, Garda Shea?' Dr Crosby said.

'Well, it would be luckier and a damn sight warmer than being born here, in front of half of Ireland,' I said. My suggestion wasn't as playful as Dr Crosby's, but it got Bridie moving towards the convent. I knocked on the door and a small woman in a habit answered. 'Hello, Sister...'

'Francis,' she supplied.

'We need your assistance,' Dr Crosby said and the nun swung the door open to allow us past.

–

The room she gave us was her own and she assured us the sheets had been washed fresh that morning. Dr Crosby ordered Sister Francis to get warm water and towels, and she asked Debbie to help her mother take off her undergarments. I was painfully aware that my place was within the walls of the church, observing the crowd, looking for a suspect, yet here I was, an unnecessary extra, now that Bridie was safe. I looked to Dr Crosby. 'Can you take it from here?' I asked her.

'I can,' she said.

'Good luck, Bridie,' I said. 'It'll be all right, Debbie,' I said to the quivering wreck beside me.

If she heard me, she didn't say. By the time I'd returned to my position, communion was being handed out. After that there were prayers said, and people started to leave. I watched them, now facing me: great sorrow, grave concern and pure piety on display, but no guilty faces – no one looking as though they were about to bolt or fall on the floor and confess to the Almighty, the Garda Síochána and the people of Kerry that they had the blood of Baby Crónán on their hands. There were too many sets of eyes on us for there to be any real chance of a private burial, so Baby Crónán was driven away from the church in McGuire's hearse and returned to the funeral home. After that, people started leaving the town but not before some of the locals had time to open their cafés, restaurants, shops and bars to make a good profit during the off-peak season. We returned to the hotel. Once inside the incident room and when everyone was settled, Foley stood in front of us, but before he said anything at all, he glared my way. *Oh no*, I thought, my guts twisting. *I've blown it.*

'Where were you?' he said.

'There was an emergency.'

'An emergency?' he asked, pushing the words out between gritted teeth.

'That's right,' I said, and I could see Dicey folding his arms and a smile slipping across his face.

'What kind of emergency would make a member of the force leave a position when assigned a specific duty?' he asked.

'Bridie Fitzmaurice went into labour,' I said.

'Bridie Fitzmaurice…'

'One of the women we interviewed.'

'I know who she is, Shea,' he said and Dicey McCarthy was only short of snorting. 'You had no business leaving your post. I put you in prime position, for God's sake.'

'I'm sorry but there was a woman in distress—'

'And a room full people who could have helped her,' he shouted, and he was right. I left my post and I shouldn't have.

'I understand,' I said.

'Do you?' he said.

'I messed up,' I admitted. He couldn't bring himself to look at me one second longer. He turned to face the men. 'Anyone? Anyone suspicious at all?' he asked and they all shook their heads.

'Nothing? No one?' he was shouting again.

'I'm not sure what we were supposed to be looking for,' Liam Kenny said and, God love him, Foley lit on him.

'A bleedin' suspect, Kenny, what in the name of God do you think you were looking for? A pony in a pair of high heels?'

Some of the Dublin lads dared to laugh but one glaring look from Foley put a stop to that. I think Foley might have given someone a good dig if it hadn't been for the phone ringing. Quinn picked it up, listened and hung up. 'That was Brian from the station. The bloods are back on the baby girl, Lily O'Reilly, and the boy, Eamon Kelly.' Everyone fell silent and waited. He cleared his throat. 'She is blood group A and Eamon Kelly is AB.' We were all silent.

'And Joyce O'Reilly is A,' O'Neill said, from the back of the room, where he was sipping tea. 'A plus AB can make an A,' Quinn stated. 'At least according to the fella on the phone to Brian.'

'Is that it?' Foley said. It was clear none of us were scientists. 'So the girl is Joyce and Eamon's?'

'Well, she could be,' Quinn said.

'Crónán is O. Can an A and an AB make an O?' Foley asked.

Quinn shrugged. 'He didn't say.'

'For the love of God, have you been banged on the head, Quinn? Get that man back on the phone,' Foley said.

'Will do,' Quinn said. Foley looked to O'Neill. 'You're with me.'

I watched as they left. Dicey McCarthy looked to me and chuckled. 'Looks like you and Foley are breaking up,' he said, delighted with himself, which made it all the sweeter when he tripped over his own shoelace. As undignified as it was, he managed to save himself before he hit the floor, but he saw that I saw. *Gobdaw*, I thought. The problem is I was a gobdaw too. I'd messed up, and I knew it. I felt sick about it. Now demoted, I spent the rest of that day typing up statements, still to be recorded. The men were slow enough at it, so there was plenty to get through. That's when I read Fidelma Regan's statement. She had no insight to offer regarding the matter. She had been out that night watching a film, *Kramer vs. Kramer*, in another town with her friend Brenda Wall. She said she got a minibus home and she couldn't be sure, but she'd say she was in bed and asleep by eleven p.m. She saw nothing suspicious but I recognised her name; it took me a minute to recall that it was her prescription for Valium that Bridie Fitzmaurice had by her bed. Sharing prescription medications wasn't advisable, especially with a pregnant woman. It wasn't illegal – unless, of course, she was selling them. She was a schoolteacher at the local primary, a single woman. I considered talking to her about it and decided that, instead of taking any formal action, I would speak to her when I got the chance, give a friendly warning and hope she'd heed it. I typed up that statement and many more besides, and it felt fruitless. I wondered what was happening with Foley and O'Neill. They were obviously talking to an expert on blood groups. I didn't see Foley for the rest of the day. By the end of my shift, it was clear I had been cut out of the real action. I thought about my mother telling me how proud she was of me. *I let you down, Mammy.*

–

At home, I had a hot bubble bath. I lay there, berating myself. I should have never left the church, for nothing or no one. I allowed myself to be distracted. I failed Foley, I failed Mammy, Daddy… I failed myself but, worst of all, I failed Baby Crónán. Seamus knocked soon after I got out. I opened the door in my housecoat. He was still in his work clothes and wellies, so he stayed standing outside.

'Are we going to the disco tomorrow night?' he said.

'Sorry, I'm not in the mood.'

'It was a hard day,' he said.

'I didn't see you there.'

'I wasn't,' he said. 'Sounds like I was the only one in the whole country who wasn't there.'

'Felt like it,' I said.

'We'll dance next week.'

'You never dance.'

'Well, I might next week.' He rubbed his hands together. That made me smile. 'Okay.' I closed the door behind him and, exhausted, emotionally spent, disappointed and angry, I took to my bed. I didn't think about Bridie at all. I didn't wonder if she'd had the baby; my thoughts lay with Baby Crónán, still in Tony McGuire's funeral home, and myself. And I wondered if Dicey McCarthy was right when he'd said, 'This is what happens when you let a woman do men's work. She makes a bollocks of it.' I was tired of myself and my worries. I fell asleep early.

Knocking to my front door woke me. I pulled on my robe and answered it. Ruth McEvoy, Seamus's mother, was standing there in her housecoat and her hair in curlers. 'There you are,' she said. Ruth McEvoy started every conversation with the words 'there you are'.

'Is everything all right, Ruth?' I asked.

'Oh, it is. Well, as much as it can be under these circumstances,' she said.

'Right,' I said, waiting to hear what was coming next.

'There's a phone call for you up at the house, it's a Detective Foley.'

'Oh,' I said and I checked my watch. It was eleven thirty at night. 'I'm sorry, it's so late.'

'Oh, don't worry at all, important business,' she said and patted my arm. 'We're all behind you.'

'Thanks, Mrs McEvoy.' I followed her to the farmhouse. The phone was in the hallway. 'I'll leave you to it,' she said, and I thanked her again and picked up the phone.

'Foley?'

'How long does it take to answer a phone?' he asked.

'Sorry,' I said. I wasn't about to waste time explaining my living situation.

'We're burying him after midnight. After the disgrace you made of yourself today, I wasn't going to say anything but you were first on site, you and Dicey McCarthy, so you should be there,' he said.

I didn't bother trying to defend myself – sure, what could I say? He was right. I was a disgrace.

'Where?' I asked.

'Meet us at the hotel,' he said. I hung up the phone and left the house without saying a word. I ran down the lane and into my little cottage, where I changed into a black wool dress and tights, put on my heavy black coat and tried on a black hat I'd bought for an occasion a few years before. I drove to the hotel. Foley and Dicey were in the small bar to the side of the reception. It was closed, so Dicey was pouring the Guinness. There was only one light on, a lamp in the corner perched over the booth they were sitting in. It was all very cosy; Dicey had the look of a cat who'd got the cream.

'Do you want a drink?' he asked. It was the first time he'd offered me anything.

'No,' I said, sitting at the booth.

'Are you always so dry?' Foley asked.

'Yes,' I said, and he chuckled at that. He looked to Dicey as he walked towards him, holding two freshly poured pints, before glancing at his watch. 'We'll need to polish these off fast,' he said and then I sat there as two grown men silently played a game of who can neck a pint faster. Dicey won, but only by the virtue that he had a bigger mouth on him. Foley was a moment or two behind. They both slapped their glasses on the table. I wasn't sure if they were waiting for some kind of round of applause. They weren't going to get it from me. I just got up and walked outside.

Day Six

We were sitting in the car, when I asked if we were the only ones attending the burial.

'Yeah, and it's enough,' Foley said. He drove through the darkness, hitting every pothole along the way. Dicey sat in the passenger seat, his head hitting the roof of the car every time. Although demoted to the back seat, it was an enjoyable sight. We drove the back roads to the old graveyard, one that hadn't been used in years. There, waiting for us in the dark, were Father Cunningham and the funeral director Tony McGuire, who was holding Baby Crónán's coffin.

'No one will find him here,' Tony said as soon as he saw us, stepping out of the car. 'He'll be safe.' Tony carried and cradled the coffin alone. We followed him to the spot where a local gravedigger, Terry Doherty, was standing over the hole. He was a big man, wearing two coats – one over the other – a thick woollen hat and a pair of leather gloves with a pair of wool fingerless gloves over them. Tony placed Baby Crónán in the ground, and all of us stood in front of Father Cunningham and recited ten decades of the rosary. The frost was beginning to settle on the ground and gravestone; the fog was thick and heavy, and our breath could be seen trailing as we mumbled our prayers. When we were done praying, Tony McGuire sang 'Nearer, My God, to Thee'. He had a lovely voice; I'd heard him sing before in the pub a few times and then at the Fitzmaurice funeral. There, at the gravestone of Bridie's husband and son, he sang 'Home Boys Home', a song about sailors returning home. Bridie wasn't even showing then but she probably knew she was pregnant as they put her husband and son in the ground, and as her tears fell, I remembered Lisa, clapping and signing along to her daddy's favourite song, unable to grasp the notion that she'd never see him again. Now, in a graveyard in the pitch-black after midnight, his impressive vocal range was on full display, effortlessly hitting the high notes, maintaining control and clarity in the lower register, his projection so powerful it's a wonder he wasn't heard for miles – his warmth, his emotion, his gritty timbre reaching into the night sky and beyond. *He's singing for you, Crónán*, I thought as he filled the void with song, and despite the cold, we stood there long after he was done. It was hard to leave that little boy in the small box in the cold ground. Finally, it was Terry Doherty that broke the tension. 'Go on home, let me do my job,' he said and he picked up the shovel.

'Thank you, Terry,' Tony said, and Father Cunningham sighed and squeezed his arm. They started to walk away; next to peel away was Dicey. Foley and I stood there as Terry shovelled earth onto the coffin. 'Come on,' he said and he linked my arm. 'We're done here.' As we walked, I remembered to read the headstone beside the unmarked plot where they lay him. There were a number of names etched into the stone but they were all so old that the only one legible, at the bottom, was Catherine Goggins, born 10 November 1880 and died 12 May 1945. The graveyard was big enough, and it was dark, but I needed to remember Catherine Goggins so I could come to sit with Crónán when it was all over and lay flowers on his grave.

It was after two in the morning when we dropped Dicey McCarthy to his door. He jumped out and ran inside, hugging himself because the heater was broken in the car. I was a block of ice by then, inside and out. When Dicey was gone and we were halfway down the road, Foley asked me how Bridie got on.

'I don't know,' I admitted.

'You didn't follow up?' he said.

'I had a lot of other things on my mind.'

'You're hard to work out,' he commented and I said nothing. 'I hear you are taking a couple of days off,' he said.

'I am.'

'Going to your parents' for dinner?' He was there when my father summoned me home; it was interesting to me that he'd taken note.

'That's right,' I said.

'Your father will want to know where we are with things.'

'I suppose he'll hear that from you,' I said, wondering what Foley was getting at.

'Ah, but he'll also want to hear it from you,' he insisted. *Ah.* He's fishing for information.

'What are you asking me, Detective Foley?' I said as he parked up outside my small cottage.

'O'Neill is a good man, one of my best,' Foley said. I waited for him to make his point. 'He didn't mean to break that fella's arm, it was an accident.' Now I understood. The O'Reillys were making a complaint, and it was clear my father had been made aware of it. Foley wanted me to vouch for O'Neill and I knew that this was my way back onto the case.

'Well, I wasn't there,' I said with my hand on the door handle.

'But you've worked with O'Neill now, you've seen the kind of man he is,' he said, slightly more urgently than I believed he intended. I had a feeling my father's reaction to the complaint hadn't been good. I turned to face him.

'Not really, I've worked with you. I've seen the kind of man you are,' I said and he eyed me. I could tell what he was thinking... *What's she playing at?*

'And what kind is that?' he said.

'The kind who sees talent and uses it, someone who listens and is encouraging. Someone who gave me a chance when no one else would.' It was a compliment, but it was also my way of asking him to let me back in.

He sighed. 'You let me down.'

He was right. I had. 'I won't do that twice,' I said.

'And O'Neill?'

'If you say he's a good man I have no reason to doubt that.' Was I blackmailing Foley? I don't know, but if I was, it worked.

He looked at me right in the eye. 'You're a hard one to work out,' he repeated. I took off my safety belt and was about to step out of the car, when he told me they'd spoken to an expert on blood groups. And just like that, I was back in the fold. I stayed where I was.

He took out a box of cigarettes and offered me one. I took it. He lit his own, then he lit mine. We both inhaled deeply. 'Well?' I said.

'Joyce is an A. Eamonn is an AB—'

'So Lily is Joyce and Eamon's, but what did the specialist say about Baby Crónán?' I asked.

'He's an O. And apparently an A and AB cannot make an O,' he said and he blew a smoke ring for effect, before putting his finger through it as it dissipated.

'So Lily and Baby Crónán can't be twins,' I said. I was relieved. I wanted to jump for joy. Joyce would be free to heal, to put this all behind her, to move on. She'd have a rough road ahead of her. The whole of Ireland were her judge and jury, she'd been demonised in the press, her reputation lay in tatters, but she was young and smart. She could still turn things around. And now we were free to do our jobs and find the real murderer. I must have been smiling.

'Don't get so excited. A woman with a blood type A can make an O,' he said. *So? What does that matter?*

'Yes, but her boyfriend Eamon is AB, which you just said can't make an O,' I said, my head already starting to ache.

That's when he said those two words: *heteropaternal superfecundation* – I don't think he even pronounced them right, I wouldn't have known if he had or he hadn't. I'd never heard those words before in my life.

'In rare cases twins can be conceived through sex with different men in a very short timeframe,' he said, and I think my mouth fell open. I definitely felt a draft. 'I know it sounds bizarre,' he said, taking a long drag.

'More than bizarre,' I said. 'It doesn't sound right at all.'

'Emer Kelly said she was flighty.'

'Emer Kelly was protecting her son.'

'She concocted a good story about the handsome carnival boy. You believed her. What if it was true?' he asked and he was right, she had been convincing. If there was such a thing as a woman being able to give birth to twins by different fathers, it was our duty to look into it.

I looked at him and sighed. 'If it's possible, we can't discount it,' I said and he nodded.

'What about the clothes found on the rocks, the three sightings of wandering women?' I asked.

'We'll look into all of it, Mary, but right now the wandering women are a fairytale, and Joyce O'Reilly is very real.' We finished our cigarettes.

As I got out of the car, my stomach felt queasy. He drove off as soon as I walked inside, and I slipped to the floor and leaned against my front door. *Heteropaternal superfecundation? Is it really possible, or am I part of a witch-hunt?* I just didn't know.

CHAPTER TEN

Day Seven

From my house in Nead Mara to my parents' in Bantry it was just under an hour's drive on a road that cut through a tapestry of rolling hills and lush green fields, and offered dramatic coastal views, often kissed by the mist in the early part of the morning. Having slept till after twelve, I hastily dressed in the jeans and the blouse I had intended to wear to the disco. I arrived fifteen minutes late for lunch. I parked outside our grand house that sat on its own half-acre, under my favourite tree, there for over one hundred years. I knocked on the black wooden front door using the brass knocker, because the bell hadn't worked in years. My father answered. He looked at me up and down to make sure I was in one piece. 'Good, good,' he said, and then he turned and shouted into the air, '*She's here.*' My mother appeared, wiping her hands on a tea towel, her bobbed blonde hair cut sharply to her chin.

'You've done your hair,' I said and she enveloped me into a big hug. 'Yesterday.'

'It's pretty,' I said as I leaned in to inhale her sweet perfume. My mother was a model for three years before my dad married her. She worked for a clothes catalogue that came out once every season. Mum featured every season during those three years, modelling cardigans, dresses, trousers and even swimwear. She was beautiful back then; she was still beautiful. I used to wish I looked more like her, but I had my dad's nose. It wasn't a bad nose but it wasn't pretty enough to feature in a catalogue either.

'Come in, come in,' she said, ushering me into the kitchen. Mammy sat me at the table while she mashed the potatoes.

'I have news about your sister,' she said.

My heart skipped a beat. 'What?' I said, terrified it would be something that would upset me.

'She's getting married,' Daddy said as he sat on a chair right beside me.

As against marriage as I was, that did not upset me. *Thank God.* 'Since when?' I asked.

'Since yesterday,' Mammy said, taking a large gulp from a glass of white wine. 'She wanted me to tell you, to make sure you'd be all right about it.'

'Why wouldn't I be?'

'Well, she's eighteen and you are… you,' my mother said.

'I think she's too young but he's a nice fella and all she's ever wanted was to be a mother,' I said. I knew she loved him, because she talked to me about him all the time.

'So…' my mother said.

'So… You can tell her to relax. I'm happy for her,' I said and she chuckled. 'She will be so relieved to have her big sister's approval.' She raised her glass.

'I'll call her tomorrow,' I said. Although ten years apart and nothing alike, I adored her as if she were my own, and she thought of me much the same way. We were different but bonded by pure love. That was our strength. Thinking of her made me smile. *Sweet Caroline.*

'Speak to her next week, at the party.'

'Oh God.'

'Don't start,' she warned.

I grinned at her. 'Fine. There better be dancing.'

'Oh, there will be dancing,' my mother said and drank deeply once again.

'Your mammy has been drinking since she found out,' Daddy said, pointing to her and making glug-glug noises. She laughed.

'She'll get pregnant right away – you know she will – and I'm too young to be a grandmother,' my mother said.

'Not really,' I said.

'That's what I told her,' agreed Daddy.

'You're both dead to me,' she said without a hint of irony, and she finished the contents of her glass.

'Now tell us about the case,' Daddy said, pouring himself a glass of wine. It was surprising: before, he would have used my sister's engagement as a way to hold yet another conversation about my life choices, but now he was talking about work. My work! As if it mattered.

He was interested. It was a dream come true. He held up the bottle of wine.

'Drink?'

'No, I'm driving back this evening.'

'Ah, sure, you're eating a meal, you'll be fine.' He poured the glass. 'Now where are we?'

'What do you want to know?' I said as Mammy grabbed her home-grown tarragon and started chopping.

'Start with the girl. Joyce O'Reilly, what's happening with her?' he said.

'Her blood type is A, the boy we've identified is AB. Lily, the baby found in the yard, is A.'

'So she's a match,' he said.

'Yes.'

'And the baby was stillborn, she never drew breath?' he asked.

'Not outside the womb, according to Frank Waters,' I said and he paused to take a drink.

'Well, Waters knows his stuff.'

'How is the girl… Joyce?' my mother asked and her tone was gentle. She knew what it was to lose a child. She'd lost six, between my sister and me.

'She's in an awful way,' I said.

My mother sipped from her wine. 'The poor girl.'

'And what about the baby boy, anyone suspicious turn up at the funeral?' Daddy asked.

'No,' I said. 'At least, if they did, they weren't acting suspicious.'

'It was always a shot in the dark,' he said. I didn't mention I'd left my post. I was enjoying his favour too much to ruin it.

'We buried him, last night in the old graveyard, after midnight,' I said. Mammy blessed herself.

'That must have been very hard,' she said.

'It was but Tony McGuire sang "Nearer, My God, to Thee". He has a lovely voice. Above us, the stars were out and everyone there wanted to be there. It was peaceful. It was nice,' I said.

My father wasn't interested in funerals. 'So where are we with the parentage of Baby Crónán?' he said as Mammy sprinkled tarragon on the carrots before serving up a chicken roast dinner.

'Dig in,' she said before grabbing another bottle of wine and joining us.

'The current theory is heteropaternal superfecundation,' I said injecting great authority into my voice just like Foley had.

'Heteropat— what?' he said, looking from me to my mother. 'What in the name of God is that?'

'I don't know, but eat your dinner before it gets cold,' my mother said. He shoved his fork into the food, lifted it off the plate and shovelled it in his mouth.

'It's when a woman becomes pregnant with twins by two different men,' I explained. He nearly choked. Mammy already had her glass to her lips, so she responded by draining it of wine. Daddy just looked at me. 'Two babies by two different men?' he said.

'That's what they are saying.'

'How does that even happen?' my mother said, her face distorted by confusion.

'Don't even think about it,' Daddy said. No one wanted to think about that. I moved on to what was pertinent.

'Baby Crónán is blood type O, so if Joyce O'Reilly is his mother, then his father can't be AB because A and AB can't make an O.'

'So the principal's son and the father of Lily is AB, and *if* there's another fella, he needs to be what... An O?' Mammy said.

'I don't know, maybe.'

My father was silent. He needed a minute to think things through. 'Twins by two different men. God almighty, that's a new one on me,' he said.

'It's new to us all,' I said.

'And who could the other father be?'

'When I questioned her—'

'You questioned her?'

'Yes.'

'On your own or with Foley? You weren't on your own in the room?' he said in a tone that suggested he wasn't quite comfortable with that. *And things had been going so well.*

'On my own,' I said, injecting steel into my voice. Mammy sensed what was going on. 'Don't ruin things,' she warned my father.

'I'm not ruining anything. I'm just asking a question. Go on, Mai*me*,' he said.

'When I questioned her, she told me the father of her baby was a handsome boy she met at a carnival. She said he was tall and dark and handsome. Eamon Kelly is none of those things.'

'And?' he said.

'And Baby Crónán had a head of black hair. He was beautiful,' I said and suddenly I wanted to cry. I could see him again, his little rosebud lips, his grey eyes. I didn't cry. I held it in.

'Two boys, two babies?' my mother said in a whisper. 'Well, every day is a school day.' She refilled her glass.

'It's just the current theory,' I said.

'And what do you think?' my father asked, leaning over his dinner – he really wanted to know. It made me want to cry again. This was what I'd always dreamed of: Daddy and I, colleagues, chasing criminals together.

'I think it's rubbish. Joyce O'Reilly nearly died on that farm giving birth to her little girl. She was in no fit state to walk or cycle or hitch a ride to the beach, which is fifteen miles down the road. And even if she could, why would she do that? Why would she kill her boy and then display him for all to see, while her little girl, who'd died of natural causes, was concealed in the engine of a tractor on her land?'

My mother nodded. 'Good point.'

'It doesn't make sense,' my father agreed.

'What if she gave birth to the boy first?' my mother said.

'Then did she kill him, get on a bike to lay him out and cycle all the way home before giving birth again? I can't see how that would be possible,' I said.

'Until two minutes ago I wouldn't have thought twins by two different fathers was possible either,' my father said thoughtfully. 'And Foley. What does he think?'

'He said if he had a pound for every person who did something that didn't make sense, he'd be a rich man.'

'He's right about that but if the girl was damaged it's a matter of how, not why,' Daddy said.

'I agree. The same night, at around nine fifteen, there was a sighting of a woman in a heavy coat, with a matching hat and a scarf around her face, walking down Appletree Lane and carrying a heavy shopping bag. Then there was a sighting of a brown-haired girl in a white nightdress soaked to the skin, sometime between midnight and morning, on

Potters Road. Then again, a girl in a white nightdress, bone dry, around Hillcrest; she was spotted around four thirty a.m.'

'Can you find a link between them?' my dad said, clearly intrigued.

'Not yet,' I said.

'I'm confused… If any of these girls were Joyce, where was the baby in this scenario?' Mammy asked.

'In the bag,' Daddy and I both said at the same time.

'Mother of God,' she said and she blessed herself. Then she stood up. 'I'll get dessert.'

Daddy and I sat in his study after dessert, talking things through. 'And the ex-jockey was sure the clothes found in the water were the same items worn by that woman on Appletree Lane?' he said, lighting up a cigar.

'That's what he said when he looked at the photos.'

'But it was dark and foggy, and how much attention does a man give to a passing woman's garments?' he said before sipping on his brandy. 'Are you sure you don't want a drink?' he asked.

'No. I'm driving,' I said.

'You should stay. Your mother can make up your old room.'

'No, thanks, Daddy, I'm up early,' I said. He nodded. 'But you're right about the clothes. Still, it's a coincidence.'

'It is,' he agreed. 'You've your work cut out for you,' he added.

'We do,' I said.

'And then there's the matter of O'Neill,' he said and my stomach twisted a bit. 'Did he break that man's arm on purpose?'

'No,' I said, absolutely sure he didn't.

'He was way too heavy-handed. It could cause problems down the line. What do you make of him?' he asked me, wanting me to express my opinion. Another dream come true, but I had an arrangement with Foley, to get back in his good graces and finish the job I'd started, so I lied to him.

'I think he's really good, we'd never be where we are without him,' I said and felt immediately sick, but I told myself that he was Foley's man. If Foley thought he was worth something, who was I to argue? I needed Daddy to back off. I needed Foley to see me as a valuable asset. I did it, and I hated doing it but if it meant staying on that case, I knew I'd do it again.

I spent the drive home contemplating everything, mulling over what we knew and trying to imagine the things we didn't. It was a mind muddle. I just couldn't work out what might have happened that night. At home I dressed in my nightclothes and sipped on what was left of the bottle of whiskey. To escape my thoughts I listened to music; I put on a Bee Gees record and sat in an old broken-down armchair that looked terrible but was very comfortable – comfortable enough to fall asleep in. I drifted off to sleep and dreamed of Baby Crónán, and his grey eyes were lit up, his rosebud lips were parted in a wide smile and his little dimpled hands were reaching out to me.

Day Seven

We were all still working overtime but I didn't sign up for a double shift. I needed the morning to myself, to clean up the house and to clear my head. I tore into chores, vacuuming carpets, scrubbing the kitchen and bathroom vinyl floors. I dusted, wiped down shelves and cleaned the toilet. I took a good couple of hours at it. It was a great morning's work. I found cleaning deeply satisfying – a clean house meant a clear head. Fulfilled and mentally refreshed, I took a shower, ate something bland and then drove to town. I still had an hour before work and decided to visit Bridie Fitzmaurice on the way. Frankly, Foley had shamed me into it. Of course, I should have followed up on how she was after the birth of her baby. I didn't even know the sex or whether they were both healthy. It was a terrible indictment of me as a person that I hadn't even considered it. I scolded myself for my single-mindedness, which I recognised as a flaw. I pulled up onto their street and as soon as I did, there was Lisa Fitzmaurice running towards me, and poor Debbie chasing after her, calling her name. I stopped the car, jumped out and grabbed Lisa. She was strong, fighting against me. 'Lisa, it's me, Garda Mary Shea.' She stopped fighting me as soon as she recognised me.

'I want to explore,' she complained.

Debbie slowed her run to a walk. 'I don't have time to explore. I have to clean the house – it needs to be like a new pin before Mammy gets home,' she said.

'I want to explore,' Lisa said again. 'I want to get out.'

'Sorry, Lisa, but you'll have to go back inside,' I told her. 'Anyway, it's going to rain again.' I could already feel it, heavy in the air.

'I didn't like getting wet,' Lisa said and she shuddered. By then Debbie had reached us.

'You don't like getting wet,' Debbie corrected her. She held out her hand; her thumb was sticking out through the hole in the arm of the faded knitwear that fitted more like a dress than a jumper, and Lisa took it.

'Thanks,' Debbie said to me and she smiled. It was nice to see.

'How's your mammy?' I asked.

'She's very good. She had a boy. He's over ten pounds,' she said. *That makes sense of the size of the poor woman*, I thought. 'He looks like my dad and he curls his lip the way my brother Tommy used to,' she said and she rubbed Lisa's head. 'Doesn't he, Lisa?'

'Mammy's friend took me to visit her yesterday. We were in Cork city,' Lisa said, delighted.

'That's good news,' I said.

'Mammy's calling him Johnny. My dad's name was John. It's John mixed with Tommy. She's happy and Dr Crosby has been brilliant altogether. She says we can get money from the state and she's helping with the forms. Mammy thinks maybe our luck has turned around,' she said, and I could see the weight lifting from her.

'I'm delighted to hear it.'

'Maybe Dr Crosby was right, maybe having the baby in the convent was meant to be,' Debbie said. 'It's a blessing.'

'Sounds like a new beginning,' I said and she beamed at me. 'Please tell her I was asking for her.'

'I will,' she said, and she and Lisa walked away from me. *At last some good news*, I thought to myself.

–

I felt a little lighter as I entered the incident room. The good news and Debbie's happy demeanour had rubbed off on me. I must have been smiling, and my smile was surely off-putting, because when O'Neill glanced my way, his face changed. 'What's wrong with you?' he said.

'Nothing.'

'You don't look like yourself,' he said.

'I'm smiling, O'Neill,' I explained. A few of the others were there too: Quinn was making coffee, Dicey was standing by the printer.

'It looks weird. Did you have a nice morning off?' O'Neill asked.

'I did,' I said and then I thought about his poor wife having just given birth to a baby girl, on her own in Dublin. 'How are your wife and your little girl?' I asked.

He smiled. 'Good. She wants me home but her ma's there so it's better off that I'm not,' he said and snorted.

'How long do you think you'll be here?' I asked.

'It won't be too much longer. You missed a lot during your time off. The McNight family, who run the carnival, have a son, Patrick – he's seventeen and fits the description Joyce gave. He's blood group O, same as Baby Crónán.'

I nearly fell over with the weight of his words. I sat down to prevent myself from doing so.

'God almighty,' I said.

'I know. To be honest, I didn't think the stupification thing was a goer.' He messed up the word on purpose, which made me smile. 'But… looks like I was wrong.'

'When did all this happen?' I asked.

'We got lucky. We traced him yesterday through an article. Patrick was fixing one of the rides when he ended up with a crush injury and needed a transfusion, it even mentioned his blood group.'

'What now, then?'

'The parents are in Blackpool at some carnival conference… The boy's seventeen, so Foley drove up to Donegal yesterday to question him. He had to tread lightly because of his age. The boy denies having anything to do with Joyce and Foley didn't get much else out of him. He's driving back as we speak and he needs us to visit Joyce O'Reilly in prison to get a confession.'

'A confession.'

'It's time to put this business to rest,' O'Neill said.

'But it still doesn't make sense.'

'So we'll talk to her to make sense of it,' he said.

'We?'

'You'll come in, but I'll be doing most of the talking,' he said.

'You think she'll talk to you after everything that happened with her brother?' I asked.

'She'll have no choice and, anyway, that's why you're there. Foley insisted.'

'You won't hurt her,' I said. He gave me the side-eye. 'I won't let you,' I warned.

He chuckled at that. He held his hands up. 'If you knew me better, Shea, you'd know I'd never lay a hand on a lady, unless of course she asked me to,' he said and he gave me a look. Suddenly, there was tension in the air. I think he was flirting. My stomach fluttered. *No, no.* It was very confusing. He stood up, grabbed the car keys.

'Come on, let's go and find out the truth,' he said.

–

O'Neill was driving. We were on the mountain road when the rain started pouring down, heavy and in sheets. It was a difficult road to navigate at the best of times. Above us, mud from the mountain rolled onto the narrow, winding road, which was lined with low rock walls barely separating us from a steep, grassy drop into a lake far below.

O'Neill was sweating, he wasn't able for the journey at all. When two sheep made a leap from the mountain onto the road in front of him, he braked sharply and the car spun to a stop. 'How do you people live like this?' he said as they ran off, unbothered. He was winded. His confidence had taken a dive. Not that he'd admit it.

'I can drive,' I said. 'I know this road like the back of my hand.'

He thought about it. 'I'll be fine,' he said and he started the car up again. He drove so slowly, we'd have been quicker walking, but I didn't want to talk to him so I didn't complain. Being that close to him unnerved me a little; the air between us was fraught with something that felt almost like electricity. *Stop it, Mary!* I kept my back to him, to stare out of the window, distracting myself by watching the raindrops hit the lake like bullets shot from the sky. I reflected on the muted palette of browns, blues, greys and greens laid out before us. *How do you people live like this?* he'd asked, the cheek of him. *Very well, most of the time*, I thought.

–

It was well after three p.m. when we reached the prison. We were back in the same interview room. Joyce shuffled in five minutes after we arrived. She was drawn but she looked much better, less pained than she had the last time I saw her. She sat down in front of us.

'When can I go home?' she asked me. She ignored O'Neill.

'It's not that simple,' he said. She didn't take her eyes off me.

'My baby was stillborn. My solicitor told me. I didn't kill her, she was already gone,' she said and tears filled her eyes.

'That's true,' I said quietly.

'But Baby Crónán was very much alive,' O'Neill said, and she kept her eyes on me as fat tears spilled from them.

'He's not mine. Lily was mine.'

'But Lily is Eamon Kelly's child,' O'Neill said. 'Baby Crónán is Patrick McNight's child.' She sat perfectly still, her eyes on me, tears still streaming, but now her pupils widened and I could see her processing the information in real time. 'You remember him: tall, dark and handsome? Detective Foley says he's a real prince,' O'Neill said.

'I lied to you, Garda Shea,' she said. 'I'm sorry. I was scared.'

'What did you lie about, Joyce?' I asked.

'I was seeing Eamon Kelly, it wasn't Patrick McNight. He didn't do anything to me. I'm not pretty enough for him,' she said.

'Why did you lie?' O'Neill said.

Now she found a way to look over at O'Neill, as she spoke quietly and carefully. 'Because if my dad found out Eamon got me pregnant, he'd do to him what you and your friends did to Thomas. The difference is, he'd go to prison for it,' she said and O'Neill didn't like that one bit.

'That's enough,' he said, 'the evidence is stacking up against you.'

'I wasn't with him,' she told me. 'Garda Shea, honestly, I was only ever with Eamon.'

'So why describe Patrick?' I asked.

'All the girls liked him, he was so handsome and friendly, always smiling – well, mostly, and flirting with the pretty girls. He's been coming with his family for years, and every year he gets better looking. When you asked me, he just came into my mind,' she said.

'And the story about you not knowing if you wanted to be with him... It was very believable,' I said.

'Because that first time with Eamon was behind a caravan at the carnival, and I didn't want to but...'

'But what?' I said.

'After that it got easier... Better.' She flushed red.

'Which lie are we supposed to believe?' O'Neill said.

'Patrick was seeing a girl in town,' she said. 'He had no interest in the likes of me.'

'Who?' I asked.

'Eileen O'Connor,' she said in a whisper.

'Thank you, Joyce,' I said.

—

I drove us back. I didn't seek permission. I just sat on the driver's side and put my hand out for the keys. O'Neill didn't even argue. He was exhausted from the drive over and we both wanted to get back to town before nightfall. He radioed Brian Keating the girl's name. The road was a good bit darker but the sheep had all sought shelter somewhere beyond it and the rain had cleared, so it was an altogether smoother drive home and I put my foot down.

'You did good,' O'Neill said, and then he sunk back in the passenger seat and closed his eyes.

Foley had returned from Donegal and he was waiting for us in the station carpark. We followed him inside. He believed Joyce was lying but we needed to investigate this new line of inquiry. Eileen O'Connor's name was written in white chalk on the board. Foley had already precured a photo of Eileen from the school yearbook. He handed it around.

'Eileen's dark, McNight's dark and Baby Crónán too,' Foley said. Baby Crónán's tuft of black hair and the smell of bleach wafted into my mind. 'But you still believe Joyce is the mother?' I asked.

'Eileen is an A student, never missed a day of school, and frankly she's not fat enough to hide a pregnancy,' he said.

'Joyce wasn't fat. She isn't fat,' I said, insulted on her behalf.

'She's a hell of a lot fatter than Eileen O'Connor… Right, let's go waste some time,' Foley said. He was annoyed that we hadn't returned with a confession. He wasn't keen on going back to Donegal to re-interview Patrick McNight when his parents returned from their trip to Blackpool. From his whisperings with O'Neill, it seemed they didn't conduct their business the same way up there. In the meantime, he'd requested his medical records to confirm his blood type.

'We'll need a doctor to take a look at her,' he said, referring to Eileen, and this time I was ready for him.

'Dr Ciara Crosby will do it, and I'm not taking no for an answer,' I said and both men looked at me as if I had two heads. 'You weren't in the room with Nora. What was done to her is something she won't forget in a long time. You might not understand that, but a woman will,' I explained.

Foley nodded. 'Fine, then, if that will make you happy,' he said. I sighed with relief. If Eileen had to endure an examination, at least Dr Ciara Crosby would treat her with the kindness and dignity she deserved. It was a small win for me and for Eileen O'Connor.

CHAPTER ELEVEN

I sat in the back seat of the car. Foley took over at the wheel and O'Neill sat in the front passenger seat. It was just after eight p.m. when he pulled up outside the O'Connor house. It was in a fairly new estate, built only five years earlier. Most of the people in it were from outside the town, but the O'Connors had bought the show house after their chemist shop on Main Street burnt down due to an electrical fault. They had lived above it for many years and, thanks to their neighbours' help, they had escaped with their lives, but Declan O'Connor, having saved his family by shielding them with his own body, suffered third-degree burns to his back. They renovated the chemist shop using their insurance but, following the trauma they had endured, they never moved back into the upper floor. I didn't recognise Eileen's name when Joyce first uttered it – there were a lot of unrelated O'Connors in the town – but I knew her mother and father. We were on friendly terms, but I wasn't familiar enough with them to have formed an opinion on the kind of people they were.

–

Dr Crosby was waiting in her parked car, and we all headed for the house together after we arrived.

Declan O'Connor opened his front door. Brian had rung ahead to let them know we were coming. They weren't told much, only that the matter we needed to discuss related to their daughter, Eileen. Declan was stooped – the skin grafts on his back were tight and painful, pulling him out of shape. His wife Betty stood by his side and, behind them, stood Eileen. I recognised her from the shop as soon as I saw her. She wasn't just pretty, she was beautiful. Her brunette hair was long, shiny and luxurious, and her brown eyes were deep; she was as slim as she was tall, and perfectly proportioned. I immediately realised we were knocking on the wrong door. Foley introduced himself and O'Neill. I said hello and nodded to the family members. We moved to the sitting room at the front of the house: it was modern, with cream walls, a tiled floor, two big windows and a wooden fireplace. Above that was a large cross with Jesus Christ nailed to it, slumped and dying. The two sofas were still wrapped in plastic and at an angle to one another, one against the back wall, the other facing the fire. There was no sign of a TV in the room. Betty was instantly embarrassed. 'We tend to live in the kitchen at the back of the house,' she said by way of explanation. Eileen seemed worried about what she could have done to attract police interest. Clearly, her parents had questioned her for the thirty minutes it took us to organise ourselves to get to the house.

'I presume you've heard about the Baby Crónán case,' Foley said.

'There are men in spaceships who've heard of it. What has it to do with Eileen?' Declan asked.

'Joyce O'Reilly mentioned your daughter,' Foley said.

'We're in the same class but we're not friends,' Eileen said.

'There's a boy who might be Baby Crónán's father, and Joyce O'Reilly has made an allegation that your daughter was seeing him...'

'What boy?' Declan said.

'Patrick McNight,' Foley told him.

'I'm still clueless as to what you want with Eileen,' Declan said, and to be fair it was hard to explain. Eileen was standing before us in white, slim-fitting tennis gear.

'We need a doctor to confirm that your daughter isn't the mother of Baby Crónán,' Foley said, looking embarrassed. Declan looked to his wife and almost chuckled.

'Sure, that's obvious to a blind man,' he said.

'We just need to tick the box so that we can move on,' Foley said.

'It will just take a second,' Dr Crosby assured Eileen's parents. 'You won't even have to undress,' she said to Eileen.

'Okay, we can go to my room,' Eileen suggested. The two of them started to move away, when Eileen looked back at me. 'You can come too,' she said.

'Right,' I said and I followed them while Betty offered to make tea.

Eileen's room was painted a pale lavender, and her white duvet was adorned with lilacs. On her wall hung a framed poster of Clint Eastwood, arm in arm with an orangutan, from the film *Every Which*

Way but Loose. She perched on the edge of the bed. 'What now?' she said. Dr Crosby explained she just had to examine her stomach. Eileen pulled up her top and Dr Crosby rubbed her hands together to warm them before beginning her examination; it took less than five seconds.

'Patrick wasn't with any other girls,' Eileen said.

'How do you know?' I asked.

Eileen got off the bed, walked to the bedroom door and opened it. She cocked her head outside, listening to ensure her parents were nowhere within earshot. Then she closed the door again and leaned against it.

'He's not the father of that baby,' she said.

'Boys wander,' I said.

'Not this one.'

'Spit it out, Eileen.'

'He was injured a year ago.'

'Yes, a crush injury.'

'And guess what was crushed,' she said. Dr Crosby and I shared an awkward look. 'I don't know if he's recovered by now, but nine months ago he was a mess down there,' she said, pointing to the ground with her finger.

'Thanks, Eileen,' I said, taking notes.

'He just told me. I didn't see it… Or touch it,' she said to be clear. We left after that.

'Well, that was an interesting way to spend an evening,' Dr Ciara Crosby said to me as we walked together, following Foley and O'Neill outside. 'You're welcome,' I said and she slowed down as we reached her car. 'I heard the good news about Bridie,' I said.

'You should have seen her when I put that baby in her arms, she was elated,' she said. 'I've never seen a mood change so quickly – and Debbie, that poor girl, she was deeply traumatised by it all but she wouldn't leave her mother's side.'

'It is a traumatising sight to see,' I said with great authority. The men were now sitting in the car, smoking.

'You sound like a woman with experience,' she said.

'A girl with experience. I was there when Mammy had my sister. I can still see it,' I said, making a face that made Dr Crosby chuckle.

'It's beautiful, though, too, isn't it?'

'About as beautiful as a butcher's bin,' I said and she chuckled again. 'You're funny.' It was a compliment. I wasn't used to them.

'Right. I'll go,' I said, about to join the Dublin boys in an already smoke-filled car.

'Mary?'

I turned to face her.

'Could we maybe have a coffee or lunch or something? I left my family and friends behind in Galway, it gets lonely,' she said. I knew how she felt.

'Oh. Okay, I'd love to.'

'Yeah?'

'Great,' I said, genuinely delighted. I pointed to my uniform. 'And you know I'm a garda. People don't usually like gardaí,' I explained and she laughed.

'Well, I was always different,' she said.

'Me too,' I said and it felt nice just to chat to another woman my age. Then O'Neill rolled the window of the squad car down, releasing a plume of smoke into the night air.

'Will you come on, it's not a hen party,' he said. Ciara and I both laughed.

'Meet me on Saturday?' she said.

'I'll be working in the morning but I'm rostered off at two,' I said.

'Great. Say in the Green Cafe at two thirty?'

'See you then,' I said. She grinned at me and waved as she got into her car. *A friend*, I thought to myself. *Wouldn't that be a fine thing.*

I sat in the back seat.

'What was that about?' Foley said.

'Ciara wants to be my friend,' I told him and the two men arched their necks around to face me.

'Are you twelve?' O'Neill said.

'I'm twenty-eight.'

Foley turned to O'Neill and shook his head. 'She wants to be friends. *Women!*' he said and O'Neill tutted. They threw their cigarette butts out the window, as the ashtray was already overflowing. We drove on, with me in the back wearing a wide smile on my face.

'So we're back to O'Reilly and McNight,' O'Neill said after a minute or two of driving down the road.

'That crush injury Patrick McNight suffered, it was to his manhood,' I said. The two heads in front of me turned to face one another. 'That boy wasn't making babies with anyone last summer,' I said, before advising that the medical report we were waiting on would probably confirm it.

'For the love of… Why didn't he just say that?' Foley shouted.

'You know what men are like,' I said. The two men turned to look back at me, neither seeming impressed, and we were back to square one.

'So where does that leave us?' I asked. Neither man answered.

–

We parked the squad car at the station, not far from my own. 'Good night, so,' I said but Foley wasn't in the mood to return to his hotel room. 'We're going for a drink,' he said.

'Good for you.'

'You're coming.'

'I'm not,' I said. I was only fit for my bed.

'It's not a request,' he said. I didn't know what to make of that. 'Look, Shea, do you want to play with the big boys?' he asked.

'Yes, I do,' I conceded.

'So you need to *play* with the big boys,' he said. I didn't know what that meant and from the look on O'Neill's face, he didn't know either. He leaned over Foley's shoulder. 'Can I speak to you for a moment?'

Foley nodded. They moved away from me, but it must have been the way the wind was blowing, because despite his attempt to lower his voice, his words carried in my direction.

'It's bad enough she's working with us. Why are you asking her to drink with us?'

'We're a team, O'Neill.'

'Not with her, and anyway, the pub isn't designed for women,' O'Neill said.

'She's hardly the usual,' Foley said. 'She'll be grand.'

They both turned to me. 'Right, are you coming or not?' Foley asked.

'I'm coming,' I said, if only to prove a point to O'Neill.

The place was busy enough for a Monday night. It was small, with a square bar in the middle of the room, surrounded by stools. A bench seat lined the walls; mostly, it was standing room only. The word in town was that you didn't go to Pete's for comfort; you went there for the best pint in the county. I was not a pint drinker, and I'd been on my feet since vacuuming at first light, so O'Neill was proved right: the place didn't suit me at all. Dicey was at the bar, shouting a round. 'Is it a pint, boss?' he asked.

'Lovely,' Foley said.

'Same,' O'Neill shouted. When Dicey saw me, his face dropped. 'And a...?' Foley looked to me.

'Whiskey and ice,' I said.

'A whiskey and ice for the lady, Dicey.'

Dicey nearly choked on his own tongue. He turned away from us. We found a space to stand in amongst some of the Dublin lads and the Kerry boys. It was when Dicey was on the way back to us with drinks that I spotted Thomas O'Reilly. Standing beside him, near the dartboard, was Seamus. We noticed each other at the same time. Seamus nodded to me. I was annoyed. I'd warned him to stay away from Thomas. He told me he would, and there they were, together in the pub in full view of the guards. I wouldn't mind, but there were at least twelve other places they could have gone for a game of darts and a pint. Thomas noticed O'Neill and Foley just as Quinn walked into the place. Thomas wandered towards us as though drawn by a magnet. I could see the dart in his left hand, which he was clutching like a weapon. I walked up to him.

'How are you, Thomas?' I said and I was between him and the Dublin boys as Dicey turned to face us with the tray of drinks. Thomas didn't look at me, instead he was staring over my head. 'Why is my sister still in jail?' he asked, looking at O'Neill, not Foley. O'Neill stepped forward. 'Because there are still some outstanding questions to be answered.'

'Like what?'

'It's a police matter.'

'My innocent sister in a prison cell is a family matter,' Thomas said and Seamus was standing by his side by now.

'She's not so innocent, though, is she?' O'Neill said unnecessarily. This brought out a rage in Thomas that would be hard to quell.

'It won't be long,' I said, trying to calm things down, but Thomas wasn't for calming. He'd a few pints in him, I could see that by his stance. He was ready for a fight.

'Shut your mouth about my sister,' he said, raising his arm, still in a cast. 'You've some neck coming in here.'

'Last I looked, it was a free country,' O'Neill said.

'Step back,' Foley said to Thomas. 'Time to step back.'

'You're an animal,' Thomas said to O'Neill and that's when O'Neill stepped up to him. Dicey turned his back on the action to gently place the tray of drinks back onto the bar counter, as if his primary concern was saving them.

'What did you say to me?' O'Neill said. Foley watched, slow to intervene.

'You heard me,' Thomas said.

'Come on, Thomas. Let it go,' Seamus said.

'Let it go?' Thomas said to Seamus, 'Let it go?' He was looking from Seamus to Dicey and the Kerry lads. 'We were friends, we played together on teams, and you all stood back and watched that *animal* assault my father. They beat us so badly, my mother lied about my sister just so they wouldn't kill one of us.' He was shouting now, and the whole pub had fallen silent, everyone listening. No one raised a glass to their lips; everyone sat or stood, unmoving and quiet. No one even seemed to breathe. Thomas looked around at the statues surrounding him, all of them men, except for me.

'Joyce's face and our faces are on every newspaper in the country. The things they say about her, about us – every word is a lie. My sister is in jail for the sin of being afraid, my mother can't eat or sleep, my father is a shadow of himself,' he said, pointing at us. 'You've destroyed us.'

'We're just doing our jobs,' Foley said and that did not help matters one bit.

'Your jobs?' he said, raising his broken arm. 'Nice job you have there, Mr Foley.'

'It's Detective to you,' Foley said, and he was done with allowing Thomas the floor. 'Your sister is in a predicament of her own making. She is by no means in the clear. Do you understand?' he said to Thomas.

Then he looked around the room at all the people struck dumb. 'A baby boy was murdered... here... In this place... And it's my job to find who did it. Whatever the cost, I will do just that,' he shouted so that even people out on the street could hear him.

'Now go home to your family, Mr O'Reilly,' he said. Foley looked past Thomas, to Pete, the barman.

'Go home, Thomas. We don't want any trouble,' Pete said. The wind was taken from him; all the adrenaline that had kept him upright, had fuelled him, dissipated at the mere mention of Baby Crónán and what was done to him. Thomas O'Reilly was spent. Seamus grabbed him by his good arm. 'Come on, don't make things worse for Joyce,' he said.

'I've lost my appetite for drink anyway,' Thomas said, pushing past Quinn, who was standing just inside the door. They were a few feet down the road before people regained their senses and a new normal resumed. Dicey appeared in front of us with the tray of drinks. He handed out the pints but waited for me to pick up my own whiskey and ice. I smiled and said, 'Thank you,' sweetly to him but my mind was with the two boys. I watched the door to make sure no one followed them. Dicey looked to Foley and O'Neill. 'Never liked him anyway,' he said, referring to Thomas. 'Not much of a hurler, too soft.'

That word 'soft' played on my mind – where was he going with this? What did he know? 'Soft like his bones,' Dicey said after taking a sip of his drink. He was trying to get on side with the Dublin lads. It was pathetic.

O'Neill was fuming. 'Animal! Bleedin' neck of him,' he said.

'Let it go,' Foley told him.

'Easy for you to say. You don't have an investigation looming over your head.'

'It will go away,' Foley said.

'Doesn't look like it,' O'Neill said. 'I've a kid now. I can't have this...'

Foley put his arm on O'Neill's shoulder, 'We'll sort it.'

And that was it. I drank whiskey and listened to the men argue about football.

Afterwards, Foley insisted on walking me to my car.

'We've posters of the discarded clothes found in the bag going up on poles and in shop windows in every town in the county tomorrow morning. They were featured in the paper today and they'll feature on the evening news tomorrow evening.'

'Why not this evening?' I asked.

'The photos weren't good enough quality for TV or some other nonsense. Anyway, they are now,' he said.

'Okay.'

'I want you to read through all the statements tomorrow. Go through them with a fine-tooth comb. There's more coming in every day but if we could just place that woman, or women, who were wandering around this town in middle of the night, it would be something,' he said.

I agreed. 'It would.'

I got to my car. He opened the door and I got in. 'O'Neill is a good man,' he said.

'You've told me,' I reminded him. He closed the door and walked away.

I was halfway home before I spotted Seamus stomping along by the ditch. I slowed to a stop and rolled the window down. 'Get in,' I said.

'You're all right,' he said. 'I'd rather walk.' He was wearing jeans, a T-shirt and a jumper – no coat, no hat, no nothing. He was hugging himself as he walked. The only thing keeping him from freezing to death was his temper.

'It's too cold and you're not dressed for the weather. Get in.'

He thought about it and then he got in. As soon as I was driving, I said it, 'You promised.'

'I said I'd stay away from Thomas for a few days. That's what I did.'

'I meant until it all blew over, and you know that,' I said.

'But it's not blowing over, is it?' he said. 'And are you any closer to finding out what happened here?' I said nothing. 'Exactly,' he said. 'And now...' He was emotional. 'Thomas is talking about leaving.'

'Where?'

'Dublin. He wants me to go too.'

Seamus was an only child. His parents were getting on in age. It was hard enough to manage the farm with him, never mind without.

'Your parents will have to sell the farm,' I said and he remained silent.

'Will you go?' I asked. He continued to remain silent.

'Is that why you stayed all these years?' I said. 'For them?' He nodded slowly.

'It's no reason to stay anywhere,' I said.

'Well, thanks for your valued opinion.'

'You're welcome,' I said, ignoring his feeble attempt at sarcasm.

'Our farm has been in my family for three generations,' he explained.

'Well, you've had a good run at it, then,' I said and he laughed and then he laughed some more before becoming sad again. 'I can't leave.'

'What kind of life is it for you here?' I said and by then we were parked outside my small rented cottage.

'What kind of life is it for me anywhere?' he said.

'It's better in the city. Easier to hide. Easier to find people like yourself.'

'I've found a person like me right here.'

'But even if he stayed, what kind of life would you both have here?'

'Don't know,' he said and then looked at me. 'I wish it was you.'

'Me what?'

'That I wanted. I wish it was you.' The pints he'd consumed were clearly doing the talking.

'Why me?' I asked out of genuine curiosity, as opposed to any kind of vanity.

'Why not you?' he said.

'Well, I'm hardly pick of the litter,' I said and he chuckled again.

'You're smart and funny, even if you don't mean to be. You're a straight talker and you appreciate the quiet.'

'Sexy,' I said and he laughed. 'I do like the quiet, though, and I admire that in you too.'

'Can I kiss you, Mary?' he asked, out of nowhere.

'Why would you want to do that?' I said, and maybe it was because I had a whiskey in me, but the notion appealed to me. While my stomach never fluttered in his presence, he was handsome and kind, and part of me wished for a man to hold. *Why not him?*

'Just to see if I could bring myself to,' he said.

'No offence taken.'

'You know what I mean.'

'Go on, then,' I said, trying to stop from trembling. He leaned over and he placed his lips on mine. They felt solid enough. He placed his hand on my cheek and he rubbed his lips around a little. Then he pulled away, suddenly and sharply.

'It felt like kissing a wall,' he said.

'Or something rubber,' I said. That's when he cried. I felt like crying too. 'I'm sorry,' I said after a minute or two.

'It's not your fault, I'm the one whose wiring's all wrong.'

'And I'm wired right?' I said. He laughed as though I was joking but I was admitting something that worried me. 'I don't want to be alone forever,' I said honestly. 'But I don't know how to be anything else.'

He nodded. 'I understand that.'

'I should go inside,' I said. 'I'm doing a double tomorrow.'

He looked up the road towards his house. 'I don't want to lose him,' he said.

'So don't.'

'Easy to say.'

'Most things are easy to say. Doing things no one wants you to do, that's hard but it's worth it,' I said and smiled.

'Is it, Mary?' he asked.

'To be yourself? No doubt about it.'

'No matter the danger?'

'Every day, I walk into rooms filled with men. Tonight, in that bar, I was surrounded – some were drunk, and violence was in the air, as it often is. And I'm a woman, vulnerable to their anger, their egos, their sense of propriety. I can feel their force, their hatred, and sometimes their lust. That's the one that frightens me most. But I still do it. I still walk into those rooms.'

'Why?'

'Because I am Mary Shea and I choose the doors I walk through, that's why,' I said.

He pulled my head towards him and gently kissed me on the forehead. 'Good night, Mary Shea.'

'Good night, Seamus McEvoy,' I said, and in that moment, I wished we were different people, living different lives. It could have been nice.

CHAPTER TWELVE

Day Eight

I was surprised to see Thomas O'Reilly sitting in his van, parked in my yard, as I left for work at five thirty that morning. He didn't move when he saw me. He just stared my way. I walked up to the van, but he remained frozen in his seat so I knocked at the window. He rolled it down, and still he said nothing. I asked him to come in, if he wanted to talk. He clearly wasn't sure if he did or he didn't. He was mute. 'What is it? You didn't come here for no reason,' I said and it was then he came to life and stepped outside. He paced the muddy ground, looking out over the fields that Seamus worked and maybe beyond to where they found comfort in one another in the caravan. Still no words came from him. Maybe his thoughts were there, in that caravan, his refuge, or somewhere entirely darker; it was hard to tell. He had his back to me.

'I have to get to work,' I said. That made him turn my way.

He finally spoke. 'Seamus said I can trust you.'

'Okay,' I said.

'What does that mean?' he asked as he climbed up on the fence that separated the sheep in the field from the muddy path. 'Can I or can't I?'

'You can trust me with the truth and to act on it,' I said. He sat and thought about that.

'How is my sister?' he asked.

'She's afraid and grieving,' I said. 'But medically, she's fit.'

'That's something,' he said. I stood in front of him, looking up at him, the sky behind him showing a hint of blue.

'What is it, Thomas?'

'The pictures you put in the newspaper, they weren't clear,' he said and I realised he was talking about the clothes and the bag. Then he mentioned the coat and hat specifically. He told me he recognised them; his mother had a coat and hat like the ones in the photo. She told Thomas that she had given them to a local charity shop, along with other items of clothing.

My heart began to race. 'When?'

'A couple of months ago.'

'Did she drop them herself?' I asked. That's when he looked away from me.

'No. She said she gave them to Joyce to drop off.' *Heteropaternal superfecundation*. Two words Thomas O'Reilly didn't know existed, and with all roads leading back to Joyce O'Reilly... *Is it actually possible?*

'Why are you telling me?'

'Because if I don't, someone else will and you're the only one who hasn't decided against her,' he said.

'How do you know that?'

'Seamus said so.'

'How does he know that?'

'I don't know, but I trusted his instinct enough to come here,' Thomas said.

'I'll have to tell the Dublin boys,' I said.

'I know that.'

'If your sister did this, I can't change the outcome,' I warned him.

'I understand,' he said. He jumped down from the fence, strode to his van and drove away.

—

The Dublin boys were in the incident room, as well as Dicey and a few of the Kerry boys. Everyone was scattered around but there was talk about what had happened the evening before as I entered the room. I walked up to Foley.

'I need to speak to you,' I said. O'Neill and Quinn were standing by his side.

'What about?'

'Joyce O'Reilly,' I said.

'Go on.' I was hoping for a quiet word but he was unwilling to move. So I told them exactly what Thomas O'Reilly had told me. Foley sighed deeply.

'It was her. It had to be her,' Quinn said.

'And the mother? What if she's in on it?' O'Neil said.

'Well, clearly Joyce didn't drop those clothes anywhere,' Quinn said. Foley didn't speak; he just listened to us debating whether or not Joyce O'Reilly's mother had been lying to us all from the start. The coincidences were mounting and if there was two of them in it, it might help us make sense of how Baby Crónán made it to the beach. Maybe Breda disposed of one baby on the beach while Joyce gave birth to the other on the farm. If that was the case, could Breda O'Reilly have been in that coat and hat, carrying that bag on Appletree Lane? The jockey didn't get a look at her face and if it was her, what was she doing there? Why didn't she drive? She had a car. But maybe she did drive... Maybe she parked up – she's local, lived here all her life, she would have known about the access to the beach via Hickey's field. Foley ordered the boys to see if anyone could identify Breda's red Ford Escort parked in the vicinity of Appletree Lane on the night in question. There were still so many questions and theories. We just talked and talked.

'What if Joyce had the baby girl... She was dead, so she hid her away on the farm. Then she went into labour again, the mother found her and she killed the second baby.

'Maybe the plan was to bury him at sea but she was disturbed or...' Foley said before drifting off. It still didn't make sense. Why didn't Breda bury the baby on the farm?

'We need to bring her in,' Foley said with finality.

'Can we talk to her at home? They've been through enough,' I said. Foley thought about it. 'The press are still outside, it might bring problems in the long run,' O'Neill said. Foley nodded. 'Okay, let's go to the farm, hear what she has to say.'

–

Breda O'Reilly was cooking when we called. As soon as she opened the door, she asked about Joyce. 'How is she?'

'She's okay,' I said.

'Did you tell her I'm sorry?'

'I told her.'

'What did she say?'

'She cried,' I said and Breda looked like she might cry too. 'She was relieved to hear it,' I added and Breda nodded to me.

'We need to talk,' Foley said, pushing past her. She followed us inside.

'Should I call my husband and Thomas? They're at the yard,' she said. Then she looked up at the big clock on the wall and added, 'They'll be back for lunch in fifteen minutes.'

'That's time enough,' Foley said. We all sat around the large wooden kitchen table.

'You're here about the coat,' she said.

'Yes,' I confirmed. She repeated the story that Thomas had told me earlier that morning. Foley asked her to list the other items she had donated and she told him what she could remember: jeans, T-shirts, a denim jacket with a patch of Donald Duck. Foley asked about the scarf and the bag, but Breda maintained she didn't recognise them. 'They're not ours,' she said.

That's when he asked her if she was lying. She was taken aback. 'Did you see Joyce give birth?' he said.

'No. I did not.'

'Did you kill that baby boy?' he insisted.

'No, and neither did my daughter,' she shouted and rose up.

'How do you know she didn't kill the baby if you weren't in the shed with her?'

'Because she didn't give birth to that baby boy.' She was shouting louder now.

'You're so sure about that?'

'I am absolutely sure about that, Detective Foley, and since our first encounter I have been briefed on my rights, so I have nothing more to say until my solicitor arrives.'

Foley looked to me. 'Make a list of every vehicle on this farm, and check they are registered,' he said, before returning his gaze to Breda.

'If you know what happened, this is the time to tell me, because if you don't and we find that you were lying to us, covering for your daughter, yourself or any member of this family, it won't just be Joyce going to prison,' Foley said, but his threat wasn't going to work. Breda O'Reilly refused to be intimidated this time around. Foley moved to leave but I had one question I needed to ask before we went.

'The coat and hat... They were nice, in good condition too. Why did you give them away?'

'Too many people bought that set. It was just too common,' she said.

As we were leaving, Foley laid out the next steps of his investigation for Breda O'Reilly's benefit; he told her we'd list the vehicles at the house, in the yard, every last one of them. The Kerry boys would be sent out to canvass the people on Appletree Lane, Hillcrest and Potters Road to see if they recognised her or her daughter. We were going to speak to Joyce again and interview staff from the charity shop, and all the while he'd have men posted outside their house. She didn't respond, except to tell him that police were not welcome to park on their land. 'You can park on the main road, opposite the main gate,' she said.

Foley nodded. 'Fine.'

'And I'm not going anywhere,' she said.

'Not for the moment,' he said.

I found it hard to look at her. Thomas had come to me in good faith, but he came with information that looked very bad for both his mother and his sister. It was a tough conversation. But we had to know. We had to find who killed Baby Crónán and make sure something like that would never happen again. I'd be lying if I said it didn't make me feel uncomfortable.

—

The charity shop was small, cramped, and it reeked of mould. Rails and rails of clothes hung side by side, creating narrow pathways in and out of the place; toys were piled in one corner, books in the other. On the counter were two plastic butter boxes filled with broken bits of jewellery. I followed Foley through the narrow passageway between the rows of clothes. We made it to the counter where Aisling Quinn stood with a wide smile, welcoming us in and asking us to have a look around. Foley showed her his badge, explaining he wasn't shopping and this was in fact a police matter. Aisling's face fell a little. Then something clicked in her head. 'Oh, I know you,' she said, pointing her finger. 'From the news.' She was in her late fifties, a big lady with big hair. 'Ohhh.' She pointed at him again. 'Is this about the baby?' she said and there was a hint of excitement in her voice.

'It's about clothes,' he said. Suddenly, her finger was shaking.

'The hat and coat from the newspaper, did they come from here?' she asked, almost breathlessly.

'We're hoping you can tell us that,' Foley said.

'Oh God, I see.' She shook her head from side to side. 'I can't answer that, I'm afraid, I've only been here the past two weeks, covering from Lena Herrman.'

'Well, where is she?'

'Germany, visiting family, she's due home any day now. I'll be finishing up next week.'

'For the love of God,' he said and sighed. 'Anyone else work here?'

'Cara Lynch used to work here until a month ago.'

'Right, then, we'll need to speak to her,' he said.

'That would be hard,' Aisling said.

'She dropped dead on the shop floor,' I said and Aisling nodded.

'She was eighty-nine. Still, it was a shock.'

Foley rubbed his temples. 'Get Lena Herrman's details,' he said, deputising me, which felt good. He stepped outside and lit up.

–

Back in the incident room, some of the boys were on phones, ringing people in the area of Appletree Road or Hillcrest to see if they remembered any of the four vehicles registered to the O'Reillys; others were out, going door to door. 'What now?' I asked Foley.

'I need more before we go back to Joyce and before I talk to the press,' he said. 'I need more,' he mumbled. He looked tired.

'Maybe you should rest,' I suggested. He looked at his watch. It was after four p.m.

'I'd prefer a pint,' he said. He turned to the men standing there. 'Find me that vehicle, and anyone with information on those clothes, bring it to me.' Then he turned to me. 'Fancy a drink?' he said.

'It's four o'clock in the afternoon.'

'And I've been working since six this morning.'

I nodded and scanned the room to check where Dicey was; I didn't want him seeing me with Foley and presuming anything. In all honesty, I was worried that Dicey was right and Foley was looking for more than my input into this inquiry. It wasn't because he was sleezy – he wasn't, not at all – but he wanted my company, and I couldn't help but wonder why.

The hotel bar was a quiet lounge, suitable for their female guests. With the benefit of daylight I could take in the patterned carpet and the mirrors on the walls, all emblazoned with the word 'Guinness', along with old black-and-white historical photos of the town. The black leather-covered booths by the entrance were private, so that's where I headed while Foley ordered a pint for him and I asked for a shandy. Jenny was serving. She told us she'd drop the drinks over to us as soon as the pint was pulled. O'Neill and Quinn were nowhere to be seen. We sat in the booth, facing one another. He played with the beer mat while we waited.

'I think you should have something to eat,' I said.

'What are you, my ma?' he said, amused.

'No,' I said.

He called out to Jenny. 'And a packet of crisps.' He looked to me, 'You want some?'

'No.'

'Grand.'

She arrived with the drinks and placed them, and the crisps, in front of us. When she left, Foley sipped on his pint.

'Good stuff,' he said.

'Foley?'

'Yeah?'

'Where are the Dublin boys?' I asked. Their absence in the incident room was noticeable.

'They're making a statement about the night Thomas O'Reilly broke his arm,' he said and it was interesting the way he phrased it… broke *his* arm. Thomas didn't break his arm, O'Neill did. I didn't argue the point but I felt anxious, sitting in the lounge of the hotel in the afternoon, when there was so much work to be done. We were focused on Joyce and Breda O'Reilly, and nothing and no one else. It felt as though Foley had found his answer and it was only a matter of wrapping this up.

'So that's it? Joyce is the mother of Baby Crónán?' I said, disheartened and in disbelief at where we'd found ourselves. He took another sup from his pint.

'What do we know for a fact, Shea?' he asked.

'We know Joyce had a baby girl who was stillborn.'

'And?'

'And that Baby Crónán was born and died the same night.'

'We know Breda O'Reilly owned a coat and hat that match the ones worn by a woman carrying a heavy bag on Appletree Lane at nine fifteen that night,' he said.

'We know that there is access from Appletree Lane to Hickey's farm, which leads to the beach,' I said.

'What else?' he asked.

'The baby ended up on the beach. The bag and clothes ended up in the sea. And before dawn, our local vet saw a woman in only her nightdress walking on Hillcrest, the other side of Hickey's farm,' I said.

He drained his pint and opened the packet of crisps. 'There's a lot more we don't know. Still, it's a lot of coincidences,' he said, lifting his empty glass, signalling to Jenny he was ready for another pint. She was already halfway through pouring it when I spoke.

'It is,' I admitted, taking my first sip of shandy.

'I received the medical report on the crush injury. Patrick McNight did a real number on himself. One testicle was rendered infertile, but you only need one to work,' he said before offering me a crisp. I refused.

'You think he could have… Well… used his equipment… effectively… only a few months after such a significant injury?' I said, searching for the right words and blushing with embarrassment. He seemed to enjoy that; he chuckled to himself as Jenny handed him a second pint.

'You'd be amazed at the challenges a young man can overcome to use his equipment effectively. Joyce identified McNight in the first instance, and his blood type is O. The fact is, he's still the potential father of Baby Crónán,' Foley said. I thought about this.

'So *if* heteropaternal superfecundation is possible… It's a big *if*,' I said as he sat silently, sipping.

'Maybe it is, but it's what we've got. A case doesn't build itself,' Foley said, holding his glass in front of his face, examining it. 'And we'll need a fresh confession,' he added. The admissibility of Joyce's initial one was compromised.

'It still has to make sense,' I mumbled. And to me, it just didn't.

'Even if we build a strong case, killing an innocent will never make sense,' Foley said before draining the end of his pint and holding it up, indicating to Jenny that he was ready for the next one. 'Nothing odder than folk, Mary,' he said. 'Remember that and you'll go far.'

I drank from my shandy, wondering if my superior had just solved the murder of Baby Crónán or if he was blinded by prejudice, and the real answer lay far from the O'Reillys' door.

–

With Lena Herrman in Germany, Foley decided it would be best to go ahead and feature the clothing on the evening news. 'To jog memories.'

I was manning the phones, when Quinn and O'Neill came back and I joined Foley to greet them in the middle of the room.

'Well?' Foley asked.

'It's fine,' O'Neill said.

'And what does that mean?' Foley said.

'I told him it was an accident and Quinn backed me up.'

'Right, then,' Foley said. 'Let's hope that's the end of that.' The words weren't out of his mouth when Liam Kenny knocked on the door and opened it.

'Hi, lads. Sorry to disturb you – we got a call to the station. Raymond O'Reilly had a heart attack in the scrapyard this afternoon.'

'Is he dead?' Foley asked.

'No, but he's critical,' Liam said and O'Neill raised both hands in the air theatrically.

'Well, at least they can't blame me,' he said. Foley and Quinn didn't quite laugh, but they both smiled at him.

Liam and I shared a pained look. Maybe O'Neill didn't cause Raymond's heart attack, but he certainly didn't help. None of us did. The Dublin boys interpreted it differently; they saw it as a sign of guilt.

'We've got them,' O'Neill said. 'It's only a matter of time.'

–

I watched Foley address the press that night, standing tall on his podium outside the station. The items Foley was about to describe had been photographed and sketched in detail. A blown-up black-and-white photograph of the coat and hat rested on an easel beside him, and smaller copies were being handed out to the press. He was perfectly cast, framed by the dim glow of streetlights and the flickering bulbs of the cameras. 'These items were recovered as part of the ongoing investigation,' he began, gesturing to the first photograph on the easel. 'The coat is a royal blue with black square patterns and large black buttons. It has two side pockets and is accompanied by a matching royal blue bobble hat, with smaller black squares around the rim.' He paused, scanning the crowd of reporters and onlookers before continuing. 'We've traced the coat and hat to a specific chain of shops, and we're appealing to anyone in the local area who recognises them to come forward. Maybe you've seen someone wearing them recently or know of someone, locally, who owns a similar set,' he said and a journalist in the front row raised his hand.

'What do you consider local?' he asked.

'The county of Kerry,' he replied. 'But we're not ruling out connections beyond that.' It wasn't a lie. We weren't ruling anything out but we'd be hard-pressed to rule anything in that didn't align with our current theory.

He shuffled the photographs, showing one of the scarf and describing it as, 'burnt orange, made from recycled polyester'. He went on to explain that while there was no branding, it was obvious it wasn't homemade. The next photograph was of the shopping bag, which he described as, 'made of a thick woven plastic, size seventy by seventy centimetres by thirty centimetres, with red and blue stripes and red woven handles'.

The cameras clicked and whirred as Foley went on to describe the importance of public co-operation in the investigation. *We'll be overrun,* I thought. The press erupted, firing questions at him thick and fast.

'What more can you tell us?'

'Has anyone else been identified?'

'What about Joyce O'Reilly?'

'When are you letting her go?'

'This is an appeal. Our aim today is to identify who these items belong to, so it will help us build a picture as to what occurred on the night of Sunday 20 January, leading into the Monday morning of 21 January,' Foley said, dismissing further questions with a wave of his hand. He was done. The press conference was over. I walked across the road and into the hotel, where I saw Dicey sitting on the chair just inside the door, smoking a cigarette. Jenny was behind the reception, typing. I moved to go past him.

'Too big-headed to say hello now?' he said. We never said hello to one another.

'Still the same sized head as ever,' I said. He started to walk behind me, closing in as I moved towards the incident room, hoping that someone was in there. I was unlucky. It was empty. The lads had used the press conference as an excuse to go for a bite to eat in town. I told myself to be calm and turned to face him.

'Is there something I can do for you, Dicey?' I asked.

'You can rein in your attitude,' he said, pushing up against me.

'Step back,' I said.

'Step back? I'll step back when I'm good and ready,' he said and I could feel the warmth of his breath on me.

'You think you're something special – you're not. You're just some skirt.' He was leaning down over me, and his hand moved to flick my skirt. I pulled back, thinking a million thoughts, all of them related to how I could get out of this without punching him square in his face, with my dignity intact and without causing a fuss. He had me by the skirt, his hand sliding slowly up my thigh, when there was a knock at the door. It was Jenny.

'Garda Shea?' she said in a loud voice.

'Yes, Jenny,' I said, my voice betraying a slight wobble. His grip released. He leaned over me, picked up a file.

'There's a call for you at reception.'

'Thank you,' I said. I moved, and Dicey moved to block me.

'It's urgent,' she said. He slid out of my way. I tried to stay calm but I was walking at pace. I followed her into the hall and reached the desk, but the phone was on the hook.

'There's no call,' she said and I sank onto the chaise longue, needing just a moment to collect myself. She sat beside me. 'I heard some of the boys making jokes about Foley favouring you over Garda McCarthy. He didn't take it well. I thought he might be waiting for you,' she explained. She'd saved me from whatever indignity he had conjured in his mind.

'Thanks, Jenny,' I said almost in a sigh. 'Thank you so much.'

'We have to stick together,' she said.

'That's right,' I agreed, nodding to her. 'I really appreciate it, Jenny.'

She stood up and moved off towards the bar, where a man was waiting to be served. I looked at my watch; my shift was done with and I was desperate to go home.

I left the hotel and in an effort to avoid the press, who were still standing between me and my parked car at the station, I walked down the street, turned the corner and found myself outside Dr Ciara Crosby's practice. The light was on. I rang the bell and I could see through the glass door that her receptionist had gone home. I was about to walk away when she came out of her office, her glasses perched on her head. She pulled them down onto her face as I waved through the glass. She smiled, picked up some pace and opened the door.

'Hello?' she said.

'Hi,' I said, and my face must have given me away.

'You okay?' she asked.

'No,' I said and that's when I started to cry. I couldn't stop myself. The tears poured out of me, an unstoppable torrent. Ciara wasn't bothered by it in the least.

She put her arm around me and closed and locked the door. 'Come on in.'

I found myself in a back room she'd turned into a small kitchenette. There was a sink, some white cupboards and a little counter. A table with two chairs was all that could fit in the space. On the wall above the table hung a framed poster of a whale leaping out of deep blue water. 'You just cry till you're empty,' she said, pouring water into the kettle. 'I'll make tea.'

So I cried for Baby Crónán, for Nora, our terrorised witness, for Lily, for the widow Bridie Fitzmaurice, for Thomas and his broken arm, for Raymond's broken heart, for Seamus and his terrible dilemma, and for Joyce and Breda, whose fate hung in the balance. But mostly I cried for myself. The kettle was boiled and the tea poured by the time I ran dry. Ciara was sitting opposite me; a box of tissues had magically appeared on the table between us. I was clutching a handful, already sodden through. She lifted the bin and I threw them in it, before grabbing some more and drying my face.

'You needed that,' she said.

'I did. I didn't know how much,' I agreed, then I apologised.

'Don't be sorry. Drink your tea,' she said. I drank my tea even as the sadness was threatening to overwhelm me again.

'Dicey McCarthy laid his hands on me,' I said. She leaned forward in her chair and I could see the anger rising in her. 'He didn't get further than my thigh, but I just froze, like a dead fish on ice in a supermarket. If Jenny hadn't come in, what would he have done? What would I have let him do?' I asked.

'It's not your fault,' she said.

'I'm trained.'

'No one is trained for that,' she said. She was right. 'He has everything on his side, Mary, and we... We have to be wily. It's all we have.'

'Wily?' I said and she nodded.

'That's right,' she said.

'Can I ask you something?'

'Depends on what it is.'

'What would you do?' I asked.

'You mean what did I do?' she said. Of course, it had happened to her too. 'I laughed. I threw my head back and I laughed at him. He asked me what was so funny, and I told him he wouldn't understand – but his wife would. It threw him right off.'

'Well, aren't you the wily one...'

'The wiliest,' she said and suddenly we were both laughing. Jenny and Ciara had reminded me of how important it was for us women to stick together. I was reminded that my gut was screaming that Joyce was a victim and Breda was telling the truth. As easy as it would be to conform, to go with the flow, to reach an easy conclusion, to build a case around it, I couldn't and I wouldn't. I needed to make sure we weren't getting it all wrong.

'What do you know about blood groups?' I asked.

'What do you want to know?'

'Joyce O'Reilly is blood group A. Baby Crónán is blood group O – how many different blood groups mixed with an A make an O? And does that question even make sense?' I asked as her eyes clouded over. I was tired, it had been a long day.

'It only makes sense if you still believe Joyce is the mother of Baby Crónán, but she can't be.'

'All I can do is ask questions. It's my job on the line.'

'Okay, I'll play along. If Joyce is blood group A, she could have had sex with a male whose blood group is, A, B or O. The only blood group incapable of producing O is AB,' she said. *That's what Foley said.*

'So what you're saying is O is as common as muck.'

'Exactly,' she said.

'So two people having it in common is not particularly coincidental?'

'Not at all,' she said.

'Thanks, that helps.'

'I'm glad.'

I stood up to leave. 'Don't let them get you down,' she said, as though she could read my mind.

'Be wily.'

'Always.' She grinned.

We walked to the door and she let me out. 'Thanks, Ciara,' I said.

'Are we still on for lunch on Saturday?' she asked.

'Definitely.'

—

The carpark was empty; all the cars were gone, except for mine, which sat alone in the dark. I glanced around as I walked to it – no one was in sight, but then suddenly Foley managed to pop up out of nowhere. 'There you are,' he said.

I jumped a million miles into the air. 'God alive!' I shouted.

'Oh sorry, I didn't mean to frighten you,' he said.

'You didn't frighten me. You startled me, there's a difference. Where were you hiding anyway?' I asked him.

'I wasn't hiding. I was bending behind your car to tie my shoelace, there's a difference,' he said. I chuckled, not because I was amused but because I was relieved. 'You disappeared,' he commented.

'My shift was over. Actually, I was speaking to Dr Crosby about blood groups. The fact is O is really common.'

'Mary,' he said.

'It's one less coincidence, that's all.'

'Joyce O'Reilly admitted an hour ago that she gave birth to, killed and disposed of Baby Crónán. She says she acted alone.' My heart sank in my chest. I needed to sit.

I opened my car door and slumped on the seat with my legs out. He stood looking at me. 'It's over.'

'But she couldn't have taken Baby Crónán to the beach on her own,' I reminded him.

'She's signed a confession,' he said.

'It's not true.'

'Sometimes you have to know when to take the win,' he said and he walked off. I jumped up and I called out, 'Foley?'

He stopped and turned to face me. I ran towards him and stopped just short of him.

'Did someone tell Joyce O'Reilly her mother was in the frame for this?' I asked.

'Yes,' he said.

'And her father's condition?'

'Her solicitor passed on the news,' he said.

'This isn't a win. This is failure,' I told him and he didn't protest. He just walked on. I got into my car and drove home. I locked and bolted my front door. I undressed and soaked in the bath. I thought about Joyce, in a cell somewhere, facing years if not her whole life in prison, and my gut was screaming. *No.*

CHAPTER THIRTEEN

Day Nine

Now that Joyce O'Reilly was charged with the murder of Baby Crónán, the boys from Dublin were just dotting their i's and crossing their t's. They didn't need much local assistance and Brian Keating made sure we were all aware that any overtime we'd signed up for was now finished. It marked the end of me being useful, no doubt about that. Dicey McCarthy went back to using me to type his statements, ignoring me, abusing me at will. It was worse now; he felt the need to put me back into whatever box he thought I belonged in. I was slowly overtaken by a sense of doom.

I needed to shop for food, as there was none in the house, but I didn't have the will or the energy. I needed to wash clothes, but I spent much of the morning sitting on a hard chair at my kitchen table, staring out the window, unfocused. I wasn't due into work until two p.m. It was cold outside, really frigid, and I was so spent, I had to fight the urge to curl up and hide.

After some time, I mustered the strength to rise and start moving; a single thought propelled me forward – the thought of Baby Crónán and the promise I made him. I pulled on a pair of woollen tights under my jeans and wore a long-sleeved vest under my cable-knit jumper. I grabbed my wellies and coat and put them on before walking out of the house. It was already mid-morning. I drove to town and stopped at the flower shop. I went inside and picked up a nice small bouquet; the woman behind the counter was new to town and I'd never met her. She had a foreign accent that was unidentifiable but her English was very good. She offered me a choice of chocolate in exchange for a donation of money to the charity box. I hadn't eaten, so I popped some change into the box and chose something with caramel in it. I ate it on the way to the graveyard. When I got there, my fingers felt sticky from the caramel which, on further inspection, turned out to be out of date. It started to rain but it didn't put me off; instead, it just spurred me on. I closed up my coat, right up to my neck, and held the bunch of flowers close to my chest while following the path I'd mapped out in my head.

I kept moving, head down, towards the tall weeping tree, then past the broken bench, and after a couple of turns, I reached the grave of Catherine Goggins. Beside her I found the fresh earth covering the tiny box holding Baby Crónán. It was mucky but I sat anyway. The coat could be cleaned and I wanted to feel close to him. I placed my hand on the soggy earth; it was freezing but I didn't care.

'Hello, Crónán, I thought I'd just sit with you awhile. If that's all right.' The sky was heavy with cloud and rain but there was a crack above us, revealing a hint of blue sky. I fought the urge to lie down with him in the mud.

'Father Cunningham says you are in the arms of the Lord, that you're in heaven. Whatever or wherever that is. If you are sentient, if you have a life somewhere other than here, I hope you are safe and happy.' I was numb, verging on despairing. I grieved the boy I didn't know, while facing my own demons too. I wasn't myself. My mind was weighed down with so many troubles that I was finding it hard not to drown in them. So I just talked to him. 'They say you are the son of a young girl, her name is Joyce O'Reilly. They say you are some sort of twin. I don't think that's right. Maybe I'm wrong but… Are you Joyce O'Reilly's son? Did she kill you? Did her mother, her father or even Thomas? Is she covering for one of them? I wish you could talk to me. Am I right to question my superiors?' I looked up to the sky in time to see the tear above us widen, revealing more blue sky. 'Is that a yes? Is that you, ripping a hole in the sky, Crónán?' I asked. *How desperate am I?* I thought. *Do you even care about matters on earth?* I wondered. *I care.* 'I care that you are in the ground and that Joyce is saying she did something she couldn't have done.'

The more I thought about it, the surer I was. *She couldn't have done what she said she'd done, not alone. It's impossible. Isn't it?* It was at that point that I realised I might be unfit for duty, sitting in the rain and mud, talking to a dead baby in a box. I wondered about myself. Was this job too big for me? Were my father, Dicey McCarthy and the likes of him right – was policing no job for a woman? 'What do you think, Crónán?' I asked him. 'Am I just banging my head against a wall?'

No answer came, no sign from God or those beyond; it just continued to drizzle with rain and I sat there in the cold mud, feeling dejected.

–

Seamus was waiting for me when I arrived home. He was sitting in his car. He got out to greet me and, seeing me covered in mud, he asked the question anyone would ask, 'What happened to you?'

'Nothing,' I said. I opened my door before pulling off my wellies and walking inside. He followed. I pulled off my coat and dumped it on the floor. I washed my hands. He sat at the table.

'Do you want tea?' I asked.

'Yeah,' he said. I poured water into the kettle and clicked it on to boil.

'You heard,' I said, referring to the news about Joyce.

He nodded. 'She confessed because she's scared for her family.'

'I think that's true.' I kept my back to him. 'But a baby is dead and someone murdered him. What evidence there is points to her, that's also true,' I said.

'So is that it? Her life is over?' he said and I turned to face him.

'I don't know, Seamus.'

'And what are you going to do?' he asked me, and his voice was thick with emotion.

'Part of me feels like giving up,' I said and I plonked down on the chair beside him. 'Life is so unfair.'

He nodded. 'Can't let them win, though,' he said after a time. The kettle had long boiled, but neither of us felt the need to actually pour or drink the tea, so we remained sitting.

'I don't know what to do,' I admitted. That was the thing, I was lost. Unsure. For the first time in my life I didn't know what to do. It was unnerving.

'Do your job,' he said. 'You have a nose for things, nothing gets past you. Keep digging. Please.'

I expelled the air from my lungs, rubbed my nose, and asked him and myself the same question. 'What if I'm wrong?' I'd never been involved in something with such high stakes. The burden was becoming heavier with each breath I took.

'You are not trying to hurt anyone, Mary, all you are doing is looking for the truth. If you find it, I'll believe it,' he said.

'What if it's her?' I asked him. 'Thomas's sister. What if his mother or any of them were involved?'

'Then they deserve to be punished.'

Suddenly, I felt a little energy return. The gloom still hovered above me but it had lifted from my bones.

'So, I'll keep looking,' I said to him and he smiled.

'Thanks,' he said.

'Don't thank me, I'm as lost as you are.'

I took a shower and changed into my uniform. I dreaded going into the station or that room where Dicey had threatened and touched me. I remembered the look in his eye, the viciousness, the hatred that sent shivers down my spine. I couldn't report it – what could I say? I'd have to be more careful around him, around them all. I parked in my usual spot and headed inside. Brian was in his office. He called out to me.

'Mary?'

I walked in. 'How are you feeling about things?' he said.

'Fine,' I replied, lying.

'It's a good result, Mary,' he said and I ignored the bait.

'Where's Foley now?' I asked.

'He's in the incident room, waiting on Dr Boyne.'

That gobdaw, I thought. 'For what?' I said.

'He may have a theory as to how Joyce could have been solely responsible for the crime.'

My feet were walking out of the place before my brain kicked into gear.

'Mary?' I heard Brian shout out. 'I have something else for you,' he said as the door of the police station slammed behind me. I ran across the road and into the hotel, saluting Jenny before running into the room where Foley was introducing Dr Boyne to the men. The Dublin fellas were there, as well as some of the Kerry lads. Dicey was nowhere to be seen.

'This is Dr Fredrick Boyne. I spoke to him earlier this morning about what could have occurred on the night of Sunday 20 January,' Foley said as I pulled up a chair, focusing on hearing Boyne's opinion of what had happened and how it was all medically possible. I didn't respect him. I'd been in the room when he unnecessarily asked a young woman to spread her legs. I was there when he turned his back on her, leaving her lying there exposed while he basked in his own power. I'd heard the joke he made at Nora's expense: *There was only one virgin to have a baby.* It struck me as ironic that this man deemed himself capable of putting the case together for us. His arrogance was astounding, but from the demeanour of everyone else in the room, it was clear I was the only one astounded by it. They were all leaning forward, rapt, waiting for Dr Boyne to solve all our problems.

'Gentlemen,' he began. If he saw me, he certainly didn't attempt to include me. 'I've spoken with Detective Foley and although I can honestly say I hadn't heard of heteropaternal superfecundation before, I do concede that having reviewed an article, it's entirely plausible.'

He read an article?! Great expert.

'But the question Detective Foley is currently wrestling with is how Joyce O'Reilly could have birthed twins and managed to get herself from that yard through the field and onto that beach, in that state she was in,' he said.

'What state is that?' I asked.

'Excuse me?' he said.

'Well, do you have the hospital report?' I asked.

'Detective Foley explained to me—'

'No disrespect, but Detective Foley has personally admitted he has no idea of the intricacies laid out in the medical report and, as a result, he has no real understanding as to the true extent of Joyce O'Reilly's injuries,' I said.

Foley raised his eyes to heaven. Boyne seemed less sure of himself, all of a sudden looking over to Foley. I could hear grumbles from the Dublin boys.

'Garda Shea,' Foley said.

'Yeah?'

'Shut up,' he said and a few of the Dublin fellas laughed. He nodded to Boyne. 'Go on.' Boyne straightened up a bit and, facing the men, he began to speak again. 'When I was training in the late 1960s in Cork, there was a woman who had given birth at home. She was alone at the time – her husband was a sailor, away at sea. It was her first child, stillborn, and the injury you described, Detective Foley, sounds very similar to the one she sustained. She lived four miles outside of

Cork city. She didn't drive. It was the dead of night. She arrived at the hospital, carrying the dead child. She'd walked the whole way.'

'Four miles at a leisurely pace is around four hours,' Foley said. 'Not to mention how much longer it should take with an injury...'

'Well, she arrived to us in the hospital just after midnight, and her child was born at ten thirty-two that evening – the woman could tell us because there was a clock in the room and she made sure to check it,' Boyne said.

'So you're saying she jogged?' I asked.

'I'm saying it's a proven fact that with a certain level of adrenaline in the body, a person is capable of incredible things,' he said.

'Or she wasn't as injured as Joyce, or maybe her clock was broken...' I said and Dr Boyne's mouth formed a sneer. I stood up in disbelief.

'Is this what we're going to hang the case against this young girl on?' I asked, looking around the room. I pointed to Dr Boyne. 'Using an ancient anecdote told by this gobdaw,' I said and Dr Boyne blanched. The Dublin boys laughed, some of the Kerry fellas too, but Foley wasn't amused. Neither was I.

'Shea,' Foley said.

'Yeah.'

'Get out.'

I left. Joyce O'Reilly was a vulnerable, grieving, shamed young girl, who would do anything to save her mother and her family from further harm. I wasn't there when she pleaded guilty but I saw how they worked, those Dublin boys. I wondered whether or not O'Neill and Quinn had paid a visit to her while they were giving their statements. Was it O'Neill who had whispered into her ear that her mother was being implicated, or the fool Quinn? I wanted no part of it and instead of allowing the feeling of doom to overwhelm me, the anger that was rising within fuelled me. I needed to do something. I needed to work things out for myself. I got into my car and drove to the O'Reilly scrapyard. I opened my car boot and grabbed an old ratty gym bag that had been in the car when I bought it. There was a box with tools in it. It probably weighed around six pounds. I placed it in the bag. Thomas saw me and walked over.

'Can I leave my car here?' I said. He eyed the bag. I kicked off my shoes and threw them in the boot of the car. Wearing no shoes wasn't the same impediment as being ripped apart but in rougher terrain it would slow me down. I shut the car boot down.

'What are you doing?' he asked.

'Trying to make some sense out of this madness,' I said.

'Good luck,' he said before walking away. I swung the bag into my arms and started off from the edge of the farm,pu planning to walk along the back roads and up through Appletree Lane, timing it all the way. I hopped the wall and followed my nose towards the sea; it wasn't the exact trail she followed – it couldn't be, the farm was vast – but I knew to head south so I walked the land, passing the cows and sheep in their fields, and through the trees and over the fences, and it was cold and the bag got heavier with each minute. I kept going, holding the gym bag, imagining it was him, Baby Crónán, hugging it close to me. Finally, I cut through the bushes and found the gap in the large fencing that separated Paddy Hickey's field from the small road that backed onto the beach. I made my way through it, crossed the road, found my way onto the grass and the dunes, and kept walking until I saw the lifeguard tower. The rain had stopped an hour or two before I set out. The cold was still in the air but without the damp, it felt crisper, the atmosphere not as depressing. I saw the tall grass, and I made my way to it – that dune, the place where he had briefly rested, the cradle. The beach was empty; the tape had been taken away days earlier, and the boys no longer blocked people's passage, but no one came here. It could have been the bad weather but that hadn't stopped them before; maybe they just needed time. I continued along the rough path until I reached my destination and there, in the dune, sitting crossed-legged and with his eyes closed was Detective Matt Foley.

'God almighty!' I exclaimed, stumbling backwards. He opened his eyes in time to see me land on my behind.

'Sorry, I didn't mean to startle you,' he said, his tongue firmly in his cheek. I wondered if he'd had a vision or some sense I'd appear. He didn't seem fazed at all.

'What are you doing here?' he asked innocently. I sat cross-legged, the same as him, except I tucked my skirt under my knees. He was staring at my bare feet. 'I walked from the O'Reillys' scrapyard,' I said, holding up the gym bag.

'How long did it take you?' he asked. I looked at my watch.

'Three hours, ten minutes.'

'You're a slow walker,' he said.

'I'm a reasonable enough walker and it's not exactly a straight line.'

'From the farm, it took me two hours and forty minutes, but of course, I was wearing shoes,' he said with a smile.

'And you weren't torn in two either,' I said before thinking on. *Hold on.* 'When?' I asked.

'As soon as we worked out the triangulation between Appletree Lane, Hickey's Farm and the beach. I got the farmer, Hickey, to show me the old shortcut. Still, that only shaved off a few minutes,' he said.

'It had to take her much longer than both of us if she was injured, carrying a baby. I don't care what Boyne says,' I told him.

'Say four hours,' he said. 'The problem is because of the decomposition of the poor creature, Waters can't get a tight enough timeline on Lily's death, but he told us that Baby Crónán was dead just shy of twelve hours when Nora Fitzgerald's dog found him here.' He sighed a sorry sigh, looking around at the place: the beauty of the blue sky with passing white clouds above us, the white powdery sand that seems to go on for miles beneath us, the green of the tall marram grass that offered small protection from prying eyes – for us this gentle place would be forever juxtaposed with the horrifying image of a murdered infant.

'Even injured, Joyce could have made it here within the timeframe,' he said.

No way, I thought and I didn't care what the idiot Boyne said. I inhaled the crisp clean air and closed my eyes.

'You don't want it to be her,' he said.

'That's not true. I don't want to be wrong about her,' I said.

We sat there in the cradle and I told him I wanted to visit her.

'No.'

'But I—'

'The answer is no.'

'Why not?'

'Because I'm in charge of the investigation and I say so,' he said.

'What if she wants to see me?' I asked.

'You tell her it's not permitted,' he said.

'And if I go on my day off?'

'I'll make sure you're fired for it,' he said. He wasn't joking. I relented.

'So what now?' I asked.

'The case is going to the DPP. He'll decide whether there's enough evidence to charge her.'

'Why wouldn't he, if she's admitting it?' I said.

'Oh, he'll charge her all right. Her solicitor has already indicated that he wishes to defend her on the basis of diminished responsibility.'

Joe O'Callaghan was already discussing pleas? My gut was screaming now. *She didn't do this.* I felt sick. If I was wrong and she did it, well, then she deserved what she got and there were plenty that were willing to make that happen. *But if I was right, there was only me left to fight for her. I just didn't know how.*

'Okay. When are you leaving?' I asked. The boys were already talking about all the things they were going to do when they got back to Dublin. Mostly it was drinking, golf and a bit of *how's your father with the missus.*

'A few days, all going well,' he said.

'Well, thanks,' I said.

'For what?'

'For including me, for letting me do my job.'

He nodded. 'You have talent, Shea,' he said and, stupidly, I blushed. It was nice to hear it.

'Thanks.'

'But...' he said. I put up my hand to stop him.

'Don't ruin it.'

He laughed. 'You have a lot to learn.' He said it kindly. Helpfully.

'And no one to teach me,' I lamented. Brian Keating wasn't going to and Dicey would do anything but teach me; given the chance, Liam would let me have a go but, sure, he wasn't that confident of things himself.

'I know it must be hard for you, being a woman... in this business,' he said.

'Can I tell you something?' I asked him out of nowhere. He nodded. 'There's only one thing that makes it hard.'

'What's that?'

'The people I work with,' I admitted. I said it because despite me believing with everything in me that he was wrong about Joyce, I trusted him too. I can't explain why, except that he was the first person in the job to trust me.

'You mean the men you work with,' he said and I nodded. He thought about that. 'I hope I'm not one of them.'

'You're not like them,' I said and then I thought about it. 'You're not like anyone.' And I meant it. He could really see people. He could really see me for who I was. He smiled at me.

'Well, I'm going to take that as a compliment.'

'You should. But Foley, I still think you're wrong about Joyce,' I said, jumping up.

'Oh, I know, Mary. I know.' Then he told me he had the car parked nearby and asked me where I'd parked mine.

'O'Reilly's yard.'

'Grand, I'll drive you back.'

'Thanks.'

'But first you're going to have to pull me up, my bleedin' leg's gone dead,' he said, offering me his hand. I chuckled and pulled him into standing. 'And we need to stop to get some food, I'm famished, and then Brian Keating is looking for you. He's not happy.'

'Okay,' I said and walked through the dunes and towards the carpark, where Foley had left his car. As we were walking back, I saw Fidelma Regan across the road from us leaving her house and I thought to myself, *I need to speak to her about the pills.*

–

The Green Fields was a pub out on its own, near the O'Reillys' place. Back then people could still have a drink and drive, so it was busy enough when we arrived after eight o'clock that night. They didn't offer anything more than sandwiches wrapped in cling film. They were egg mayonnaise, and had been sitting behind the bar counter for most of the day, but were tasty enough. Foley insisted I eat mine with cheese-and-onion crisps. 'It's lovely. Trust me,' he said. It sounded wrong but it was a pleasant enough combination. He drank Guinness, referring to it as dessert. I asked him about his wife; it was my subtle way of reminding him that he had a wife, *if* he was sniffing around after me. Despite everything, Dicey McCarthy's voice was still in my ear, telling me that I was only good for one thing, and it wasn't solving cases. Foley smiled warmly when I brought her up.

'Imelda,' he said. 'I call her Mellie.' And immediately, he was touching his gold band with his thumb.

'Where did you meet?' I asked.

His smile widened. 'I saw her on the street and I just froze. She was the most beautiful thing I had ever seen.' He was back there, lost in that moment in his head, on that day, seeing his wife for the very first time. 'She kept looking at her watch and just as she moved to walk away, I found the courage to walk up to her. I told her I was really glad that some fool had stood her up because I wanted to take her for a cup of tea and, if that went well, a walk on St Stephen's Green. We were married six months later.'

'That sounds lovely,' I said, and I meant it; he obviously loved her deeply. My concerns about him having any designs on me faded. 'Any kids?' I asked.

'Mellie likes to paint. You should see her landscapes, something else...' he said, shutting down the question.

'I love a landscape. Does she sell them?'

'Nah, she paints because she loves it.'

'If she's that good, why doesn't she sell them?' I asked.

'Not everything is about making money,' he said.

'I never said it was, but why keep a talent like that hidden?' I asked.

'It's not hidden, it's all over our house, at her mother's place, her sisters', her friends'. We have boxes of it... I'm sure I could root out a few for you and send them, when this is over.'

'I'd like that,' I said and I meant it. The cottage walls were bare.

'She's sick,' he said out of nowhere and, quite suddenly, he was brimming with sadness. It was as though he'd just remembered it.

'I'm sorry,' I said, embarrassed by him fighting emotion.

'Hmm. Me too,' he said, seemingly happy to stay in the moment, to think of her, to lament her.

'Can I ask what's wrong?' I asked.

'A heart condition,' he said, now attempting to conceal his pain with a smile.

'Shouldn't you be with her?' I said.

'She's had it for years, keeping it at bay, she's a survivor, my missus... Anyway, she likes it when I'm away, we talk on the phone and I tell her all about my days. She has a nurse when she needs one, but mostly she manages okay.' He stopped talking abruptly, before changing the subject. 'I told her about you.'

'And what did you say?' I asked, not really sure that I wanted the answer.

'I said I was dealing with a horse that wouldn't be broken.'

I wasn't that taken with the analogy. *A horse? I suppose it's better than a donkey.* 'What did she say?'

'She told me to enjoy it, there's nothing quite like seeing a wild horse running free,' he said and smiled to himself.

I wasn't sure what to make of that. 'I'm not much of a runner,' I said and he laughed at me. He finished his pint. 'Let's get that car of yours.' It was nine thirty; my shift was over at ten.

As I left his car, I turned to tell him once again how sorry I was about his wife. 'Don't be. She plans on being around as long as you or me, and my wife gets her way,' he said and he grinned.

'Good night,' I said.

'Good night,' he replied. I drove back to the station to seek out Brian Keating, who had wanted a word, but he'd left hours earlier. I left a note on his desk, just to cover myself. O'Neill was sitting at a typewriter, smoking a cigarette.

'You see Foley?' he asked.

'Yeah, I think he's gone back to the hotel,' I said.

'Where were you?'

'At the beach, where Baby Crónán was found.'

'Why?'

'I walked it from the O'Reillys' yard to time it.'

'And?' he said, leaning in. 'Was Boyne right?'

'They'll say it's possible.'

'Who'll say?'

'You'll say.'

'And what about you, Mary?' he asked.

'I'll disagree,' I said.

He shook his head. 'Then it's a good thing no one cares what you think.'

'Not for Joyce,' I said.

He sniffed and talked to himself. 'My love, my baby girl, I'm coming home.' He was looking above him, as though his family were in the sky. Quinn walked in with two teas.

'Why are you smiling?' Quinn said to O'Neill.

'Because in a couple of days we are out of this kip,' he said, turning to me. 'No offence,' he added.

'None taken. I'm not the biggest fan of Dublin, myself,' I said. 'It's very dirty.'

They both looked at me as though I'd farted. That's when Foley strolled in. 'Bad news, O'Neill,' he said. 'Thomas O'Reilly has hired a solicitor and he's escalated the complaint into a legal case against you.'

O'Neill shook his head. 'Will it affect our case against Joyce?' he asked.

'It certainly won't help,' Foley said.

O'Neill mumbled something I couldn't hear but it sounded like a swear word. Silence fell and the atmosphere between the men changed. I got out of there as fast as I could. I drove home without stopping. It was obvious the O'Reillys knew by now that Joyce had confessed and this was a strategic move to mitigate that. I hoped that Seamus would call. I waited up for hours but he didn't, and I fell asleep in the chair.

CHAPTER FOURTEEN

Day Ten

Quinn was standing outside the door of the station as I drove in for the two p.m. shift. He waved at me. 'Foley wants to see you,' he said. I followed him inside to find O'Neill, Foley, Dicey McCarthy, Brian Keating and Liam Kenny, all seated. It was a full house.

'What's going on?' I said.

Liam's sweaty brow suggested his nerves were at him.

'Sit down, Mary,' Brian said. I sat. Quinn came in behind me and grabbed a chair.

'Due to Thomas O'Reilly's potential lawsuit, the matter has escalated and Superintendent Lynch wants statements from all of us about what happened on the night when the O'Reillys were being questioned,' Brian said.

'I wasn't there,' I said.

'No, you weren't, but you were there the next morning and you made a call to a local doctor to have Thomas O'Reilly's arm set in the cell.'

'That's right,' I said.

'And what did you think happened?' Brian asked. All eyes turned to me. *Really?* I thought. *This is what we're doing?*

'I think O'Neill broke his arm,' I said. O'Neill bit his lip and his eyes darted Foley's way. Foley remained looking straight ahead, taking me in, taking my answers in.

'Why do you think that?' Brian said.

'Because when I left the place, Thomas O'Reilly had two unbroken arms. The next morning, he had one broken arm,' I said. Liam's eyes were on stalks; I feared if they bulged any further they'd fall out of his head.

'So why do you think it was O'Neill?' Brian said.

I looked to Liam, who had told me what the Dublin boys – and particularly O'Neill – had done to the O'Reillys. *Quinn gave Raymond a few good clatters but O'Neill gave Thomas an awful leathering*, he'd said. He stared at me, his bulging eyes pleading with me to say nothing. I faced Foley. 'You told me,' I said.

Foley laughed to himself. 'I did not.'

'You did. You said to Quinn that O'Neill broke the boy's arm. And O'Neill confirmed it when he said, "How was I to know he has bones made of butter?"'

Everyone was staring at me. A relieved Liam Kenny bowed his head. 'I think you misheard us,' Foley said. I said nothing. 'The boy does have bones made of butter, that's true enough, and the men spent a long night in that cell… who knows what went on between them,' Foley continued, but he wasn't looking my way or meeting my gaze. 'O'Neill, Quinn or any of the boys didn't use excessive force at any time, did they, Kenny?' he said, looking Liam's way.

'No,' he said. 'Not that I saw.' He was shaking and he was lying. As clever as I was trying to be, I was lying too, by omission.

'An internal investigation is no easy thing. You weren't here, no one spoke to you about what happened and other than mishearing me, you have nothing to say on this subject. So when you're asked, you're unable to help because you were off shift. The end,' Foley said and now he was staring straight through me. I thought about this. He was right, except that I did not mishear him, but it was the word of four men against mine. I didn't stand a chance. 'So I misheard you,' I said.

'You did. Yeah.'

'Fine,' I said. What else was I supposed to do? If a superior was going to lie, I wasn't going to risk my career telling an unwanted and discredited truth.

'We've been asked to write statements,' Foley said and he gave me paper and a pen.

'And I suppose that's what you want me to say,' I clarified, just to be sure.

'Well, that's what happened, isn't it, Shea?' he said.

'Fine,' I said. It was a battle I couldn't win and if I wanted to survive to win the war, it would have been foolish to even try.

After we wrote our statements and they were signed, our Station House Officer, Brian Keating, drove to Tralee to hand-deliver them to the superintendent himself. Before he left, he mentioned that there was no tea, coffee or biscuits left in the break room. 'Go and get them,' he said. 'The lads need a bit of sustenance.'

'No problem,' I said. I wanted to get away from them anyway. I drove to the village and headed into the local supermarket. I picked up the tea, coffee, milk and a selection of biscuits. I filled the basket and as I was walking up the aisle, I saw Bridie Fitzmaurice with her newborn baby boy, Johnny. She was wearing a dress, her face was made-up and her hair was freshly washed. She was a good-looking woman when cleaned up.

She was cradling him, hugging him to her chest. I said hello, and when she turned to me and smiled, I saw him – the baby in her arms. Slung over her shoulder was a blue towel. Of all the colours, it threw me. His black shock of hair against the blue towel instantly took me back to that beach and my first glimpse of Crónán. Suddenly, I smelled the bleach. My stomach turned. I looked at his little button nose, and all I could see was Crónán – cold, black at the tip, and those grey eyes that matched the sky. I lost my grip on reality and on the basket. It slipped from my hands, and the biscuits went everywhere.

'Are you all right, Garda Shea?' she asked.

'I'm fine,' I said, scrambling to put the biscuits, some of them broken, back into the basket. I rose up and told myself, *It's not him. It's not him. Calm down, Mary.* She pushed her baby towards me. 'His name is Johnny,' she said and I tried to avoid looking at him but I couldn't and, of course, he wasn't Crónán. He looked just like him but then all babies look the same. *Don't be silly now, Mary.* I wanted to cry so badly. *Stop it. Stop it now,* I told myself when my breath threatened to catch in my throat. If she noticed my discomfort, she pretended not to.

'He can't seem to keep anything down today,' she said to me before turning to her newborn son. 'And I'm not letting you ruin my nice dress, am I, Johnny?' she added, while pulling the towel over to cover her lapel. She looked to me. 'But other than a little reflux, he's a dream, the easiest I've ever had. He was sent from heaven,' she said. I managed a smile.

'He's beautiful,' I said and he was, just like Crónán was beautiful. His fingers were gripping hers. His tiny chest heaving, his eyes blinking in the light. *It's not him, Mary. It's not him.*

'Thank you for helping us. I meant to get a card but this is my first day leaving the house.' She looked at her son. 'We've been in a little bubble, haven't we, Johnny?' she said and he yawned.

'No need for a card,' I said. 'I was glad to help.'

I ran out of the place with the dented box of tea and broken biscuits. I couldn't face returning to the station. I needed to escape the boys' shenanigans, Dicey's stare, my own head… And then seeing Bridie reminded me of Fidelma and the word I'd been promising to have with her. It would be an excuse to stay away. It was well after four so, taking a chance, I drove to her house to see if she was home.

Fidelma answered the door with a pair of large yellow rubber gloves on, and a tea towel tucked under her arm. She looked at me, standing there in my uniform, unsure and slightly alarmed. 'Is something wrong?' she asked, her eyes searching me for an answer, her body tense, preparing to react to the worst. I smiled. 'Nothing to worry about,' I said and her shoulders dropped. 'Maybe we could just have a word,' I said, and she nodded and pulled the door open, allowing me to come in.

The house was plain, crisp and clean. Fidelma wasn't one for decoration or clutter. The kitchen had little in terms of personality but it sparkled. You could eat your dinner off the floor. She pulled off the gloves and placed them in the sink. She pointed to a chair. 'Sit, please,' she said and so I did, and she joined me at the kitchen table. She didn't offer me tea. She just waited for me to explain my visit. 'Fidelma, I was in Bridie Fitzmaurice's home the day we found Baby Crónán – in her bedroom, to be exact.'

'I know, she told me.'

'During my visit I saw medication – specifically, a relaxant drug for the purposes of dealing with anxiety,' I said and her shoulders stiffened. She knew what was coming.

'It was your medication.'

She nodded, her face drawn. 'She was in a terrible way,' she said.

'She was pregnant. Did you know it could harm the baby?' I asked.

'No, I didn't, but if I hadn't given her something she would have harmed herself and the baby,' she said.

'I see.'

'Do you think the baby was harmed by the drugs? Is that why you're here?' Fidelma said, alarmed at the notion of it. 'Because I think she only took it once or twice – it didn't suit either of us, really. I just had one bottle.'

When I saw the bottle, it was under half-full. She'd taken enough. The baby was perfect, at least physically, and he didn't seem sick at all, but then I hadn't been able to really examine him. The memory of how I felt when I saw him washed through me. I tried to shake it off and I wondered if that's how I'd be around babies from now on.

'I think he's fine but medication is administered by doctors for a reason. They know what they are doing,' I said.

'Nobody was helping her. Dr Pierce just told her she was pregnant and she had to pull herself together. That's what he said, *pull yourself together*. Her husband and her son had just drowned. He saw how desperate she was and he walked away,' she said. She bit the inside of her cheek and scrubbed away the tear that threatened to fall from her eye. 'What would you have done?'

'I don't know,' I said honestly. 'She seems to be doing okay now?'

Fidelma smiled. 'She's great. I'm seeing signs of her old self, and Debbie is so relieved. These few months have really taken a toll on her too.'

It was nice to hear some good news amongst all the bad and terrible. The Fitzmaurices brought in some light to a town still shrouded in darkness. 'Well,' I said, 'I'll take my leave of you.'

'Is that it?' she asked.

'It is,' I said.

'Oh. Okay.'

I stood to leave. 'Except… you're all right yourself?' I said. I asked it awkwardly, not wishing to ignore that she had tablets prescribed for her nerves.

She blushed. 'I'm fine. I was feeling down for a while but it passed.'

'Good,' I said.

Fidelma lived five doors away from Irene Lacey, the old woman with a drinking problem who believed a girl in a white nightdress was her dead daughter coming to visit. As she opened the door to let me out, I could smell the sea. 'That night, when Baby Crónán was placed in a dune across the way… You were at the cinema?' I asked.

'Yes, my friend Brenda drove us home. I went straight to bed.' She looked down and away from me; it was only for a split second, but I noticed it. Her face changed a little, her lips tightened, but surely it was nothing.

'And you didn't see a young woman in a nightdress?'

'No,' she said. Her jaw tightened just a tiny bit. 'I saw nothing.'

'Okay, thanks,' I said and I moved to walk down the small pathway that led to the iron garden gate. 'Garda Shea,' she called out. I turned to face her. 'I'm so sorry about the baby,' she said and she was suddenly filled with sadness. I felt it.

'Me too,' I said.

—

Dicey McCarthy was the first face I saw as I walked back into the station, and a chill ran through me, but he wasn't interested in me – he was animated, pumped even, as he stalked out of Brian's office. Something was going on. The Dublin boys were in a circle.

'Quinn could be right,' Dicey said. The lads all sat up, and O'Neill stood.

'Right about what?' I asked, focusing on Foley. That's when Dicey said those words, 'Thomas O'Reilly is a queer.' My heart surged, my mouth went dry. I didn't say a word.

I just listened as the men spoke excitedly, and the things they were saying were as childish as they were ugly. Over the course of the conversation, I pieced together that Quinn reported to Foley that he'd noticed something between Thomas and Seamus in the pub. *Oh Seamus.* Quinn decided there was a closeness between them that wasn't natural for men. Foley, O'Neill and the others were happy to run with it – after all, what better way to discredit him?

'That's rubbish,' I said quietly – too quietly, no one was listening to me.

Liam scratched his head. 'All I saw was two fellas playing darts and threatening a fight. They seemed pretty normal to me.'

'Because they are normal,' I said. Again, I was ignored.

'Then you weren't looking close enough, Kenny,' O'Neill said.

'When's the last time someone was arrested for bumming?' Foley said and my stomach turned.

'A couple of years ago,' O'Neill answered. 'Usually we just give them a beating these days.'

'Stop,' I said.

'Still, it's an illegal act,' Foley said.

'*Stop*,' I said, louder now.

'Absolutely,' O'Neill said. 'Disgusting.'

'Seamus is not with Thomas, he's with me,' I said, and that got their attention. All eyes were on me now and I could feel the temperature rise.

'Is that right?' Foley asked.

'I think your radar must be off, Quinn,' I said, turning to him to avoid lying to Foley's face.

'Can I see you in the office?' Foley said and then turned to the lads. 'Find out where the queers hang out, see what they have to say,' he instructed, before I followed him into Brian's office.

We sat opposite one another.

'Are you telling the truth?' he said.

'We go to the disco every Saturday night, if you want to ask around,' I said, avoiding lying to him directly.

'Do you love him, Mary?'

'No, but I care for him,' I said honestly.

'Maybe he's using you.'

'Maybe you're using him,' I whispered. I could see it, Foley was torn. His skin was greyer than usual, his eyes cloudier. He raised his big hand to his face, squeezing his temples with his thumb and third finger, his gold wedding band shining at me.

'Go home,' he said. I looked at my watch – it was just after eight. I still had two hours.

'I'm on shift,' I said.

'Conflict of interest,' he said. I didn't move.

'Go home,' Foley repeated. 'Don't make me ask you again.'

–

I arrived at the farm and walked up to the house. Mrs McEvoy answered the door. 'Hello, Mary, do you need to use the phone?' she said.

'I'm looking for Seamus,' I said.

'He's somewhere out in the fields,' she said, looking out over her land.

'Any idea when he's due back?' I asked.

'No. I don't know what he does out there till all hours,' she said. *I do, and now so do the police.* I asked her to tell him I was looking for him and, thankfully, she didn't ask any questions – I'd had enough of obfuscation for one day. She agreed to pass on the message, and we said good night. I was going to go home, but then I thought about his caravan and wondered if I'd find him there – maybe Thomas too. It was obvious the boys were cooking up something to force Thomas to withdraw his case, and I didn't want Seamus to be a part of it. Word would spread in a small town, and life would be over for him. His parents wouldn't handle it well. They were too religious, paragons of the parish. It would kill them. They had been good to me. He was my friend. I wasn't going to allow an injustice to occur to him just to save O'Neill and the threadbare case the boys had.

Pulling my hood up, I started walking. From what Seamus had told me, the caravan was placed in the yard furthest from the house, where only he ventured. I walked for a while before I saw it in the distance, propped up on bricks. It was small, its joints a little rusty. Once white, it had yellowed over the years. There was no light coming from inside. The yard was a dead, silent, lonely place. No doubt it had its beauty – surrounded by green fields and under a blue sky – but now, under a veil of darkness, it felt empty.

The door was locked. Of course it was. But I knew the key would be close and it didn't take long to find. It was just behind the bricks at the back of the caravan, close enough to the door. I opened it. I didn't go there to stick my nose into Seamus's business, but I couldn't walk away. The Dublin lads were on to him now, and I needed to know what we were up against. Inside, it was plain but cosy. Lots of blankets, a fridge stocked with beer and some food in the cupboards. A kettle and a box of tea. A jar of powdered coffee. The bathroom was tiny – nothing in there except a toothbrush. Just one. *Good.* I was going to leave. It was Seamus's private space, and I knew I was stepping over the line. But something held me there –probably my own curiosity. I lifted the seat that would turn into a bed. That's when I found the gay porn magazines and other things, and that's when I was confronted by his sexuality. It seems silly now to be shocked by the images I saw, but I was.

It was only when the rusty hinge screeched and he was upon me that I registered his presence. It was too late. I was caught. I could feel the anger radiating from him even before he raised his voice. 'What are you doing here?' he shouted. I placed the magazines back where I found them and slowly turned around to face him.

'I'm sorry,' I said. He looked from me to his personal, private magazines.

'Why?' he said, and his face, his entire being, crumbled before me. Any shock I'd felt was quickly replaced by my own shame. I needed to explain myself. I told him what I knew and what the Dublin boys were up to. 'They are talking to people who frequent…'

'Queer bars,' he said.

'Yes. Do you and Thomas go there?' I asked. He moved past me and placed the cushion over the seat, to cover the magazines fully. To hide them from sight. To disappear them, but we were both acutely aware they existed in this space. It was hard to see past them. 'Why did you come in here?' he asked, his voice even and strained.

'I came to find you and then I couldn't help myself,' I said.

'So now you really see me and you hate me too,' he said.

'I don't hate you. My stomach's turned a bit but I definitely don't hate you,' I told him. 'Besides, who hates you?'

'I do,' he said.

I was sorry to hear that but I didn't have anything to say that could help, not in that moment.

'You have to get rid of this stuff. All of it,' I said.

'We go to a bar in Tralee,' he said.

'They'll find out,' I warned him.

'How did they know?'

'Quinn says he spotted something between you and Thomas in the bar,' I said and he scoffed, a bitter, humourless sound.

'Quinn… He's one of us,' he said.

That took me by surprise. 'What do you mean?'

'He's queer, Mary.'

'How do you know?'

'The same way he does. We just know.' It took the wind out of me, more than seeing those pictures, which is saying something. I found my way to the cushioned seat. He sat opposite me at the small table.

'He'd do that to one of his own?' I said.

'He's a guard first. He's picked his team.'

'But his team would arrest or beat up the real him!' I said and now it made sense why Quinn seemed so bland to me, why he was so utterly forgettable – he was a chameleon, purposefully melting into the background, hiding in plain sight. I wanted to have pity for him but I couldn't; instead, I held him more in contempt.

'Get rid of the evidence,' I heard myself saying. 'They will come knocking.'

'And what are they planning?' he asked.

'They won't tell me. They know we're friends,' I said and that's when I asked him to talk to Thomas, to tell him to withdraw his complaint and to call off his solicitor. 'They'll leave you alone then. It's the only way.'

He refused, he said Joyce was throwing her life away and Thomas was going to fight to stop that from happening. I warned him, he was up against the state. He was risking his own future, his own liberty, for a case that would no doubt be thrown out.

'It could destroy you both,' I said.

He thought about it. 'Warn him,' I urged. 'But don't let them catch you together,' I said and he nodded his agreement. I left him alone, to bin or burn the evidence of his sexuality. I slept uneasy that night. I'd made a decision to put my friend above my job. I saw how Foley and the boys drew outside the lines and I didn't like it, but here was I, the first opportunity I'd been given and I was doing exactly that. I didn't like myself for it, but I did it just the same.

Day Eleven

It was four a.m. when I woke to banging at my window. I looked up to see Seamus's face pressed against it and lit up by the moonlight – it was a startling sight. *Jesus*, I thought. The goofy face on him – he stopped knocking to point at my door, as if he was guiding me towards it. *I know where my front door is.* I checked the time as I got up, put my robe on and let him in.

'It's the middle of the night,' I moaned. He boiled the kettle and put two teabags in cups. He was energised, nervous but almost happy.

'I spoke to Thomas. His dad got out of hospital yesterday afternoon,' he said.

'That's a great recovery,' I said, unsure.

'He discharged himself. He wants to be home with Breda, and here's the thing...' He was building himself up to say something. I knew whatever he was about to say would be serious, maybe even life changing.

'We're going to Dublin, Thomas and I. We're leaving tonight,' he said.

'Tonight?'

'You're right, he's got an uphill battle ahead of him but Joyce didn't do this. He needs people to know why she's pleading guilty,' he explained.

'And you think you'll be safe in Dublin. The Dublin boys are from Dublin, the clue is in the name.'

'Let them come for us, but let them come for us there, not here, not around our families,' he said.

'But there doesn't have be an "us",' I said.

'I love him.'

'Right,' I said and to be honest, it was unusual to hear one fella talk about another in those particular terms, and I didn't know where to look. He stood up, manoeuvred me to a chair, sat me down and continued making tea. I sat in silence, thinking through all the things that were wrong with them running away together, but also admiring them, hoping for them. Then I was sipping my tea, and he was opposite me, a smile on his face. Despite everything, my friend was happy. I reached across the table, placed my hand on his.

'Good luck so,' I said.

He nodded. 'Thanks for changing my mind.'

'God, how did I do that?'

'I didn't want to leave because this farm has been in my family for three generations,' he said.

'Well, like I told you before, you've had a good run at it, then,' I said and he smiled.

'You were right. We have. My parents have made their money and there's plenty of land there to sell off if they need to. I don't want to give up my life for green pastures. This land will exist whole or in parts forever, but my time in this world is fleeting.'

'That's very poetic of you,' I said, impressed by both word and deed.

'I was composing it the entire drive home,' he said and he laughed. He was walking taller, speaking louder. I was happy for him and scared for him too.

'Are you sure about this, Seamus? It's a huge decision. It's your life,' I asked.

'We're leaving tonight,' he said firmly.

The reality of losing him took the wind from my sails, but they were right to leave quickly. The Dublin boys wouldn't wait long to pounce. By the time we finished our tea, it was close to five a.m. I walked him to the door.

'They'll be watching, Thomas, they'll have alerts out on his car and possibly yours,' I said.

'Don't worry. I'm handling things.'

'Be careful,' I warned.

'I will,' he said. 'And thanks.'

'Goodbye.'

'I'll write,' he promised. It was an unexpected gesture and enough to pick me up.

'I'd like that but wait a while, won't you?' I said, nervous I'd be dragged into the whole mess too.

'I will and I'll sign it from your cousin George,' he said. Everyone knew Dicey McCarthy's sister-in-law, Doris, read half the letters that passed through her post office.

'Good luck,' I said. I closed the door and, even though he'd crept into my life and my world without me noticing much, I took a moment to register how much I would miss him once he was gone.

CHAPTER FIFTEEN

I had the day off. It made me nervous that I was left out of things, unsure what I could or should do now that the case was slipping away from my grasp. I had no leads of my own and was being slowly pushed out into the cold. It was agitating and I couldn't just let it happen. I knew Lena Herrman, the charity shop worker, was due back from Germany and scheduled to work in the shop that morning. I also knew Foley and O'Neill would be there, waiting to speak to her. I couldn't help myself, I needed to know what she knew. The phones had been ringing off the hook in the incident room since the actual clothing had appeared on the news. Half of Ireland were walking around in those coats. I put on a pair of jeans and a thick woollen jumper; my warm coat was soaking in the sink and my good one was a bit too fancy for a Friday morning in town, so I put on a woollen hat and got in the car. I shopped for essential food items in Nolan's Supermarket. It was only a few shops down from the charity shop, which didn't open until ten a.m. The closed sign was still on the door so I sat in the car, watching and waiting. At about nine fifty, I saw Foley and O'Neill walking towards the shop. They passed by the supermarket carpark without looking left or right, deep in conversation, and I wondered what it was about. Maybe it was related to Thomas and Seamus. My thoughts went to them and their plan to escape the small town, this unforgiving place. They knocked on the door, no answer. They sat on the bonnet of a random car parked in front of it, arms crossed, still talking to one another. It was quiet for a Friday, very few around – even the last stragglers of the press had moved on by now. I had been kept quite apart from the circus, as Foley liked to call them, so I couldn't speak much about their presence. But it had a profound enough effect on the town, deepening old wounds and suspicions. There was a chill in the air that had nothing to do with the Irish climate – an unease.

All those dark deeds and silent screams, hidden behind closed doors and so carefully brushed under the carpet that we all had a hand in weaving, were now threatening to burst through its seams. Baby Crónán's murder and Lily O'Reilly's lonely, tragic stillbirth were a poor reflection on our society – a stark reminder of who we really were, as opposed to who we pretended to be. The people of the town were grieving, but they were also angry – angry at the intrusion from the outside, at the glaring exposure, at the judgement passed by those with little right to judge. They were hiding away from each other, and perhaps even from themselves. I wondered if Lena had stepped off the plane to be confronted by the news of what had happened in the town she'd adopted many years before, or had she learned of it abroad? The story had become international. Maybe she chose to stay away. Maybe she'd never turn up. I didn't have long to wait and wonder, because at ten Lena Herrman seemed to materialise as if from the ether, her key turning in the lock before Foley and O'Neill had time to unfold their arms. I could see she was a tall woman, with short hair, and she wore a long sweeping fur coat. I sat up straight, watching as they called to her, and she turned to greet them. I hugged the steering wheel as they followed her inside the shop and the door closed behind them. Not sure of what I was doing or why I was sitting there, I waited. They emerged half an hour later, both looking stern. They were walking my way so I shrunk down in my seat, just in case they glanced my way. I waited for ten minutes and after they were well out of sight, I stepped out of the car, casually walking outside, making my way to the charity shop.

–

Lena was behind the counter; she was an attractive woman in her mid-sixties, fit and healthy, and adorned in chunky silver jewellery. Every time she moved, she jangled. She wore round spectacles and looked over them at me as I entered. We silently acknowledged one another while I moved to one of the rails, holding skirts and dresses. I was flicking through the endless items when I decided my pretence was silly and I just needed to come clean with my intention.

'Ms Herrman,' I said.

'Garda Shea,' she said.

'You know me?'

'You are the only female guard in the town. Of course I know you,' she said.

I dropped all pretence. 'I wanted to ask you about—'

'The clothes. Joyce O'Reilly dropped them into this shop, just as Breda said she did.'

So Breda was telling the truth. *This is huge, isn't it?* I thought. 'What did you do with the clothes?' I asked.

'They had been cleaned and ironed, so I put a price on them and placed them on the rails before close of business,' she said.

'Who bought them?' I asked, my ears and head buzzing.

'I don't know. Cara sold them.'

'The woman who died,' I said numbly.

'Afraid so.'

'That's what you told the boys from Dublin?' I said.

'Of course.'

'And you don't take note of who buys items? Surely there's a receipt book?'

'We detail price, the date and item sold, not names and addresses,' she said. 'Those men have it. I hope they give it back. I don't want trouble.'

'They will,' I said and she offered me a smile of sorts in response to my despondence.

'Do you have regulars?' I asked.

'I do, a great many. I also have people who come in once in a blue moon or once and then never again,' she said.

'And you don't have CCTV?' I asked, already knowing the answer.

'This is not the Allied Irish Bank, Garda Shea. People don't come here to steal, they come to donate.'

'Can you do me a favour and make a note of the regulars who shop here?' I said.

'They are mostly pensioners.'

'Humour me,' I insisted and Lena hunched. 'Okay.' I moved to leave.

'Detective Foley said you'd be paying me a visit,' she said.

'Right,' I said. He knew me well. No flies on him.

'He said you wouldn't be far behind them. He was right.' She smiled. He had my number all right.

I left after that, torn in two. Foley was at least one step ahead of me and probably ten. He knew I'd go into the charity shop asking questions, of course he did. He was smart as a whip. And as smart as I thought I was, he wanted me to know I wasn't smarter than him. Still, this changed everything. Didn't it? I wanted to walk to the station and ask him where this left us. If the family no longer owned the coat and hat, how could Joyce O'Reilly or her mother Breda be wearing them that night? It was one fewer coincidence. I walked straight into the cafe next door. I'd been awake since four a.m. but I hadn't eaten and felt the worse for it. I hoped if I ate a full breakfast my brain might switch on. I was in the queue, the radio was on and Simon & Garfunkel's 'Bright Eyes' was playing. The young girl behind the counter was singing along. She was around Joyce's age. She took an order from an elderly man with a combover, just ahead of me, and as he shuffled past me, she looked up and grinned. 'Can I help you?' she asked.

'I'd take a full Irish.'

'Brown or white toast?'

'White.'

'Do you want black pudding?'

'Yeah.'

'We've no beans left.'

'Fine.'

'I'll throw in an extra sausage.'

'Thanks,' I said.

'Tea or coffee?'

'Tea.'

'You're the lady garda,' she said. I nodded.

'Bad news about Joyce O'Reilly…' she said.

'What bad news?' I asked.

'Well, she's been officially charged. It was on the news at ten,' she said, signalling to the radio to demonstrate where this news had come from.

'Right,' I said and suddenly I lost my appetite.

'I was in school with her.'

'Did you know her well?' I asked as she took my money for the breakfast I knew I'd only barely pick at.

'We weren't friends,' she said. She rang up the bill, opened the till and gave me my change. It was my cue to move off to a table but as

207

she placed the change in my hand, she leaned in. 'The papers are saying that she walked for miles after she had the baby. It's weird.'

'Why do you say that?' I asked.

'Because of her asthma,' she said.

I wasn't aware she had asthma; no one had mentioned it and as far as I knew, not one of us had asked. 'How bad is it?'

'She never did PE because of it, she had a permanent note. I remember she was taken out of school in an ambulance after a game of skipping in primary school. I was only nine but I remember it well.'

'Did you mention it when you were interviewed?'

'No. I only thought of it when I read in the paper that she'd gone on a hike. It didn't sound like her at all,' she explained.

'Thanks,' I said and as I walked out, I heard her asking about my breakfast, but I didn't have time to reply. I left the car and ran up the street to Dr Pierce's surgery. He was the O'Reillys' GP. I'd seen a referral note addressed to him on Joyce's hospital chart. I walked in and his snotty assistant looked me up and down, registering my woollies.

'Do you have an appointment?' she said.

'No, but I need to speak with Dr Pierce.'

'He's busy,' she said. The waiting room was full, to be fair. He appeared just then, and I was sorry to interrupt those sick people's day, but not sorry enough to back off. 'Dr Pierce, I'm Garda Shea, I need to speak to you urgently,' I said.

He looked me up and down the same as his assistant, but without her spite. 'I've a full house,' he said.

'It's about Joyce O'Reilly.'

'You have five minutes,' he said. I took it and followed him into his room. It was plain enough: white walls, a leather examination table, a desk, chair and a notepad. He pointed to the hard chair parked in front of his desk. He sat in his own chair, opposite me.

'I can't talk about Joyce's medical record without her consent,' he said.

'I know that. I want to ask you a general question that may or may not relate to her.' He thought about his answer for a few moments.

'Well, I hope it relates to this ridiculous theory that a young girl can give birth to twins by different fathers, honest to God, it's the biggest load of rubbish I've ever heard,' he said and I must have smiled because it was then he realised I was not his enemy.

'This is what I know: Joyce confessed to giving birth to Baby Crónán and then walking for miles to the beach. I saw the hospital report on the injury she sustained. I can't work out how she could have walked that far. In your opinion could any woman walk that far with that kind of injury?' I asked.

'In my opinion, no woman could,' he said, warming to me and my line of questioning.

'There's a doctor in this town that says he's heard of a woman who did just that,' I told him and Dr Pierce rolled his eyes. 'Well, that could be only one fella – Boyne,' he said. 'Fool.'

'But what if the woman had a birth injury and asthma. How would that further affect a person in that situation?' I said and Dr Pierce cottoned on immediately.

'Well, some asthma's brought on or made worse by exercise – the irony is that controlled exercise is a remedy but a lot of patients are terrified of bringing on an attack. The asthma would no doubt have affected a woman during a difficult labour, and it would further impede her taking a long walk afterwards,' he said.

'What about an inhaler, would that help?'

'A woman with the kind of tear Joyce had and a woman with the type of asthma I just described, in frigid temperatures, would not have made it fifty yards with or without an inhaler,' he said. I smiled. I shouldn't have, it was unprofessional. Dr Pierce smiled too. I offered him my hand. He clasped it firmly.

'For the record, do you think Joyce O'Reilly gave birth to twins by different fathers that night?' I asked.

'Absolutely not. It's a fairytale. That's just my opinion,' he said. We shook hands.

'Thanks,' I said, heartened that I wasn't alone in that belief.

–

Dr Pierce's insight was important enough for me to risk Foley's ire so I went straight to the incident room. Foley knew what I was up to anyway, and aside from my new intelligence, I needed to get a feel for what the boys were thinking and doing. It was quieter now; lots of the other fellas had been sent back to their own stations, and it was just the Dublin lads and Dicey McCarthy. They looked up when I entered.

'What are you doing here?' Dicey asked, clearly annoyed by my presence.

'Just saying hello,' I said, lying with a smile.

'Feck off,' he said. I ignored him. He glanced around at the Dublin boys, clearly hoping for a laugh, a chuckle or at least some nod of agreement. It was obvious he thought he'd finally earned his place with them. He hadn't – none of them liked him, he was just too stupid to realise it. Foley walked out of Brian's office.

'Joyce dropped off the hat and coat to the charity shop, just like Breda said,' I told him before he had a chance to acknowledge my presence. He raised his eyes to heaven.

'How long after us?' he asked.

'I was there before you. I watched you go in,' I said.

'So, the hat and coat aren't the lead we thought they were. Joyce confessed to the murder and disposal of Baby Crónán. She's been charged,' Foley said.

'She's lying. The case you're building is falling apart at the seams,' I said.

Foley stood up. 'Mary, I let you interview the girl, it was helpful, but while you've been having a few chats, the team have followed over 400 lines of inquiry and I've been overseeing the lot. Listen when I tell you that we're done here,' he said and I couldn't tell how he was feeling. He managed to keep that hidden behind the invisible wall he'd built over years on the job. *A few chats?* Is that what my contribution amounted to? I looked around the incident room at the boxes upon boxes of statements, the chalkboards filled with details, questions and theories. He was right – I didn't have a grasp on every aspect of the case, whereas he did. I deflated, like a balloon pricked by a sharp needle. Was he right? Was my contribution really just a few chats? What did I know about real police work? My mouth went dry again, and I started to wonder if I should be checked for diabetes. I think I coughed. I couldn't even make Dr Pierce's argument – it wasn't in me at that moment. I'd lost confidence in it, in him, in myself, in my judgement and in my skills as an investigator. So I made my excuses and pretty much ran out of the place.

I headed downtown to fetch my car and planned on driving wherever the road would take me, just to get away, to escape it all. I slowed down, passing the chemist, and practically walked into Liam

Kenny as he exited. I looked past him and waved to Eileen O'Connor standing behind the counter, pretty as ever. She grinned at me and waved back before I turned to Liam.

'Are you all right?' he said.

'Grand.'

'You're white as a ghost. I hope you're not coming down with that dose I had. It's only starting to really shift now. I've enough vitamins here to knock a horse,' he said, raising a paper bag that rattled.

'They're acting the fool, Liam,' I said and he nodded.

'Things aren't as clear as I'd like, all right,' he admitted.

'Dr Pierce doesn't believe in the heteropaternal superfecundation theory.'

'Well, some doctors do and some don't.'

'He doesn't believe it was possible for her to walk to the beach.'

'What about Boyne's story, the woman in Cork?'

'Joyce O'Reilly suffers from a type of asthma brought on by exercise,' I said and that caught him off guard. He thought about it for a few seconds.

'So he'll testify in her defence,' he replied.

'What if they don't believe him?'

'That's not something you can control,' he said and I knew he was right. We started to walk together. 'All we can do is our best,' he continued, attempting to pat me on the shoulder. He missed and instead slapped me on the back.

'Mary,' he said and his voice had changed, becoming quieter. I leaned in. 'Does Seamus McEvoy mean something to you?' We kept walking but I nodded. 'I played hurling with Thomas O'Reilly and Seamus for a while...'

'Okay,' I said.

'They're good men,' he said. I waited for him to get to the point. We crossed the road together.

'Why are you telling me this?' I asked.

'Because the Dublin lads know he's leaving town. They seem to think maybe Thomas is leaving too.'

'Based on?'

'Seamus rented a car first thing this morning, and he's dropping it to a place in Dublin tomorrow evening,' he said.

'How would you know that?' I asked.

'Do you ever wonder how Dicey McCarthy knows about every blade of grass growing in this town?'

'I have,' I admitted.

'His sister-in-law works in the post office, his brother works in the bank, he has an aunt in the hairdressers', a cousin is in the ambulance and his sister runs the car rental place,' Liam said. I had no idea he was connected to so many people in the town.

'Oh,' I said.

'If Seamus is on the move and he's alone, then that's fine, but if he intends to leave with Thomas, you need to get word to him,' he said.

'What are the boys planning?' I asked.

'They'll stop them, arrest them for a lewd act, take them in,' he said.

'Since when has driving been lewd?' I asked.

'Since two fellas intend on going off together into the sunset... Since Thomas O'Reilly might cause the Dublin fellas trouble.'

'Will they hurt them?' I asked.

'No, but they'll drag their names through the mud. They won't leave a stone unturned, they'll publicly humiliate them both, to discredit Thomas. Whatever it takes,' he said. 'It will be the local lads who trap them, the Dublin fellas can't be involved.'

'Is there someone still watching the O'Reillys' place?' I asked. He nodded. There was.

'Thomas is not getting out of there unseen. Warn them,' Liam Kenny said before he peeled away, heading in another direction, leaving me alone on the street to digest what he'd just told me. I had no idea where Seamus was, but I thought he'd be gone most of the day. Time was running out and as far I could see, I had only one option available to me.

–

Dr Ciara Crosby's office was not as busy as Dr Pierce's. She had a free appointment and I took it. There were only two people ahead of me, waiting to see her. She was puzzled when her secretary showed me into her room.

'Are you sick?' she asked. I waited until the door was closed.

'No, but I do need your help,' I said.

'What is it?' she asked and I told her the sorry tale regarding the beating Thomas took, the case he was taking against O'Neill and the love between him and Seamus.

The plan the Dublin boys made to disgrace Thomas and how it would take Seamus down with him. She was intrigued.

'What do you need from me?' she asked.

I asked her to go to the O'Reillys', pretending it was a house call to see Raymond, following his discharge. I asked her to tell Thomas that whatever their plan was, they needed to abort it.

'He can't get in that car,' I warned.

'Hmm… but what then?' she asked.

They would have to stay apart, keep their heads down, wait it out. The Dublin boys couldn't keep a squad car watching the O'Reillys' house, not indefinitely. 'Or…' she said and she grinned and her eyes twinkled.

'I have a better idea,' she said and to be fair to her, it was a better idea, if not a far riskier one.

–

I drove to the phone box by the beach. I parked up and rang the McEvoys' house, and when Ruth McEvoy answered, I didn't give her time to speak. I asked to speak to Seamus. I was in luck — he'd just walked through the door. She handed over the phone.

'Mary?'

'I was looking for you,' I said.

'Well, you found me. What's going on?'

'They know you've rented a car, they know you're leaving together.'

'So?'

'So they're going to pull you over. They're going to say you were having relations, they're planning on charging you,' I said as I leaned against the square glass window.

'Jesus,' I heard him whisper. 'We have to get out of here.'

'I know,' I agreed, and then I relayed the plan that Ciara and I had concocted. It was simple, really. Thomas would take his rental car and drive it to The Green Fields pub, down the road from the O'Reillys'. The local cops would keep eyes on Seamus, presumably waiting for Thomas to join him in the pub. Meanwhile, Ciara Crosby would do a house call to checkup on Raymond O'Reilly, passing by the garda car parked on the road. Once she got there, Thomas would conceal himself in the boot of the car and she'd drive him to the next town. An hour later, Seamus would appear and instead of driving to the O'Reillys' yard, he'd drive away from town alone. He'd keep going until eventually the car following him would realise that Thomas wasn't joining him, and they'd turn back. As soon as they did, and after dark, he'd double back and pick Thomas up.

'You think it will work?' he said.

I told him that it would have been safer for them to leave town separately. 'I'm not leaving without him and I'm not letting him go alone, especially now that they are after him.'

'So does it matter what I think?' I asked.

'I suppose not,' he admitted.

'I can't be any more involved than I already am,' I said. I knew I was breaking every rule in the book but, then, so were the Dublin boys.

–

I drove home, past Liam Kenny, who was sitting in an unmarked car at the side of the main road opposite the McEvoys' farm. Seamus was being watched now, which meant that, indirectly, so was I. I pretended not to notice him. I went inside my small cottage and made dinner, tried to think of other things, put on some music, danced, ironed some clothes, washed the floor – an hour passed and then Ruth McEvoy knocked on my door. She told me that Detective Foley rang the house and requested I come in to work to do some overtime. I thanked her and I felt terrible because I knew no matter what happened that evening, her life would change. If the boys were caught, she'd face humiliation; if we succeeded, she'd lose her son to the city. I put on my uniform and drove into town, worried as to why Foley wanted to keep me close. Was he keeping an eye on me to make sure I was on board or did he know I was acting against him? *Do you want to play with the big boys?* he'd said in passing. Turns out I did want to play, but I was determined to play it my way. *Hold your nerve, Mary.*

At the station, the Dublin boys were all sitting around. Brian Keating was manning the radios, listening intently for updates. When Liam Kenny's radio crackled to life with the report of Seamus McEvoy's whereabouts, it was seven p.m. 'Keep your eyes firmly on the place,' Brian said. He had a habit of sitting on the table, leaning back, with his legs propped up on a chair. Now, there he was, dead centre in the room, perched on the table with the radio in his hand, commanding attention like a performer holding court. We, his audience, were gathered around, watching him set the stage.

'I'm looking at Seamus McEvoy,' came Liam Kenny's voice.

'Where is he?' Brian asked.

'Walking out of his farm… Wait, no, he's ducked behind the wall…' he said and we all waited.

'He has a suitcase,' he said.

'Looks like Seamus didn't plan on saying goodbye,' Brian said, stating the obvious.

'He's walking down the road, to the parked rental,' Liam Kenny said.

'And?' Brian asked.

'He's putting the case in the boot of the car now.'

Foley smiled. 'They're legging it all right… Sneaky feckers.' He was delighted with himself.

'How do you know? What if Seamus is going somewhere alone?' I said. I mean, after all, it was entirely plausible.

'Timing,' he said and he seemed satisfied enough with that answer, as though it meant something significant.

'Timing?' I said with as much incredulity as I could muster.

'I've asked around, that fella hasn't gone anywhere in over ten years and now suddenly he's renting a car and taking a suitcase – that tells me he's going for good,' he said.

'Why would he?' I asked and maybe the wobble in my voice made him confuse my fear with heartbreak, because he softened. 'I know you think there's something between you, Shea, and maybe there is, but men like him often use women like you…'

Ah, it was then I knew why I was there. 'Women like me…'

'Decent women…' he said, and I could feel all the eyes in the room boring holes in me.

'And you want me to see for myself who you think he is?' I said and realised he thought he was doing me a favour, so I bit my lip.

O'Neill was more tense than the others; the outcome of this mattered for him, for the case, for his career. I made myself small, tucking myself away on a stool in the corner of the room, simply there to bear witness to these clever men doing clever things. It just annoyed me how smug they were. Yes, Seamus and Thomas were together, so in this instance, they were right – but even a broken clock is right twice a day. We waited as Liam Kenny followed Seamus McEvoy.

'He's stepping into The Green Fields, now,' Liam said over the radio.

'That's the place we stopped in for a sandwich, close to the O'Reillys'?' Foley said, looking my way.

'It is,' I confirmed.

'Get on to McCarthy, Brian… See what's happening at the yard,' Foley said. Brian shifted the weight on his arse cheeks on the desk and flicked on the radio, calling out to Dicey, who I believed was parked on the main road outside the entrance to the scrapyard.

'Any news?' he asked.

'The last of the workers left half an hour ago, and I followed Thomas to his front door. No move since,' he said.

'We think the other fella is waiting for him in The Green Fields pub,' Brian said.

'Well, he won't get past me,' Dicey said, self-assured. 'My eyes haven't left the house.'

I couldn't believe my ears. He followed Thomas to his front door? How? His front door was down a long avenue that was private property. He had no permission to be on that land. 'How close to the house is he?' I asked in as calm a tone as I could muster.

'He's in the front yard,' Foley said.

'The O'Reillys' front yard? He's parked outside the house?' I said, confirming this as fact, my heart racing. 'How?'

'There's been credible threats against the welfare of the family, so we felt it was necessary to post a man on the grounds of the house for their own safety,' Foley said.

'Credible?' I mumbled. *There are no threats.*

'A fella rang the station threatening to burn the house down…' *Liar.*

'Tonight?' I said, incredulity dripping from my lips. *They know I know they are lying.*

'Bingo,' he said. *And they're pleased with themselves.* O'Neill was too nervous to be smug and Brian was delighted to be part of some action happening in the station. He was having a lovely time, his arse on Dicey's desk and in the centre of it all. I was quite scared by that point, I'll be honest. I swallowed hard because my heart was in my mouth. I hadn't foreseen that a man would be posted in the yard; it complicated a very simple plan, but it was out of my hands now. All I could do was sit in the corner and wait.

'I wouldn't mind a tea,' O'Neill said, looking my way.

'Oh yeah, lots of milk for me,' Brian said. He loved a milky tea, it put me right off.

'I'll have one,' Foley said before looking over to Quinn. 'Quinn?'

'I'm grand,' he said, his voice faint. I wondered if he felt sick about what he'd started here. I hoped so. He deserved to feel that way.

'Right,' I said. I stood up and walked a few steps, and I thought about making a run for it, but I couldn't. I was stuck there. I just hoped against hope that Dr Ciara Crosby would see the police stationed right outside the house and abandon the plan. But knowing her, even as little as I did, I worried she was the type that wouldn't take the easy option. *Please don't do anything stupid, Ciara*, I thought. *For both our sakes.*

As I moved away, my stomach tightened, and I could feel the vein in my neck start to throb a little. I walked into the small kitchenette and I closed the door behind me. I inhaled and exhaled. I held myself, hugging myself tight, and my thoughts ranged between, *Hang in there, Mary,* and, *My God, what have you done, Shea?*

–

The teas were made and drank before the radio crackled to life again. It was Dicey.

'We have a bit of action here,' he said. We all leaned forward in our seats.

'It's that doctor, the woman,' he said.

'What about her?' Brian said.

'She's after driving in... Holy God on high, will you watch what you're doing!' he shouted.

'What's going on?' Foley said as the sounds of a roaring engine and wheels spinning filled the air.

'Ah, she came in fast, nearly hit the bloody house,' he said. 'She parked up right against the feckin' door,' he said, breathless.

I could hear Ciara's feet crunching on the gravel as she approached Dicey. She must have leaned into the window, as she could be heard clearly on the radio in his hand.

'Sorry, Guard. It's a new car, I'm still not used to it,' she said.

'Well, that's obvious to a blind man. You'll get yourself killed,' he said.

'I didn't expect a car to be parked here, in the middle of the yard, it took me by surprise.'

'Well, open your eyes and slow down, woman.'

'Good advice,' she said and then I heard more crunching as she walked away.

'What's she doing there?' came Foley's frustrated question.

Brian relayed it to Dicey, and I could hear him shouting out to her, 'What's your business here?'

'There's a sick man in the house,' she said. 'Raymond O'Reilly,' she reminded him. Foley grabbed the radio from Brian. 'Pierce is the O'Reillys' doctor, what's the woman doing there?' he said clear enough for Ciara to answer herself. 'They sent for me,' she said.

'Right so,' Dicey said and the radio went silent for a minute or two. Then he spoke to us, after she had gone in through the door.

'Well, Thomas is still there, he answered the door to her. Looks like Raymond O'Reilly's home from the hospital,' he said, as though we all hadn't been a party to the previous conversation.

'Keep eyes on the house,' Foley said and Brian repeated it for Dicey's benefit.

We waited, the knot in my stomach tighter by the moment.

The radio crackled again; this time it was Liam Kenny. 'Well, that's Seamus McEvoy leaving the pub now. He's getting into the car.'

The room spiked with energy – everyone sat up except for Quinn, who remained slumped in the corner of the room.

'Keep your distance but keep on him,' Foley said.

They fully expected him to stop somewhere close to the O'Reillys' yard, so when he kept on going, we received a pretty miffed call from Liam Kenny. 'Eh… lads, he's well past the yard now…'

'Keep on him,' Foley said but his voice was quieter, he was thinking. He asked Brian to check in with Dicey McCarthy to ask if there was any way that Thomas could have got past him. He turned to O'Neill to explain his theory that the lads might be meeting somewhere on the road. Dicey confirmed he was looking at Thomas, currently chasing the chickens loose around the yard after they had somehow managed to escape their small coop.

I took the opportunity to interject. 'Well, it looks like this is not happening. Is it all right if I go home?'

'Stay where you are. The night's not over,' Foley said. He thought for a moment. He looked at Brian.

'Tell Kenny to pull him in.'

'Seamus McEvoy? For what?' Brian said.

'I don't know, how many pints did he have? How's his driving?'

'But what's the point if they're not together?' Brian said. Foley was panicking. He didn't know the answer. 'Fine, stay back from him, keep following.' But something was gnawing at Foley; things weren't working out the way he thought they would. He was busy trying to understand why and with each moment he wrestled with his thoughts, my heart beat harder and grew bigger in my chest. I was waiting for him to look at me and see the deceit, written all over my face. *Calm down, Mary. Calm down.* It was Dicey's voice that brought my mind back into the room. 'Lads, the doctor needs help.'

'What now?' Foley said.

'It's Raymond, he needs shifting into bed. Breda and Dr Crosby can't shift him.'

'Well, what about Thomas?' Foley said.

'He's got a broken arm,' Dicey said, sheepishly.

'Oh, for the love of...' Foley said. 'Go in, help them.'

I didn't know what was happening. Foley was smelling a rat, I was sure of it, but as the plan had changed, I had no idea what was going on. Dicey came back on about five minutes later.

'Raymond's fine. He's settled now, the Crosby woman is gone,' he said.

'And Thomas?' Foley asked.

'Last I saw he was making tea,' Dicey said. They must have aborted the plan. *It's over,* I thought as relief washed over me. We waited another hour, with the lads calling in with updates. Liam Kenny was in another county on his way to Dublin, and Dicey reported that the lights were out and the O'Reillys were in bed by the time Foley called it off.

'Turn Kenny around but have someone watch the house till morning,' Foley said to Brian. 'Let Dicey go home.'

O'Neill was agitated. He argued he was never up for this gay nonsense anyway, he just wanted to get his hands around Thomas's throat and make him some promises. Foley reminded him that that was how he got into trouble in the first place. Quinn was mute. Brian was a little disappointed that the night had ended in such an unexciting way. I asked if I could go home. Foley agreed and walked me to the door. He opened it and held it, and we were face to face, looking into the whites of each other's eyes.

'I don't know what happened here tonight, Shea,' he said.

'You'll find out,' I replied, plastering a smile on my face as I pushed past him, hoping he couldn't see that I was a traitor. 'Good night,' I called out to the wind as the heavy blue door shut behind me.

—

At home I paced the floor, desperate to talk to Ciara, to hear things from her side, but without a phone... It was clear that Seamus left town alone – with eyes directly on the house, they wouldn't have been able to get Thomas out as planned. *But did he get out?* Night was rolling into morning and I'd agreed to meet Ciara Crosby for lunch. I'd get my answers then, but in the meantime I'd feel foolish because it all felt foolish, us all carrying on a charade while an innocent young girl was sitting in a jail cell. I thought I was better than those men. I wasn't. I was just as corruptible in my own way. *What had it all been for? What were we doing?* Those were the last thoughts that washed through my mind as I finally closed my eyes and fell asleep.

CHAPTER SIXTEEN

Day Twelve

I had the day off and a lot on my mind. I wanted to get out of the cottage and away from the farm. I knew the McEvoys would wake up to their son's empty bed and a note to explain he'd left them. Their lives would change irrevocably. Their future was now uncertain. Seamus was right, financially they would be fine, but the loss of their only child would have a devastating effect. I didn't want any part of that; life was too difficult as it was. I decided to walk to town – it would take thirty minutes, but the clouds had cleared, the sky was an icy blue and the air felt cold enough to sweep the cobwebs and maybe even some of the misery away. I moved quickly through the lower yard and then to the long muddy track that separated the fields. I was nearly jogging by the time I was halfway down the path. Then I saw the familiar battered old van that Ruth McEvoy drove. My heart squeezed in my chest. She slowed to a stop. I did the same. I heard the window jerking down before I turned to meet her eyes. Her face was red, burnt by the salt of her tears.

'How're things?' she asked. 'Would you like a lift?'

'I'd rather walk. Thanks.'

'Did you know he was leaving us?' It wasn't an accusation. She just wanted to know.

'I did,' I said. 'But only since yesterday.'

'We had hoped that maybe the two of you…' she said but she couldn't manage to finish the sentence.

'It was never on the cards, Mrs McEvoy, but he's a good friend, better than I'd realised. I'm sorry he's gone,' I said. That made her smile the slightest smile.

'He wrote that he was sorry, but he couldn't live someone else's life any more… Whose life do you think he was talking about?' she asked.

'Yours,' I said before I had a chance to stop myself. I didn't say it to hurt her, it was a thing that was true.

'We just wanted him to be happy. Farming is in his blood,' she said and I nodded. Of course that's all they wanted for him. They loved him. He was their son. Their only child.

'I knew he was different, of course I did. A mother knows.' She wiped an invisible tear from her face. 'Now we've lost him.' She was grieving, I could feel the weight of the pain that seeped from deep inside her. Her boy was gone. What could I say? I scrambled for words of comfort but found none.

'Do you think he'll ever come back to us?' she said in a voice threatening to crack.

'I don't know the answer to that, Mrs McEvoy. All I know is that Dublin isn't America. He might not live in the same county but that doesn't mean he can't be in your life,' I said.

'You make it sound so easy.'

'I didn't mean to. I know it's not easy, but you raised a good and kind man, and I'll miss him,' I said and she reached out through her open window. She took my hand in hers and held it to her broken heart before kissing it and letting it go.

'Thank you, Mary,' she said before driving onwards. I watched her disappear down the long avenue before I turned away and headed for town.

–

I had time and I was drawn to the beach and to the cradle, where I sat for a while cross-legged, before the weight of my worries forced me to lie on my back, facing the heavens above. 'I'm sorry, Crónán,' I said out loud. 'I'm letting you down, we all are.'

I lay quietly after that, thinking – processing every moment I could remember from the time Dicey McCarthy and I were in the garda car, when the call came in about a hysterical woman and a dead baby on the beach. We'd gone after the O'Reillys straight out of the gate, and all the evidence we'd collated against them turned out to be circumstantial. I could see her now, the lost and crying girl, gripped by shame, confusion, physical pain and mental anguish. What was Joyce O'Reilly telling me when she wasn't saying a word? She was guilty, yes – but of what? She was guilty of getting pregnant and lying about it, concealing it. She was guilty of giving birth alone, unattended by a trained medical professional, of being unable to deliver a living child. Guilty of panicking and concealing evidence that the child ever existed. And the shame she carried… that was our fault. It was rooted in how we viewed young women like her, how we treated them, judged them, demonised them. Her mother's reaction said it all: she knew Joyce's predicament and instead of helping her, she turned her back. Unable to cope with the awful truth: her daughter was one of *those* girls. Loose. Lacking in moral fibre. A stain on the family name. That's what Joyce O'Reilly told me without words. She said nothing about a baby boy or his murder because she knew nothing about it. *So who did?*

The sky brightened, the white light hurting my eyes. I closed them and felt my lids warm. I could have slept there, in the cradle, with the soft sand underneath me and the long grasses surrounding me, protecting me, the sky bearing down like a heavy blanket. *Who did this? And how? And why?* The answer was there, I just had to open my eyes and my mind.

I decided to refocus my energy upon my return to work. The boys could do what they liked. I was all but out in the cold anyway. I'd make their estrangement work for me – I'd carry out my own investigation. Maybe I was naive, and God knows I wasn't sure what I was doing, but I knew one thing: I'd try. That's all I could do. I opened my eyes, sat up and called out to him, 'It's not over yet.' I stood up, brushed myself off and as I stepped out of the dune, I whispered, 'Rest now.'

–

The cafe was busy enough at lunchtime. I was five minutes early but Ciara had made it there before me. She waved and smiled when she heard the jingle of the bell above the door as it opened. My heart lifted a little. I'd been afraid she'd be angry with me for asking her the impossible. But she was grinning widely, a large cardboard box sitting on the table in front of her. She stood up and grabbed it.

'Let's go,' she said.

'Where?' I asked, looking into the box to see a few sandwiches and some cake carefully packed inside it.

'I have a flask of tea in the car,' she said, before she waved to the girl behind the counter and the girl waved back. I followed, not yet understanding what was going on.

'Ciara?' I said as we walked onto the street and the bell over the cafe door jangled behind us.

'We've a lot to talk about and there are far too many ears inside. Come on,' she said and I followed her to her car. She handed me the large box and started driving.

'They didn't have anything smaller?' I asked and she grinned. 'No.'

'Well?' I said as she took off down the coast road.

'Well,' she said, and she giggled. The tension was killing me.

'What?'

'Where is Thomas O'Reilly?' she asked.

'Well, I presume he's at home, where you left him,' I said.

'Ah, but I didn't leave him at home,' she told me and I'll be damned if her eyes didn't sparkle.

'You didn't?' I said, wondering how it was possible.

'Nope,' she said, shaking her head emphatically.

'What did you do?' I asked and now I was grinning too. Surely this story had a happy ending, the positive vibes were rocketing off her.

'Let's find a spot,' she said, pointing towards the forest. 'I'll tell you everything.'

With our coats zipped up and our woollen hats tight around our ears, we walked between the towering trees that formed a canopy above us, shielding us from the worst of the cold, but the air was still crisp enough to redden the tips of our noses, and it carried with it the faint scent of moss and damp earth. It wasn't long before we found a cosy spot, where Ciara spread a soft blanket on the ground, covering the carpet of fallen leaves that crunched beneath our weight. She served us tea from the flask into two small plastic red cups and we indulged in triangular-shaped sandwiches with the crusts cut off as we shared our experiences of the previous evening. I explained I'd been called into the station, so I was aware that Dicey was sitting right outside the house. In fact, I had borne witness to everything – or at least, I thought I had. I was soon to be disabused of that notion.

Thomas didn't know why Dr Ciara Crosby had come to his door, but she quickly made it clear she was there to help him escape. Breda and his father were both aware that Thomas needed to leave town to successfully launch a legal case against the Dublin boys. But, with Dicey having a direct line of sight, our original plan was scuppered, so Ciara devised a simple yet risky solution. They would carefully help Raymond out of bed and onto the floor, then call in Dicey to assist in putting him back. While Dicey was distracted, Thomas offered to make tea – he'd boil the kettle, slip out of the house and hide in the boot of Ciara's car. Once Dicey left, Ciara would drive Thomas to safety. The plan worked – barely. Ciara managed to distract Dicey as he left the house, ensuring he didn't stop to speak to Thomas as he passed the kitchen door, even as the kettle whistled. Shortly after, she drove away, passing Dicey parked outside, with Thomas hidden in the boot of her car. She drove to her practice, where she hid him until she received a call from Seamus later that night to advise that the coast was clear. From there, she drove Thomas to meet Seamus in the town of Macroom.

'What time did you get home?' I asked.

'It was well after four in the morning,' she said.

'You must be exhausted,' I said.

She grinned. 'Exhausted? I'm elated. I felt like I was in a film.'

'You're a wild woman, Ciara Crosby,' I said.

'I believe you're right,' she said and we celebrated her escapade by eating cake. Seamus and Thomas had got away. I was happy for them, but I couldn't deny the enormity of what I'd been a part of. Had I interfered with an investigation? *Hardly*. The Dublin boys weren't looking for truth that night, they were looking to cover themselves. They were seeking to threaten and destroy the lives of two innocents. *Right?* It wouldn't prevent us from finding the real truth… *Would it?* In the end, I couldn't have known either way, and it did bother me. It did scare me and I wondered, *Who am I? What am I capable of?* I knew it wouldn't be long before the boys realised Thomas was gone, and Foley put two and two together. He'd suspect Ciara's involvement – and mine – and all I could hope for was that Dicey was as weak a man as I believed him to be. He had claimed to have seen Thomas making tea before he left the house, and I was relying on him failing to correct himself.

–

That night we went to the disco, Ciara and I. She should have been too tired but she was still pumped and as soon as we walked inside the door, we were swathed in an explosion of lights and energy. The room was pulsing with drumbeats and guitars pushing us towards the busy dance floor, filled with men in brightly coloured shirts, glittering women, and the scent of perfume, sweat and cigarette smoke. It was good to dance, to shake and shimmy, to leap around, to spin and lose myself in the beat of the music, to get lost in the shimmering reflections of the disco ball on the mirrored walls and the fog that the machine coughed out every fifteen minutes. The stool at the bar was missing Seamus; some other fella was sitting on it, drinking a green cocktail and chewing on a tiny paper umbrella. I wondered how Seamus was. I hoped he was all right. Luckily, Ciara liked to dance as much as I did, and so we lost ourselves and our cares on that floor. I didn't know it then, but our lifelong friendship had just begun.

It was on the way out, while I was queuing for the coats, that I heard one of the boys ask a girl if she wanted a lift. She said no, she'd get the bus. It's funny, the way the mind works – I can't remember if it was in that exact moment, when I heard the boy ask the question, or a few minutes later, when I saw some women jumping onto the minibus and others getting into cars, but something clicked. *My friend Brenda drove us home…* That's what Fidelma Regan said to me when I asked her about the night Baby Crónán died. But her statement said something different. She had lied to me.

Day Thirteen

The incident room was empty, the boxes packed and ready to go to the prosecution office. I found one containing witness statements and rifled through it until I found Fidelma's. I sat down to read it: she had been out that night watching a film, *Kramer vs. Kramer*, in another town with her friend Brenda Wall. She said she got a minibus home and although she couldn't be sure, she believed she was in bed and asleep by eleven. Did she lie in her statement or to me? Or did she just forget? Hard to forget how you got home on the night a baby was murdered and his body had been lying not far from your home.

Hard to forget when you were asked about it and made a statement a day later. But if she was lying… why? Foley and the Dublin boys were staying in the hotel. They were probably taking some downtime. *Should*

I go to Foley? And say what? A witness lied about how she got home? Did it really matter? I didn't know, I wasn't sure what to do. I picked up the phone and I placed a call home. My father answered.

'Hello, you've reached the Shea residence,' he said.

'Hi, Daddy.'

'Mai*me*. How are you?'

'I'm fine,' I said.

'Do you want me to get your mother?'

'No, Daddy, I'd like to talk to you,' I said and he made a little noise. I wasn't sure, but it sounded like he was surprised and happy.

'What can I do for you?'

'A woman lied in her statement, or maybe she told the truth in her statement and she lied to me about how she got home the night Baby Crónán was murdered,' I said.

'Do you think she could be a witness? Or involved even?'

'I don't know, but she lives on Potters Road, a few doors down from a woman who saw a mysterious girl in her nightdress, not far from the beach,' I explained.

'I take it you don't believe that girl was Joyce O'Reilly,' he said.

'No.'

'They've charged Joyce.'

'And they're wrong.'

'You're so sure?'

'I'm almost positive.'

'What about Foley?'

'He's only short of packing up to go home,' I said. He thought about it for a moment.

'You've always had a good gut,' he said and I felt myself smiling. 'Go with it. Talk to her, see what she says.'

'Okay, Daddy. Thanks.'

'And Mary, girl… mind yourself,' he said and hung up the phone. I looked up Brenda Wall's number in the phone book. Luckily, although there were a number of Breda Walls, there was only one Brenda. She lived in a smaller town, six miles away. She was off the beaten path, down a narrow and winding road. It was a tiny house, surrounded by dense vegetation, hidden amongst trees that seemed to have been growing there forever. I could picture the spread of wildflowers that would no doubt carpet the place in spring and summer. I knocked and she opened the door almost immediately, dressed in welly boots and a raincoat, and making her way past me while asking if I was lost.

'No,' I said. Then I asked her name. She confirmed to me that she was Brenda Wall.

'Friend of Fidelma Regan?' I asked. She nodded, before an alarm set off in her head.

'Did something happen to her?' she asked.

'No,' I said. 'But I'd like to ask you a few questions.' It was then I showed her my credentials. She turned her key, locking the door behind her.

'I need a walk but you're welcome to join me,' she said. Brenda was a woman in her late thirties, of medium build, with dark hair to her shoulders, and attractive enough without make-up. As we walked, she took an elastic band from her pocket and tied her hair up in a small bun.

'What do you want to know?' she asked. We were walking away from the road and deeper into the property.

'Can you tell me about the night Baby Crónán died?'

'I was with Fidelma, we went to *Kramer vs. Karmer*, she liked it. I thought it was depressing. That's all, really,' she said.

'How did you get home?' I asked.

'I drove. Living out here, I drive everywhere.'

'Was Fidelma with you?'

'No,' she said.

'How did she get home?' I asked. I could see the tension tighten on Brenda's face.

'She said she was getting the minibus.'

She said… Funny way to phrase it.

'And did she?' I asked, and I knew she was fighting an internal battle – her loyalty to her friend versus lying to the police.

'What did she say?' she asked.

'I can't tell you that, but I need you to be honest with me, Brenda,' I said.

'No, she didn't. I saw her waiting for it all right, but as I was pulling away, I saw her get into a car.'

'Whose car?' I asked.

'I don't know. It was a dark car, I think it was a BMW. It looked smart.'

'And you never asked her about it?'

'Fidelma's very sensitive and I didn't want her to know I'd caught her in a lie,' she said.

We continued to walk through the wood of evergreens. It felt like shelter. 'Watch your step, this ground has a mind of its own,' she warned. There were roots and vines all around us; I did as I was told.

'You didn't get a glimpse of the driver?' I asked.

'No. He drove off at speed, you'd swear it was a race car he was in,' she said.

'Is there anything else you can tell me?' I said.

She thought about it and shrugged. 'But what does this have to do with the baby found on the beach?' she asked.

'We take statements from so many people because one of them might have seen or heard something that leads us somewhere entirely different – a piece of the puzzle that is meaningless on its own but, when placed in the right spot at the right time, reveals a picture that tells us a story,' I answered honestly. 'If someone isn't honest with us, it corrupts the story. A girl's life is on the line,' I said and Brenda sighed wearily.

'Fidelma was with a fella called Damien Brady when they were younger, and they were together for a long time. She thought they'd marry, but he had other ideas. They split up, and he got married and had two kids. She never got over him. I don't know who was in that car, but I do know that after going through a hard time over the last few years, Fidelma has been happier in herself, lighter – and Damien Brady drives a dark-coloured BMW,' she said. She suspected her friend was having an affair. It was a good enough reason to lie. Maybe that was all it was, a woman hiding an affair with a married man. It had been done before. It would be done again.

I thanked her, and we walked for a bit. Somehow, we must have made a circle, because we ended up in front of my car. As she was walking away, Brenda turned back to face me. 'She's a good person,' she said, before she was quickly swallowed by the trees. So Fidelma Regan lied both on her statement and to my face, which meant she wasn't home and in bed alone by eleven. *So did she see something?* I drove to Fidelma's house and banged on her door. She wasn't there. I parked in the carpark by the beach opposite her house and waited for her.

It was a good vantage point – I could see right down the road. About an hour later, a dark BMW slowed to a stop much further up the road. Fidelma jumped out, and then the car took off like a bat out of hell. I wondered why they even bothered; they weren't exactly practised in covert behaviour. I watched her walk inside. I got out, followed her and banged on her door. When she opened it, her face fell – she knew this wasn't a social call.

'Garda Shea,' she said, her eyes already filling with tears.

'Hello, Fidelma,' I said as she ushered me inside, before closing the door behind us.

We sat at her clean table in her clean kitchen, not a drop of tea between us; her hands were joined in front of her, my arms were crossed.

'You lied to me,' I said and she nodded.

'I'd hoped you hadn't noticed. I realised as soon as I messed up,' she admitted. She was emotional but her voice was calm. I wondered if there was just a tiny part of her that was relieved to have been caught in the lie.

'Why did you lie?' I said.

'Because…'

'Does it have something to do with the man in the BMW?' I said and a fat tear plopped from her eye, splashing her cheek.

'Damien,' she said. 'He's married.'

'And you're seeing him?'

'For the last six months.' She couldn't look me in the face. 'He's not happy and they haven't been happy in a long time.'

'I'm not here to judge you. Adultery isn't illegal,' I said and it sounded more judgemental than it was meant.

'Was the baby yours, Fidelma?' I had to ask.

'God no…' she said before adding that I could check with Dr Pierce. Fidelma suffered an infection when she was younger. They had to take her womb.

'It's why he left me. He wanted kids. I couldn't give him that, so I suppose now he has them and he has me.' She sounded bitter and relieved all at once.

'You'll have to ask Dr Pierce to provide me with documentation to that effect,' I said and she nodded. 'I'm sorry,' I added and she hunched.

'I'm over it,' she said, but she wasn't — that was clear by the sadness in her tone.

'What time were you out till?' I asked. It was time for the truth now.

'It was half three in the morning.'

'You're sure of it.'

'I had school in the morning, I teach primary. Anyway, he needed to go home,' she said.

'Did you see anything?' I asked and she looked at me and exhaled, and I could see that she had and that it was weighing on her. 'What did you see?'

'It can't be connected,' she said. It was obvious that she had been torn about it.

'Let me decide that,' I told her.

'I saw Lisa.'

'Who is Lisa?' I said.

'Lisa Fitzmaurice.'

I took it in. 'Bridie's girl, the escape artist with Down syndrome?' I said. She nodded.

'She was in her nightdress, in the rain.'

'Where?' I asked.

'A few doors down from my house,' she said before bowing her head.

'Outside Mrs Lacey's house?'

'Yes. She looked distressed. I wanted to go out to her but Damien said we couldn't be seen together, not that late at night, and Lisa, because of... what... she is... couldn't be trusted to keep a secret. We argued about it. Then all of a sudden she ran off.'

'Was she alone?' I asked, my mind racing ahead... *Lisa?*

'She was, that's all I can tell you,' she said. Was Lisa a link to the missing piece of the puzzle or just another ghost to chase? I didn't know. How could I?

—

After that, I went home. I made a fire. I cooked food. I listened to music and I drank two glasses of whiskey. Then I went to bed and I lay there, mentally pouring steel into my veins because if Lisa Fitzmaurice was the missing piece to this case, chances were I'd have a fight on my hands.

CHAPTER SEVENTEEN

Day Fourteen

I wasn't sure how to approach Foley. It was hard to know if we were on the same team any more; in fact, by then it seemed obvious that we weren't. I found him in the incident room, alone. There was a large brown envelope, lying on the table, its ragged edges suggesting it had been ripped open, and he was hunched over, reading a document of some kind. I couldn't tell what it was. He didn't even turn to face me when he spoke. 'Thomas O'Reilly is gone,' he said.

'Right,' I said, injecting as much nonchalance into my voice as possible.

'Is that all you have to say?' he asked and he spun around on the chair. I sat on the closest desk to the door I could find. Steeling myself for what was to come. *Did he know? He wasn't a fool. His face of thunder suggested he'd put two and two together, surely.* I thought about what that would mean; others, like O'Neill, acted out, bended and broke the rules, and they'd be fine, but me... The rules were different for me. I would lose my job. I thought about my father – would he be happy that at least his daughter was no longer doing a man's work, or would it fill him with shame? His legacy would be tarnished, just as he had predicted.

'What do you want me to say?' I asked nervously, waiting for the axe to fall.

'Dicey McCarthy swears he saw Thomas making tea as he was leaving the house,' he said.

Yes, thank you for being you, Dicey, I thought. 'He went off shift at midnight. The local young fella that took over swears there wasn't a budge out of the place and yet Thomas O'Reilly has up and vanished.'

'Right,' I said.

'Right,' he echoed, more frustrated now. 'The people in this place are really starting to annoy me.'

Fair enough, I thought. I decided to inject a bit of honesty in the conversation, this play-acting didn't suit me at all. 'What you were doing to Thomas wasn't right anyway.'

'It that so?'

'It is and while I'm at it, Joyce O'Reilly didn't give birth to Baby Crónán. She certainly didn't kill him. We're looking in the wrong direction,' I said and expected to hear shouting, but he seemed to slump as though my words had taken all the air out of him.

'That's surprising… You've been so good about keeping those feelings to yourself,' he said sarcastically, raising his eyes to heaven. I allowed myself to smile.

'You're being sarcastic,' I said.

'Yes, I am, Shea.'

'Right,' I said. He looked me in the eye.

'Do I know there are holes the size of a small county in this case? I do. Do I think it's possible that someone else could have had that child? Of course, because I've learned that anything is possible. But everything and everyone I've looked into leads either to Joyce O'Reilly or a dead end,' he admitted, looking defeated. I hadn't thought that possible of him. I liked him more for it. And he was right – except, I had something worth pitching. Maybe he had a conscience after all. I knew it could be nothing, but no stone should remain unturned.

'I've identified the girl in the nightdress on Potters Road,' I said and that got his attention. I could almost see his spirits lifting.

'The ghost of the dead daughter?'

'Yeah,' I said.

'Who is it?'

'Lisa Fitzmaurice. She's—'

'The kid the Fitzmaurices lock in the spare bedroom,' he said, making her situation sound a lot worse than it was.

'Yeah.'

'And you think she could possibly have something to do with this?' he asked, his enthusiasm slightly dimming.

'I think we'd be in dereliction of our duty if we didn't ask,' I said.

He grabbed his coat from the back of his chair. 'Right answer,' he said and he walked out the door. I wasn't sure if he was inviting me to join him until he called out, 'Well, are you coming or what?'

–

He drove while I explained how I'd uncovered the information, by catching Fidelma in a lie about how and when she got home from the cinema that fateful night. 'Very good,' he mumbled. I went on to describe Fidelma's circumstances. 'So she was lying because she didn't want to be caught in an affair,' he said. 'I don't know how people have the energy.' It was the early shift and at six thirty in the morning, lights were only starting to appear in houses, dotting the streets. I could see the light on in the top left-hand window of the Fitzmaurice house. Bridie's room. She was awake and probably feeding baby Johnny. The idea of seeing him again unnerved me. *It's just a baby, Mary. Grow up. Toughen up.* We parked outside. Foley glanced up at the window and sighed. 'We'll give them another few minutes.' He looked at his watch and rubbed his forehead. 'It's early.' We sat there in silence for a while.

'I think McCarthy is lying about Thomas,' he said out of nowhere and my chest wall threatened to collapse my lung cage. I didn't respond. I couldn't. I could scarcely breathe. He didn't say anything else. He just let it sit there and so did I. It was a test. He had a theory about how Thomas got away, maybe even the right one, but didn't say any more. Another light went on upstairs and then one in the hall downstairs.

'That's us,' he said. I followed him to the front door. Debbie answered; she was in a white nightdress, hugging the thick knitted cream cardigan she was wearing over it. She seemed surprised to see us.

'Is something wrong?' she said and she paled. She was used to bad news and terrible things; her knees had already begun to shake. I was quick to assure her that everything and everyone was fine. She exhaled and welcomed us in. Bridie was in the kitchen, feeding a bottle of warm milk to baby Johnny. His shock of black hair brought me back to the beach, back to the body – and then I could smell bleach. A wave of nausea hit me, so intense that I had to focus on not throwing up. I don't remember the greetings, except that when she told us to sit at her kitchen table, I grabbed the chair and held on to it to steady myself.

If anyone noticed my discomfort, they didn't say anything. I sat down. Foley was playing with the baby's chubby fingers. 'He's a fine fella,' he said as I focused on the woodgrain on the table.

'He's his daddy and his brother all over, reborn. We're blessed,' she said. She was smiling, alert, glowing. Suddenly, there was a pot of tea on the table, with Debbie placing cups around it. 'I'll leave you to it,' she said, about to exit the room.

'No, stay,' Foley said and she wasn't sure what to do. Her mother nodded to her, and she grabbed a chair and sat.

'What's this all for, Detective?' Bridie said. Foley explained that I'd spotted the drugs on her bedroom locker and that they were prescribed for Fidelma Regan.

'Oh God. I only took a couple. Is she in trouble for it?' she said and he was quick to disabuse her of that notion. He explained that she'd made a statement about the night Baby Crónán died, as she lived on Potters Road, opposite the entrance to the beach car park, but new information had recently come to light. 'I'm not following,' Bridie said.

'She lied about how she got home,' I clarified.

'Sorry to hear it but I'm still not sure why you've landed on my doorstep,' Bridie said, rubbing the child's back vigorously.

'Because she saw Lisa on Potters Road that night,' I said.

'Our Lisa?' she said, looking to Debbie, who immediately bowed her head. The baby belched, his presence a distraction to me. I tried to stay focused. *It's not him, Mary. It's not him.*

'What time was this?' she asked.

'Half three in the morning,' I said and Bridie's face reddened. She shot a look at her daughter and her tone was accusatory. 'She was out in the middle of the night on her own? God almighty, Debbie, anything could have happened.'

Debbie immediately started to cry and I pitied her. She was a young girl with way too much responsibility resting on her shoulders.

'Ah now, sounds like she's a bit of a handful,' Foley said. 'And it looked like Debbie had a lot on at the time.' He offered Debbie a smile and a wink to assure her. Her tears had dried, but the colour had drained from her face, and her eyes were dark holes in her gaunt features. Bridie seemed taken aback, but what could she say? He was right. Following their tragic loss, she had fallen apart, leaving her daughter to pick up the pieces. The girl was shattered – anyone could see that.

'You're right,' she said reasonably. 'She's hard to keep up with and we can't lock her door overnight. It's too dangerous,' she said.

'Has she escaped at night before?' I asked.

'No. She's usually a good sleeper.' Bridie looked to Debbie for her agreement. Debbie nodded. 'She hits the pillow and she's gone for at least eight hours,' Bridie said, looking down at her newborn son, nudging the nipple of the bottle against his tiny red lips.

His fists were balled but his fingers flexed. His eyes were shut, he was sleepy. My heart raced. *It's not him, Mary. It's not him.*

'Do you remember that night?' Foley asked Debbie, and she seemed flustered.

'It's all right,' I said in an effort to calm the storm quietly brewing in her.

'I found her on the doorstep that morning, I don't know how she got out. I really don't know.' She sounded panicked.

'It's okay,' Bridie said. 'The detective is right, it's not your fault,' she said but I could feel the waves of fear coming off her.

'I'd never let anything happen to Lisa,' she said and Bridie knew that.

'Of course you wouldn't,' she said.

'Can we speak to Lisa?' Foley said and the question seemed to shock both Bridie and Debbie.

'Why?' Bridie said.

'We need to know if she saw anything that night,' I explained.

'And what she was doing out there,' Foley said.

'She doesn't know anything about that dead baby, we didn't tell her about it,' Debbie said, with a rush of panic.

'Lisa wouldn't understand it. She still finds it difficult to understand her daddy and Tommy aren't coming home, it's all just a bit too much,' Bridie said.

'We'll try not to upset her,' Foley said, not taking no for an answer. Bridie looked to Debbie. 'I'll get her,' she said. She got up from the table and with feet of lead she slowly walked up the stairs. I wondered if the girl was sick. She looked sick. Bridie ordered us to drink our tea. It was a few minutes before Lisa arrived, dressed in a pair of pyjamas with pink elephants on them. She was rubbing her eyes as she walked in. By now the baby in Bridie's arms was asleep, his gentle breathing a soundtrack beneath the drama unfolding.

'That's Detective Foley, Lisa, and you know Garda Shea?' Debbie said and Lisa said hello. She sat down and looked at us with childish curiosity. I wasn't sure how Foley would handle the matter.

He smiled at her. 'Lisa,' he said and she nodded. 'That's a lovely name.'

She grinned.

'I hear you like to go on walks.'

'I'm an escape artist,' she said as a matter of fact.

'Do you like escaping at night?' he said.

'I don't like the dark,' she explained. 'It's hard to see in the dark.'

'Have you ever run away at night?'

She shook her head.

'Are you sure, Lisa? Think hard, have you been walking at night any time lately?' she thought hard, biting her tongue.

'It was raining,' I said in an attempt to jog her memory and it worked, because something stirred in her, a recollection. *I didn't like getting wet…* I remembered she'd said that before, but Debbie had corrected her grammar: *You don't like getting wet…*

'Do you remember getting wet, Lisa?'

She nodded. 'I was cold.'

'I found her on the step that morning. I didn't know how long she was out,' Debbie admitted.

'How did you get out?' Foley said. Lisa thought about it, really focused. 'I don't know,' she said and as frustrating a reply as it was, I knew she was telling the truth.

'Why did you go out?' he asked.

She thought about it again and shook her head from side to side. 'I don't know.'

It didn't make sense. *How could she not remember? It was only two weeks ago.*

'Has Lisa a history of sleepwalking?' I asked Bridie. She was quick to deny it.

I looked to Lisa. 'What do you remember about being out in the rain?'

She thought about it. 'I was scared.'

'Did you see anyone?' I asked.

'An old woman in the window,' she said.

237

'What did you do?' I asked. She tried to think, hard… then the tears came. 'I don't know.'

Bridie stood up, baby in arms, and she kissed her forehead. 'It's okay, Lisa. I think that's enough,' she said.

'We need to know…' Foley started to say, but Bridie was done with us.

'I was sore,' Lisa said suddenly.

'Sore?' Foley asked.

Debbie jumped in. 'She cut her foot, she couldn't tell me how. It makes sense now,' she said. Lisa was quickly distracted, taking her sock off to show us the scar that was forming.

'Lisa, did you know a baby died?' Foley said. Lisa's eyes widened into saucers.

'Ah, for God's sake,' Bridie said. He held up his hand to silence her.

'A baby was found not so far away on the beach,' he said.

'Whose baby?' Lisa asked.

'We don't know,' Foley said.

'Who would hurt a baby?'

'That's what we're trying to find out. Do you remember something to help us find who hurt that baby?' he asked.

She shook her head. 'No.'

'Do you remember anything at all?' he said and he was almost pleading with her.

'I was sore,' she told him, looking down at her foot. It looked like a deep enough cut.

Foley stood up. 'Thank you for your time,' he said, and we saw ourselves out.

–

We sat in the car. 'What did you make of that?' I asked.

Foley made a sucking sound between his teeth. 'Another feckin' dead end?'

'It's strange, though. Why doesn't she remember being outside?'

'Find out if it's something to do with her condition,' he said.

'Okay,' I said.

So there we were, back to square one, but something wasn't right and we both felt it.

We returned to the incident room just in time to witness O'Neill's meltdown when word came in that Joyce O'Reilly's solicitor had issued a statement telling the press that she was retracting her second confession. He was hovering above Quinn, shouting the odds, and Quinn was shrinking under him, taking his abuse. It looked like he might hit him; his body was tense, he was poised like a rattlesnake about to strike, and the language coming from his mouth would shame the devil. Quinn had the look of a beaten dog. 'What's this?' Foley said. O'Neill was shaking with rage. 'If this fella wasn't such a lightweight, I wouldn't have needed to put Thomas O'Reilly under that level of pressure. It was like I was on my own in the room,' O'Neill shouted. Foley lost it – he wasn't about to go over the incident again. O'Neill might have been his favourite, but that day Foley showed his pet his own sharp teeth. 'Shut up, O'Neill, shut your mouth. You were heavy-handed. You're always heavy-handed. When it gets results, you bathe yourself in glory – so, this time it went bad, own it and move on,' he said and O'Neill was taken aback.

'But you said—'

'*I said what?*' Foley roared. '*What did I say?*' And it was clear to everyone in the room that this was not a question that demanded an answer. O'Neill took a step back. Quinn looked like he was about to burst into tears.

'It's not about you. This case is built on a house of cards,' Foley said and my knees nearly went from under me, to hear him admit it out loud in front of the boys. He was quieter now – the explosion had vented the frustration that had clearly been building up in him.

He was once again in control of himself and, more importantly, the room. We all stood like statues as he dismantled his own case, card by card.

'Baby Crónán's blood group is O. We say Joyce's and McKnight's blood groups could produce an O, but O'Neill and Quinn could probably produce a baby with a blood group O,' he said, pointing to the two men. Quinn paled slightly. 'So, what will the defence say to that? They'll say it's as common as muck – meaningless. And they'd be right. We say McKnight was with Joyce O'Reilly, but the defence will point out that he couldn't even pick her photo out of a line-up, never mind the injury he's sustained that casts doubt on his fertility. We say she had two babies, murdered one, walked to the beach and returned to the safety of her bed before morning. They'll argue that, due to the nature of her birthing injury and her medical condition, it would have been impossible for her to make that return journey…'

'But what about what Dr Boyne said?' O'Neill asked in the most timid voice I'd heard come out of him.

'Boyne's a bloody idiot. I've spoken to Joyce's surgeon, and Boyne's testimony would have the court laughing at us. As for the theory of heteropaternal superfecundation, it's as rare as hen's teeth and now, to add the final nail to the coffin, the current coroner's report suggests Lily O'Reilly was premature, while Baby Crónán was overdue. Hetero-paternal superfecundation happens when two babies are conceived during one menstrual cycle – Baby Crónán and Lily O'Reilly are three months apart. I have more chance of being his mother than Joyce O'feckin'Reilly,' Foley concluded.

Suddenly, things made sense. It was the coroner's report he had been reading when I arrived earlier that morning. His frustration and anger had little to do with the disappearance of Thomas O'Reilly and everything to do with his case falling apart. No wonder he'd listened to me and followed up on my lead. A drowning man will clutch at any straw. No wonder Joyce was retracting her confession – it had finally been deemed impossible for her to be Baby Crónán's mother. And now there would be questions. Why did she confess? Thomas would be more than happy to provide those asking with the answer. There would be trouble for the Dublin lads, but even then, as I looked at the stress and tension etched on each of their faces, I knew deep down that whatever lay in store for them, it wouldn't be anything they couldn't navigate. It was just the way the world worked.

'What now?' I said.

Foley looked at me. 'Now?' He exhaled. 'We start again.'

O'Neill sank into his chair. Quinn said he needed to go to the loo. He passed Dicey McCarthy on the way in to begin his shift. 'How ye, lads,' Dicey said. He was met with silence and icy stares. He shrank a bit, like prey sensing danger or a submissive dog, but instead of exposing his belly, he meekly asked if anyone wanted tea.

'I'll have a cup,' I said. Well, if looks could kill I'd be six feet under, but he made the tea. I didn't drink it, just in case he urinated in it. Dicey handing it over in front of the Dublin boys was all the satisfaction

I needed. Foley looked at his watch. 'Go home,' he said. 'We start tomorrow at six a.m. Don't be late.'

'What's going to happen to Joyce?' I said.

'Her solicitor would have received the same report as I did. He'll have the case thrown out.'

'How long will that take?'

'Depends.'

'On what?'

'On how quickly people do their jobs,' he said. I left the place knowing that at least that girl would get out of prison, and I was happy for her, Thomas and her family. I was happy for Seamus, because what affected Thomas surely affected him. I hoped things would resolve sooner rather than later so that they could start rebuilding their lives together, without carrying the burden of Joyce's unjustified incarceration. It was a win for the O'Reilly family; sense finally prevailed. She was lucky, there were others caught up in the system not so fortunate.

–

Ciara was waiting for me in the pub. We'd decided to go for a quick drink after work and as I opened the door, I was greeted by the unmistakable scent of peat burning in the fireplace. Finnegan's was a rustic place, with wooden beams above us and worn floorboards creaking underfoot. The walls were filled with old photographs of the town in another era. Ciara waved to me from where she was standing, by the polished oak counter. Behind that, bottles lined the shelves and I could see the various whiskeys, their golden liquid glimmering in the soft light coming from the stubby red candles about to flicker out.

'Whiskey?' she called out to me.

'I'll buy,' I said. She liked a G&T. I ordered and paid the boy behind the counter; he couldn't have been more than sixteen but he was at ease there, born for it. We moved to a table near enough to the fire to get the benefit of its warmth, but not so close as to find ourselves burning up. In no time at all we were sipping on our drinks, exchanging pleasantries, and it wasn't long before I asked her about Down syndrome and the effect it had on memory. She told me that both short-term and long-term memory can be affected, but when I outlined a set of circumstances that involved a young girl with Down syndrome going for a walk in the middle of the night and being completely unaware of how she got there or why, she said that sounded more like sleepwalking.

'What if she has no history of sleepwalking?' I asked.

'What age is this theoretical girl?' she asked.

'Seventeen,' I said.

'It's unusual but not impossible for a one-off incident, but in this scenario… you're saying she was walking about around dawn? Sleep-walking usually happens earlier in the sleep cycle. Also, typically, it lasts under ten minutes, in some cases half an hour, but what you describe went on for far longer, and it sounds more like a blackout,' she said.

'A blackout… Isn't that usually associated with alcohol?' I said before taking a sip from my drink.

'There are other causes. If this person has seizures…' I shook my head to indicate no; Bridie had made it clear that her daughter was perfectly fit and healthy. 'Or she's on certain medications,' Ciara said and I moved to shake my head no, but then I remembered the tablets with Fidelma's name on them by Bridie's bed. Fidelma said she'd only taken a couple, as they didn't suit her, and Bridie had said the same, but the pillbox was only half-filled. I asked her about the drug and whether that could cause a blackout. 'Absolutely,' she confirmed. There was still no link to Crónán, though, only a possible answer as to why a young girl found herself on Potters Road, wet and scared. She'd been drugged. The question of why gnawed at me. We spent the rest of the night enjoying ourselves; Ciara liked jokes, and not the mean-spirited mother-in-law ones that the lads favoured, but cute ones that weren't really that funny, but she had a way of telling them.

'Why don't scientists trust atoms?' she said.

'I don't know.'

'Because they make up everything,' she said and she was already laughing.

'That's a horrible joke,' I admitted.

'I know,' she said, and I found myself laughing and wondering again if I'd hit my head. Outside in the cold, we said goodbye and, before we parted ways, she asked me a question.

'Do you think Lisa Fitzmaurice is linked to the Baby Crónán's case?'

'I do,' I said. 'I just don't know how.'

'You'll work it out,' she said and I hoped she was right.

Day Fifteen

We started at six a.m., just like Foley had instructed. We were back in the incident room in the hotel and the boxes of evidence were open on the floor, and I found myself sitting on it, camped in a corner, reading statement after statement. The others were sitting too, dotted around the room, doing much of the same; every now and again someone would raise a question or highlight something, and we'd mutter ideas between us before falling into silence once more. The lads were focused on re-reading everything they had on the mysterious woman in the hat and coat. If she wasn't an O'Reilly woman, who was she?

'Did we ever get that list of the charity shop regulars from Lena Herrman?' I asked.

'Yeah, it's here somewhere,' O'Neill said and Quinn went scrambling for it.

—

Quinn handed the list to Foley. 'There's quite a few names on it,' he said. It was four foolscap pages long. Then I saw her name: Bridie Fitzmaurice. I looked to Foley.

'What if Bridie bought the hat and coat? And Lisa is connected after all?'

'If "if" was a donkey we'd all have a ride, Shea,' he said. 'And anyway, Bridie gave birth to a healthy child days later.'

My mind was firing… Everything was clicking into place. 'What if Lisa was drugged?'

'Why would she be drugged?' Foley said.

Click. 'They can't lock her up at night, it's a fire hazard,' I said.

'What has that got to do with the price of bread?' O'Neill asked.

Click. 'Bridie was hiding in her room, so she wasn't going to get in the way,' I said.

Click. The blue towel… I remembered the blue towel, slung over Bridie's shoulder in the shop that day when I was buying biscuits and tea – the faded, worn blue towel that protected Bridie's pretty dress from Johnny's reflux.

'The blue towel!' I said and I think I shouted it.

'What?'

'I saw it, it was the same as the one around Baby Crónán, that's what threw me, that's why I got so upset…' I was rambling now, the pieces all slotting into place in my head. The boys looked at me as though I was a mad woman.

'Slow down, Shea. What towel?'

'Bridie Fitzmaurice had a blue towel, just like the one Baby Crónán was wrapped in.'

I could see it happen in Foley's eyes, his mind making the same connections. I could feel excitement coming off him, his voice now as energised as my own. 'What age is Debbie?' Foley said.

'Fourteen.'

'That's childbearing age?' he asked.

'In some,' I said.

'Could a girl that skinny hide a pregnancy?' Foley said. The boys all looked to me.

'She's skin and bone under clothes that are too big for her,' I said. 'Her arms, her legs, her face even, but her stomach…' I thought back to all those times we met. 'It's always concealed.'

'So what do we have?' Foley said and that's when we pieced it all together to form our theory about what happened, leading up to and on that night. Bridie bought the coat and hat. Debbie hid her pregnancy from her mother, who was distracted with grief. The night Debbie went into labour, Bridie had already checked out. She used Bridie's Valium to sedate Lisa. Then she gave birth to the baby, killed him, wore the coat over her nightdress, placed the baby in the bag and left the house. At some point Lisa woke up and as Debbie wasn't there to stop her, she wandered.

Foley asked, 'How far is the beach from the Fitzmaurices' house?'

'Via Appletree Lane and using the Hickey's farm shortcut, about twenty minutes,' I said.

'So why the delay? If Debbie was seen heading to the beach by the jockey at around nine fifteen that night and, on the road home, by the vet at four thirty a.m. – what was she doing all that time?' he asked. That took us a while to work out. We talked it through and that's when O'Neill hit on something.

'The girl in the nightdress on Hillcrest was dry. She was sheltering from the rain,' he said. Quinn asked another question, 'So how did she get back to the house before Lisa?' But Foley re-read her statement. Debbie said that she found Lisa on the doorstep that morning.

'What if she found Lisa on the doorstep when she returned home?' Foley said. He was already shouting orders at the lads as he grabbed his coat, and I was following him out the door, my mind racing, heart beating. *Debbie, oh God, Debbie. What did you do?*

CHAPTER EIGHTEEN

It was late afternoon by the time we knocked on the Fitzmaurices' door. This time, when Debbie opened it, she could tell by the look on our faces that we weren't there for anyone but her. No words passed our lips as we took her in – the girl we'd met so early on in the investigation, in the house that was our first call because her mother was pregnant, grieving and our immediate suspect. When we discounted Bridie, had we been so blind as to miss Debbie's fear, staring back at us? I didn't know the answer then.

'Debbie,' Foley said. 'Did you have a baby?'

Her eyes filled and she blinked, tipping tears onto her face. 'No,' she said. She shook her head vigorously. 'I didn't. I didn't.' She tried to close the door on us but Foley wedged his foot against it. It didn't budge; helpless now, her shoulders were heaving.

Bridie called out to her, 'Who's at the door, Debbie?'

'It's the guards, Mrs Fitzmaurice,' I called out. 'We're here to see Debbie.'

She came to the door, baby Johnny in her arms, and I realised why he jarred me as he did. It wasn't just the PTSD, it was his likeness. Not because of coincidence, or the idea that all babies looked the same, but because they were family. My breath hitched in my throat and my pulse quickened.

'What's going on?' Bridie said and she could sense the terrible seriousness of our visit.

'Mrs Fitzmaurice, did you buy a winter coat and hat in the charity shop recently?' Foley said.

'I did,' she said. Foley described the coat and hat to her. She nodded. 'Yes.'

'Where are they?' he asked and she pointed to her daughter.

'The coat was too big on her, around the shoulders. Debbie brought them back, didn't you?'

Debbie bowed her head and hugged herself.

'Debbie? You got a credit note, didn't you?'

'Didn't you see the news or read the newspapers, Mrs Fitzmaurice?' I said.

'I sold the TV and if I had money for newspapers I wouldn't be buying clothes in charity shops,' she replied evenly.

'Nobody mentioned to you that we were looking for a coat and hat matching the description of the one you bought at the charity shop?' Foley said. She looked down at the child in her arms before directing her gaze at us.

'People don't tend to talk to me about that business,' she said. 'Debbie? You brought the coat and hat back, didn't you? Look at me,' she said to her daughter, anxiety creeping up inside her. Debbie raised her head and slowly she shook it from side to side.

'We believe that Debbie Fitzmaurice is the mother of Baby Crónán,' Foley said and Bridie nearly dropped the child in her arms. She weakened and slackened so much that I lunged for her, grabbing the baby, holding on to him tight before he landed on the floor. *It's all right, little one, it's all right*, I said in my head as I allowed myself to truly look at him, his button nose, his shock of black hair, his open mouth, his blue eyes… He was gazing at me, content. He yawned, his back stretched out and his little face scrunched. Foley was administering to Bridie, who appeared to feel faint, and he took her into the kitchen. Debbie was just standing there like a deer caught in headlights. Her brother, Richard – the boy I'd forgotten even existed – arrived home from school. He threw his bag onto the floor before noticing us: his sister standing like a statue by the stairs and me holding his baby brother as though my life depended on it. A strange sight, I suppose. He said nothing, just hopped onto the staircase, taking two steps at a time until he was out of sight. Bridie wanted to talk to Debbie, to ask her questions, but Foley was adamant that he would be the one asking the questions, and it would happen at the station. That's when Bridie found her resolve. She refused to let Debbie go anywhere without her. She called up the stairs to her son, and he came running. Taking baby Johnny from me, she handed him to Richard.

'Take him, mind him and when the school bus drops Lisa home, mind her too.'

Now he looked like a deer caught in headlights. It was clear it was a responsibility he hadn't had before, despite being a year older than Debbie. We left him there, a babe in arms, gawping after us.

–

Our first port of call was Dr Crosby's office, at my insistence. I was adamant that the intimate exam would be carried out by her and her alone. I wasn't asking, and Foley wasn't arguing – he would have agreed to anything in that moment. We radioed Brian, who called her office to ask her to clear her appointments for the next hour. Foley didn't want any gossip; there was already enough of that. We drove around to the back, where Ciara was waiting. She guided us into her waiting area. Debbie was now mute with fear. Bridie wasn't much better. Ciara looked at Debbie, a trace of confusion on her face. The jumper she was wearing was the same oversized, faded knit with the hole for her thumb that I'd seen her wear before. Ciara knelt in front of her. 'Debbie, do you mind if I touch your stomach?' she asked, and Debbie nodded. Ciara slipped her hand under the voluminous jumper. We all stood rooted to the floor – no one had expected the examination to begin in our presence. She pressed gently, then lifted the jumper to reveal a tatty but tight vest over a taut, skeletal frame. She lifted the vest to reveal Debbie's skin, only for a second; she didn't need any longer. Ciara looked from Debbie to the rest of us. 'This child hasn't had a baby,' she said, and the case we'd built in our heads fell apart in an instant. *How? It didn't make sense.*

'You're wrong,' Foley shouted, letting his emotions rule him.

'I'm not wrong. No signs of stretch marks, distension, loose skin or muscle separation. She hasn't had a baby,' Ciara said and Bridie burst into tears while mumbling a prayer under her breath. Debbie didn't move an inch, nor did she utter a word. I looked from her to Foley. Ciara was right, that child's body hadn't birthed a baby. It was impossible. Foley was only short of punching the wall.

'We're going home. Come on, Deborah,' Bridie said, finding her voice. 'Let's go.'

'We need to talk to her,' Foley said, but his heart wasn't in it, such was the blow he'd just received.

Bridie held on to Debbie while asking a valid question. 'Why?'

'Because something happened and Debbie has the answers,' he said, staring at the ghost of a girl as tears streamed down her face.

'I'll be contacting a solicitor. Any questions you might have we'll answer in the morning with a solicitor present,' Bridie said and I'm not sure if she really knew her rights or was just bluffing, but Foley nodded in agreement.

'Make sure he comes early, Mrs Fitzmaurice. I'll be at your door by ten a.m.,' he said before warning her that, until then, there would be a guard posted outside their home.

'Fine,' she said and she pushed Debbie out of the surgery. When they were out of sight, Foley turned to us. 'What is going on?' he said before collapsing into a chair with his head in his hands. 'What is going on?' he repeated. I shared a look with Ciara. She hunched and shook her head before offering us tea.

'I need something stronger than tea,' Foley said, standing up. I said my goodbyes to Ciara and followed him outside. It was raining heavily now.

'Before you say a word, I just need to think,' he said. 'Just leave me to think.' He was walking away from me, down the street, through the rain. I couldn't help myself, I followed him into the night.

She was drugged, she had a blackout. She said she was scared and that she was sore…

'It was Lisa who gave birth. It has to be,' I said, wiping the rain from my eyes. He turned to face me, his suit and hair soaking wet.

'You think that girl capable of lying to us?' he asked.

'No… I think… She didn't know what was happening,' I said.

'I just need to think,' he repeated and walked away from me, leaving me standing drenched in the rain, utterly convinced that I was finally right. Lisa Fitzmaurice was Crónán's mother. Debbie's face plagued me – her gaunt, haunted look, her fear, her pain. I thought she was grieving because of the loss of her father and brother. I thought the responsibility of taking care of her mother, sister and brother was what creased her young face with worry. But it was guilt. *Oh Debbie, why?*

–

I made my way to the car; as soon as I sat, rain pooled on the leather seat, soaking into the foam through the tear, barely held together with a piece of curling tape. Cold water streamed down my face and neck, forging a path down my back under my jumper, sending chills up my spine. I drove with the windscreen wipers struggling against the torrent, barely able to see. Pulling in by the deserted phone box, I ran outside under the falling sky, yanked open the squeaky door and sought refuge in the glass box. The small square windows instantly steamed from the heat of my breath. I lifted the phone off its hook and shoved coins, slippery in my wet hands, one by one into the coin box. Dialling the number, connecting the call.

Please, please, please. Click.

'Hello, you've reached—'

'Mammy?' I cried.

'Hello, love,' she said.

'Oh, Mammy,' I said and the tears fell as I sank down onto the dirty concrete floor, hugging the phone to my ear.

'Whatever it is, you're going to be fine,' she said.

'I don't know. I don't know anything,' I told her, hugging my knees to my chest as the cold took hold of me now, shrinking me into myself.

'None of us do,' she soothed. 'We just do our best.'

'I know what happened to Baby Crónán. I thought I'd find the devil but I think I just found more victims,' I said.

'It's rarely the devil, Mary. It's often just some lost and desperate soul who does the worst of things.'

I nodded to myself while sobbing my heart out – for Crónán, for Lisa, for Debbie and whatever hell she had endured to drive her to such a terrible act.

'I can hear the rain beating against the glass. I want you to go home now, Mary. You'll face what needs facing tomorrow because you were made for this,' my mother said, in a tone that made it clear she wasn't taking no for an answer.

'I was?' I asked.

'You were,' she confirmed.

'I don't know, Mammy,' I said.

'I know. Go home. Go to bed. Go to sleep. You'll put down a hard day tomorrow and when you come home, I'll be there with dinner on your table and a shoulder to cry on,' she said.

'Thanks, Mammy,' I said. I wasn't going to argue. I wanted to see her and for her to wrap her arms around me. I needed her. I drove straight home, crying all the way. I went to bed but sleep was beyond me, so instead I listened to the rain beating on the roof, with my red-rimmed eyes staring at the ceiling, not caring if it came down on me.

Day Sixteen

Dicey worked the night shift guarding the Fitzmaurice house. Foley and I arrived there at ten a.m. on the dot, just as he'd promised. He banged on the roof of the car, waking Dicey from his slumber.

'Were you sleeping?' he said.

'No, just closing my eyes for a minute. The solicitor's inside the house, he arrived two hours ago.'

'Do you know him?' Foley asked.

'Never seen him before,' Dicey said.

'Right, let's knock on the door,' Foley said and I followed him down the path. He rapped on the door with a closed fist and when it opened, it was the solicitor. I could immediately tell he was free, legal aid – young, with a cheap suit.

'I'm Detective Foley, and you are?'

'I'm Debbie Fitzmaurice's solicitor, Paddy Clarke,' he said. The door swung open and the house looked like a foreign place: it was upended, as though a bull had passed through it. Richard, the forgotten boy, was sitting on the stairs, his eyes red raw from crying, staring blankly at us. In the kitchen, Bridie was sitting on the floor, holding on to her baby, tears falling as soon as she saw us.

'Where is Debbie?' Foley asked.

'She's upstairs, packing her things,' Bridie said in a hoarse voice.

'Debbie has made a confession,' the young solicitor said. He handed Foley a statement.

'I'll need to take a statement myself,' Foley said.

'Of course,' the solicitor agreed. Bridie sobbed.

'And Lisa?' Foley said.

'She had a baby,' Bridie said, wiping the never-ending stream of tears from her eyes with the back of her hand. 'Debbie told her she had food poisoning. She told her to close her eyes really tight and not to open them, and if she did that, the pain would go away.' She shook her head from side to side. 'Lisa had a baby boy and, while her eyes were closed,

Debbie killed him.' She placed her hand on baby Johnny's head, stroking it gently, before looking up at us. 'And it's my fault.'

'Why is that, Mrs Fitzmaurice?' Foley said.

'Because I told her we were cursed, that the devil was in this house – and she believed me.' And there he was…

'She wanted to save Lisa, me and Richard from the devil between Lisa's legs,' she said, and she closed her eyes and placed a light kiss on baby Johnny's head. The young solicitor blessed himself. Foley and I shared a look. *God almighty*. Except he wasn't the devil – he was an innocent. A little boy who would never smile or kick, never gurgle or laugh or speak… forever silent. Baby Crónán, the little dark one. An angel.

'She needs to come to the station now,' Foley said. The young solicitor offered to fetch her and as soon as he left us, I asked after Lisa.

'She's fine. She knows nothing. Debbie drugged her, but it must have worn off, that's when she went wandering,' Bridie explained.

'She'll need to go to hospital for a check-up,' I said.

'Fine,' she said. Her eyes were dead. The solicitor came thundering downstairs and nearly tripped over Richard, still stuck to the bottom stair.

'She's gone,' he said.

'What? How?' Foley said.

'The back window is open, it looks like she jumped onto the back wall.'

'Oh, for the love of God,' Foley said, hightailing up the stairs. 'Tell Dicey to get the boys over here now,' he shouted. I went to the car, Dicey was snoozing. I banged on the door. He opened his eyes, saw me and closed them again.

'Debbie's gone,' I shouted. His eyes opened. He cursed a blue streak.

'And I suppose this is my fault.'

'Just call it in,' I shouted, fear gripping me. *Don't do something stupid, Debbie. Please…* He picked up the radio and called it in. When I went back into the house, Foley was already in Lisa's room; she was lying in bed, hugging her pillow, still groggy. I slipped in behind him and waved to her. She smiled and stuck out her tongue.

'Lisa, can you look at me?' Foley said as the young solicitor pushed his way inside the door.

'This isn't appropriate,' he said.

'It might save Debbie's life, unless you'd rather she did something stupid?' Foley said.

'Right,' the young man said, aghast.

'Lisa, it's very important. Do you know where Debbie has gone?' Foley asked. Lisa thought about it. 'She likes the swing by the river. She takes me there,' Lisa said. The swinging tree... *Oh Jesus*... I looked to Foley. 'I know the spot, it overlooks the bay.'

'Move,' he said and we ran out of the place.

We parked up and sprinted down the path that led to the small hill above it. That's when I saw her. She was dangling, swinging from the old swinging tree. She had wrapped one end of her father's old fishing rope around her neck and tied the other to the thickest branch of the tree. She'd balanced on the swing seat and then stepped off it. As we ran to her, the knot in the rope gave way just in time for Foley to scoop her up in his arms.

'It's okay, missy,' he said gently. 'You're all right now.' He tapped her face as I unravelled the rope from around her neck as quick as my fingers could work. I could see the colour return on her face, her bulging eyes open and tears fall from them; her tongue looked too big for her mouth and her head fell backwards onto Foley's chest, but she was alive. 'Call an ambulance,' he said to me and I was already running away from him, down the hill and onto the pathway that led to the rusty green gate out to the car, where I called out to Brian Keating on the radio, 'Get an ambulance... Get an ambulance.' They weren't long, ten minutes, maybe twelve. I heard them before I saw them, sirens pealing, red lights flashing. I opened the gates wide and they barrelled down the narrow pathway over stones and rocks, until they couldn't drive any more and two of the lads bailed out with bags and a stretcher. I ran behind them, following them to where Foley held Debbie in his arms.

'We've got her now,' one of the men said, taking her from Foley, who looked as dazed as I felt.

'There now,' Foley said as he handed her over. 'There now.' She looked like she was dying. They took her away in the back of the van, and Foley and I sat in the dirt under the swing, recovering, regrouping, gathering strength before moving on.

'You did your best,' I said and I pretended not to notice the tear that fell from his eye. He stood up, sniffed, shook himself off. 'We have work to do,' he said and I suppose the shock got the better of me because I don't recall much of the rest of the day.

–

It was that evening before Debbie was well enough to speak to us. She lay in a single room, looking tiny in the bed, her neck wrapped in soft bandages. An IV was in her arm, saline dripping into her undernourished, broken body. Her mother sat next to her, holding her hand, silent as the grave except for one moment when she looked up at Foley. 'You saved her. Thank you,' she said. After that, she was out of words.

Debbie's voice was hoarse when she spoke. 'I'm sorry,' she said.

'What happened that night, Debbie?' Foley asked.

I had brought a small battery-operated tape recorder, and both she and her mother agreed to let me record her statement there, in the small hospital room. They had nothing to hide now. She told us she'd been so tired, and her mother was in a bad way – unable to get out of bed, crying all day. To calm her, Debbie gave her a tablet from the pill bottle that Fidelma Regan had given her after witnessing an incident that had frightened her.

'What happened?' Foley said, taking Debbie further back in time. She looked to her mother, and Bridie nodded, squeezing Debbie's hand. She told us that she had to run to Fidelma's, begging her for help when her mother threatened to hurt herself and the baby. She said that she was screaming and shouting about the devil being in the house, inside her. She was pulling at herself and she grabbed a pair of scissors; Debbie took it away from her and locked her in her room using the same key she used on Lisa's door. She brought Fidelma back to the house to witness Bridie's despair. Bridie was banging on the door, calling out to God, begging for forgiveness. She was shouting at Him, swearing at Him, screaming about the devil and saying that God had cursed her. A tear slid down Bridie's face as the whispered words drifted from Debbie's mouth. 'She just kept screaming, "The devil is here, inside this house."' Bridie bowed her head, slowly catching her breath. Fidelma came to the house and calmed Bridie down by giving her one of those pills. 'It knocked her out, calmed her down. She left the bottle,' Debbie said.

'The night that Lisa gave birth to the baby... Tell me about that?' Foley said.

'I gave Mammy a pill. She fell asleep. Richard was out with his friends. I washed up from the tea and I realised that Lisa had taken herself off to bed at seven. Normally it's a fight to get her up the stairs at nine. I checked on her and I found her in a ball on the bed.'

Bridie started to cry. Debbie was desperate to speak now, to unburden herself. Her voice was raw; her words came slowly, but no one interrupted her, and with her eyes closed, I could see that in her mind, she was back in that room, looking at her sister on the bed.

'She was crying out in pain. She said she had a sore tummy. I tried to touch it but she pulled away and she wouldn't stop crying, so I went to Mammy's room to tell her but she was asleep, there was no waking her. I went back to Lisa and by then she was on all fours on the floor, grunting and groaning, and her eyes and tongue were bulging. She was panting like a dog.' Debbie looked from Foley to me. 'She didn't look like herself at all,' she said. 'She looked like something possessed.' Foley and I shared a look in that moment. *Oh God.* 'The next thing, there was a bulge in Lisa's knickers, and she was pulling at them, desperate to get them off, so I tore them and that's when I saw the head. I saw the black hair of the devil and I screamed.' She was crying now, tears burning red tracks into her pale skin. 'Lisa was grunting and the head was just there. So I told her to close her eyes or the pain would get worse. I knew how to make pain stop but I needed her still while I got what she needed. I ran to the kitchen and grabbed the kitchen knife and some towels. By the time I got back, he was all but out, and his eyes were open and staring at me but he didn't make a sound… Then he plopped onto the floor behind Lisa and I remember shouting at her to keep her eyes closed. I think I heard him cry or maybe it was Lisa. I'm not sure because my eyes were closed and I was praying to God to save us from this demon, this monster, and I begged Him not to curse our house again. We had enough, we couldn't take any more. Then I closed my eyes and brought the knife down on him… And then I cut the cord that tied the devil to my sister.'

'Oh God,' Bridie cried out. 'Oh God, forgive us,' she muttered, bringing her hands together in prayer.

'What happened next?' Foley said and Debbie thought for a second.

'I grabbed the sheet from Lisa's bed and I told her that as long as she kept her eyes closed, the pain would stay away. She squeezed her eyes shut. I lifted her into bed and I told her I was going to help her get clean, but first I needed to fill a basin. I took it downstairs and I placed it in the shed. I cleaned Lisa and I told her it was safe to open her eyes.

I changed her sheets. I snuck into Mammy's room and I took a few of her tablets, and I fed them to Lisa with warm milk. I prayed I'd saved her from Mammy's curse.'

Bridie took Debbie in her arms. 'It's my fault,' she said. 'It's my fault.'

Debbie leaned into her mother. 'I thought when you had Johnny in the convent it was a sign that we were free. You were so happy and back to your old self again, I was sure of it, except that I couldn't escape from the horror of what I'd done. He calls to me, Mammy… every time I close my eyes, he's there.' She stopped talking. She looked from her mother to Foley and then to me. 'But he's not frightening, he's just a little baby like Johnny and not the devil at all.' Tears spilled from her; she was drowning in sorrow, right in front of us. Her mother held on to her. 'It's my fault, Debbie. It's my fault.' She looked to us. 'She's only fourteen,' she said, holding Debbie tight to her. We left them both weeping.

'You did good work,' Foley said as we walked to the carpark via the narrow lane, flanked by stone walls, parting the peat-rich soil that stretched out on both sides for as far as the eye could see.

'Thanks,' I said.

'This is the worst of the job,' he said and I nodded. 'So I've heard.' We were quiet after that. I lost myself in the stillness and serenity, where nature seemed to pause, awaiting the arrival of spring.

–

My mother was true to her word: she was making dinner at the stove when I dragged myself through the door. She welcomed me with a hug. 'Your dad is asking for you, he's so proud,' she said and I wanted to cry but I didn't have any tears left in me. I showered and changed my clothes, and just as dinner was being served, Ciara knocked on the door. I opened it to reveal her holding up a bottle of whiskey. 'I just examined Lisa Fitzmaurice,' she said.

'Come in. Come in,' my mother called to her. 'There's plenty to go around.' It was my favourite, beef stew with dumplings, and there was enough to feed ten. I made the introductions.

My mother smiled. 'You're Mary's new friend,' she said and then we sat down to dinner and we drank whiskey, and they asked questions about the case and I answered them. No need for secrecy any more; Debbie had made a verbal and a written statement, pleading guilty to the murder of Baby Crónán.

'Was the baby in that bag that they showed on the TV?' Mammy asked.

'Yes,' I said. 'Debbie wrapped him in a blue towel and put him in the bag. She put on the hat and coat because they were big enough to cover her, disguise her,' I said. Debbie knew the shortcut from the lane through the farm to the beach. That's when the local jockey spotted her. She was heading for the beach when it started to rain, so she found shelter in an old disused shed.

'She waited until it stopped raining?' Ciara said.

'She did.'

'Why? I would have thought the rain was the least of her worries,' Ciara said.

'She said her mother didn't like them getting wet,' I explained. Ciara sighed deeply, then she drank deeply. Mammy shook her head. 'The mind is a mysterious thing,' she said.

'So why place him in the dune and not have the sea take him away?' Ciara asked.

'She wanted him found, so that the priest could bless him,' I said.

'But if she thought he was the devil…?' Mammy said.

In her statement, the one she'd made for the young solicitor the previous night, Debbie had explained that she thought the baby was possessed by the devil. She killed the devil but she wanted to save the baby's soul. After he died, she washed him. She didn't have holy water in the house, so instead she used bleach to cleanse him and then she placed him in the dune, so he'd be found and so the priest could send him to heaven.

'She laid him out under the sky so God could find him,' I said. We sat quietly for a time, letting that sink in.

'And poor Lisa?'

'She'll be fine, the birth didn't damage her,' Ciara said.

'Does she know about the baby?' I asked.

'I had to explain why I was examining her. Bridie left permission to say what was necessary.'

'Did she understand?' I asked.

'I think so,' she said. 'She'd like to visit with him.'

I exhaled. Crónán had a mother, he was no longer unknown. A tear slipped down my face.

'And the father?' I asked.

'A boy, just like Lisa, the same age, from her special school. She says she loves him,' Ciara explained. It turned out all those times Lisa ran away, she was running towards him, Jeremiah, her love. Neither knew she was pregnant, no one had talked to them about sex and relationships; no one had thought them capable of what is natural.

'God love them,' my mother said.

We stayed up till dawn and my mother told my friend inappropriate stories about my childhood, and we laughed and cried. We talked until the sun rose and a new day began. I wasn't sure what lay ahead for me, but I knew I needed to experience something more than the dreary life I'd been leading. I couldn't go back. I wouldn't. I just didn't know how to move forward.

Foley took me out for a pub lunch to celebrate a successful end to the case. He raised his glass to me and I to him.

'Good luck, Mary,' he said, and I said the same to him. He spun his big gold ring around his finger. 'Thanks,' he said, looking down at it. 'We need it.' He was thinking of his sick wife as he tried to smile for me. It was sad; he was far from a perfect man, but I liked him. He had it in him to see me as more than just a woman – we were two colleagues exchanging respect. It felt good.

Then came the blow. I watched him and the Dublin boys stand at a press conference, taking all the credit for solving the case. My name wasn't mentioned. I was nowhere. I was no one. The Dublin boys cleared out of town a day later, and it hurt. The hurt burrowed deep.

'It's a man's world, love,' Mammy said.

'Bastards,' Ciara said.

I thought about leaving the force. I just couldn't think what else to do.

–

Debbie didn't want visitors, and it wasn't appropriate for me to visit anyway. I did visit with Joyce O'Reilly as soon as she was freed from her prison cell. I was welcomed into the O'Reillys' home by Breda and Raymond, who was still recuperating from his heart attack. We didn't mention my connection to Ciara or to the escape plan that got Thomas successfully out of town, but a big lunch was laid out and Joyce hugged me tightly as tears fell from her eyes. I was embarrassed. 'I didn't do much,' I said.

'You saw the truth,' Breda said. 'You saw my Joyce for who she is.' She squeezed my shoulder as I sat down on a chair at their big old wooden table. Joyce was excited that her brother Ricky was coming home from America to visit, and Thomas was coming home too.

'It will be nice to have them both back for a holiday,' I said.

'Thomas is coming home for good,' Raymond said. That threw me. I knew he no longer needed to pursue a case against the garda now that Joyce was free, but what about Seamus and their life together in Dublin? They didn't mention Seamus, and if they knew about a relationship between the men, it was no business of mine. Joyce walked me to the door, and before I left, I offered her a warning: after what she had been through, her life would be forever tarnished. 'But only if you let it,' I said.

'I know.'

'So don't let it,' I said.

'I'll try,' she promised. I left her in her doorway, waving at me with a smile on her face.

A week later, I received a letter from Seamus.

> *Dear Mary,*
>
> *You probably know I'm on my own now, but I think I've found my place here. I miss walking the land. I miss the air, it's different here, cloggier, dirtier, heavier, but I love the noise, the energy, the lights. I like being anonymous. Despite the poor air, I can breathe easier here.*
>
> *Here's my address: 7 Slipper Street, Northwall. Use it. If you come to Dublin, find me.*
>
> *Seamus.*

I missed him but I was happy for him.

I had a new friend in Ciara and a fuller life outside work; the days were getting longer, the sky brighter, but life in my station was becoming more difficult and I more restless. Dicey McCarthy was a wounded animal and, in his mind, I was the one who'd wounded him. His bad behaviour towards me was tolerated by the others; excuses were made for him and my discomfort ignored, every injustice overlooked. I thought about leaving. Then one month and four days after the case of Baby Crónán was closed, our Station House Officer, Brian Keating, called me into his office. He made me sit in front of him, wearing a serious face, as he pushed a piece of paper in front of me. I read it. My brain went into shock. The words blurred on the page. I attempted to read it again.

'It's a job offer,' he said.

'I see that,' I said, trying to cover my surprise.

'In Dublin… You'll have to do exams, but Foley's recommended you for a detective spot,' he said and his voice betrayed his own shock and surprise, with a hint of bitterness thrown in.

'With the Dublin boys?' I said agog.

'Yes.'

'Right,' I said.

'Right,' he echoed. I got up to leave.

'Well, will you take it?' he said as I moved towards the door.

'Does a bear shit in the woods?' I said and I giggled to myself as I walked out, clutching the offer, and past Dicey McCarthy, who had tried but failed to break me.

'Hey, Dicey,' I said from the doorway. He looked up.

'They want me in Dublin,' I told him and his mouth fell open, tea spilling out. 'I win,' I said and Liam Kenny clapped his hands together. Dicey gave him a death stare. Liam stopped clapping.

I walked down the road to where Ciara was waiting. As sad as she was to see me go, she was happy for me. We hugged and made promises to be friends forever. Together, we made our way to the phone box by the beach. She waited outside under a blue sky while I stepped inside. I fed the box with coins, listening for the clink as they dropped, the hum of the dial tone, and the click of the receiver. I didn't wait for my mother's greeting.

'Mammy?'

'Hello, love.'

'Guess what?'

'What?'

'The Dublin boys want me to work with them. I'm going to be a detective,' I said and I could feel my own heart pounding. Aside from some static on the line, I could hear nothing else except the slightest intake of breath. Outside and through the dirty glass, I could see Ciara hugging her knees, her eyes closed and her head thrown back.

'Mammy,' I said.

Silence. I worried I'd caused a heart attack.

'Mammy?' I repeated, worried now, urgency in my voice.

'I'm fine, I'm fine,' she finally said before sighing heavily.

'You're worried. You think I'm not able,' I said, my own doubts sweeping to the surface and my heart threatening to break.

She laughed. 'Worried! I'm elated. I just needed a moment... just to feel it... the joy of it.' She was crying now. 'My girl... a detective.'

I relaxed, letting go of my fear, my worry. 'It's going to happen, Mammy.'

'Oh, I know it is... Begs not tell your father,' she said.

We were both laughing now. If Ciara noticed the mad woman hysterical in the box, she didn't flinch or let on. I was serious then. 'I'll always of think of him,' I said about the little baby boy whose loss inadvertently gave me new life.

'I know you will, love,' she said.

It was a Friday when I drove away from Nead Mara in my old Ford Escort that smelled of peat briquettes, had a tear in the driver seat's leather upholstery and a steel hanger that replaced the long-gone radio aerial. I stopped at Baby Crónán's new grave. He now lay with family – his grandfather and his uncle. I placed flowers by the headstone, which included his name: Anthony Fitzmaurice. I sat with him a while, staring up at the grey sky and singing a lullaby before finally saying goodbye.

Acknowledgments

My love and gratitude go out to all the women who raised me and taught me how to be strong and joyful, beginning with and in memory of my mother, who fought her illness valiantly, loved fiercely, and – even back in the dark days of Ireland – never allowed society to tell her who she was or what she could and couldn't do. In memory of my two grandmothers, Nora and Anna – completely different women, yet both rebels.

My aunt, Mary O'Shea, for taking me in when I needed care most, for loving, defending, and minding me my whole life, for being that voice in my head that tells me to be better and demand better. To my aunt, Mary Flood, for your kindness, humour, and for being there whenever my back is to the wall. In memory of Catherine 'Terry' McPartlin, my mother-in-law – so fierce she'd frighten the dead, so loving and caring she deserved sainthood, and except for that potty mouth of hers, she could have been a contender.

All the women and girls in my life – my sisters, sisters-in-law, and friends – I love you more than I can express. The joy and peace I feel in your presence is unmatched, and our laughter lives on in my head long after we're apart.

My nieces. I love and adore you, and I want so much more for you. So fight the good fight – for yourselves and for the next generation.

The authors who took part in the podcast What's in the Water, especially my co-host and work wife, Sinéad Moriarty – this idea originated during our time on the podcast, listening to all those amazing Irish female writers talk about our origins as storytellers. You all inspired The Mary Shea Murders.

My agent, Sheila Crowley, who is a constant inspiration, a firm hand when needed, and a joy to work with. My TV & screenwriting agent, Jessica Cooper, for her patience and for being a joyful warrior.

My editor, Louise Cullen, and her team in Canelo, including Alicia Pountney and Daniela Nava – thank you for your incredible work in helping me bring The Mary Shea Murders to life. Thanks for believing in this project and taking a risk on a story that is incredibly dark but, as it's inspired by real events, also means so much to so many women of Ireland.

Although this one is for the ladies, I can't not acknowledge the men in my life.

To my uncle Tony O'Shea, the only father I've known, for his love and support. My father-in-law, Don McPartlin, for his warmth and kindness and my husband, Donal, for you unwavering support and whom I love and adore. And finally in memory of my dear uncle Paudie McSwiney – he would have loved this one.

CANELO CRIME

Do you love crime fiction and are always on the lookout for brilliant authors?

Canelo Crime is home to some of the most exciting novels around. Thousands of readers are already enjoying our compulsive stories. Are you ready to find your new favourite writer?

Find out more and sign up to our newsletter at canelocrime.com